THE
10:12

THE
10:12

ANNA MALONEY

RAVEN BOOKS
LONDON · OXFORD · NEW YORK · NEW DELHI · SYDNEY

RAVEN BOOKS
Bloomsbury Publishing Plc
50 Bedford Square, London, WC1B 3DP, UK
Bloomsbury Publishing Ireland Limited,
29 Earlsfort Terrace, Dublin 2, D02 AY28, Ireland

BLOOMSBURY, RAVEN BOOKS and the Raven Books logo
are trademarks of Bloomsbury Publishing Plc

First published in Great Britain 2026

Copyright © Anna Maloney, 2026

Anna Maloney is identified as the author of this work in accordance with the Copyright,
Designs and Patents Act 1988

This is a work of fiction. Names and characters are the product of the author's imagination
and any resemblance to actual persons, living or dead, is entirely coincidental

All rights reserved. No part of this publication may be: i) reproduced or transmitted in
any form, electronic or mechanical, including photocopying, recording or by means of
any information storage or retrieval system without prior permission in writing from the
publishers; or ii) used or reproduced in any way for the training, development or operation
of artificial intelligence (AI) technologies, including generative AI technologies. The rights
holders expressly reserve this publication from the text and data mining exception as per
Article 4(3) of the Digital Single Market Directive (EU) 2019/790

A catalogue record for this book is available from the British Library

ISBN: HB: 978-1-5266-8916-0; TPB: 978-1-5266-8917-7; EBOOK: 978-1-5266-8915-3

2 4 6 8 10 9 7 5 3 1

Typeset by Six Red Marbles India
Printed and bound in Great Britain by Clays Ltd, Elcograf S.p.A

To find out more about our authors and books visit www.bloomsbury.com
and sign up for our newsletters
For product-safety-related questions contact productsafety@bloomsbury.com

To Kathleen and Eddie, my parents, and siblings Mary, Hugh, Paul, Catherine and Sean for such an enjoyable and interesting childhood.

Note from Editor:

Hi Claire,

Here are the latest proofs. Almost there! We've dropped in some of the court transcripts in what looks like the right places, see what you think. And check out the texts we discussed. I've added a few comments or queries. We're so excited by the book, Claire, but appreciate how hard it has been for you. I'm glad that you've found it useful to send us the MS sequentially, although we won't be able to have it legalled until it's ready for sign off. Lawyers like to see everything, and in context! I know some of the additional information that's cropped up in the process has been difficult for you, but from what you've said, sending it to us in sections has made the MS easier to modify. Hopefully publication will be cathartic for you.

Have you spoken to Laurence recently? He mentioned he's had difficulty getting hold of you. Also, I believe our rights and publicity teams are still waiting to hear from you about the serialisation and Radio 4? From a commercial perspective that could make a big difference but, more importantly, I'm sure you want to get your story out to as many people as possible. I know you like to go off the radar from time to time, but it would be good to get everything sorted asap.

We've noticed you've taken out some of the testimony from a couple of the contribs and assume it's re permissions. Obviously, we need to be super careful about legals. Have you had clarification on what you can say regarding your previous employment? I think Legal may be concerned about the Nancy material — perhaps we can talk about that. I know you accept you may have gone a bit off-piste with your investigations, although, as you said, it is interesting what routes you take when trying to discover the truth!

Let us know your thoughts,

Our very warmest wishes to you,
Loretta

Loretta De Silva
Editorial Director, Ashgrove Publishing

Prologue

First of all, I didn't kill the dog. If you've picked up this book then you're probably familiar with that element of the story relating to the 10:12 NorthRail train from Manchester to London in April 2023 and my supposed role in what occurred on that train. The dog was unharmed – but that didn't bother the people spreading rumours and misinformation. Facts, truths – they are so easily distorted in today's world.

What happened on that train made news all around the world: the people who died, the people who survived and how it all ended. But by the time the trial started almost two years later, the world had moved on. I don't think I was alone in assuming it would be a reckoning, an opportunity to rationalise what happened and help those involved come to terms with the events of that Tuesday in early spring. I had imagined the trial would be the point at which the full story of what happened on the 10:12 would emerge. But it wasn't like that.

Witnesses provided glimpses of the day from often conflicting different points of view. One of the defendants refused to participate, another accused all the witnesses of lying. Despite that, I think justice was largely well served by the jury and the right decisions made over people's innocence or guilt. But what wasn't justified was the personal attack on me by the defence barrister who asked if I believed I had committed murder. *[actual words 'righteous murder' – Loretta]* Given that I wasn't in the dock but a lead witness for the prosecution, I believed I had every right – and need – to refute that horrendous slur in the most robust way possible. Only it turns out that's not how things work in a court of law. I tried, but His Honour Justice Chartwell, while showing some sympathy, shut me down. I could see that word – *murder* – hanging like a dark cloud above my head. And I wasn't allowed to blow it away.

That was the germ of this book. The need to explain what we really experienced on the 10:12, and why things transpired the way they did. Many of the people on the train were not fully aware of what was going on, while other passengers and crew members were fighting for their lives. I realised I needed to investigate further. I decided to contact the people who I had come across on the 10:12, or who I knew were directly involved, and find out what they thought had happened, and why. That's different from deciding who is guilty but, for me and many of the others caught up in the events of that day in April, it's perhaps more important. The story that emerges is very different to that heard in court. When you start digging for the truth you don't know what you might uncover and I certainly had no idea that the hijack would turn out to be only the start of a far more complicated – and dangerous – story.

I wish to thank all of those who have kindly given me their time, answered my questions and offered their own perception of events. Any testimony from a named person has been included with their approval, so their story remains unfiltered. Some interviewees requested their names be changed to protect them from reprisals or intrusive public interest. Others did not want to be mentioned at all. One of the police officers involved was given permission to contribute and, crucially, two of the perpetrators eventually agreed to talk to me.

There are people at the heart of what happened whose stories we can never hear as they either died on the 10:12, or later, from their injuries. The conversations with those people included in the book are based on my memory, and those of other people who were present. Family members of the deceased have also contributed. I have tried to be as thorough as possible in exploring why what happened, happened – and why it happened in the way it did. Because that is what was missing from the judicial process. The culprits were rightly found guilty and sentenced – but what led them to do what they did was never fully explored. And that is what those of us who were caught up in the events of that horrific day deserve to know. Not because we're expecting closure, or any other trite psychobabble; I'm sure none of us are going to forget that day, or necessarily want to. We need to understand why it happened, not just for ourselves, the survivors, but to properly honour the memories of the good people who died.

Claire Fitzroy
January 2026

I

Setting Off

> Hope all OK with Em and Derek and train on time.
>
> Meeting at 7 but shouldn't be too late.
>
> Took ragu out of freezer xx

It was a Tuesday morning and every car, van, tram and bus in the Greater Manchester area seemed to have decided that the city centre was the place to be. Crawling our way through the traffic, conversation had been awkward. I was anxious about missing the train and preoccupied by what Derek had let slip. He was embarrassed. When we finally reached Piccadilly station, Derek stopped on a double yellow and, after hasty farewells, I ran through the busy, red-brick Victorian entrance, past the shops and onto the concourse. I'd already checked the platform number, and as I pushed through the crowds, caught a glimpse of my train under the pigeon-netted glass roof. I was childishly pleased to see it was one of the upgraded models, sleek and shiny. A new company had recently taken over the franchise and their gleaming livery – all silver and black, with *NorthRail* on the side in a traditional-looking font – looked classy. I hoped the interior would be clean and comfortable to match.

But the platform gates were closed. An announcement that the 10:12 to London was delayed due to an electrical fault explained the presence of hundreds of people milling around the concourse. With a sinking heart, I came to a halt, almost tripping as something wrapped around my legs. Looking down I saw a small wiry excitable dog, some kind of Jack Russell cross, bouncing around as if on springs, ears flapping at every jump. It started to yap. The owner, an elderly woman neatly turned out in a tweed coat, was holding a lead with one hand, while struggling to carry a large old-fashioned brown leather handbag, plus a copy of the *Telegraph*, in the other. 'Monty, Monty, sit!' she commanded, with little success.

Moving away from the mutt, I navigated around stationary people, their eyes on the electronic noticeboard, heads raised as if in supplication to the god of the railway timetable. It was the usual snapshot of the British population, albeit with fewer children as it was a school day. I ended up beside a pretty woman with long dark hair and a backpack, trying to manage a baby in a buggy and a large case while talking on the phone. She looked anxious, scanning the crowd, and I heard her say, 'Stop worrying, Dad, it'll be fine,' just as she stepped back and knocked the case over. I went to help, but a young, slight man with glasses beat me to it, lifting the case back up, and nodding in response to her flustered 'Thank you'.

There was a young couple, seemingly unconcerned about anything else but each other, a painful reminder to me of the simple joy of being in love. A woman, mid-fifties, with blue hair and cat eye diamante frames, moved gently to the music that I assumed was coming through her earbuds. *A character*, I thought dryly.

Now I see that crowd differently: all of us setting out on a journey, randomly thrown together, and shortly to be enclosed in what are effectively metal cylinders. None of us could imagine how important we would become to each other, for good or bad. Or that among us were people who would not live to see their destination.

Sudden movement among the waiting crowd indicated the display had changed and before any announcements were made, passengers were surging towards the ticket barriers, with the usual chaos ensuing until the staff conceded and the gates opened for people to scurry through. I held back to avoid the stampede; with a booked seat, I had no need to fight to the front.

My carriage, J, was the last but one. The carriage behind, K, appeared to be shut off, and there was a handwritten sign on the connecting door saying it was closed due to electrical problems. I presumed that was the cause of the delay. So much for upgraded models. As I passed the large disabled toilet at the back of my carriage, the door slid open and a skinny young man came out, sniffing. He bumped into me, and I muttered 'sorry' as Brits often do, automatically apologising for something that's the other person's fault. He briefly stopped and looked at me but said nothing. It was long enough for me to notice the traces of white powder round his nostrils and the acne on his pale skin. But it was the look he gave me that made me step back. Disdain? Hatred, even? It shook me but I wasn't going to let a cokehead have a reason to go off on one, so I let him push past me, and was relieved to see his seat wasn't close to mine.

First class means wider seats, more space and better fittings. The seating was upholstered in smart dark grey leather, the lighting expensive and subdued, with grey and muted red carpeting throughout. It looked elegant and relaxing, the polished overhead parcel shelves of dark grey glass with a slick silver metal trim reflecting the seats and passengers beneath them. It was just what I needed in order to sit and consider what my next steps should be, and how I would confront Jim when I got home.

I was right at the back, by a window. There was a magazine on every seat with the beaming face of the new MD of NorthRail, May Leung, pictured in the driver's cab of a train. I remembered there had been something of a media fuss when she was appointed: the first woman, the first British Asian to run a British railway service. The daughter of Hong Kong migrants, she'd grown up in a Chinese takeaway in Liverpool. But I wasn't in the mood to read puff pieces. I settled into the plush seat and hoped the one beside me would remain vacant.

I like travelling by train. You can get up and move around, watch cities and countryside pass by through the window and they're usually dependable, largely running to schedule. Planes have lost their glamour, not least because of the fuss involved before you even board. On the train, I could relax and think in comfort. And did I need to think.

I'd been visiting my sister-in-law, who I'll call Em, as she was recovering at home from breast cancer surgery. I'd been through it myself a few years earlier and wanted to offer support, I knew how easy it can be to catastrophise. Jim, my husband, had recently called in on his sister when he'd had a meeting in Manchester and agreed she'd welcome a visit. I'd packed a small heart-shaped cushion for her – he didn't think she had one – and I knew from personal experience how they can help make post-surgery more comfortable.

Resting at home, my sister-in-law was tired but optimistic, and Derek, her husband, was trying to give the same impression. I could tell Em was on the mend when she commented on my grey hair, which I'd stopped cutting and dyeing in the pandemic and then decided I preferred it that way.

'Brave,' she said. 'Still rocking the granny look.'

She stroked the sleek blonde wig she had decided to wear before she even started chemo in order to get used to it. 'I might go all Joan Collins and stick with the wig. It will save on salon prices.'

Em is one of those elegant Northern women who are always beautifully turned out: perfect make-up, smart outfits with high heels. I knew she'd thought her brother had made an odd choice when we first met many years before. I was introduced to the family wearing a leather bomber jacket, jeans and Converse trainers. She probably still thinks I'm a scruff, but over the years we have developed a warm friendship, discussing our children and the different challenges life has thrown at us, usually over a bottle of wine. But I was still surprised when an arm was suddenly around my shoulders, encasing me in a warm hug as she asked how I was. Just fine, I said, a little bemused. She was the one who was sick.

Derek ambled off to do something in his workroom – after he burnt out in a stressful career he turned to hand-making axes and knives. He's the first to admit it was an unusual path, but to be fair to him, they are objects of surprising practical beauty. Em and I sat across from each other at the table in her gleaming kitchen, nursing mugs of tea. We talked about our kids for a while; theirs are older than mine and long gone from home, when suddenly she said: 'I keep on trying to think of a reason. Have I drunk too much, eaten the wrong things, not done the right exercise? I know it's stupid, but I want to know, why me?'

[I've removed more identifying details re 'Derek'. I assume that's not his real name but thought he actually might be a burnt-out social worker? – Loretta]

[You're right. Glad you picked it up. – Claire]

I took her hand. 'Em, you've done nothing wrong. Unless it's inherited, you know it's random. And common. One in seven women in the UK. We're just the unlucky ones. But also lucky. Because we got it older, our hormones aren't up to supercharging it, so we have good survival rates. And we live in a time where there's great treatment available.'

She didn't seem completely convinced. I tried again.

'It's a bastard, and the cure's not pleasant, but you've got every reason to be optimistic. You didn't ask for it, you didn't cause it. We always look for reasons, but most shit things that happen are just random. Wrong cell, wrong place. Wrong place, wrong time.'

She looked at me for a moment, and I could see she was tearing up, then she nodded, chinked her mug to mine: 'Bollocks to cancer.'

I chinked back with a smile.

A pre-ordered dinner delivery from a local posh restaurant, my treat, went down well. Afterwards, I was delighted when Derek presented me with a kitchen knife, about 20 cm long, a dark green resin and olive wood handle anchoring a strong, well-honed blade. Less delighted when he explained why. I slept badly that night.

The usual hustle and bustle occurred at the last minute as passengers wrestled with luggage, finding the right carriage and the correct seat. A strong odour of unwashed clothes suddenly hit me, a smell I imagine everyone was used to a hundred years ago, but which is jarring nowadays in our ultra-hygienic society. Before I had time to discover the source, I was hit on the head by a supermarket 'bag for life', apparently full of tinned food.

It wasn't a major incident, but the cans hurt. I turned and looked up angrily, prepared to remonstrate, however, the culprit appeared more in need of help than a telling off. He was a big anxious man, perhaps in his early thirties, gold-framed glasses with smeared lenses perched on his nose, patchy stubble on his chin and beneath that, zipped up to the top, a grubby high-vis yellow vest over a grey jumper. An incongruous pair of pink trainers completed the look, along with a mauve backpack, threads spooling from the seams, strapped to his shoulder. He was clutching a ticket in one hand and the shopping bag full of tins in the other.

'Which carriage is your seat in?' I asked, selfishly hoping he wasn't going to be my neighbour.

His eyes darted, as if he didn't know what to do. I smiled, and he relaxed a little then handed me his phone with his ticket displayed. He was in a seat a few carriages ahead and, relieved, I explained carefully how many carriages he needed to walk through, while trying not to breathe too deeply. If I was a better person I would have taken him to his seat, but I desperately wanted some peace and quiet to consider my future after Derek's accidental revelation. It hadn't come as a complete surprise, but I knew I had to think carefully about my next steps.

I ducked as the anxious man swung the shopping bag and lumbered away up the carriage. People were settling down, moving the last bits of luggage out of the aisle and onto the parcel shelf, when a middle-aged man appeared at my side; tall, red-headed, he was swaying before the train had even moved.

It just wasn't my day. He shoved a backpack onto the overhead shelf then sat down beside me and spread his leg into my space. Booze, sweat and cigarettes; he looked like he'd been up all night. A crumpled shirt pulled tight across his substantial stomach was topped by an expensive wool jacket. He leant across.

'You're in my seat,' he slurred, Scots-accented.

I showed him my ticket and the numbers on the seats. 'I booked the window seat,' he said emphatically. He clearly hadn't, but at the thought of how uncomfortable the journey would be, trapped by his manspreading for a couple of hours, I offered to swap. At least then I could escape into the aisle, and he might face the window which could minimise the alcohol fumes wafting in my direction. He was muttering, and a few people glanced our way. We exchanged seats, but instead of thanking me, he just said: 'This was my seat anyway, woman.' I let it go. Funny how the factual word 'woman' can sound like an insult, said in a certain way. But a man who is drunk at ten o'clock in the morning is not a man to argue with in an enclosed space.

The carriage wasn't full, and I considered moving, but if I sat somewhere that turned out to have a last-minute booking, it would mean even more disruption. The seat I assumed should have been my neighbour's wasn't reserved, so with any luck he wouldn't be on the train for long. There were two quick stops after we left Manchester – Stockport and Wilmslow – and with any luck he'd stagger off at one of those. On a day when I really needed peace and quiet, I'd only been on the train a matter of minutes and already suffered aggression from a coke-addled arsehole and a soused seat-stealer – and been banged on the head by a bagful of baked beans. People say bad things come in threes. Perhaps now I could have a peaceful journey. What else could go wrong?

The train hissed softly and set off with a light whoosh, creating the sensation we had been hermetically sealed in the carriage. The sounds were hushed, the swaying movement gentle. There was a brief and friendly announcement and apology for the delay from the train manager. A low hum of conversation from a few passengers didn't pause for the security announcement that starts 'If you see something that doesn't look right' and ends with 'See it. Say it. Sorted.' and a number to text. The usual routine. Most people were silent, watching out the window, looking at phones or other devices. There was the occasional rustle of a paperback and, more rare, a newspaper.

At last, I could turn my thoughts to what Derek had accidentally revealed the previous night. I remembered how my stomach had lurched when he had produced that beautiful kitchen knife and said that he'd made it for me because he thought Jim would take his when he moved out. He had patted my hand sympathetically, assuming I knew. And was deeply embarrassed when he realised I didn't.

Sitting on the train, I tried to imagine how the next conversation with my husband would go and how I'd manage to control my fury with him for not talking to me first. Of course, I knew things weren't right between us. But to just walk away after all those years, and two children? I could feel my heart starting to thump and decided to try not to think about it for a while and let the possible end of my marriage percolate somewhere in the background instead.

My neighbour, who I later learned was Patrick Harbour, 48, a Glaswegian businessman and divorced father of two, continued to be unsettled and unsettling. He fell asleep shortly after the train pulled out of Manchester Piccadilly and his leg sprawled further into my space, pressing against me.

My phone vibrated. It was Jim. I rejected the call. Then I saw there were three texts from him. The last one:

> please please ring, we need to talk.

I felt my heart rate going up again, caught my breath and deleted them all. He could wait. Let him find out what it's like to not know what's going to hit him. It would do him good to sweat while I decided what to do.

I put the phone on silent and tucked it away in my bag. I had to find a way of reducing the tension throbbing through my system. Taking a few deep breaths, I looked across the aisle and out of the window at a wet Manchester and studied the grey clouds overhead. I focused on the quiet thrum of the train. Sleep had been elusive at my in-laws, and I was hoping for a snooze to refresh me. But, inevitably, Charlie came to mind, which he did whenever I was facing a dilemma. What would he do?

We weren't very similar, my twin and me. He was fair, I was mousy brown, although we were alike in other ways: tall, brown-eyed and both with a penchant for arguing, particularly with each other. Having my own children had brought back memories of our battles. They bickered too as kids, but it lacked the ferocity that Charlie and I brought to our fights. No wonder our parents, who were surprised by our arrival in their late thirties, were exhausted by us. But when we weren't fighting, we got on well. We understood each other in a way no one else could. Together, up against anyone else, we were united and implacable. I wished he could help me work out what to do. Maybe punch my husband in the face? Not really his style. Or mine.

The drunk's knee pressed into my thigh, pulling me away from thoughts of my twin. I attempted to gently move him back to his side by pushing with my left leg. He woke, confused, then angry. 'No, thanks. I don't screw oldies.'

His blue bloodshot eyes were like marbles that had failed the quality check. Two angry misogynists in one carriage – what were the odds. I told him that if he carried on being offensive, I'd fetch the train manager and have him thrown off at the next stop. I sounded calm: my teacher voice. I'd been a university lecturer for years and knew how to project, and I wanted other passengers to hear in case I needed support. He muttered something unintelligible and turned back to face the window, moving his legs and freeing up the space between us. People had turned to look, and I caught the eye of one young woman, brown-skinned with a pierced nose. I rolled my eyes, and she shook her head in sympathy.

Outside, the hinterland of Manchester passed by, bearing the marks of industry from a previous age, the occasional Victorian brick mill chimney still standing proud among all the new-build apartment blocks. The drifting grey clouds and sporadic rain seemed entirely appropriate for the outskirts of the city where spring had not yet sprung. It looked almost dark: the light played differently with the red brick of the area, compared to the warm yellows of the London stock brick with which I was more familiar. We steadily moved from the post-industrial landscape to suburban rows of houses backing onto the railway line with their strips of gardens; as ever, some neat, clipped and planted – who knew so many families had trampolines – others just a dumping ground.

The 'oldies' comment stung a little, I admit. I smoothed my navy-blue Margaret Howell jacket, enjoying the feel of the material. I don't go for glamour, but I like to wear well-made clothes. Underneath, I was wearing a blue- and white-striped shirt with a grey jumper, topping tapered dark grey trousers. I'd never taken to wearing heels and had fully embraced the trainer revolution, although today I was in black brogues. I remembered Em that morning, looking me up and down as I was leaving, and saying that my look was 'very arty'; that she could imagine Grayson Perry wearing it, which I thought was odd as he's most famous for ornate takes on dresses. But 'arty' was fine.

A friendly young woman in a red uniform came through with a trolley of drinks and croissants. I took a coffee, then checked my phone. I couldn't help myself. Another call from Jim. I contemplated texting something to wind him up, but decided silence was better. I noticed a new email from my daughter, recently moved abroad to study, and read it, my heart sinking. She was anxious, not sure she'd made the right decision. I replied quickly, with love and sympathy and encouragement. Pressing send, I hoped my message would work. It was tough to be in a new country without any friends, but if she stuck with it for a couple of months, I was sure she'd come to enjoy her new life. If she returned now, I was just as sure she'd feel a failure.

The cokehead was standing and fiddling with a bag on the parcel shelf. He turned and looked round the carriage, and I ducked my head. Perhaps I'm a snob, but I wondered what he was doing in first class. Maybe he was a successful dealer who was developing a taste for the product. He looked restless, wired, and I didn't like the way his eyes prowled round. And why take a hit when you're going to be sitting on a train for a couple of hours? He put a phone to his ear then sat down. My neighbour belched, more stale whisky fumes, but at least he stayed asleep.

We had been moving for less than ten minutes, when, suddenly, the train lurched, and then slowed. A bag fell off the parcel shelf onto a man beneath, who, startled, gave a surprisingly high-pitched yelp. Passengers turned to each other with questioning looks or peered out of the windows in case an obstruction could be seen. People in Britain have lived with terrorist attacks for decades, and the monochrome posters on public transport with the mantra we'd heard on the recorded announcement, '*See it. Say it. Sorted.*', are a reminder to stay alert. But people aren't that bothered. The man hit by the bag made a joke of it – 'leaves on the line'. Within moments any slight tension had dissipated, and the train's speed picked up, rather slower than before it seemed, but smoothly.

I was just beginning to doze off, when another unpleasant odour hit my nostrils. I've a more sensitive sense of smell than most people, but it really was olfactory hell in coach J that morning. Now I was assaulted by a sharp chemical odour caused, I quickly discovered, by a woman across the aisle doing her nails. She had an open bottle of remover on the table, a few cotton wool pads, plus a pot of varnish and what looked like a bunch of miniature torture tools. A full mani was in progress and I hate the smell of acetone. I would have taken a deep breath to try to calm down – but that would have meant filling my lungs with the toxic fumes. The train pulled into Stockport station.

It was a short stop, a few people joined the train, a few left, but none from our carriage. We were just pulling out from the platform when the Scotsman's leg shot out again, kicking my ankle. This time I decided to avoid confrontation and take the opportunity to use the loo and stretch my legs, so I grabbed my navy leather tote bag – a present from Jim, I suddenly remembered, a catch in my throat.

The manicurist was facing the window, texting. As I passed, I swept the bottle of nail polish remover into my tote, pushing the click top closed. Childish, I know. If she is reading this, I apologise. I suppose it was a reaction to all the inconveniences I'd already experienced in the brief time since we left Manchester. But no excuse, it was petty behaviour.

The disabled toilet was spacious and clean, and I took my time, brushing my hair in front of the mirror and wondering if I should start dyeing it again. It felt thick and healthy in a way it never did in the years it was dyed various shades of brown. I suddenly wondered what Jim thought of it. When I was recovering from cancer, he'd often tell me how much better I was looking, until I retorted, 'I must have looked really crap last week, because apparently I've improved every day since.' He hadn't mentioned my appearance again. But he was now looking at someone else, apparently. It was so humiliating. I was distracted for a moment by a noise; was it a shout? I wasn't sure, it could have been a squeal of brakes or just the scraping of wheels on a worn piece of line. But the train was still moving smoothly, taking me home, to what?

Lost in thought, I emerged from the toilet and stopped suddenly as I heard a man shout aggressively: 'Shut up and sit down!' The anger in his voice made me freeze and then, instinctively, I tucked myself behind the heavily laden luggage rack.

It took a few moments for me to understand what I was seeing. The cokehead was in the aisle not far from my seat, with his back to me. He was the one shouting, and now, I could see, also waving a gun. My heart missed a beat. Was it real? Someone said, 'Calm down, young man. It'll be OK,' with misplaced optimism. It didn't work. He shouted louder, his accent Liverpudlian, sounding like a petulant child unleashing a tantrum.

'Do as I say. Put ya phones, ya laptops on the floor in the aisle. Nobody speak. Do as I say, and I won't have to shoot ya, OK. And shut the fuckin' blinds. Now!'

Armed robbery? On a train? How did he think he would get away with it? Or was he off his head on whatever he'd put up his nose? There was a stunned silence; someone choked a sob. The woman with the nose ring was standing beside her seat in the act of putting her bag back up and looked straight at him. Then things happened very quickly. The gunman yelled at her to sit down, and a middle-aged Black woman stood up and approached with her arms held out, saying something like, 'I am a pastor, god is watching us...' at which point Cokehead advanced towards her, pointing the gun.

'Stupid bitch. Shut up.'

She backed away, head still held righteously high. As Cokehead reached her, he raised his gun. With unexpected speed, my red-headed neighbour launched himself down the aisle at the gunman. There was a tussle. The pastor sat down hurriedly, out of the way. Others stood and tentatively moved to help – I particularly noticed a wiry man with a shaven head – and then a gunshot rang out. It was deafening. Shocking. Who knew they were so loud? Blood and human tissue exploded out of Mr Harbour's back, spraying across the carriage as he fell to the floor.

2

Out of Sight

COACH J

10:35

> Sorry. We need to talk. cancelled meeting. when will u get home?

How do you know someone's dead? In Patrick Harbour's case, there was no need to try and find a pulse; his fatal injuries were obvious. As was the blood. The young woman with the pierced nose and the shaven-headed wiry man started towards him, but quickly stopped. There were screams and sobbing, topped by Cokehead yelling. I could see his gun hand was shaking. Then another man, squeezed into a shiny black jacket which made him look like a club bouncer, appeared at the far door from the coach further up the train and called out in a loud and firm voice. 'Sit down and shut up, everyone. Now! And you,' he said to Cokehead, 'get their phones.'

Black Jacket appeared to be in his thirties, tougher looking than Cokehead, with a woollen grey beanie pulled low on his head and a black backpack strapped on tightly. He glanced at the dead man then threw an annoyed scowl at the shooter, shook his head and muttered furiously. His brown-skinned face was battered, like a boxer's, and muscles strained at his jacket sleeves. The carriage was quiet, although my ears and probably every one else's were still ringing with the noise of the gunshot. It was hard to take in what had just happened. It didn't seem real.

Did Cokehead really murder a man just to steal some phones? Tucking myself back against the wall as far as I could, I peered through the gaps between bags and cases undetected.

Why didn't I sit back down with everyone else? There wasn't time to think about it and make a considered decision. It just felt safer to be out of sight, however long that might last.

Black Jacket surveyed the carriage. In his right hand was a long, thick, scary-looking knife. His cool demeanour was terrifying. He came down the aisle and I shrank back even further, searching for the passenger emergency stop handle to alert the driver, then realised it was in the carriage – if I went for it, I would be clearly visible to the man with the knife.

'Pull the blinds down,' he said, loud and clear, in what seemed like a Manc accent. Passengers began to fumble and do as he commanded, and as they did, the world was shut out, detaching us further from normality.

Whereas the first hijacker was a bundle of nerves, Black Jacket looked at the passengers with detached disdain. 'This man's dead cos he did something stupid, OK? Didn't need to happen. Do as we say, and you'll be fine. We're not here to hurt yer, all right?'

An odd thing to say when someone's been shot dead and the man speaking has a large knife in his hand.

People kept their heads down while Black Jacket started picking up phones and putting them in a plastic bag he produced from his pocket. He handed another bag to Cokehead to do the same. There was the occasional whimper and people kept glancing at the body. I caught a glimpse of a sprawled leg, dark blood spreading across the floor and stepped back without thinking, which accidentally opened the automatic vestibule door. But as luck would have it another train went past in the opposite direction at that exact moment, and no one noticed the noise, so I slipped through, then tried the door to the out-of-service end carriage, thinking it might be a good place to hide – but it was locked so I ducked back into the toilet. I had to ring the police.

It turns out that it's not easy to use a phone when your hands are shaking. I locked the door behind me as quietly as possible, trying not to think of a gunshot blowing it open, and sat on the toilet, lid down, bag on lap and pulled out my phone. Focus, focus, I remember telling myself. I tried to recall the text number for the Transport Police thinking it might be quick and direct – the 'See it. Say it. Sorted.' one – but couldn't. How's anyone supposed to remember that when they need it? Instead, I dialled 999 and after what seemed like an age, but I learned later was only twelve seconds, got through to the police.

Can you speak up?

No. Listen. There are at least two armed men on the 10:12 train from Manchester to London. They've shot one man dead already. In the second to last carriage, J.

What's your name please, caller?

Claire Fitzroy.

And your address?

Fuck my address. There's a madman with a gun. More than one. Do something. They're…

Where are you right now, are you safe?

No! I'm in the toilet. Not safe. No one's safe!

Please try and stay calm.

Please try and fucking do something. Shit. They're at the door.

I hung up. I could hear someone outside the toilet. The handle was being shaken.

'Open the door!'

I slipped my phone under a ledge over the sink. 'Sorry. I'm on the toilet. I'm sick.'

I tried to make my voice sound weak. Which turned out not to be that difficult.

'Open the door!'

Banging and scraping noises made me realise he was trying to smash the lock. There was nowhere to hide. I raised the toilet seat lid and sat down again, bag on lap. Bent over, my hair hung down about my head. Holding my breath, thoughts of my children almost paralysed me. Would I ever see them again? I pushed the thoughts away and concentrated on slowly breathing out. The door opened and he came in. I saw his black trainers. Cokehead. I hoped he'd see an old lady, bent over and sobbing, her grey hair covering her face.

'Please, I'm not well.'
'Give me your phone, bitch.'
'I don't…'

He moved closer. I could smell the laundry detergent on his clothes and briefly, madly, wondered if his mum did his washing. He grabbed me under the chin and lifted my face. As he looked into my eyes, I brought the kitchen knife up and out of my bag and held the point against his neck. Could I get him to back off? He frowned: a strange nanosecond of intimacy where I noticed one of his brown eyes had a slight squint. He was lifting the gun, when, suddenly, the train jolted, his head jerked forward and the tip of the knife pierced his throat. The blade was sharper than I had imagined. Dropping the gun, he tried to grab it, and I tried to pull it away, but somehow, in the struggle, the knife slipped across his throat. Arterial blood sprayed out as I stood up and backed away to avoid it. His hands moved to his neck, the blood escaping between his fingers, and he looked at me, surprised, then swayed to one side. I think I muttered an apology as I gently helped him sit down on the ground, resting his head and back against the wall while trying not to get covered in blood.

As I moved back, the blood continued to spurt from his throat through his fingers and onto the floor. His bloodied hands slipped down. There was a gurgling noise coming from his mouth. He was dying. I couldn't see any signs that he was in pain, he just looked shocked, then vacant, his mouth slackening as he slid to the floor. Ducking down, I tried to use his jacket to stop the blood. Then looked at him again.

I started the morning as someone upset that her marriage might be over. And now I was someone who had accidentally killed a man.

3

Misdirection

COACH J

10:50

> Ready to go stick to plan

> aok

There was no time to think. I couldn't believe what had just happened, but there was nothing I could do to save him and Black Jacket was still in the carriage. There was a shout: 'Hey, brother. Hurry up.'

He sounded more irritated than nervous. I battled with my fear. Fight or flight or… There was no escape. I'd have to stay where I was and try to… I didn't know. I'd have to wing it. Shifting to the side, I pressed against the wall so that the gunman's body would be the first thing someone coming through the door would see. And the blood. There was a lot of it, spreading across the floor in a growing pool. I wiped the knife on his trousers and put it back in my bag and noticed blood on my shirt. Grabbing a fistful of toilet paper, I wiped my face to remove any spray and then picked up the gun from where he had dropped it. It looked old and was heavy and clearly loaded, although the safety was on. Somewhere in my brain I registered that the train continued to move, as if nothing had happened. I wondered about CCTV, if someone might come to help. I felt numb, but intensely aware of everything around me. I dropped my head down again, trying to control my breathing.

Black Jacket was closer. He shouted: 'Come here, you. Shut the fuck up. If anyone tries anything, she gets it, OK?'

So much for *we're not here to harm you*.

'Brother, what's up...? What the fuck?'

I raised my eyes and saw Black Jacket in the doorway. He was holding the young woman with the nose ring, one hand at her neck, the knife in the other. Her face was frozen, her lips clamped together. His jaw dropped open in an expression of disbelief that was almost cartoonish.

I sobbed: 'A man with a knife. He went down there...' and pointed towards the closed carriage at the end of the train. It didn't make sense. But I just needed him to be distracted. As he turned to look where I had indicated, the young woman leant back and I jumped up, years of yoga coming into play, while dropping my bag and bringing the gun up to his head.

'Let her go,' I said firmly. For just a moment Black Jacket looked puzzled. Then the shaven-headed wiry man I'd seen in the carriage appeared behind him, swiftly removed the hijacker's hand from the woman's neck and grabbed him firmly as the knife dropped. There was a half-hearted struggle, but Black Jacket's eyes kept returning to what was on the floor.

The newcomer glanced too, then looked at me. 'You all right, pet?'

I nodded, keeping the gun trained on Black Jacket. He turned to the other woman. 'You OK?'

'Fine. Thanks.' She managed a brief smile and moved back, rubbing her neck.

'I'm Stuart Deaver, call me Deavey.' He seemed alert but calm. We were in close proximity in the train toilet, the smell of fresh blood with its metallic tang winning out against chemical air fresheners. I registered piercing green eyes, light brown skin, plus the shaved head, and a tattoo I couldn't decipher on his neck. There were burn scars on one side of his face and he was wearing a neat Harrington jacket in navy, with jeans that looked ironed. Military, I thought. A 37-year-old ex-corporal originally from Sunderland, as it turned out.

Before I could respond, Black Jacket came back to life.

'Get off me,' he shouted, and he tried to struggle free, his eyes blazing in fury. Deavey grabbed him more firmly in an armlock.

'Stay still,' he barked.

'Do you know anything about guns?' I asked him.

He nodded. 'Ex-military.'

Bingo. I held out the gun to him. 'A water pistol's about my limit.'

He kept Black Jacket in a firm grip with one hand and quickly took the gun with the other, checked it over then pointed it at the hijacker's head. I noticed a slight tremor in his hand. The young woman was still behind him, pulling her dark ponytail into shape and smoothing the grey sweatshirt she was wearing over her jeans.

She spoke softly. 'I'll ask everyone to be quiet in case there are more of them.'

Black Jacket produced a mixture of a laugh and a grunt. 'Course there are. Do as you're told, and you might live.'

He looked at me, perhaps trying to work out what had happened and what my role had been. He didn't seem to find an answer so turned to Deavey.

'You fight back, you'll all be dead.'

This was definitely not a robbery. 'Why are you doing this?' I asked.

He started to say something I didn't catch, and the woman interrupted.

'This is not what is taught in Islam. It's not right to hurt innocent people.'

'Is that it?' I added. 'Some kind of jihad? Really?' That was puzzling. The man dead on the floor hadn't mentioned religion.

Black Jacket didn't answer.

'Just another fruit loop, the flavour makes no difference,' said Deavey, breaking the moment.

'We need his jacket and hat. If one of us puts them on and keeps our back to the next carriage, it might fool them for a bit. If there are more,' I said.

'What about his phone?' said the young woman.

Deavey nodded and dug a phone out of the squirming man's pocket and handed it to her. It was an old green flip phone, cute, but not smart. Calls and texts only, I assumed. I turned to the young woman. 'I'm Claire, by the way.'

'Anita. We need a passcode.' She waved the phone and squeezed out a quick smile. I was impressed by her sangfroid.

'What is it?' I asked Black Jacket. He ignored me. The phone wasn't capable of fingerprint opening let alone face recognition, which we might have been able to force him to do. Getting a passcode was a different matter. 'Let's have his jacket.'

Between us we removed it and his hat while he swore at us and tried to resist, until the ex-soldier gave him a sharp slap. I noticed a red badge on the captive's jacket that said *My Vaccine Passport* on top of an image of a hand giving the finger.

Anita took the clothes. 'I'll put them on. I'm not far off the same height. Might get away with it.'

She was slim, but with the volume of the puffer jacket it could work. 'Remember not to get too close to the doors or they'll open,' I said. 'I already made that mistake. And on the way through, can you ask passengers for scarves, belts, anything we can tie him up with, and get someone to bring them to us?'

She nodded and left.

I looked to Deavey. 'We should gag him, so he doesn't alert anyone. But we could do with the passcode.'

He nodded as Black Jacket began to struggle again. He shook him, then lightly slapped him with the gun. 'I'm military, OK. I don't have a problem using a gun, so behave and tell us your passcode.'

[Hijacker's testimony said Deavey's words were: 'Or I'll blow your fucking head off and you can join your friend in hell.' Not correct? – Loretta]

Black Jacket stopped wriggling but laughed. 'You're all dead anyway.'

'Why?' I asked.

He smirked.

'We'll keep Laughing Larry in here. With his chum. Don't want to scare the horses,' said Deavey.

He turned to Black Jacket again. 'Are you saying there's a bomb on the train?'

Black Jacket decided he'd said enough. He looked away from Deavey and me but began shuffling when he realised his colleague's blood was spreading towards him. Deavey checked the dead man's pockets, keeping the gun trained on Black Jacket, and came up with another green flip phone.

I stepped through the doorway. 'I'll get something to tie him up.'

COURT EXHIBIT No. JH01
(Group text from Gold Command main
channels – authenticated)

10:50: Move to highest alert. Loss of life confirmed. Extreme danger to public. Code red.

As I came out of the toilet cubicle, I realised we were going through Wilmslow station: small, low-slung buildings, almost empty. We had been due to stop, but instead we appeared to accelerate. That meant either the driver had been told to keep going by the rail company, or hijackers were in the driver's compartment. I assumed the latter. Now the outside world would take us seriously. A runaway train was dangerous. A man with a gun was dangerous. So, apparently, was a late middle-aged woman with a kitchen knife, but I couldn't think about that for now.

Passengers turned to look in my direction when I stepped back into the first-class carriage, finger to my lips. There were about thirty of them, and even the ones facing ahead were turning and raising themselves from their seats and passing along ties, scarves and belts to a young man near the back. A few looked stunned. Someone said, 'What happened out there?'

Hopefully the noise of the train and the doors between carriages would limit what could be heard, but I didn't want to risk any potential hijacker, or whatever they were, in the next carriage hearing something to make them curious. I noticed one woman look at me with horror. I'd forgotten about the bloodstains on my shirt and cashmere jumper. If I'd known I'd be in a bloodbath, I would have worn polyester.

Mr Harbour's body was slumped partly across the table where we had both been sitting. Someone must have moved him off the floor. I glanced at him, and for a moment felt sick, until I reminded myself how brave he'd been and tried to focus on that. My jacket was over the back of the seat, and I grabbed it in passing and put it on, concealing most of the bloodstains. At the far door, Anita was standing to one side and glancing into the carriage ahead. Two young men had found the robbers' bags that contained phones and were passing them round. The manicurist, ashen-faced, looked up at me and said softly, 'The poor man, his poor family,' then put her face in her hands, one with turquoise-painted nails, one without.

Someone asked again what had happened in the toilet.

'One of them, the murderer, is... out of action. And the other one is being tied up. But he says there are more. If anyone can get through to the police, tell them that. Please keep calm and quiet.'

Suddenly the Tannoy came to life and a strained male voice spoke. '*This is your driver. Please stay seated and do what you are asked to do.*'

There was whispering and clicking over the speaker. Then the tense-sounding driver spoke again. '*Don't use the emergency brake handle. It's been— What did you—*'

There was a click as the Tannoy was switched off. Everyone seemed frozen in their seats, waiting, as if we were at the top of a rollercoaster. Another click.

'*The emergency alarm mechanism in the carriages has been rigged with explosives.*'

The driver's voice sounded flat, tentative. I suddenly realised he was repeating what he'd been told to say. They were in the driver's cab.

'*If anyone pulls one of the emergency alarm handles, there will be a series of explosions throughout the train.*'

Explosives. Somebody screamed. There were gasps and a muted shout of 'Oh my god'.

The driver paused and when he spoke again, he sounded different, as if he was speaking for himself this time.

'Please, everyone, keep calm for all our sakes. Let's try and stay safe. Let's try and get—'

There were more clicks, then silence. Passengers were turning to each other with dawning realisation. Some people were crying, others were trying to comfort them, while some just sat in silent shock. It was a long train. We were at one end and the driver was at the other. I wondered how many more of those bastards were between us – and where were the explosives?

4
Moving On

COACH J

11:00

ring police trubleon train 10:12 frommanc. Gunshots

wtf u OK

Frank u OK? rang cops– don't know if they believed

cops rang back. let me know you OK.

stay strong

sorry sounds stupid. thinking of you

[Texts inserted as you suggested. Some from trial. Some from that obtuse Texts in Crisis article you suggested. Amazing what academics will research but actually rather moving. Author says OK, as long as credited. Great that he did the research! Also, others you sent. See what you think – Loretta]

'You heard that? They've got the driver.' I'd nipped back to the toilet carrying the swag of a few belts, ties and more scarves that the passengers had collected and put the bundle down beside Deavey. Just as well the disabled loo was relatively roomy. Deavey seemed to have used the dead man's jacket to wipe up some more of the blood and had placed it over him but was keeping close to the door and the fresher air.

He nodded grimly and Black Jacket barked another laugh, playing into the evil villain stereotype. Deavey asked me to hold the gun while he tied the hijacker up with a variety of scarves and belts. The hijacker resisted as much as he could, while swearing uncreatively. There was no point trying to get someone else to help, as we'd reached maximum occupation. I did what I could, holding the gun, but Deavey had to take it off me and smack him in the face to stop him fighting, before he eventually pushed a light but long floral scarf into the man's mouth for good measure. The hijacker didn't like that, his nose was bleeding; he started to gasp.

'Will he be able to breathe?'

'Don't know, don't care,' replied Deavey, giving him a kick which sent him to the floor beside his dead co-conspirator. 'Unless you want to tell us where these explosives are, matey?'

Black Jacket turned his head away. Deavey efficiently tied the man, who was trying to kick him, to the pipework. He landed a kick and Deavey retaliated by punching him in the face again, and the hijacker flopped back, stunned, his lip bleeding. Deavey watched for a moment until it was apparent he could breathe, then bound his feet and legs more tightly. 'Better safe than sorry.'

Deavey moved past me to the door. It was a tight squeeze. He stared at me curiously. 'You ex-services?'

I shook my head.

'Police?'

'Art lecturer.'

'Art lessons must have changed since I was at school.'

I suddenly caught sight of a woman behind him who moved away when I saw her. It was the righteous woman who the Scotsman had leapt to defend, a noble intention that resulted in his murder. Melissa Ngozi, a church pastor from London, in her forties, I found out later, smartly dressed in a burgundy suit with a cream pussy bow blouse, and what looked like an expensive handbag on her arm.

'Do you need the toilet?'

She hesitated, then nodded. I assumed she'd seen the blood and was shocked. She was fumbling with her pocket and seemed nervous but given the circumstances that was hardly surprising. I could have done with a soothing hug and a cup of tea too. Instead, I gave what I hoped was a reassuring smile. 'I'm afraid the closest available one is in the carriage ahead, and there could be more of these men,' I said, pointing up the train. 'The door to the carriage behind us is locked.' She said nothing and walked away, which I thought was odd, but shock can take people in many ways. I put her out of my mind and turned to Deavey.

'We should see if we can put the two of them in the empty carriage. Force the door.'

He shook his head. 'No time for that now. The others could find out any minute.'

The others. Were they planning to use us as hostages for something? 'What do you think they want?'

Deavey shrugged. 'No idea. But we need to move.'

We walked back into the main part of the carriage. Passing by Patrick Harbour's body, I focused on Anita, standing at the far end, with her back to the door into the vestibule between ours and the next carriage but not close enough to set off the opening mechanism. A tousled blond-haired head was stuck out into the aisle, trying to look past her, into the carriage behind. As I watched, Anita also hazarded a quick glimpse over her shoulder. The blond, a young man, turned and saw me, and raised one finger. Most people were watching him and Anita, but now other passengers were turning round to look at me and Deavey. There was a low murmuring, and I shushed everyone as I crept up the carriage and squatted down beside the blond man. This was Alex, on his way back from Manchester on a first-class ticket provided by his tech company. He was in his twenties, looked like he might play some kind of energetic sport and lift weights, and seemed, somehow, to be ready for action, but calm at the same time.

Ready for action. We know the expression and what it means without probably thinking about it too much. Focus? A level of contained energy? Looking like you're keen to get on with it while not looking like you'll lose your shit at the same time? I think back to the events of that day, the journey through the train, making snap decisions about who could be trusted not to freak out. I wouldn't call myself a particularly good judge of character if I'm only given a few seconds to assess someone, yet mainly those decisions were correct. Deavey later told me that, based on his experience, he'd concluded it was instinctive. If you stay calm yourself under stress, you pick it up in others. I'm not sure. It could just have been luck. Everyone on that train was certainly lucky that Deavey, Mr Super Calm, happened to be a fellow passenger.

The young man leant towards me. 'You OK? Where are the hijackers?'

'I'm fine. We've got one tied up in the toilet… and the killer's… out of action… dead, actually.'

'Wow.' He paused, then nodded. 'Good. I'm Alex. It's hard to see properly, with the two sets of doors and the gap between carriages, but a big guy came through the far door for a moment, and looked in. I think he saw the back of the hijacker's jacket and must have been reassured because he turned back without investigating.'

He looked at me. A serious face. 'What can I do to help?'

'The live hijacker is currently unconscious, but probably not for long,' I whispered. 'Can you keep an eye? He's not armed, and he's been efficiently tied up by Deavey, that man there, he's an ex-soldier. I'm Claire, by the way. And, Alex, be prepared, it's not a pretty sight in there. A lot of blood. Do you think you'll be OK?'

He nodded as Deavey joined us.

'Alex will keep an eye on the guy in the toilet,' I whispered.

'Great. I'm Deavey. Hijackers' phones,' he murmured, as he passed them to Alex. 'He won't give us a passcode, and we need to hurry. If his mates don't hear from him soon, I'm pretty sure they'll come looking. When the bloke comes round, see if you can get him to give it to you. It would be good to know what the hijackers are saying to each other. Don't guard him on your own, get some help, and be careful. He's tied up but he's a nasty piece of work. Try and find some kind of weapon to defend yourself.'

'If you get access, maybe try some disinformation, like there's police at the next station or something. It might help,' I added. 'They probably are there, or on their way.'

'I've got something in the luggage rack that could be useful,' Alex said, turning to fetch whatever it was. He seemed a remarkably cool young man.

A woman I hadn't noticed before, in a window seat near the front – thirties, sturdy, auburn bob, tense and dressed for the office with flat, brown leather ankle boots on her feet – cleared her throat for attention. 'Alice Hartley. I'll help – I can run messages, alert anyone – or take one of them down with a rugby tackle.'

I could hear anger, but it seemed controlled. Her hand was on the back of the seat in front and there was a pretty tattoo of a bird, a swallow maybe, just beneath her thumb joint.

'You could check if anyone's got anything we can use as a weapon. Also, we need to exchange phone numbers, to keep in touch and keep safe.' Maybe it was my age, I thought, but both she and Alex spoke to me as if reporting for duty. Fine by me. The last thing we needed were arguments about who was in control. Much better to just get on with it.

I could see Alex near the luggage rack and noticed Deavey had taken Harbour's jacket off and covered him with it. It was respectful, and sensible. No one wants to look at a dead body. It's not good for morale. Deavey was now moving along the carriage, crouching, talking to passengers in a soft voice. I glanced into the space between carriages behind where Anita stood, a serious sentinel, but could see nothing. 'Are you OK?' I mouthed, and she nodded. It takes a lot of courage to stand with your back to a glass door with who knows what behind you.

People were checking their bags for anything that could be used as a weapon. Alex had a cricket bat in his hand. He told me later it had been passed on by a friend in Manchester who had stopped playing. I've a feeling Alex would give most sports a try. Deavey joined him and handed him something, then came back up the train, his progress followed by curious eyes, to join me.

'I gave him a Swiss army knife – more discreet than a bat,' he said and then produced a metal ruler and a bottle of Prosecco from an M&S shopping bag.

'Bit early, isn't it?' I muttered. He rolled his eyes.

Alice joined us. 'Why not barricade the door?'

I shook my head. 'Then they'll know we're in control in here. And that could have other consequences. For now, best to pretend they're in charge, don't you think? Perhaps later, though.'

An older, frail-looking woman pulled gently on my arm. 'I've been trying to reach my son. But he's not answering.'

Her voice was little above a whisper and I wanted to reassure her. I took her hand for a moment. She was scared, but trying not to show it, which I admired. 'It'll be all right,' I said. 'There's a lot more of us than them. Why don't you leave him a message?'

I'd told her it would be all right, but would it? Fake optimism, perhaps, but sports psychologists say it helps to believe you stand a chance of succeeding when you are up against it, even if you know you're probably kidding yourself. Cognitive dissonance, to a certain extent. Me, I just chose not to fixate on failure, although of course the thought of it popped its ugly little head up from time to time, and I chose not to think about my children, except fleetingly. I sensed that if I gave them much bandwidth, it could stop me in my tracks.

Deavey took the hijacker's jacket and beanie from Anita and put them on. The two passengers in the seats closest to the doors, one either side of the aisle, made room, and Anita crouched on one side, her body half on the seat, while I slid into the other, close to Deavey standing at the door. I could sense a change in atmosphere throughout the carriage. People wanted to help. Thought they might have a chance. Alice was at the back trying to pull cushions out of seats, preparing for an eventual barricade, I guessed. With luck, there were enough passengers to deal with this carriage and the prisoner. We just had to face whatever was in the carriages in front of us.

It was hard to see through two sets of doors, with the added distance, perhaps three metres, of the vestibule between the carriages. But it appeared H was an empty carriage apart from one man standing talking on a phone. Where were all the passengers? I slid into the seat beside a bald man in his late thirties, dressed country casual, with a waxed cotton jacket. He seemed jumpy and spoke too loudly in a posh voice.

'I box. I can take the bastards out.'

I was briefly tempted to ask why, in that case, he hadn't had a go already. But then again, it can take a while to process a murder in front of your eyes. 'Good to know,' I whispered with a nod. I've often found if you speak softly the person you're speaking to drops their volume accordingly. 'Can you stay in this carriage for now?' I added.

'Who put you in charge?' Still too loud.

'No one. But the training never leaves you and I'm working with that ex-soldier and policewoman over there,' I lied, pointing to Anita. At that point I had no idea what she did. And I don't know why I said what I said about training, but it seemed to do the trick. I could see him check out Deavey and Anita.

'After we've gone into the next carriage could you keep an eye on the door? If a hijacker comes through, we'll need a second line. Have you got anything you could use as a weapon?'

Baldy clenched his fists and I nodded. He seemed mollified. Alice joined us, carrying a pair of scissors and some knitting needles, and I handed one to the bald gent, who examined it as if he'd never seen one before. Alice was followed by a middle-aged man, bespectacled, suited, with a full head of short grey hair, and a jacket that was having a bit of an argument about meeting over his stomach. I'm pretty sure he wouldn't mind me saying that. 'Paul. I was in the TA for thirteen years. How can I help?'

'Thanks, mate,' Deavey replied softly. 'Fusiliers, ex-corporal. Bit of backup for now maybe? Can you handle this?' He reached behind his back to pull something out, and the long blade he'd taken from the hijacker appeared in his hand. Paul nodded, and took it, testing its weight. He looked as if it was just what he had been expecting when he'd got on the 10:12 that morning to head into London for a services charity meeting with donors.

I did my best to peer into the next carriage, but the train jerked, I lost my balance, and the door opened. Suddenly Baldy was there, standing on the seat, steadily holding it open to stop the noise it would make shutting. I revised my opinion of him. Through the next door I could see the one man standing, his back to us, seemingly oblivious to the noise. My mistake with the door was useful. We might be able to get closer to each carriage before anyone knew we were there. The trouble with modern train carriages is that, for good reason, there is nowhere to hide. But the recesses at the exits in the vestibules, I realised, gave welcome space to tuck yourself out of anyone's eyeline.

I turned to Deavey, Paul and Alice, who had joined us. 'Shall I take a closer look?'

'I'm happy to go,' said Paul.

'Me too,' added Alice.

'And you're not leavin' me out of the party,' muttered Deavey.

Baldy joined us. 'I'll hold the fort here.'

We crawled in and arranged ourselves out of view from the carriages, two on either side while Baldy placed a large case behind us to keep the door open into the liberated carriage J, in case we needed to run back, or they needed to come to our aid.

We crouched, wedged in our hiding places. Alice whispered: 'Are they suicide bombers? Jihadists?'

Good questions. But I didn't have any answers.

'Maybe. But who knows?' said Paul.

'The driver said there were explosives, he was obviously told to say that, and that moron in the toilet was laughing as if he knew we were buggered,' said Deavey as he peeked round across from me, and lower down, I did the same.

We watched the man in the carriage ahead checking seats and picking up phones. Only one guy, but he was big, over six foot and broad with it, even if you discounted the added heft provided by his grey puffer jacket. Anita stuck her head round the door. She was going to stay in J, to help in case things went wrong. We agreed the next steps and Deavey handed over the jacket and beanie to Alice.

Stepping back into J, I stood to one side of the door, raised my hand for silence and spoke quietly to the passengers. 'Pass this on to anyone who can't hear me. If someone comes through that door who isn't one of us,' I indicated the people in the vestibule, 'duck down, OK? We're going into the next carriage. There might be people in there needing help.'

I just had time to notice Melissa Ngozi shaking her head, before turning back into the vestibule. There Alice, in the black puffer and beanie Deavey had taken from Black Jacket, moved to stand with her back to the door into coach H. Deavey and Paul crouched in the recesses by the outer doors and I moved to position myself in front of Alice. Alice glanced behind her then looked at me with a nod and a wink, of all things. It was so unexpected that I had to stifle a smile as she started towards me. We each screamed as loudly as possible, I launched myself at her and we fell to the floor, opening the door to coach H.

Extract from Cross-Examination of Jason Fellowes by Defence Barrister Eleanor Masters

DB. *When did you first see Ms Fitzroy?*
JF. *I was waiting to see when the hijackers would return. I'd said we should jump them, and then the young Asian woman came up, shushing people and stood by the door. And then I saw Corporal Deaver and Claire Fitzroy come in.*
DB. *You told the police that you thought Ms Fitzroy was retired military, or police. Did she tell you that?*
JF. *Perhaps she was talking about Mr Deaver, and I misunderstood.*
DB. *That's not what's in your statement to the police, Mr Fellowes. I'll read it to you: 'Claire Fitzroy said she was retired military when I asked her why she was in charge.'*
JF. *It was a misunderstanding. It was a brief conversation in chaotic circumstances.*

DB. *But she was the leader, in your opinion?*
JF. *Not exactly. The corporal and Paul from the TA also made decisions. Actually, we all threw in ideas at different times, or did things on our own initiative.*
DB. *How would you describe Ms Fitzroy's demeanour?*
JF. *Calm. Focused.*
DB. *Focused on getting the hijackers.*
JF. *Yes. But…*
DB. *Leading the pack, as it were?*
JF. *I was going to say she was focused on getting the hijackers, to stop them hurting anyone else. We all agreed on that. Apart from the religious lady who wanted to pray for them.*
DB. *Did you know that Ms Fitzroy's brother was killed by terrorists?*

5
Big Guy

COACHES J–H

11:15

> aok cab

> ffs pickup bro

> coming

Perhaps you will question our actions and think of better things that we could have done, or better ways of doing what we did. I know I do. Usually in the early hours of the morning when I've been woken up by the technicolour nightmares that invade my sleep. But on the 10:12 that day, every decision we made had to be acted upon so quickly that there was no time for discussion or reflection apart from a brief nod or shake of the head. And sometimes there wasn't even time for that and individually we had to act on instinct.

In the swaying space between coaches J and H, we couldn't be sure that only one hijacker would come through the door. I tried to quell the image of a hoard of armed maniacs thundering through from carriages further up the train. Any more than one would have posed a much bigger problem for our small band of brothers and sisters, although the enclosed space played to our advantage rather than to theirs, I thought.

Fortunately, in response to our little pantomime, it was only one, the big guy in the grey puffer. He was pumped up at the sight of the person who he thought was his colleague wrestling on the floor with a mad woman. Pumped up and armed. A long machete had appeared in his hand, which, even as I was grappling on the floor, gave me a moment of cold terror.

In his hurry to help his mate, he ignored the door recess. As he passed, Deavey and Paul leapt out, Deavey smashing the machete out of his hand with the gun as Paul got him round the neck. Baldy, who had introduced himself as Jason Fellowes, lunged through the J carriage doors, launching a kick, which missed. This was no neat, choreographed battle. Alice and I were trying to get up from the floor and keep out of the way of the fight at the same time, which proved largely impossible. It was a mess. But Jason made himself useful again by helping to drag a yelling Big Guy to the ground and keeping him there. There was a melee of punches, grunts and kicks. I disentangled myself from Alice and tried to keep an eye on what was happening while checking to make sure I hadn't caused her or myself any injuries. Deavey managed to force a scarf in the hijacker's mouth, while Paul and Jason contained him, and Alice searched him for a phone. Then Big Guy was dragged struggling back into coach J by Paul and Jason, with passengers joining to help – or hinder – and a menacing Deavey coolly pointing the gun at him. There were kicks and curses and one woman slapped him. Out of the corner of my eye I saw Ngozi filming it all on her phone. And then, horrified, I noticed that other passengers were filming too. If any of them were livestreaming this, and the other hijackers saw what was going on, we were in trouble. I was livid.

'Stop filming!' I called out. 'They'll know what we're doing.'

But the phone holders either looked puzzled or ignored me.

'We don't want them to know we're fighting back! Stop filming – don't upload anything to social media,' I said furiously.

We had very little time, and potentially even less than we had hoped for if any of that footage had already been uploaded. Images could move quickly through the internet. Just because the phones we'd found on the hijackers so far weren't smart, it didn't mean there weren't others. But people were gormlessly holding out their sodding phones. It was as if getting them back meant they had to be used. Alice was arguing with an outraged twenty-something who waved his around as if he was glued to it. Meanwhile Deavey and the others had got Big Guy to the back of the carriage where he was still trying to wriggle out of their arms, and was, I'm sure, playing to the phone cameras, moaning as if he was being murdered. It was chaos.

I looked down the carriage to Deavey with a WTF expression. He caught my eye, swore, then barked: 'Listen! Don't send anything to anyone. If they see it, they'll come down and kill all of us – or set a bomb off.'

That had an impact. It wasn't just people responding to male authority – although Deavey does a good bark. It was the word 'bomb', even more than 'kill', which sent ripples through the carriage. Phones were lowered, and people started to mutter to each other, looking scared. A young woman with lank ash-blonde hair put her head in her hands, whimpering. Paul grabbed Big Guy's grey jacket and wrestled it off him with some help from Alice, then pulled it on over his suit. Lifting up the hood, he spoke calmly: 'Any volunteers to tie this guy up? We need to act fast.'

It was a good distraction. Jason and a few others were quickly all over it, so we left them to deal with Big Guy and moved into H, the next carriage. Deavey first, then me, Paul, Alice – with Anita, who had joined us, to bring up the rear.

It was eerily empty: blinds down, spilt coffee cups dripping onto the floor, abandoned food, jackets and coats strewn across seats. We had taken down three hijackers already, but glancing at the plan of the train layout on the wall at the end of the carriage I could see there were six more coaches. How many more hijackers were there, armed and ready, further up the train?

Deavey picked up a sandwich from a table, took a bite, then walked up to the plan. Paul and Alice joined us. Echoing my thoughts, Alice said, 'How many more of them do you think?'

'If they're squashing passengers into fewer carriages, it could mean they don't have the numbers to keep an eye on everyone if they're spread out, so fewer than ten? And we've already taken care of three,' I replied.

I noticed Paul and Deavey exchange a glance.

'What?'

'It might be about where they've placed an IED,' shrugged Paul.

'They're moving passengers to keep them safe?' asked Alice.

He shook his head. 'Not necessarily.'

'Shit,' she replied, looking sick.

'But they could be negotiating. With the police,' I said, trying to be positive. 'We need to find out what the cops are doing.'

'Alex said the police say they can't get hold of them,' said Alice.

'So we can't hang about. Let's get moving... while they don't know about us.' Deavey was already edging to the connecting door to coach G. He ducked down, looked through then turned to us and whispered. 'Plenty of passengers, from what I can see. All squashed in. Can't see a hijacker.'

He looked at me. 'I'll do a quick recce, can you keep watch? And if it goes tits up, don't leave me dangling.'

He crouched low and approached the door. It swooshed open, and he went on through, dropping the rest of the sandwich and holding the gun low and steady. I grabbed a bag from the luggage rack and wedged the door half open. Paul, Alice and I clambered over it, pushing the door back and ducking into the recesses by the external doors. I could see Paul was preparing to stand with his back to coach G and do Alice's trick, but Deavey glanced through the door, shook his head and walked through. No shouting, no gunshots. Quiet.

The rest of us waited. We had to, but it wasn't what I wanted. Waiting allowed unwelcome images to surface. A knife sliding across a throat. Blood on the floor. A cold shiver seemed to go down my spine. It all seemed unreal.

I didn't wake up that morning planning on harming anyone. If only he hadn't decided to get on that train. If only he hadn't had a gun and shot a man. If only the train hadn't jolted at that moment. I had seen him murder someone for very little reason. Even if he didn't kill me, it was more than likely that he'd kill someone else if they resisted. Surely it's right to resist dangerous people to save innocent lives, I remember telling myself. Was I wrong? Was it wrong to put my own life at risk? And tucked away in the back of my mind was the thought, I'm unemployed, my children don't need me, and Jim doesn't want me. What have I to lose? The train rocked, and I stumbled and realised I had to focus on the now. Through the window I could see grey sky with scudding clouds and a flock of crows flying past. Was that a good or bad omen?

In the next carriage, the blinds were down and the passengers were squashed in together, some three across two seats and others sitting awkwardly on tables or on the floor in the aisle. A mistake by the hijackers. It impeded their movement.

I watched as passengers facing back noticed Deavey. A few looked terrified. I realised they might think he was another hijacker, armed and ready to fight. But he ducked and muttered to a few people and the message seemed to spread. Watching, I realised that compared to the hijackers, he looked professional. Deavey had spent a few years living on the street after the army, before he pulled his life together, but he moved like a trained soldier and somehow packed an intensity into his presence that could either be chilling or comforting depending which side you were on. Crouched low, Deavey exchanged a few words with a young man, then beckoned to us. I assumed he meant that there was no hijacker present in the carriage but even so, I held my knife firmly in my hand. As we entered at the back, Deavey crept up to the front of the carriage and was peering through. I was about to follow when a dog started yapping loudly, which made me and everyone else, I imagine, jump.

Nerves jangling – who knew what the noise might bring down on us – I quickly found the culprit, a small noisy mutt, some variation on a Jack Russell, sitting wriggling on an older woman's lap about halfway down the carriage. I realised it was the same dog that had almost tripped me up on the concourse.

'Shut your dog up, missus,' hissed Deavey.

'Miss Atkinson to you,' she snapped back while trying to hold on to her dog.

Miss Atkinson appeared to be in her seventies, with sharp blue eyes behind her gold-rimmed glasses. She was still wearing her tweed coat, with sensible leather shoes, and had short curly salt and pepper hair. I squatted down. 'Please. They might come to investigate why he's barking.'

'There's no need to take that tone. Hush, Monty.' A middle-class accent with a touch of the West Midlands. There was the *Telegraph* in front of her, open at the crossword.

The dog ignored her. Such a loud noise from such a small animal. I spoke firmly. 'Please take him back up the train. Now.'

She didn't move. I grabbed the barking dog, made my way through the passengers back to coach H, where I handed him to a startled Pastor Ngozi who was standing by the door. I told her to take him back into J, before the barking brought the hijackers down on us, and then turned back.

Miss Atkinson stood in the aisle, outraged. 'What have you done? Where's Monty?'

I pulled her down as gently as possible back into her seat. I think she was so surprised she forgot to resist. The rest of the team were similarly tucked in among the squashed passengers. Crouching, I spoke softly, but clearly to everyone around me. 'Someone is taking the dog to the back of the train. Out of danger. The carriages behind us, J and H, are under passenger control. We've got two of the hijackers in the end toilet in coach J. They're secure. Anyone who wants to move back can do so after we've gone through. Anyone who thinks they can help us, please talk to Corporal Deaver, there. Pass this on to anyone who can't hear me, but we need to keep quiet and alert as they may come to check.'

Miss Atkinson ignored what I'd said. 'Where's Monty?' She spoke querulously and too loudly.

I took her arm. 'Please be quiet – or the hijackers may make sure Monty won't have an owner to come back to. He's safe. Go back down the train and you'll find him. We've got more important things to do than deal with a dog.'

She shook me off and gave me a filthy look. I didn't have time for this. I've never been a fan of yappy little canines in normal circumstances let alone in extremely abnormal circumstances. I stepped round her and reached the door to the vestibule between G and E – there was no F – and joined the others, who had picked up some more 'weapons'. In Alice's hand was a multi-function bottle opener. You can do a lot of damage with a corkscrew. We opened the door into the next vestibule, and I slipped through quickly followed by Deavey, Paul and Alice, with some helpful passengers who had come up behind us, holding the automatic door back and promising to prepare a second line of defence if needed.

DOGGY WORLD ONLINE
HOT DOG NEWS – APRIL
Post your stories/comments via socials

THE 10:12 HIJACK – WHAT HAPPENED TO MONTY?

'I was in the carriage. Woman who looked like a witch wrestled little Jack Russell cross from its owner, an old lady who was doing her best to keep the pup quiet. Witch woman was so rude. The hijackers weren't even in that carriage. No one knew what happened to little Monty. Someone said she'd chucked it out the window. The poor old lady was very upset.'

'I heard a hijacker stamped on the little dog. Hope he dies a horrible death.'

'I think dog's OK. Owner not said anything.'

'Owner too upset to talk. Her pet was thrown out of window of fast moving train.'

Extract from Cross-Examination of Claire Fitzroy by Defence Barrister Eleanor Masters

DB. *When you left carriage J after killing Mr Afiri, what were your intentions?*
CF. *Mr Afiri stumbled onto the knife when the train jolted. I reject your implication that I'm a murderer.*
DB. *Perhaps we can agree Mr Afiri died as a result of a wound caused by your knife. Moving on, what were your intentions at that stage?*

CF. It seemed likely there would be more hijackers ahead in the train – Black Jacket, Mr Jefferson, had said as much.

DB. Why didn't you stay put and let the authorities deal with them?

CF. What authorities? There were no authorities on the train, just passengers. The train manager was in no position to help, and the driver was driving the train under duress.

DB. But we have heard that various people, yourself included, had notified the police of the problems on board, and that the police and security services were putting a plan in place to deal with the situation. And you were advised numerous times by them not to attempt to tackle the hijackers. Why didn't you wait for the professionals?

CF. Wow. That's what we're doing is it?

DB. I'm simply asking, Ms Fitzroy, why you didn't do as you were requested to do by the authorities?

CF. I had watched the callous murder of one innocent man not long after the train left Manchester. I heard threats to others. Waiting for the experts would have probably resulted in more deaths. And how were these experts supposed to even get on the train when we weren't stopping at any stations? They weren't going to drop down from helicopters. The cavalry wasn't on the way.

DB. These were your assumptions, is that true to say?

CF. Yes. Based on common sense.

DB. Action was being taken by the police and security services, but we'll leave that for now. Let's come to your role. You are a woman in your late fifties with no official combat experience, is that correct?

CF. I don't know what my gender or age has to do with anything, but yes.

DB. You've studied martial arts, is that correct?

CF. I've done some self-defence classes, like a lot of women, perhaps you too, Ms Masters.

DB. Were these classes just about defence, or were they also about attack?

CF. We were encouraged to assess threat quickly and react quickly. A fundamental element of self-defence generally.

DB. Would that include the possibility of threat?

CF. Isn't a threat always a possibility? Until it isn't, then it's not a threat, it's a reality. In the case of the 10:12 the possibility quickly became the reality. A man was murdered minutes after leaving the station.

DB. Two men died. One in the toilet, where you were waiting with your knife. Isn't that what happened?

CF. I wasn't waiting for him. I hoped he'd go away and leave me alone. He chose to break into the toilet and put my life in danger.

DB. Were you endangered though? Ms Ngozi, who witnessed some of what happened, thought you could have talked him round. You are an educated and articulate woman, didn't you think it was worth trying?

CF. Look what happened when she tried talking and an innocent man died going to help her. And she didn't see everything. I was already aware that Mr Afiri had taken drugs, seemed unhinged and most of all had killed an innocent man. He broke down the door of the toilet. He loomed over me, with a gun, yelling threats. It didn't feel like the moment to attempt a social chit-chat.

DB. No. Instead, you cut his throat with a very sharp seven-inch blade, that you conveniently had in your bag. Is that correct?

[silence]

Judge. Ms Fitzroy, I understand this may be distressing for you, but you do need to answer the question.

CF. I didn't set out to cut his throat, I held it to his throat and before I could say anything he moved unexpectedly as the train jolted, and the blade cut him. I wish I hadn't had to defend myself. But without that kitchen knife, I doubt I would be here today.

DB. Ms Fitzroy, that's...

CF. As I've already explained, it wasn't as if Tom Cruise was going to drop down from a helicopter and give us a hand, Ms Masters. The hijacking was taking place on a speeding train. No one was coming to help.

DB. If you could just answer the questions, please. Apart from the fact that you were carrying a dangerous weapon, what made you think that you should be the person to deal with the hijackers?

CF. I wasn't the person. I was one of several people who seemed to feel that doing nothing wasn't an option. In the toilet I didn't have a choice.

DB. But you were the leader.

CF. Is that a question or a statement?

DB. My apologies. Do you agree that you were the leader of this little band?

CF. As far as I was aware there wasn't a leader. We never took a vote. We did what we had to do and discussed plans as quickly as possible. There wasn't time for strategy. A number of passengers were involved, using their skills or simply their bravery. We had to move fast. I don't think it was particularly organised. We just wanted to save lives.

DB. Yes. Saving lives. I'll come to that. But I'm curious, I can see that the ex-services personnel had the required training, and that others had youth and fitness on their side. But forgive me, what did a fifty-something art lecturer bring to the team, apart from a few self-defence classes, and anger about her husband's affair?

CF. My marriage had nothing to do with it. As for me, determination? An element of surprise? Ask the rest of the team. Perhaps, as you are demonstrating, people tend to underestimate fifty-something women.

DB. Not me, I assure you. Perhaps it was because you had already proved your determination when you killed Jay Afiri. Isn't that right, Ms Fitzroy? You were responsible for Jay Afiri's death.

CF. I think that's another statement, not a question.

DB. The team knew they had someone with them who was prepared to kill. They banded together, led by you – passengers thought you were in charge as you were giving orders. Was that the case?

CF. I didn't give orders. We followed agreed courses of action or followed our instincts.

DB. What strikes me, is that you set out like a hunting party. Is that not so?

PB. Objection!

Judge. My learned friend, I've given you some leeway, but Ms Fitzroy is not on trial here. What is it that you are trying to explore in reference to your clients?

DB. The mood of the team that would come to violently engage with the hijackers.

6
The Quiet Carriage

COACH E

11:20

> Somethings going on ambulances, cops cleared platform won't say what's happening.

> Shit, armed cops

> Crap u come out with for being late as usual. Our sister's wedding. Can't believe u do this

Deavey crawled to the door into E and peered in. He retreated quickly and joining us in the recess by the external doors, broke the bad news: a full carriage, with a hijacker standing at the far end looking back down across the passengers to the door. Deavey could see a knife but didn't see a gun.

'And no one's tackled him? One man and a knife?'

'Think of the damage one woman and a knife did—' started Deavey.

I quickly interrupted. 'But it's a full carriage. A lot of people, working together, although… maybe there's another hijacker sitting down.'

Paul nodded. 'Exactly. We don't know the full situation.'

'We need a different plan,' I said, thinking about the best way to continue. Standard-class carriages had double seats on both sides of the aisle, unlike first class, which had a double on one side, and single on the other. I couldn't see that would give us any advantage apart from the fact that there should be more people to help. And more people to get in the way.

As we were considering our options, the train suddenly lurched and we grabbed handles or each other to avoid falling. Through the window, I saw a station speed by. We were travelling too fast to read the signs, but I recognised Crewe; it's a big rail interchange and another station where the train would normally have stopped. I thought I saw flashing blue lights to one side, and a large group of police officers in reflective stab vests on the platform. A large poster of a dog from the RSPCA – and was that a couple of ambulances on the road? Then it all disappeared, like a mirage.

Our lack of external support, or of assistance coming any time soon, hit us all properly then. The authorities knew. They'd been ready, just in case the train stopped, with plenty of officers, no doubt some armed, and ambulances. That was fast work. But there was no 'just in case'. We sped past. We were on our own.

Suddenly Paul, Deavey and Alice's phones started vibrating. Mine was on do not disturb. Alice spoke first. 'Alex says the hijacker in the loos is going on about a bomb set to blow up at Euston. There might be others that will go off earlier.'

'That could be bullshit,' I said.

Paul shook his head. 'But we have to prepare for the worst-case scenario.'

We had to move. I had an idea – it wasn't met with enthusiasm, but no one came up with a workable alternative in the brief time we had. Bombs were on all our minds. I stood at the door of carriage E and stepped through as it opened, hands up and head bowed in what I hoped looked like a submissive pose. I tried to walk as if I had mobility problems, although the movement of the train pretty much did the job for me.

The carriage was quiet. The blinds were down and the seats looked to be full. I noticed a blond, curly-haired little boy wearing large headphones sitting on his father's lap, mercifully asleep, a protective arm around him, his dad's puzzled face one of several turning in my direction. It was stuffy, with a tense atmosphere. The door I'd come through didn't shut, and I heard Alice cough behind me. That hadn't been the plan. It was going to be me on my own. I was momentarily irritated, but it wasn't as if I could send her back.

I studied the man at the other end of the carriage. He was young, thin, dark-haired, brown-skinned, bespectacled and nervous. He looked like a nerdy sixth-former. He also looked familiar, but I had no time to think about it. I quickly scanned for signs of another hijacker, then spoke, making my voice loud enough for him to hear but at the same time trying to make it breathy and quavery, just an unthreatening old lady.

'I, we were sent here. It's too crowded back there. The man sent us. He said he'd tell you.'

He tried to peer round me. 'You, the woman in the back. Get in front with your arms up.'

He sounded tense. Alice shuffled round me, doing what he said.

'Sit on the floor. The young one. Keep your arms up, both of you.' Alice bent down in front of me, toppling a little as she tried to keep her arms up and sit down on the floor of a swaying train at the same time. Good core strength, though.

The Nerd moved down the carriage towards us. 'Don't think of trying anything,' he said to the carriage at large. 'Remember,' and he waved a green flip phone at no one in particular. That's how you quell a whole carriage of people when you're just a scrawny kid. You tell them there's a bomb and that you control it.

He got close to us and then made a noise like a small explosion, his arms going out, the knife slicing through the air in one hand, the mobile twisting in the other. I flinched and he laughed, but it sounded fake. I could see he was scared; his hands were trembling. I suddenly remembered where I'd seen him – he'd helped the young woman with the baby and the case at the station. He'd smiled at her.

'Describe the man who sent you.'

'Black, big? In one of those puffy jackets. A black one. He's a carriage back.'

Nerd checked the phone.

'Nothing.'

'Signal's crap that's what he said,' responded Alice, in a soft voice.

He made an exasperated noise. 'Deep State. They're blocking the signal.' He spoke to himself.

I didn't know if that was even possible but didn't comment. Instead, I looked him in the eye and asked in a pitiful voice, 'Please can I sit down? It's hard for me to stand for long.'

He held my gaze for a moment then, seemingly embarrassed, turned to a table of four to one side, pointed at a young man in a window seat, and said: 'You, fuck off up there and sit on the floor or squash in with someone.'

The man he'd singled out, young, a boy really, maybe sixteen, East Asian looks, nodded and stood quickly, waiting while the woman next to him in the aisle seat stood and moved out of his way. Curly-haired and in black leggings, her long floral shirt stretched across her pregnancy bump. The hijacker indicated for me to sit, and I obeyed.

'Come with me,' he said to Alice, and she followed him for a few rows until he told her to sit and passengers moved up for her to squash in. There was silence in the carriage. Across from me sat a middle-aged woman with shoulder-length pink-to-silver balayaged hair, and next to her a young East Asian-looking girl, probably a student, in a blue hoody. She and the pink-haired woman avoided looking me in the eye, but the pregnant woman on the adjacent seat gave me a small, sympathetic shake of the head. She must be terrified for her unborn baby, I thought. I noticed her knitting on the table. Pale yellow wool, a cardigan for her baby. Her first, I discovered later. The whole carriage felt like a room where people have been having a big argument moments before – tension thick in the air.

The young hijacker seemed relieved by the obedient silence. The stuffiness was unpleasant. Doing nothing was stressful. I wondered what Charlie would have done.

As teenagers, I was on peace marches while he was in the army cadets. And while I was choosing a university, he signed up. Spitefully, I enjoyed my parents' bewilderment at his choice, although I agreed with their fears – soldiers have a nasty habit of dying before their time. 'Fighting for your country' seemed such an outdated idea. But Charlie wasn't interested. 'Why should someone else fight our battles, if I'm not prepared to do it myself?'

The train lurched and the Nerd stumbled. A young Black man near the front started to rise, perhaps seeing a chance to grab the Nerd, but quickly sat down as another hijacker appeared from the coach ahead. He looked like he was in his early thirties, perhaps five foot ten and wore a leather jacket. Short curly black hair topped a face with angry eyes and a scar down one side of his chin. He looked in, raised his hands, one holding a gun, in a WTF motion to the Nerd who quickly joined him at the door.

'You.' Scarface pointed at the young Black man who had stood up. 'Get a bag and wedge this door open.' He looked back over his shoulder as he spoke. I wondered if he was the only hijacker in D and if that door was wedged open too, so that he could keep an eye on both coaches. Scarface suddenly seemed to notice the young man who had been moved to let me sit down.

'Put your head down, Chinky, unless you want it blown off.'

I heard a sharp intake of breath from the student opposite, and the pink-haired woman took her hand, then indicated that the girl should pull up her hood. She did and turned her head down.

The young man at the front pulled out a bag from the luggage area and placed it in the doorway, the door bumping into it, while the hijackers continued to talk to each other in hushed tones. I noticed the Nerd point me and Alice out to Scarface, then they both looked at their phones, compared what they saw and exchanged a few more words. I stood up.

'Excuse me. What is it you want? Perhaps we can help find some kind of solution…?'

I trailed off as I saw Scarface indicate with his index finger that I was to sit down. I sat down.

He cast his eye along the carriage at Alice, and then me. Looking down, I slid my knife carefully out of my bag, concealed by the tabletop. Next to me, Elaine, only four weeks off her due date, noticed the knife, and made a little more room. She looked uncomfortable, her baby bump almost touching the table. The two women opposite continued to look hard at the table; the pink-haired woman now had rosary beads in her hands while her lips were moving in silent prayer. The student was statue still. Under cover of the train rattling through another station, I whispered to my neighbour that the carriages behind us were under passenger control. She should go back, when she got the chance. I scooped the knitting into my bag and slipped the knife down the back of my trousers. Not comfortable, but I didn't like the way the hijackers were looking at me and Alice. She shouldn't have followed me.

'You!' Scarface suddenly shouted, pointing at Alice, and then 'You!' pointing at me. 'Come here.'

7
One More

COACH E

11:30

> Key back of bathroom cabinet keep you going for a while. Love you xxxx

> Are you leaving us? key to what? scaring me.

> Sorry tin box in cellar under bottom shelf. Just in case.

> there's £££££ where's it from what you up to!?

> train hijacked check news love you

I don't believe you should judge someone on appearances. But despite the Nerd's theatrics with the phone, the way Scarface studied us made me sure he was the more dangerous of the two. There wasn't a shred of humanity in the older man's cold eyes. Or perhaps it was my own fear that interpreted his look that way. Or perhaps he was stoned out of his mind. Whatever the case, he was terrifying. A man who didn't care about anyone or anything and was more than happy to kill.

Obeying orders, Alice and I made our way up the aisle. Following her, I muttered, 'If it comes to it, you take the Nerd and I'll take Scarface.' Her head inclined slightly. I wondered what Deavey and Paul could see from the door behind us, and what, if anything, they could do. I thought of the little boy in his father's arms and hoped he was still asleep.

The hijackers pulled us into the area by the luggage racks where there was more space. Scarface waved his phone at Alice. It was another green flip-up. 'No message 'bout you.'

His voice was surprisingly high, now he wasn't shouting, and an original accent from somewhere I couldn't place, was overlaid with London. He looked at Alice.

'Who sent you here and why? You a fed? And don't give me any shit, cos I ain't got time for it.'

Alice replied, 'I'm an accountant. The man in the puffer jacket told us to go up the train.'

Scarface turned to me, almost shouting. 'Talk, old woman, or I'll stab your friend, your daughter, or whatever, in the heart, here,' his finger jabbed at Alice's chest, 'right in front of your eyes.'

There were audible gasps from along the carriage. Alice looked away.

'We don't know each other, young man, sir,' I replied, breathlessly. 'We were sent together because there were no seats. The one in the puffy jacket watched us till we came through this door. I didn't see him use a phone.'

'He was very busy,' said Alice.

That didn't help. I spoke again, before she could say anything else. 'It was all so sudden.' I hoped I sounded pitiful.

He got closer. I could feel his hot breath on me. It was minty. Fresh breath confidence for the everyday hijacker. Then he grabbed my bag and as I staggered, I deliberately stumbled onto my knees, partly to get away from him. Alice turned to help, but the Nerd pushed her behind the luggage rack. There were more gasps in the carriage. People don't like the sight of two armed men pushing two women about. Most people anyway. And if it motivated some passengers to consider resistance, that could be helpful.

Scarface tipped the contents of my bag onto the floor. Along with a make-up bag, purse, the purloined nail polish remover, tissues and pink stainless steel water bottle, the knitting needles fell out, with a few rows of knitting attached to the yellow ball of wool. Thank goodness I'd left the knitting on when I'd scooped the needles off the table. Scarface ignored them. I backed myself up against the seat where the Black lad who had wedged the door open was sitting – Ty, a second-year design student and drill performer, I later found out.

'Where's your phone, granny?' demanded Scarface.

'We had to hand them over,' I said in a nervous voice. All the while I could feel it digging into me from my back pocket under my jacket. He looked at me briefly, then, as if bored by my answer, turned suddenly and grabbed Alice. This wasn't clever, because it also surprised his co-hijacker. The Nerd stepped back and stumbled, dropping the phone he'd been waving in his hand. I stood up quickly, trying to get the knife, but fumbled and dropped it so instead grabbed the steel water bottle – which was quickly snatched out of my hand by Ty, who smashed it hard into Scarface's forehead before he could turn the gun on us. The Nerd was reaching for Alice who had slipped out of Scarface's hands, but a stunned Scarface staggered back and got in his way. Those small spaces again.

A part of my brain registered that the Nerd hadn't gone for the supposedly lethal phone he'd dropped. But there was work to do before I could work out what was really going on. Under attack by Ty wielding the pink metal one-litre water bottle (almost full), Scarface tried to get his gun in line but, after a particularly hard wallop on the wrist, dropped the weapon. Out of the corner of my eye, I saw Alice smash her fist into the Nerd's face. I grappled with Scarface who seemed groggy but still aggressive. Ty hit him again with the bottle across the face. I heard something snap as he fell back. Other passengers were scrabbling to join the fray. I dropped on the floor to get the gun, my knife, the stuff from my bag and the hijacker's phone, if I could find any of them in the melee. People who were trying to help were getting in the way, or worse, treading on us, the good guys. Then there was a shout from the rear of the carriage.

On my hands and knees, pushing my belongings back into my bag, I looked over my shoulder and down the aisle. There stood Deavey with Paul right behind him, passengers shrinking away at the sight of the gun in Deavey's hand.

Deavey's voice carried down the carriage. 'Hijackers, get on the floor or I'll shoot, and I don't miss. Calm down, everyone else, and go back to your seats. I'm not one of them.'

Confusion continued. Some passengers thought Deavey and Paul were hijackers, or maybe they didn't hear what they said or couldn't take it in. The two men were having trouble getting through the chaos. Ty had fallen, Scarface was struggling to his feet and I received a couple of painful kicks from him. I retaliated without thinking, shoving one of the metal knitting needles hard through his jeans and into his calf and leaving it there, a piece of yellow wool dangling off it like a flag. He bent to pull it out but stumbled as the train jerked again. With various passengers scrambling around me, I continued my search. I still couldn't find my knife, but I did pick up Scarface's gun. It looked meaner and newer than the one we already had. I stood up and stuck it into Scarface's neck as he was trying to get to his feet.

'Don't think I won't use it,' I hissed in his ear, in the most aggressive way I could. I thought this was a cliché he'd understand. But he didn't seem to care. Although his nose was broken and bleeding, he was still in fighting mode. He shoved me out of the way, then landed a severe blow to Ty's chest, who doubled up, gasping for air. Fortunately, just as Scarface turned his attention back to me, Deavey got through and thumped him. Deavey's presence and the blood flowing from Scarface's broken nose and injured leg where I had stabbed him meant the hijacker was finally looking beaten. Alice was sitting on a whining Nerd. Despite the blood coming from her lip and nose, she looked very pleased with herself, as if she'd just scored a try. She bounced hard on the boy's chest when he resisted, while another passenger, a stocky man in his thirties, had his trainer-clad foot on the Nerd's face. There was blood oozing from under the shoe.

Deavey smiled grimly up at me while he tied Scarface's wrists together with a black tie. I briefly wondered if the donor had been en route to a funeral. What a day they were having.

'You OK? Can't leave you for a minute.'

'Got delayed, did you? Somewhere else you needed to be?'

I handed the gun to Paul who examined it.

'Waiting for the attack, as agreed,' answered Deavey.

'If I say that again, I don't mean it.'

Paul shook the gun and laughed.

'What?'

'It's an air pistol. They make them to look like the real thing. In this case, a Glock.'

Scarface distracted me from answering by struggling with Deavey, pulling at the tie round his wrist, and snarling. I caught a few impolite words, and he looked at me fit to explode with anger. He might not have a real gun, but he had guts. As Paul got him round the neck, I turned to the carriage. 'More stuff to secure these men please – scarves, belts, ties… And does anyone know where the bomb is?'

8

Chopper

COACHES E–D

11:40

<u>COURT EXHIBIT No. LE3</u>
<u>(Letter extract – authenticated)</u>

Mum, one day you'll see the truth and be proud. Dad left me the gun for a reason. I have a path to follow. If I die, I die for a good cause. People have got to be made to see they're sleepwalking into destruction. They've got to see through the Deep State lies and find the truth.

While carriage E bustled with activity, there was the mystery of the missing knife to solve. I had an idea who might have it, but first we needed to ensure our new captives were tied up securely and look for an IED. I checked with Elaine, the pregnant woman, and she confirmed the Nerd had threatened to 'set off a bomb' with his phone if passengers didn't do as he said. She smiled when I apologised for damaging her knitting, then when I suggested she head to the back said she badly needed a pee. There was a queue for the two cubicles, but when people noticed her bump, she was ushered to the front. A nice moment.

The woman with the pink hair went past with the two young students, Chinese, I later learned. The girl was sobbing. A younger woman gave her a tissue and an older man patted the boy on the shoulder. 'You'll be all right now, lad.' There were murmurs of agreement, and someone said, 'We all need to stick together.'

Paul led Ty and a few passengers in the search for the IED, starting tentatively where the hijacker had been sitting.

Alice handed the Nerd's phone to Paul.

'I don't want to touch the wrong thing accidentally.' She shuddered, then took a tissue from me and dabbed nonchalantly at her bloodied lip and nose, as if being smashed in the face was an everyday occurrence. All the men had the same model phone, even the same colour, worrying evidence of a degree of organisation and planning behind the attack, despite our successes being evidence to the contrary.

'I'm not sure there is an IED,' I said. 'The hijacker whose phone was supposed to detonate the bomb seemed uninterested in recovering it after he'd dropped it. What better way to make a group of people do your bidding when there's only one of you than to claim you can set off a bomb?'

'They should have done that in every carriage,' Deavey said.

Paul thought we couldn't rule out the possibility that there was a real IED somewhere, although he doubted there really was one connected to the passenger emergency stop system – far too complicated, he said. But we couldn't take any chances.

Anita appeared and said all was still well down the train, although coaches were filling up. She had a habit of appearing, then disappearing. She was calm, but she didn't want to be involved in any confrontation. Which was fine, particularly as she was being useful in her own way. She stood by the back doors, helping to ensure people moved through in an orderly fashion. Strangely, given the presence of hijackers and the possibility of bombs, some people were in good spirits, or perhaps it was mild hysteria.

One jolly chap incongruously wearing a trilby and a yellow bow tie, patted me on the back as he passed and said, 'Good job.' It made Deavey laugh.

As well as the split lip and bloody nose, Alice had the beginning of a black eye, but unfazed by her injuries, was busy ensuring noise levels remained low among the passengers. Her bashed face and direct manner certainly lent authority to her requests.

The man with the toddler hadn't moved and I stopped by his seat. 'Be safer if you go to the back.'

He looked up at me with a serious expression. He was in his thirties, dark hair flecked with grey and metal-framed glasses. 'I don't really want to wake him. He had a bad night.'

We both looked at the little boy. 'Just as well. It's great he slept through what happened.' I said. 'But it will be safer.'

He nodded. 'Yeah, we'll go when the rush dies down. It's just… peaceful, you know, watching him sleep. I don't want to spoil it.'

I could only agree. Suddenly there was a bittersweet memory of Jim with our baby son snuggled in his arms, both asleep. A moment of pure love. Another life.

Anita offered to take a peep at the next coach, D, which we thought looked empty. I was following, when her phone vibrated and she answered, and then said to the caller she'd pass it to me. It was Alex.

'The police.' He was trying to sound businesslike but couldn't keep the tension out of his voice. 'We've got a good link now. Apparently, the hijackers aren't interested in negotiating. The cops are a bit puzzled, I think. There's something weird about these guys. They're not blowing anything up, but they're not negotiating either. Be careful, won't you. The cops said they're going to try and help in a different way.'

'How?'

'Don't know yet. They said for you to move back.'

Wouldn't you have to be weird to hijack a train? No one so far had been wearing a suicide vest, the typical TV terrorist accoutrement. Perhaps they didn't want to die. And how were the police going to help, unless they shunted us off onto another line – which could prime the remaining bad guys to blow us up. If there was a bomb.

Suddenly I heard the sound of a helicopter over the phone, and then outside the carriage.

'They're here!' Alex said, the sound of cheering behind him. I said we'd speak later and hung up, handing the phone back to Anita who headed up to coach D. The remaining passengers in

E were excited. I shushed them, pointing further up the train. Deavey was peering out of the window, and I checked the other side. He spotted the police helicopter first.

'We should put signs up in the windows showing which carriages are clear,' he said. 'It might keep the passengers safer. Things can go wrong with phone messages.' His phone vibrated, he walked away down the aisle to answer it.

I wondered what they were planning. Would the security services attack the train? Would they decide it was better to let it explode in the countryside, with the only victims being passengers and staff, rather than in crowded central London? Would we be sacrificed? And was there a bomb timed to go off at Euston? Surely they'd evacuate the station and neighbouring buildings. Too many questions. I hoped there might be a news chopper soon. Witnesses to whatever happened. Paranoia is contagious. And speculation wasn't helpful. I gave myself a quick talking to and focused on the job in hand.

Ty was on the seat behind, looking up at the helicopter. 'I've got my folio with me. I'm a design student. Could use the backs of some of my drawings, do a few big "SAFE" signs for each liberated coach.'

'Great. You took a few punches, are you OK?' I asked quietly. He nodded. He was a handsome young man, with an air of confidence despite having taken a few hard blows. There was a fine scar from the edge of his right eye to the corner of his mouth. 'Can I have my knife back?'

He looked embarrassed. 'Yeah. Sorry 'bout that.'

'Why did you take it?'

'Knives. Once you get 'em out, there's no knowing who'll end up on the end of the blade. Often it's the person who thought the knife would protect them.'

I looked again at his scar. He touched it and gave a slight nod.

'Yeah. Sorry. Thought you was out of your comfort zone. Didn't want you to get hurt. Clearly, I was wrong, Mrs Ninja.'

I laughed and it felt good. He pulled the knife out from his jacket. 'I hate 'em. Although that's,' he examined Derek's craftsmanship, 'a sweet one.'

Deavey joined us in a hurry, putting his phone in his pocket as he spoke. 'The cops have told Alex someone's been stabbed, needs help. They think he's near the cafe. Coach C. I'll try and find some first-aid stuff.'

I ran to the doors, grabbing a discarded sweatshirt on the way. I could hear the helicopter buzzing loudly above us like a giant wasp over a picnic. Coach D was now empty, apart from Anita, who was leaning over a row of seats. Bags and clothes were strewn on the racks and seats, and a few phones were ringing. It was eerie. She looked up as I came through the door.

'Is that the injured man?'

'How did you know?'

'Someone reported it to the police. Here, I've got a sweatshirt to use to pack the wound, and Deavey's getting help.'

'It's too late.'

I quickly joined her. Stretched across a table about five rows up from the disabled toilet, legs wedged under the table, head down on a backpack, was the body of a man. His short black hair showed beneath a rust-coloured beanie. He was in a black jumper and jeans with Adidas trainers. He looked to be in his thirties or forties from the small part of his face I could see, but it was hard to say. There were stripes of dark blood pooling on the table and in the adjacent aisle.

'He's dead,' she said.

I picked up my phone and rang Deavey. 'We're too late.'

'Shit. OK. I'll be with you shortly.'

I could still hear the chopper. Then there was shouting, an amplified male voice. 'What is it you want? Let's talk.'

Anita peered out the window. 'They're trying to negotiate.'

'Hope it works. I can't see us evacuating passengers from the roof of a speeding train.'

There was a bang from somewhere towards the front of the train. Looking out of the window I saw the chopper rise swiftly. And then we were in a tunnel.

'I think that was a gunshot,' said Anita.

'So that's a hard no to negotiations then,' I replied with a sigh.

Anita picked up a black mac from the seat beside the body and placed it over him. I caught sight of the distinctive Burberry lining. There was a bunch of freesias part trampled on the floor. I gathered them up, their sweet fragrance an incongruous relief after the smells of blood and sweat, and put them on top of the coat. We moved away from the body as we came out of the tunnel.

'I'll head back down the train, see how it's going,' said Anita. As she left, I turned to the window and watched mesmerised as the train rushed through another station. We were going so fast, again, I couldn't make out the name. But through the window I caught a snapshot of another life. A few people on the platform, a bank of police officers and an announcement being made over the Tannoy, impossible to understand. I suddenly wished with all my heart that I was on that platform watching the 10:12 hurtling by, safe in the knowledge that I could go to the station cafe, buy a cup of tea and a KitKat, and not have to look at another dead body.

For a moment I felt suspended in time, the noise of the train, buildings rushing past outside, my body swaying with the movement of the carriage. A hand on my arm jolted me back. It was Paul. 'Come on. For now, it doesn't matter who he was – he's dead and we've got a bit of a problem.'

There were raised voices at the door to coach E; some kind of disagreement. Melissa Ngozi was arguing with Deavey, a few passengers around her. I quickly joined them. Deavey turned to me, annoyed. 'These people want us to stay here.'

Pastor Ngozi looked at me. 'There's been too much bloodshed already. My fellow Christians—'

'Actually, I'm a Buddhist,' interrupted a thin young man, with an American accent.

She continued without missing a beat. 'My fellow passengers of faith think the killing must stop.'

'I'm with you there,' I agreed. 'Unfortunately, the hijackers haven't got that memo. You might recall what happened to the man who went to help you. And there's another murdered man right here.' I pointed to the body.

'God rest his soul.' She paused for a moment, and shook her head. 'But you are provoking them.'

I was speechless.

'We're trying to stop them killing anyone else,' replied Deavey.

'They will not kill if you're not confrontational.'

'We just found that poor man's body. We didn't confront anyone,' I managed to say. 'And if you remember, the hijacker who died was on the verge of attacking you when that brave man stepped in to protect you.' I couldn't help adding furiously, 'And was murdered for doing so.'

'We need to find a solution, not fight a battle.'

It was as if I hadn't spoken. The woman talked in aphorisms. A tall man in a navy wool jacket, with a sad face and thick grey hair elegantly swept back, stood beside her. I glimpsed a dog collar.

'This extra death makes it even more essential that we try and talk with them.' His voice was sonorous and clear. A man used to being listened to.

A woman in her seventies wearing an elaborately embroidered coat added, 'Jaw, jaw not war, war.'

I was pretty sure which side Churchill would have been on in this particular dispute – whether or not he had actually said those words.

The vicar continued. 'We're heading up the train to talk to them. We come from a position of deep faith, like them.'

'How do you know that? They seem more concerned with Deep State rather than deep faith.'

'You should stay here,' said Pastor Ngozi, ignoring what I'd said. 'Your presence will aggravate them. We're all agreed.'

'No, we're not,' I replied. What planet were these people on? The vicar sounded like he was giving a sermon and the pastor appeared to be issuing a royal decree. I tried again, holding my temper.

'Please. They are not going to listen to you. Don't you think we tried talking? The people in the helicopter did too, and they shot at them. We don't know what they want. Maybe death and glory.'

The vicar gave me a stern look. 'The pastor here told me you're responsible for the death of a young man. You will both be in our prayers. All life is precious in God's eyes.'

'It was self-defence,' snapped Deavey.

'I've seen Melissa's film of you with the hijacker,' the vicar said turning to Deavey. 'We don't want any more of that.'

She had been filming. Of course she had. Shit. I tried to speak calmly. 'If you've posted that footage, they'll know we're fighting back.' She gave a regal shake of her head. I realised discussion was pointless and we didn't have time to argue. But I was angry. 'I suppose you believe in martyrdom too. Well, that's your choice – but you're not taking everyone else with you. Keep out of the way. We've got a job to do.'

'I haven't noticed a vote being taken, putting you in charge.' The pastor pulled her handbag across her chest like a medieval breastplate.

'I'm working on the basis that most people on this train would prefer to live. In this world. They're not ready to head for the next one just yet,' I replied.

'Come on,' said the vicar, turning to the door to go up the train.

'Please don't,' said Paul, with quiet authority, stepping in front of him. 'I know a bit about conflict; I was a major in the TA. They've murdered twice and are quite capable of doing so again.'

'Only because you wouldn't do what they asked. Which was to sit and be quiet. Something I agree with,' said the pastor.

But wasn't prepared to do, I thought. I was struck by the certainty that some religious and political beliefs give people. I suppose you need that to create martyrs. They moved up the carriage, pausing briefly beside the body, and the vicar said something.

'Don't expect us to fucking rescue you,' muttered Deavey, loud enough to be heard.

The older woman in the elaborate coat paused, turned and came back. 'I'm too old for this. But she is right. We have to try and talk with them,' she said, then shook her head sadly and returned into E.

'Better get after them,' said Alice, looking towards coach C as the others disappeared.

'If they're going to confront the hijackers, our presence might put them in more danger,' I said.

'Tempting,' Deavey muttered, then sighed. 'How about we give them a few minutes, then I'll go and scope out what's happening.'

I nodded. There were a few moments of silence. Alice leant against the seat and looked out of the window. 'I'm supposed to be speaking at an audit workshop this afternoon.'

I was stifling an unexpected giggle when the yapping dog suddenly appeared from carriage E and went running through the carriage to the door to the vestibule into carriage C, skipping through the legs of the young Buddhist who had just opened it. 'You're needed in here. Get a medic. A man's badly hurt,' he said breathlessly.

Deavey picked up his phone and we all ran to the door.

COURT EXHIBIT No. NSC07
(Screen grab – authenticated)

[ref:NOSINOCHAN Chat Group]

BOND66: Maybe bomb some takeaways. 😃😄😁😁

HERO2: Man – they be sick up over their noodles. 🤮🤮 🏯🏯 😁😁

WORDWARRIOR: Nooo dude. love a sweet and sour. 🙂 🙂 🙂 Some of them fams been here over hundred years. No cabal. ANR. Do the research.

BOND66: True. Just chattin. 😅😅😅 No one wants to get rid of gyozas.

WORDWARRIOR: Ha ha. Leave the Japs out of it maybe?

BOND66: You on it WW. Like weightwatchers innit? You a fat bwoy? Too many takeaways?

HERO2: Plenty of righteous targets. London mayor?

WORDWARRIOR: Not Chinese! Not cabal.

BOND66: Ain't about race man. Secret power, and who's got it. Chinese tech everywhere, taking us down. Giving us Covid. Takin our govmt, airport, power and railway. Trust me – I see it.
IRONMAN: Taking us over. Bond's right. It's Deep State.
WORDWARRIOR: handle change to DMITRI
DMITRI: need to protect that shit.
BOND66: right bro. seek the truth, see the truth, say the truth. and make lotta ps for us. got us a plan – big plan. big ps we ready?

9
Another Man Down
COACH C
11:50

> Dad what time does train get in? hope you didn't miss it haha.

> Dad, r u on the 10:12? r u OK? It's on the news.

> keep safe dad i love you so much best dad in the worldxxxxxx

> Stay safe dad. Kit told me you're on 10:12. Luv you so much. in our hearts. xxx

Coach C was the cafe car. It was quiet. Further up the carriage were a few rows of seats and tables. At the far end the vicar and the pastor sat together, heads down, perhaps in prayer. At least they were safe. Deavey was on the phone. In front of us was a shiny counter, and a Perspex-fronted cabinet with sandwiches, cakes and chocolate bars, and, puttering about, sniffing the carpet, Monty. Alice grabbed him quickly but gently, then moved fast to the door as he started to yap, murmuring that she'd come back, before disappearing, his bark fading away.

Through the windows, un-blinkered by blinds, a grey windswept countryside was visible. I had a momentary glimpse of a man standing beside a tractor watching the train as it thundered past. The yapping was replaced by an eerie silence, suddenly broken by sobs.

I stepped over long streaks of fresh blood across the floor, now surrounded by little bloody paw marks, to reach the counter. 'Nik, Nik,' a woman was sobbing, her voice coming from the floor.

Looking over we saw the young woman (Melanie, 26) dressed in the train company's red uniform who, in what seemed like another lifetime, had served me coffee. Behind her was the Buddhist, ashen-faced, sitting back on his haunches and holding a bottle of water. A man was sprawled on the floor in front of her, a slim figure with black shiny hair, also wearing the train company uniform. It was the train manager, Nik Bhatia, 42. His eyes were shut, and he looked to be in a bad way. An open first aid kit, paper towels and dressings were scattered on the floor, most of them soaked red. Melanie had her hands on the man's chest, trying to compress a wound with napkins and a dressing. Jonathan, the Buddhist, was trying to help the wounded man drink some water.

Melanie looked up at us with a pale and tear-stained face, mascara smudged onto her cheeks.

She stuttered out her words between sobs. 'I thought you were them come back. They stabbed him. They, they stabbed him.'

For a moment, I think we were stunned by what we could see.

'I've rung Alice,' said Deavey, as he quickly opened the door into the back of the counter and squatted down.

'I don't know what else to do. I'm just applying pressure. Can you help him?' Melanie whispered.

'You're doing the right thing,' replied Deavey, grabbing a wad of napkins and a roll of blue paper towel from the counter and applying more pressure to the manager's chest, while Melanie leant forward and stroked the hair off the poor man's face.

Jonathan moved out of the way. I asked Paul to keep an eye on the vestibule between B and C. We didn't want any nasty surprises while we were dealing with an emergency. I concentrated on helping Melanie out from behind the counter. I sat her down, and she began talking, quietly at first.

'Nik came to see if I was all right. Then two of them came in after him and they were shouting at him, pushing him. Something about a screen. Then he hit the smaller one with a metal tray. He's so brave, he's just got to be OK...' She caught her breath. 'The other one had this huge knife. He just stuck it in Nik, I couldn't do anything. I... Nik's got two young girls, he's the nicest guy.'

She was overtaken with sobs as Alice appeared, accompanied by a tall ginger-haired man of about forty, in jeans and a blue sweatshirt, who looked serious and businesslike. Alice muttered 'paramedic' and handed him a small first aid kit and a couple of towels. He looked at me and said, 'Geoff.'

'Claire. Glad you're here. The train manager's called Nik.'

Geoff went behind the counter and got down on the floor. 'Hi Nik,' he said softly, 'I'm Geoff, a paramedic. I'm here to help.'

Melanie's sobs were getting louder. I hushed her gently and put my arm round her. She fell silent, apart from her breath catching quietly in small hiccups.

'We tried to help, but there's not much room, and Melanie wanted to stay.' It was the vicar. He looked stricken. 'Melanie, will you come with us now help has arrived? It will be safer for you.'

She shook her head.

'Then we'll head back to the safe carriages and see if we can help in any way.'

I nodded. He was joined by the pastor and the American. The young man turned to me. He had kind eyes and tears on his pale face.

'Good luck,' he said softly, as they stepped out of the carriage.

To: Claire Fitzroy
cc: Laurence Walker
From: Loretta De Silva
Subject: Peace people

Hi Claire,

Just a couple of quick ones. Have you checked with the peace group that they are OK with what you've written about them? And Rights says you've still not been in touch re: serialisation? Would be really good for sales and getting your story out there. Need your sign off asap so we can get rolling.

Let me know if you want to talk about it again. The end is in sight, honestly.

Best,
Loretta

Loretta De Silva
Editorial Director, Ashgrove Publishing

To: Loretta De Silva
cc: Laurence Walker
From: Claire Fitzroy
Subject: Re: Peace people

Hi Loretta,

I've spoken to the vicar. He's not over-thrilled but as long as he's anonymous he won't do anything about it. Others untraceable and Ngozi hasn't responded. I can't see any reason not to go ahead. She's had the option to comment and chose not to.

As for the other matter, as I've said right from the start, it's essential that I remain aware of, and respectful towards, other people's sensibilities. Furthermore, I need to be protective of my own mental wellbeing. People were hurt, people died, people with friends and families. I don't want anyone to suffer any more than they already have and am acutely aware of the need to tread carefully. Conversations are taking place. When agreement has been reached, I'll provide whatever is appropriate. How aspects of that dreadful day are described by me, a participant, cannot be rushed to suit a deadline. I'll get in touch with your rights team.

Regards,
Claire

There was blood streaked in Melanie's blonde curls and on her face and hands, which were twisting in her lap. Alice joined us and gently wiped Melanie's face with a wet napkin.

'I'm Alice,' she said.

Melanie barely noticed. 'The monster who stabbed him. Be careful, he's got this knife…'

I nodded, thinking it sounded like he had made use of it more than once, both on Nik and on the dead man we had passed.

'We'll get someone to walk you to one of the carriages further back where it's safe.'

'The big one went up the train, towards the driver's cab. That's the one who stabbed Nik.'

'How many did you see?' I asked.

'Just two. He shouted at me. Said it was Nik's own fault he'd been stabbed. Bastard.'

'You've been very brave,' said Alice. She turned to me. 'I'll see if I can find anything to help.'

I heard something from behind the counter and got up to look into the galley. On the floor, Nik was slowly turning his head, his eyes open.

'Good to see you,' he rasped painfully to Geoff, clearly having problems breathing.

I kept my eyes on the manager's face. 'Nik, my name's Claire, and a group of us have taken down three of them. Do you know how many more there are?'

He shook his head and gasped between breaths. 'I saw two… I don't…'

I was silently willing him to survive. He coughed, and there was blood round his mouth.

A small, older Black woman, greying hair in braids, appeared in the doorway. She held a pack of sanitary towels, I guessed to help staunch the blood. 'I'm Rita, retired midwife. How can I help?' she said, no-nonsense and calm.

'Shall we move him?' I asked, and Geoff shook his head.

'Not now. Rita, come in here please.'

'The counter gives some protection, if anyone comes back,' added Deavey.

Deavey came out and she got in beside Geoff. I was aware of them doing the thing that medical people do – allowing the training to take over, focusing on the patient, putting everything else to one side – and saw Rita take Nik's hand and say, 'I'm going to make you more comfortable young man.' Behind me, Alice stepped back into the carriage with a bundle of clothes and handed them to Rita to place round and under the train manager.

Deavey looked at me. He was grim. 'We need to get a move on.'

'CCTV,' croaked Nik suddenly, and I looked around and caught sight of what might be a camera in the ceiling: a glass dome.

'Shit!'

I leant over the counter again. Nik was trying to lift himself up and Geoff was telling him to stay still and I saw the cost of the effort that Nik was making. 'I… CCTV feed… switched it off, from my console. So they couldn't see. In case. Someone like you. Passengers. That's why he stabbed me.'

He started coughing again and blood dribbled onto his chin.

'Don't try to speak any more Nik, keep your strength, OK?' said Geoff, lowering him back against the side, but not letting him slip to the floor.

'That's amazing, mate. Proud to meet you,' said Deavey.

'Tell my wife… she and the girls, everything to me. Tell her…' Nik stopped and coughed again. His breathing was painful to hear – gasping, straining for air. He gave up and slumped against Geoff.

'It's all right, Nik. You can tell me about your wife and kids in a while. Just rest up for a bit.'

I noticed a shelf stacked with spirit miniatures and put a few vodkas beside Geoff in case he wanted to use them as sterilisers.

Then grabbed another mixed handful, dropping them into my bag.

Nik spoke, his voice weak, but clear. 'I don't understand how they knew about this train.'

I stopped, turned back, looking over at him. 'What do you mean?'

'Two fewer coaches than usual... easier to take over,' Nik managed. 'And then the electrics in coach K...'

He started coughing again.

'Let him be,' said Geoff. 'He needs his strength.'

I thought about what Nik said. Had someone told them there would be fewer coaches – or made sure there would be – and knocked out the electrics in the end coach? Did the hijackers have someone on the inside, with NorthRail, or even on the train?

10

Surprise

COACH C

12:00

> Where r u. cab under control. Send co-ords of stop place now.

I had to use the loo, and take a moment. It was overwhelming. We were marching inexorably forward into more chaos. Maybe more death. There was one between coaches C and D, empty, and as I washed my hands, I saw they were shaking. I suddenly remembered asking my twin why he loved the army. Common purpose and comradeship, he'd said. Excitement, boredom and truly shit food. What more could a man ask for? A long life, I should have replied. Not that he would have taken any notice.

And now was my life going to be cut short? That would make things easier for Jim. He could shag who he liked. I caught sight of my reflection in the mirror; it was startling. One cheek was flaming red, and there were scratches above my eye. My hair, shirt and jacket were a mess. I rolled a wodge of toilet paper into my hand and tried to wipe the blood off, but it only made it worse. Perhaps my appearance might offer a distraction. There was a scrunchie in my pocket and I pulled it out and put my hair in a ponytail.

Sod making things easier for Jim.

I had no intention of dying today, if I could help it. I let my anger rise then looked at the bloodied tissue in my hand and squashed it into a pocket, swigged some nasty water from the tap and went to join Paul, Alice, Deavey and Alex who had just arrived.

Paul asked if I was OK and I nodded. That was when I noticed the narrow door in the vestibule leading back into D. I wondered if it covered an instrument panel, then suddenly thought there could be room for a person in there and knocked gently, whispering, 'Hello?'

Deavey gave me a *Really?* look, but pointed the gun at the door.

I leaned in, not really expecting a reply, and jumped when the door slowly opened a crack, nudging me back. A whisper. 'I'm not a hijacker. I'm a passenger. My name's Gill.' A woman's voice. Quiet but clear.

We stepped back as Gill came out; fifties, average height and comfortably built, blue hair in a choppy bob style, a studded denim jacket, large diamante-edged black glasses, and a phone in her hand. The 'character' from Piccadilly station concourse. She eyed us warily, then stepped back to the seats behind the luggage rack and took a quick look round the carriage. Deavey lowered his gun. There are no rules for what a hijacker should look like, but sparkly glasses didn't feel like it fit.

'Are you OK?' I asked.

'Yes. Managed to hide in the chaos. When they grabbed that poor man. What happened to him, do you know?'

Deavey shook his head. 'Not good, I'm afraid.'

We peered into what I'd thought was a cupboard. It was actually a tiny office, room for one person at a squash – with a smashed console and screen. Nik's workspace.

She was still holding her phone in front of her, but flat, not filming.

'No. But he's getting help. And we need to get going. How many hijackers did you see?'

Deavey and I were already moving back to coach C, the others were standing to one side.

Gill put her free arm on mine. 'Wait a minute, all of you.'

Deavey turned. 'You can go back down the train; we've got control of those carriages.'

'How many hijackers did you see?' I asked again.

'The man who attacked the train manager was a big guy. Black, with a machete. I heard the cry, and when I went to the door, saw the two of them. There was nothing I could do—'

I interrupted. 'Did you see a passenger being attacked?' I indicated back down into coach D, but the row of seats hid the body stretched across them.

'Oh god, a passenger as well.' She looked sick.

'How come they didn't see you?'

'I was just leaving the toilet, so I hid behind the door and left it unlocked so they'd think there was no one inside. There was only one of them, I think, or maybe two. When it was quiet I came out, the door was ajar to the train manager's cubby and I could lock it from the inside. I didn't hear or see anything of the other man they murdered. They must have done it when I was in there. I heard a woman screaming, but that was from the cafe area.' Gill pointed to coach C. She was tense but controlled. I couldn't figure her out.

'So, what's your plan?' she asked.

'There are two medics in there looking after the train manager. We've taken the four hijackers we've captured down the train to the last carriage. Passengers have got them tied up. You'll be safe at the back of the train and we need to get a move on,' I replied.

Alice spoke: 'I think we may need some more volunteers if we're moving ahead. I'll see who I can find,' and she set off back down the carriages, phone to her ear. It was curiously quiet again, apart from the rush of the train while another station flashed by too fast to identify. It was raining. I thought of more dead bodies and checked my knife. I thought of what the rain would feel like, falling on my face. How many casualties were there? Gill was still holding her phone in her left hand.

'Why I asked you to wait, I've been talking to gold command. They know what's going on. They're getting Euston ready.'

'Gold command?'

'The police group in charge of the response. I'm a former police sergeant. It might not look like it – but I know what I'm doing. They, gold command,' she pointed to the phone in her hand, 'are listening. You've got to talk to them before you do anything else.'

They were listening? Gill held the phone out, between Deavey and me. Deavey gave a quick shake of his head. I took the phone from her hand. A man's voice said hello.

Holding Gill's phone to my ear in the swaying carriage, I listened to DS Chambers – Steve, as he quickly introduced himself – and then briefly explained who I was. If he was surprised that he was talking to a fifty-something history of art university lecturer about a hijack counteroffensive, he hid it well. I took him quickly through what had happened and what we knew, and suggested we get photos of the hijackers we had captured and send them to him. He agreed, said they'd already received a few but any more would be good, and then instructed us not to carry on forward. We would be putting ourselves in too much danger, he said firmly.

'We're already in danger,' I said, and pointed out that it wasn't like a train in an old film where passengers could uncouple the carriages they were on and drift safely to a gentle stop while the engines chuffed away with the baddies on board. We were stuck on a potential death machine hurtling to London. The hijackers had already murdered two people – three, if Nik died – and were probably planning to kill a lot more. We were lucky to have a few people with helpful skills. I came across as tetchy, as I realised when I heard the conversation relayed in court. I tried to keep my voice level and calm but could feel the rising stress in my throat when Steve started to argue. I handed the phone back to Gill.

[I know you didn't want to use the court transcript of the recording of this call as you were concerned by how you came across, but wouldn't it be a good way of showing the stress you were under? No wonder you were shouting and hung up on him – Loretta]

[No. It's just one conversation and not representative of how I behaved in general. I say I sounded tetchy and that I was stressed. The recording made me sound unhinged, which I wasn't! – Claire]

Our police can't be seen to encourage have-a-go heroes. But the people who'd come forward understood the risk. The police activity on the platform at Crewe would have tipped off the terrorists that the outside world was aware there was something bad happening on the train from Manchester. And if they'd missed that, the helicopter had been an unmissable clue. That could force their hand. It was unlikely that the outcome would be good for the passengers on the 10:12.

Gill tried to argue but I lifted my hand. 'You're wasting your breath, and we're wasting time.'

'We're not stopping now,' agreed Deavey, and the others nodded.

'Gill, we'll keep you informed of our progress.' I didn't want to completely alienate the woman.

'We won't take any unnecessary risks,' added Deavey.

Alice reappeared.

'If you can face it, take a picture of the body back there,' I said to Gill. 'The police may be able to find out the identity of the poor man.'

'Body?' asked Alice. 'What body?'

Extract from Cross-Examination of Assistant Chief Constable June Heatherington by Prosecuting Barrister Hugh Delaney

PB. *Assistant Chief Constable, how soon after the train left Manchester Piccadilly were the police aware that there was trouble on board the 10:12?*

JH. *We had the first notification of concern at 10:29 via the Transport Police.*

PB. *Was that a phone call?*

JH. *The Transport Police received texts on the 'See it. Say it. Sorted.' number before 10:40, around a dozen I believe. And there were* several 999 calls where people used the 'silent mode' which meant we could hear a little of what was going on.

PB. Did the use of texts and silent mode raise particular concerns?

JH. Yes. The indication was that callers felt under threat. And the numbers of texts and calls, and the fact that they were coming from different carriages, also indicated a scale of threat.

PB. In these early stages, what were you able to learn about the situation?

JH. There were a few direct calls where passengers spoke to responders, including Claire Fitzroy and one from former Police Sergeant Gill Kaplan. By 10:45, we knew it sounded like a hijacking, and someone was already dead.

PB. What were your first actions?

JH. We immediately initiated the appropriate protocols along with the Transport Police, and I took gold commander role. That was at 10:41.

PB. Could you explain a little about the protocols, Assistant Chief Constable?

JH. Our first job in these circumstances is to alert everyone who needs to know, which would include the local forces, domestic counter-intelligence bodies, the government, health and fire services, and so on. We also initiated protocols with the railway bodies, alerting them to what was known about the situation on board and requesting information about the train.

PB. This was done sequentially?

JH. No. Time was of the utmost importance. These tasks were carried out simultaneously.

PB. What was your initial analysis?

JH. Twenty minutes after the train left Manchester, indications were that this was a major incident, possibly of a terrorist nature.

PB. Did you have any direct communication with the hijackers?

JH. No. We searched for any way to contact them, but they appeared to have unregistered phones and no interest in speaking to the authorities. We attempted speaking to them from the helicopter and they responded with gunfire, so the pilot had to follow out of range. We also tried the driver's phone, which went unanswered.

PB. Were you aware of their motives?

JH. *No. We kept an open mind. What they were doing was more important than why they were doing it, particularly as no demands were made that required a response.*

PB. *Why was the train not forcibly stopped or diverted, say at Crewe or another station?*

JH. *We took the decision, based on specialist advice, that any attempt to stop the train by barricades, or by taking the train off to a siding by changing points, would alert the terrorists and possibly result in them taking drastic action earlier than planned.*

PB. *What sort of drastic action?*

JH. *Hurting more of the passengers. We had to work on the basis they weren't just planning to crash the train, but possibly also blow it up in a way that would inflict maximum fatalities and injuries.*

11

Prepping

COACHES D–B

12:15

> Sian babe love you always. been hurt being cared for no pain. Thankyou for everything love our girls so much. sorrytell mum love her 2 youre the bestxxxxxxx

Deavey was already moving. Leaving Gill, I joined him, heading back into carriage D where we had left what we thought was a corpse. But it was no longer there.

The freesias were scattered on the floor where there were some bloody footprints. An awful thought struck me. 'Didn't Melanie say they stabbed the train manager in here? It's his blood, it has to be. The body we saw, he couldn't be walking about with that much blood loss, could he?'

'Whatever, he wasn't dead and we didn't check. Shit.' Deavey sounded weary, not angry.

I felt terrible. 'Anita said she had, but sorry, this is on me. And now he's back in what we thought were the safe carriages. We need to tell the policewoman. He's got to be one of them, hasn't he?'

Deavey shrugged. 'Unless he was knocked out by them? A passenger who fought back.'

I shook my head. 'We have to assume the worst. Warn Alex; tell him to check if anyone has come through. I don't think he can have gone up the train to the front, do you? No one got by us, did they, even when we were with the train manager?'

'No, although… in the chaos…' He sighed.

'If he is one of them, he'll have rung his mates in with the driver. Told them about us.'

I felt sick and returned to the cafe carriage, furious with myself for not checking. There had been a lot happening, but my lack of attention could cost lives.

Gill was talking to the people helping the train manager. She came over as we walked in.

'I saw a body in D, a man, some time ago. Seemed dead. Either he's been moved, or he wasn't dead. There are bloody footprints heading to the back.'

'A hijacker?' she asked.

'Could be, now going into the safe areas down the train. And he'll have warned his mates up front. We need to let everyone know.'

Paul lifted his phone. 'I'll call Alex now.'

'He's medium height, olive-skinned, black hair, jeans, maybe a black coat with a Burberry-type lining, and a rust-coloured beanie, though he could've dumped that,' I said to Gill. 'Could you go back up the train and check?'

Alice added, 'Gill hasn't met Anita.' She turned to the policewoman. 'Young Asian woman, pierced nose. She's been organising things and needs to know. She's not answering her phone, battery might be dead.' She thought for a second. 'I'll come with you, we might need reinforcements.'

Gill nodded. 'OK. The rest of you stay here and I'll check.' They set off back into coach D.

There was a moment's silence while Paul finished talking to Alex. Was the missing man a hijacker? Was he armed? Deavey spoke: 'We need to get on.'

Deavey, Paul and I moved swiftly through coach C and into the vestibule to B. Squatting down, I looked through the double doors. Coach B was stuffed full of passengers. A man with bleached blond hair and large tortoiseshell glasses was close to the door, seated on the ground, his legs folded in the aisle and his back against a seat frame. He turned, registered my presence. I put my finger to my lips. He gave a slight nod, then tilted his head, which I took to mean there was a hijacker close by, although I couldn't spot one. He lifted his hand to his mouth and raised one finger, then another.

Deavey joined me cautiously, a brown leather jacket in his hand.

'Two in there, probably. Man on the floor was indicating,' I reported. Deavey looked through the door.

'Thank goodness the train manager blocked the CCTV,' I said, pointing to the glass half-globe inset in the panel above the door which I assumed was a camera.

Deavey looked at me. 'You've blood on your face,' he said matter-of-factly.

'It might unnerve an arsehole just for a moment and give us a chance.' My heart was pumping, nerves jangling, thinking about Nik Bhatia.

'Fair enough. But maybe put this on.' He handed me the leather jacket. It was sturdy and had a military look about it. I realised he was now wearing one too, only his was black, rather snug and more fashion than fighting. I was puzzled.

'Better protection from knives.'

I put it on. It felt heavy and I wondered whether it would be too cumbersome. But then I pictured it deflecting a knife.

'Are you ready?' I asked. 'Shall we go in together? Or do another set piece here for them? With this on I feel like we should invade Poland.'

Deavey shook his head. 'That didn't end well. Whatever we do, we don't want them in here. Not with Mr Bhatia and the medics.'

Paul joined us. 'Gill's gone to see if she can get anything from the hijackers in J. We're to keep her updated. I think we need to hold off for a bit. If there's a couple of the bastards in there, then more in the driver's cab, we won't be able to pick them off like we did with the others.'

'And we have to assume they're going to be expecting trouble, as they're getting no answers from their mates,' added Deavey. 'We need to wait for help.'

'Just two more carriages,' I said. 'Let's make a barricade. It will keep them out of here until we're ready.'

'What about the passengers in B? Won't they feel stranded?' asked Paul.

'Maybe, but we could let them through quickly if needs be,' I replied.

He nodded, and using seat cushions, we quickly raised a barricade of sorts up against the door to the vestibule between B and C. A small gap let us check what was happening on the other side. Being busy also meant we could keep our minds off what was going on behind the counter, from where there were occasional low murmurings.

<u>COURT EXHIBIT No. ML1</u>
<u>(Group email – authenticated)</u>

From: May Leung CEO NRAIL
Subject: Urgent Alert
To: senior management team
Reply to: MLCEO.NRAIL

Check phones for updates and refer to emergency protocols. Police/Gold Command in charge. Sector team fully apprised. Essential all media enquiries go through communications team.

Alice was quick. She came through into coach C with two people. The first, a stocky, brown-skinned, middle-aged man with a canvas shoulder bag, immediately went over to the counter and ducked behind it. 'That's Dr Patel, a pathologist,' Alice explained, then pointed behind her. 'And this is Kyo. They're an MMA fighter.'

A scrawny, heavily tattooed young person in a navy-blue hooded jacket looked out from behind her with pale blue eyes, a half grin and short brown hair, bleached white in places. A cut lip and a bruised, crooked nose completed the picture. The newcomer surveyed the carriage, registering the sounds coming from behind the counter. The grin disappeared.

In their present state, Kyo didn't look like they could throw a ball, let alone a punch. But then off came the hoodie, revealing a strong, wiry torso and muscled arms, covered in bruises and scratches. 'I'm not the best. But I'm not bad. I usually win my fights,' Kyo said softly, rolling their neck. It sounded like they were from Belfast.

'But not the last one,' said Deavey with a smile.

'Youse should have seen the other fella,' replied Kyo.

'Better put your hoodie back on,' I said. 'Keep the surprise. They'll probably underestimate your potential.'

'From what I've heard about you, that'll be them making the same mistake twice.' The hoodie was pulled back on. 'How's the train manager?'

'Not good. The medics are doing their best. What's going on down the train?'

Alice was methodically laying out an array of items on top of a pile of stacked cases and bags. 'Passengers in coaches G and H are trying to find IEDs, at least the ones that aren't panicking or sobbing. They're all getting a bit nervous and narky. The high's wearing off.' She considered her collection: knitting needles, hairspray, a penknife, some of those little hammers that are provided to smash a window in an emergency. I briefly wondered just what emergencies the designers had imagined. Not this one, I'd bet.

'But there's a great crew keeping an eye on the prisoners – plenty of them, including the stroppy bald bloke, Fellowes, who keeps on calling Anita "Sarge", which is funny. She's checking out the end carriage. And there's a few organising an armed barricade at the front of coach G, including an American, so they're calling themselves "the Alamo".' She rolled her eyes. I was just cheered to hear of a collective defensive effort.

'What are you doing?'

'I like to plan ahead. Never commit to a tackle without considering all the outcomes.'

I wondered if this ordering of things was Alice's way of dealing with nerves. If so, it seemed like a good system to me. Her blue eyes calmly scanned her little collection of weapons, and her hands, with their short, square cut nails and two slim silver and turquoise rings, were steady. As she picked up the items on display and distributed them between pockets, a couple joined us, both late twenties, tall and in smart but casual clothes.

'Josh and India. Can we help?' the man said. 'We're pretty fit, triathletes.'

They looked it. 'I was in army cadets for six years at school, if that's any use,' added India. 'I can follow orders, anyway!' She smiled.

There were quick introductions then Deavey turned to India. 'Arms training?'

She nodded. 'I passed the lot. Although not much use in digital marketing.'

He held out Cokehead's gun. She took it and Deavey watched as she efficiently checked it.

'I can see you know what you're doing,' Deavey said approvingly.

'Where's the other one? The plastic one?' I asked.

Deavey fished in his pocket and pulled it out. 'Not much use.'

'Looks real enough,' said Paul. 'Particularly if you're not familiar with guns.'

Deavey looked sceptical and put it on a table.

'It could hurt someone close up, couldn't it?' I asked tentatively.

'If you shoved it in someone's ear and fired, I suppose it might give them a bit of a headache,' Paul replied.

Extract from Cross-Examination of Mohammed Abadi by Prosecuting Barrister Hugh Delaney

PB. *Does this machete on the table belong to you?*
MA. *Don't know.*
PB. *If you look closely, you can see distinctive marks on the handle. Up on the screen are the capital letters M and A carved into the wood, and then scratched over. Do you recognise it now?*
MA. *Just scratches, man. Don't mean nothing to me.*
PB. *This is the machete that was used to inflict fatal wounds on the train manager, Mr Nik Bhatia. Did you inflict those wounds?*

MA. *Don't remember.*
PB. *You don't remember whether you took an innocent man's life?*
MA. *Innocent? Nah. I wouldn't do that. They was all part of it. The takeover.*
PB. *What takeover?*
MA. *No point talking about it. You just be chatting shit.*
Judge. *Keep your language respectful and appropriate for the court, Mr Abadi.*
PB. *Were you one of the people who attacked Mr Bhatia?*
MA. *Don't remember.*
PB. *Do you at least agree with several witnesses who have identified you, that you were on the train in question, the 10:12 from Manchester to London?*
MA. *People see what they want to see.*
PB. *Mr Abadi, are you denying that you were on the 10:12 train from Manchester to London on the day in question?*
MA. *Not denying nothing.*
PB. *Are you going to answer the questions put to you?*
MA. *I'm answering. You just don't like my answers.*
Judge. *Mr Abadi, you are being evasive in your replies. Are you going to avoid answering all the questions put to you?*
MA. *I don't recognise this court. You're part of Deep State. It's fake. You can't be the judge of me.*
Judge. *My learned friend, I believe you said your client was prepared to answer questions in the dock. Would you like to have a word with him?*
[DB and defendant in the dock confer.]
DB. *I'm afraid my client has changed his mind, Your Honour.*
Judge. *Remove Mr Abadi from the dock.*

Paul looked up from his phone. 'Gill says there've been people moving about, anyone could have gone through. But she's going to pass the message on to look out for a man in a black coat and she'll come and join us when she's done that. There's been no trouble reported. They're busy searching for IEDs.'

'Let's get ready,' I said, trying to put the image of a walking dead man out of my mind, picking up the plastic gun and putting it in my bag – which was now beginning to bulge. I was fast turning into a bag lady.

Deavey spoke. 'If too many amateurs poke around, who knows what could happen. Paul – I'm guessing you've had explosives training?'

'Yes. But I want to help bring them down.'

'Of course,' I said. 'But Deavey's right. You're the one with the skills. Tell them what to look for, what to be careful about – you've got the authority. No point getting the arseholes if they blow us all up anyway.'

Paul didn't look keen.

'Please, Paul. The train's got to be searched properly and it might stop people panicking if they know your background.'

He nodded and turned to go back, taking off the hijacker's jacket and handing it to Alice.

'Good luck, bomb squad,' I muttered.

'The B team. Good luck A team,' he replied wryly.

So, there we were. The A team: me, Deavey, Alice, Josh, India and Kyo. Against how many, and armed with what? Kyo had muscles and MMA skills, Josh was a red belt in karate apparently, Alice carried a knitting needle and penknife and I had my kitchen knife and a toy pistol. At least Deavey had a loaded gun and knew how to use it.

Kyo stood up and stretched. 'The train manager. He was just doing his job. And that brave fella who got shot. Let's do it for them.'

As a call to arms, it was pretty simple. But it felt good to hear. The next carriage. The next fight. Could we survive again?

Extract from Examination of Geoff Wilson by Prosecuting Barrister Hugh Delaney

PB. *When you assessed Mr Bhatia, what were your conclusions?*

GW. *He was in a serious condition and the first aid kit that the catering manager had been using was rudimentary and more focused on burns. However, we did what we could. Mr Bhatia had lost a lot of blood and was going into shock. Melanie Draper had* done well trying to stem the bleeding by pressure, but it was a big wound, made by a big knife. A machete. Rita Jackson and I tried to pack it and stop the bleeding as best we could, but he'd already lost so much blood.

PB. Was Mr Bhatia conscious?

GW. Some of the time. Drifting in and out.

PB. Did he talk? Tell you what had happened?

GW. I was trying to keep him quiet, as I didn't want to put any further strain on him. I wasn't best pleased when Claire Fitzroy started asking questions. But he wanted to help. I could see that. I think it made sense to him. It helped him to know that what he'd done might make a difference. I think perhaps he knew he was dying. He was a brave man.

PB. What did he say?

GW. He told us that he'd tampered with the CCTV feed so that the terrorists wouldn't be able to see what was happening on the train and that they were angry. They'd guessed what he'd done. One stabbed him... But he also he wanted us to tell his wife...

Judge. Take your time, Mr Wilson. Would you like a glass of water?

GW. No... I'll be fine. Thank you. Dr Patel joined us and tried his best and someone got a phone so that Nik could call his wife. The hijackers had mine. But Nik couldn't get the number right. Then Melanie came back and helped him. Nik left a message for his wife and children.

PB. I think we can all appreciate how hard it must have been for you.

GW. I've been a paramedic for sixteen years. I've seen lots of shocking things. But I felt helpless without proper kit. Not that I think it would have made a lot of difference. Nik was effectively dying from the moment he [witness indicates prisoner in dock] *removed the machete from his chest.*

DB. Objection.

Judge. Sustained.

PB. You didn't actually see what happened, did you, Mr Wilson?

GW. No. But I saw what had been done to him. And he told me who had done it. He had no reason to lie, given the circumstances. Also, the catering manager, Melanie, was there and witnessed what happened. Abadi murdered Nik Bhatia. Rita and I made him as comfortable as possible. Melanie, Dr Patel too, and Alice — she brought in coats and jumpers that passengers donated for him to lie on. Rita held his hand and even made him smile, talking about his children before he lost consciousness. I want…

PB. Yes, Mr Wilson? Do you need to take a break?

GW. Sorry. I'll be all right… I want to say that Nik Bhatia was a very brave man and a very kind one. His only thoughts right up to the end were for other people, his family, the driver, the passengers. If he hadn't knocked out the CCTV, the hijackers would have seen exactly what Claire and the others were doing and I'm sure would have killed—

DB. Objection.

Judge. Overruled. You may continue, Mr Wilson.

GW. Thank you. Nik Bhatia is a hero. And the driver and the brave policewoman too. The best of us. As for those scum…

Judge. Thank you, Mr Wilson. You are to be commended for your humanity in such difficult circumstances. Usher, would you help Mr Wilson from the witness box, please? And the court will take a short recess.

12

Lifesaver

COACHES C—B

12:25

> sorry this is weird. trouble on train had to let you know how much I love you just in case

> leave me alone or i'll tell your wife

> omg. u on that manchester train?

> matt?

> matt?u OK?

<u>**COURT EXHIBIT No. NSC15A**
*(Post on NoSinoChan site and Facebook –
authenticated. Deleted 12 hrs after incident)*</u>

By the time this posts, it will be done. I expect I'll be bad-mouthed, a lot of trash talking, so I want to put the truth seekers right. The others don't matter, they believe the lies the State feeds them. There is collateral damage in war. And it wasn't me that started the war. This is my manifesto.

1. Takeover. As a proud Englishman, I have been forced to take a stand. I've watched our country being taken over by foreign countries like China, taking over our utilities, factories, hotels and football teams. Our heritage, our country, our once Great Britain, is unrecognisable.
2. Females. Part of the Deep State attack is the emasculation of men by women. They are feminising us through hormones in the meat and washing-up liquid, etc. The #MeToo whining feminazis trying to stop men being men. The gays and trannies, all trying to undermine what a real man is. Men know, deep down, that women should not be in charge. I'm not Stone Age Taliban, driving cars is OK, teaching, nurses, etc. But they shouldn't be in charge of powerful machines, or of the country, or of large organisations. They don't have the right analytical brains. And that's just a scientific fact. What they are designed to do is be mothers and wives. Girls are being brainwashed into thinking that's not good enough.
3. Action. I have to act, to make people listen to what is really going on. I'm not saying that all the men with me are people I agree with, or that they agree with me. Some of them don't fully understand what's going on. But I've been encouraged by those that know, to take the lead and in war, sometimes that means working with strange allies to achieve your aims.
4. Truth. In this red pill/blue pill world, I chose the red, to see the real world, the truth.

As I write, I'm struck by how much was going on and how long a reader might assume it took for those events to happen. But the reality was different. What I recall is the speed of the various transactions: we seemed to be living at a different pace to the normal world. All with a backdrop of the noise of a speeding train. Our ragtag group had had more success than most people, including us, would have predicted. But the big battle, I'm sure we all felt, was ahead. When we passed through Stafford station the driver sounded the train horn, a warning measure I assume. But to me it sounded like a war cry.

I tried hard not to think of my family but I wasn't entirely successful. If the worst happened, what would be my children's last memories of their mum? I took out my phone and sent a quick text to each of them.

> ☺. Hope you're having a good day. Love you lots! Best 'kids' ever! xxx ☼.

It would have to do. Hopefully the text was not weird enough to worry them, just enough to make them think their mother was having a rare silly, sentimental moment. But something for them to keep. As for Jim, he wasn't going to get unconditional love under the circumstances. I'd suspected an affair with a young woman at work – I met him at the office one day, and caught a look – something indefinable, but tangible. Although she didn't seem his type. Fake blonde, fake nails, fake lashes, fake smile. Derek didn't say, or didn't know. Just said Jim implied he was leaving me. Implied. Christ. What a betrayal. What a cliché. Things hadn't been great between us, admittedly, but he could have talked to me. Was it her? I pushed against the wall of fury. After all our years together, and our children, I owed him something. Maybe. He'd be worried, possibly frantic. Good. But the better part of me typed.

> Trouble with train. Will be late.

No xxx's. My finger hovered, ready to send, then I changed the '**with**' to '**on**' and sent. It didn't feel like enough. I tapped another, and pressed send.

> Knowing you betrayed me and lied has
> not helped

But maybe it had.

We checked carefully through the gap in the barricade, keeping low. I began to remove some of the cushions. Kyo, slim and small, moved round like a snake and paused to pick up a black stainless steel water bottle that was rolling on the floor, assessed its heft in their hand, and looked pleased. Deavey took up position on the other side of the door, gun in hand, and Kyo squatted down between the seats in front of me.

'Same plan?' asked Deavey. But before I could reply there was noise at the end of the carriage behind us. It was Gill with two men – Alex, the tech company employee, and another smartly dressed guy of about forty who looked like he worked out a lot. The newcomers were distracted by noises from behind the counter, but Deavey quickly waved them up to our end by the doors. They joined us, squatting between the seats.

'We need to focus on moving up the train,' I stated.

Gill spoke. 'It's all getting organised back there. I think people are glad to have something to do. We can create a line here, by the look of it. Stop them coming back down the train. But no luck getting anything out of our captives so far.'

'Any sign of our disappearing body?' asked Deavey.

'He could be anywhere. Best we can do is keep people on alert. There are a lot of medium-height men in jeans with short black hair. He could have ditched the coat. They've got a good barricade. If we can keep the remaining hijackers up front, till help arrives, it will minimise things.'

I asked Alex how the captives were.

'There are four people keeping an eye on them at any time. And more to cover. They're not going to cause any trouble. The big one keeps on laughing about bombs but won't say where they might be.'

The well-dressed man said he was pretty fit and just wanted to help. He had a penknife; Alex, the cricket bat. I decided they weren't just here to hold a line, whatever Gill said. But I'd also realised that the packed carriage meant we couldn't go charging in all together, there just wasn't the room to manoeuvre.

'Let me go in first,' I said, 'then Deavey and Kyo, so they think it's only us.'

'No. We all stay here and hold a line,' Gill spoke firmly.

'And let them win while we wait? For what? I don't think so,' I replied.

'I'm happy to go in first,' said Deavey.

'You look like you could give them trouble. I don't. It's worked so far. I'm just an old biddy. They're alert to men and underrate women. Misogyny's in my favour.' I was getting impatient.

'I can't condone any attempt to go towards the hijackers,' Gill said, holding the phone in front of her.

'Understood. But you can't stop us.'

We both looked at the phone, and then each other.

The well-dressed man spoke to Gill. 'You're a police officer?'

She nodded, obviously deciding not to get into the 'ex' bit.

'Maybe we should wait like she says?' he said tentatively.

This was turning into a full debate.

'People who want to wait with Gill should,' I said. 'But I can't sit back and let them kill people if I think we can at least save some lives. It's that simple. Anyone care to join me?'

Everyone nodded or said yes, including the well-dressed man, while Gill shook her head in resignation.

'Old lady goes first?' I asked.

Deavey and Kyo nodded agreement. I'd pretend to be injured, with Deavey and Kyo ready to move as soon as the hijacker or hijackers were distracted.

[Didn't witnesses say in court that this got quite heated? Gill told you the police were telling you to stop, in no uncertain terms? That you refused to speak to them on the phone? Just to clarify. – Loretta]

[Yes, it got quite heated. But I can't really remember the details, so much was happening. – Claire]

> Love you ma. you're the best. ta for everything. hope dad, you know...

> Some nutters on train. love kyo xxx

> keep your head down. don't start a fight, for god's sake.

We pulled away more bags and stepped into the vestibule. Slipping my knife down the back of my waistband, the toy gun nestled in one pocket of the leather jacket, I took the ball of bloodied toilet paper from the other pocket and stepped through the door, clutching it to my head.

The train lurched as I came into coach B, causing me to stumble over the young blond man sitting on the floor, an action I exaggerated, and to which I added a loud groan. The air was stuffy and unpleasant, as before, caused by overcrowding and fear. A voice shouted angrily for me to sit down. I looked up, the wodge of paper over one eye, and could see the hijacker – the only other person standing in the carriage.

Scarface. The man I'd last seen being hit over the head with my water bottle. The man with the dead eyes. Now with black eyes, and a bruised face. Now wearing a green fleece.

How had he got up here? He should have been tied up in coach J. Somehow, he'd slipped past us. Later I found out there had been a bottleneck of passengers trying to move back up the train, and in the confusion he'd got away – two different 'guards' thinking the other one had him. But there was no time to think. I held up one finger behind my back as I continued to stand. I hoped the leather jacket, the ponytail and the bloodied toilet paper would mean he wouldn't recognise me. And the fact that we had almost a whole carriage between us.

'I'm hurt.' To further distance myself from the woman he'd confronted earlier, I tried a slight Scots accent, which wouldn't have fooled anyone from north of Hadrian's Wall. I carried on with a moan. You don't need an accent for that. Passengers were trying to make space for me and some were offering to help. I could sense their fear. The hijacker had armed himself with a fresh gun since I had last seen him and now started to push towards me as I continued moaning, my hand holding the stained tissues to my face. His face looked terrible. Broken nose and possibly cheekbone. I could see he was in pain. Good.

He loomed in front of me. I deliberately staggered back into the luggage rack, discreetly pulling out my knife as he seemed set to push me down. A woman screamed: 'Don't hurt her. She's just an old lady.' He looked round and I drew my knife as Kyo came hurtling through the door. In a blink of an eye Scarface was in a headlock. I brought my knife sharply down onto the wrist of Scarface's gun-carrying hand, and he yelped as his wrist flowered with blood.

But he flung his arm back and in that confined space smacked Kyo in the face, who lurched back into Deavey. Scarface somehow got past me then turned, his gun pointing at my face, and jabbed me hard in the neck, fingertips straight into my windpipe, leaving me gasping for air and shocked by the pain.

'Bye, cunt,' he snarled, raising his gun. His head suddenly jerked back, an incongruous blue and pink piece of material yanked hard around his neck, pulling him off balance, revealing Gill behind him, twisting her scarf tightly. As he writhed, the gun went off with a loud bang, and Kyo kicked Scarface's legs from under him. Gill was still standing – the bullet had gone who knew where. Kyo smacked Scarface hard in the face and successfully held him this time.

I was trying to catch my breath and scraped out a thank-you to Gill, who muttered, '*De nada*,' and started checking my neck. Someone handed me a bottle of water, and I sipped gratefully.

'I'll be fine,' I rasped. But we'd lost focus. I heard someone mutter, 'Shit.' It was Deavey, crouched on the floor, gun in hand, watching the door at the other end of the carriage. Then there was a scream. I followed Deavey's eyes. A giant of a man was standing inside the door, holding a young woman like a shield, a knife at her throat.

13
Isha

COACH B

12:35

> Mum love you and nan everyone! good people here God is with us don't worry bout me

> We love you too baby girl come home to us be strong pray to Jesus xxxx

I stared down the carriage. The sound from the gunshot seemed to be reverberating, bouncing off the walls. The young woman in the hijacker's arms looked terrified. Even from that distance, I could see she was shaking, and her eyes were shut, as if hoping it would all disappear. From somewhere behind her, there was the plangent sound of a baby crying.

For a moment everything in coach B froze. Kyo stayed still, low on the ground, Scarface in a headlock, no longer struggling after receiving a surreptitious blow to the head from Deavey, which must have hurt his already bashed face. He was clutching the wrist I'd cut with the knife, and blood was seeping out between his fingers.

I staggered up. 'OK,' I called out. 'You win. Please don't hurt her. What do you want us to do?'

There was no immediate answer to my question. The heavily bearded hijacker holding the young woman just scowled.

Passengers were squirming in the aisle, which irritated me until I realised they were moving to conceal Deavey. Behind me, Kyo had stepped back and Scarface was trying to stand, groaning loudly. It was good to know he was having a bad day. Almost matching his groans in regularity, if not volume, was the Tin Can Man from coach J: Tony Rossi, 33, from Salford. Squashed at a table, he was fidgeting with his carrier bag, while an older man with a fringe of straggly grey hair, a rakish scarf round his neck and a concerned face, was gently trying to hush him into silence.

The hijacker attempted to retrieve the phone in his pocket without releasing his captive. He was olive-skinned, tall, 'roid wide at his shoulders and wearing a black puffer jacket – apparently hijacker de rigueur couture – and those tight trousers that are like a cross between leggings and jeans. They highlighted skinny chicken legs that jarred in contrast to his pumped-up torso. However, chicken legs or not, he seemed to fill the width of the aisle and towered over the young woman.

'Let him go and give him back the fucking gun or the femoid gets it,' he suddenly yelled out, in a light breathy voice.

I was on my feet, looking down.

'OK. OK. Whatever you say, young man,' I called out, and proceeded to put the gun on the floor. Femoid? Really? Did I hear that correctly?

Scarface unfortunately made it to his feet, eyeing Deavey with fury.

'Give me the gun,' he gasped, and slapped Deavey with the back of his unharmed hand, which meant he had to let go of his cut hand and the blood flowed. Deavey backed away, head down.

'I said give him the fucking gun!' the new hijacker echoed with more certainty in his tone.

'I'm sorry,' I called out, trying to make my voice clear, but timorous. And pointlessly Scottish. 'I'm nervous and a wee bit deaf. Sorry. I thought you said put it down. I'll get it.'

I moved about looking at the floor as if genuinely confused.

'Don't you fucking move,' said Scarface, huskily. 'I'll get it.' He cast his eyes around the crowded floor, scrutinising passengers. 'Where the fuck's it gone?'

He hadn't seen what I had. One of the passengers squatting on the floor, Ben (16, a sixth-former from South East London on his way home from visiting his grandma in Manchester Royal Infirmary) had used his foot to push the gun further away from the hijacker so that it was now under a seat and closer to Deavey. This carriage was giving it some. The baby was still crying but more softly. I called out, 'Hold on. I think I can see it. Aye. I'll pass it to him now. I'll do it slowly.'

To my right, Tony Rossi had gone quiet and while I fumbled about, I noticed he was staring at the hijacker towering over the petite young woman. At the moment I ducked as if to pick up the gun, Tony selected a can of kidney beans from his bag, stood up and sent it flying through the carriage towards the hijacker. It hit him on the head, he let go of the woman, and as another can caught him on the shoulder, he stumbled backward, still managing to hold on to his knife. From her seat, Mary King, a 72-year-old retired teacher, grabbed the young woman and pulled her down onto her lap.

Scarface started towards me, but Deavey stood and shot. There was an almighty roar, much louder than the previous gunshot, but largely, I realised, made by the screech of brakes as the train rounded a bend. The gunshot was just part of the overall racket. There were gasps and a scream as the hijacker staggered, put his hand to his chest and tried to move back into the vestibule. Kyo was pushing their way up the aisle, but several passengers got to the hijacker before them and pulled them back into the main body of the carriage, with others trying desperately to get out of the way.

For a moment, apart from a few grunts and the sound of heavy breathing, it was curiously quiet, the sound of the train speeding along the lines a constant background to the drama being acted out within the carriage.

Deavey managed to stop Scarface in his tracks with the help of Alex and the quick-thinking sixth-former. They were subduing him and trying to tie him to the rear luggage rack. Scarface was shouting, until Alex literally put a sock in it — a pair, to be exact — into the hijacker's mouth. Alex told me later that he'd taken them from his luggage with just that in mind. But I think he was winding me up.

'How did he get back up here?' I whispered to Deavey.

Deavey shook his head. 'Must have got past us when we were in the galley kitchen with the train manager.'

At the far end of the carriage, the young woman who had briefly been taken hostage was being comforted by Mary, the retired teacher, a small, slim woman with a dark grey bob and tortoiseshell glasses. Tony Rossi was standing with another can of kidney beans ready in his hand, while passengers around him were congratulating him.

'Great aim,' I said and smiled.

'Don't hurt girls,' Tony said, seriously.

'You're right,' I replied as I tried to make my way towards the two women. At least the baby was now quiet, and hopefully asleep. The hijacker was moaning loudly, and an older man told him to shut up. Someone else applied a bundled-up jacket to his wound. I suggested passengers could move back in the train to the safer carriages. A mistake. A mini stampede ensued, until Deavey raised his gun and told people they were to go row by row. Panic breeds panic, but Deavey's words, or perhaps the gun, largely did the trick. Deavey added that if they had anything that could be useful as a weapon, would they please hand it over. And if anyone wanted to stay and help that would be good. Alice was calming people down and helping them through the doorway, while Gill had arrived and was still on the phone – no doubt to gold command. I wondered if she'd tell them that she wasn't trying to stop us anymore.

'Is anyone a first aider, or have any medical experience?' I asked. Two passengers raised their hands. One was a young nurse, the woman it turned out who had already packed the hijacker's wound with a coat, the other a middle-aged male first aider. After conferring with Deavey, it was agreed that passengers should continue back along the train and that the two medics should take the wounded hijacker back too, with help from a couple of passengers. Another group had arrived to help, including Jason, the bald man from my carriage. Alice and Ben the sixth-former trussed up a battered Scarface, who finally seemed to have lost his will to fight. They all made their way back down the train.

While all this was going on, Kyo had slipped into the vestibule between coaches B and A and was carrying out a recce.

Deavey was either a brilliant shot or it was a lucky fluke. Although the hijacker looked to be bleeding quite heavily, it seemed that the bullet had made its way out of the other side of his right shoulder and then through the train wall. Lucky for him, and us. We didn't want to kill anyone if we didn't have to. Whatever anyone said afterwards.

I reached the two women. 'I'm Claire. Are you OK?' I said to the younger one, whose huge brown eyes were overflowing with tears.

Mary, the older lady, said, 'Her name's Isha.'

'They've got my baby, my baby girl,' she sobbed.

'Your baby? Why have they taken your baby, Isha?'

That must be the infant I had heard crying. How bad could they be?

'I don't know why.' She started crying again.

'Where is she?'

'That man was keeping me up front with her. Then he grabbed me and brought me in here. But he wouldn't let me bring Star,' she sobbed. 'Her name's Star. She's only nine months old. I've got to get her. There's no one to look after her.'

Isha moved as if to stand but Mary grabbed her hands firmly, and said softly but clearly, 'Wait, Isha, you need to stay safe.'

'There's no one with her?' I asked.

'No,' replied Isha struggling to free her hands, but the older woman held on.

'I know it's hard, love, but you have to stay safe for your baby,' Mary said softly.

'So there's no one else in the front carriage?' I asked, thinking about the layout. There were usually rows of seats, then a storage area and the door into the driver's cab.

'There was just the one who took my baby, who that man shot.' She pointed at Deavey. 'I don't know who's in the cab. Apart from the driver.'

Isha looked around as if she was worried about who might be listening.

'I need to get her.'

She sounded determined. I realised she was the woman from the concourse who had been helped by the Nerd. Helped by one, threatened by another. How weird was that?

'Let's see if we can.' I said, as positively as I could. 'But you need to stay here and keep safe. For your baby's sake. Your baby needs her mum.'

Kyo beckoned to me, holding the vestibule door open with one hand. Leaving Mary with Isha, I joined him, and India followed. Further back in the carriage I could see people were still jammed in the aisle trying to get to the liberated carriages, trapping Deavey at the back. Keeping low, Kyo slid through into the front carriage, where there were about ten rows of seats, two on each side, and an open storage area at the far end. Beyond that, right at the end, was the door to the driver's cab. I looked at it, wondering who was on the other side. And what they were planning to do.

The carriage looked empty, apart from Kyo, crawling along the aisle. Coming from one of the seats, about halfway up, was the sound of the baby crying. I heard a gasp. Isha had escaped from Mary and crept up beside me. I turned to her, signalling for her to go back. She shook her head, so I held her hand tightly to stop her running up the aisle. We both turned to watch Kyo edging towards the row where the baby seemed to be.

Suddenly the cab door opened. I pulled Isha down and we crouched as Kyo rolled in-between the nearest seats, and a shot rang out. The glass of the vestibule door shattered, showering Isha and me with fragments. Then the glass in the door into coach B splintered and crashed. I fell flat to the floor, hoping no one was hit. I could see a hand with a gun poking out from the cab door. India, on the floor beside me, fired her gun high, just as Kyo reappeared, crawling rapidly back towards us. Kyo jumped through the smashed door into the vestibule and pulled Isha with them to the back. Isha was unharmed, and for a moment struggled against Kyo's grasp to get to her baby, who was crying louder than ever, but Kyo held on tight. Next to me, India steadied the gun, pointing it at the cab door.

'Stop, it might hit the driver,' I said to India, thinking how easily bullets seemed to go through all the train walls. India nodded, then wiped her face. There was blood trickling into her eye from a wound at her hairline. A small piece of glass was embedded in her forehead. I picked it out. I looked at the door again. So close, but how were we going to be able to take control? And we had to help that baby.

'You better get patched up,' I told India. 'It doesn't look serious, but you need a plaster to stop it dripping into your eyes.' I looked at Kyo. 'Get back, both of you. Isha, your baby will need her mother, please go and keep safe. I'll keep watch.' India offered me the gun, but I shook my head. 'See if you can find someone to bring more bags up here for a barricade.'

When I think how I took charge, it seemed that it was just what had to be done. It wasn't that way for the whole journey, but at that moment, I felt calm and knew what had to be said. In retrospect, focusing on the immediate stopped me stressing about the future. And I could see that the people around me needed that too.

Isha hesitated in the vestibule, peering forward trying to see her baby, who was whimpering softly.

'Isha,' I said gently. 'You need to go back.'

'I'm getting my baby.' Isha was firm.

Deavey took her arm. 'We will get her for you. But you have to stay safe.'

She shook him off and tried to pass me. I held her gently.

'If you get killed, she won't have a mother.' As I said it, I thought about how, when my children were tiny, I had prayed to a god I didn't believe existed to let me live long enough to protect them into adulthood.

'I won't leave her.'

She was struggling harder now and I held her more closely. 'I know. I'm a mum too. Please, please trust me. She's going to need you. My kids are grown up now. Honestly, I'm older, more expendable, if anyone's going to be hurt fetching her, it should be me. And what kind of monster would hurt her? They probably just want money.'

Isha looked like she was going to argue, but then Deavey spoke, with quiet intensity.

'I'll have to stop you if you try to go forward. It will put you and your little girl at risk, love. I'm a dad. Please trust me. We've got to move to help your baby and you're making that harder. Please, Isha, let us get on with it.'

'My baby,' she sobbed.

I could feel her torment, the need to run and grab her child, but at the same time was aware we were wasting time.

'Isha,' said a soft voice. I hadn't noticed Mary, the woman who had helped her in the first place, come up behind us. 'Isha, love, you need to come with me, but I promise we'll stay close, so you can get to Star as soon as possible.'

'The driver—' Isha started to say, but Deavey interrupted. I could see he was becoming anxious to get her back to relative safety.

'I'm sorry, you have to go now,' he said firmly.

She looked at me. 'I'm trusting you to keep her safe.'

I nodded. What else could I do? With Mary's encouragement, Isha left. I whispered to Kyo to find people to keep Isha from coming forward again. We couldn't risk her running for her baby. Kyo nodded and followed them.

Deavey looked at me. 'She'll be OK.'

I wasn't sure about that, but knew we had to carry on. He crept up to the other side of the door and we both peeped through, quickly and carefully.

'Did that bullet hit anyone?' I asked.

'Just grazed a bloke's arm, I think. Bloody lucky in a crowded space.'

We waited. My throat was sore and throbbing and I was trying to ignore it. The baby started to cry, making me desperate to fetch her. I hoped Isha couldn't hear the sobs. Then the door at the far end into the driver's cab opened a few inches, and a flat voice came from within. 'If you shoot, we'll kill the baby.'

I looked at Deavey, who lowered his gun and whispered. 'Thank god her mum's not here. I don't think they can see the baby. The seats are in the way.'

'You're not going to shoot, are you? If they fire back, a bullet will go straight through the seat. They might not see her, but they can hear her.'

Deavey shook his head.

'We won't shoot,' I called out. 'Please don't hurt her. She's only nine months old.'

I don't know why I said that. As if they cared. But it seemed so appalling that someone could even speak of killing a child. The door shut. The baby carried on crying. It was nerve jangling, the insistence of it — would the hijackers just get sick of the noise? And then what? I felt sick.

In the vestibule behind us, Josh cleared a path through the broken glass as quietly as possible. He pushed some coats, bags and seat cushions to where Deavey and I were crouching. We made a low pile in the middle of the shot-out doorway, using the coats to avoid cutting ourselves, and keeping clear of the area where we could be seen. The crying continued, driving into our brains. Deavey and Josh looked at me — I could see we all felt the same. If the hijackers were finding it stressful…

The driver's cab door opened again and the same voice issued from within. 'We're sending out the assistant driver to get the kid. If we even see you, we'll shoot him and the brat. Get back into the carriage behind you.'

I scrabbled in my bag and took out a make-up mirror, then whispered to Deavey. 'We can't do anything. Hopefully the assistant can look after her. But maybe we can see how many there are.'

He nodded and quickly crawled to my side, took the mirror and wedged it into the pile of luggage so we would just be able to see something of the door at the far end. We crowded behind the wedged-open doors into the main carriage, protected from being seen by the bags keeping the doors open.

'We don't want anyone to get hurt. We'll move away,' I shouted.

We watched the small mirror, our heads close together as the door opened wider. The baby was really wailing now, deeply gasping for air. I remembered when I'd had babies. Was there a bottle in the baby bag? Her mum didn't have a bag, I suddenly remembered. Everyone carries a bag with a baby. I called out again. 'Please, if there's a baby bag, please take it. There might be a bottle in there. Or please give her some water. She's only a baby...'

The train jerked a little, and the mirror fell off the bags and into the carriage. I couldn't see the cab door.

'I thought you were fucking going,' the voice replied.

'Yes, right now,' I called back. Josh heard the demand and opened and closed the smashed automatic door behind us into B. If the hijackers could hear the swoosh of the door, they'd think we had left as instructed.

I noticed Deavey's hands were cut and scratched. We lay flat, using the piles of clothing to quietly push away the glass splinters, and edged even closer behind the bags, each finding a gap we could see through. Moments later, the cab door opened, and a man in the train company uniform, late twenties, medium height with sandy hair, walked slowly out, his expression fixed and unreadable. Frozen in terror, I imagined. Two seat rows in, he leant over. When he stood, he was adjusting a bag over his shoulder, then he ducked again and this time when he stood, the baby was in his arms, wrapped in a blanket. He hoisted her up and little arms came out, wriggling to get free. I was about to signal, but the door behind him was open a crack, no doubt a gun pointing his way. What could he do? And I might make matters worse. I looked at Deavey and glanced at the cab door. He shook his head. Too risky. He'd been keeping an eye on the door all the time. We stayed as low as possible behind the heap of luggage as the assistant driver took the crying infant into the front of the train, and the door shut.

The baby was gone, and I felt cold fear in my stomach. I thought of the tiny fists, the little body full of life. These people were prepared to use a baby as a human shield. We wouldn't be able to get in the cab. We wouldn't be able to stop the train.

THE MIRROR
DEAD 'HIJACKER' WANTED BY POLICE

by Sam Dean

Manchester Police reveal dead train hijacker Jay Afiri was wanted in relation to rape allegation.

Detective Superintendent Asif Patel of Manchester Police said yesterday that DNA taken from the body of a dead Manchester train hijacker after the incident in April matched him to a rape allegation and serious assault. 'We already had a good idea of who the attacker was and are now able to confirm it.'

Afiri was a violent career criminal recently released from prison with no evidence of any religious affiliations, according to the police. Photofit pictures of a man were posted around the Oldham area in February, following the serious attack which hospitalised the young woman (21). She managed to escape her attacker despite her injuries. Two road engineers working overnight on Oldham Way came to the woman's rescue and called an ambulance.

'We have kept the young woman fully informed and although, like us, she would have preferred to see him come to trial, she has some resolution to her dreadful ordeal. She is a brave young woman and is recovering, supported by her family.'

Afiri was tackled by Claire Fitzroy, 58, one of the passengers who resisted the alleged hijackers on the now infamous 10:12 NorthRail from Manchester. *The trial of the remaining hijackers is scheduled for next year.*

14

Leave It

COACHES B–A

12:47

> My darling Anthony. You have been a wonderful son and I am so proud of you and your family. Don't worry about me. There are kind people here. Whatever happens I have had a long and full life. With love and blessings from your mother. xxxx

I did what I could to reassure Isha. The assistant driver would look after her, he'd taken the bag. That was a good sign. Was there a bottle in there? She nodded between sobs. Deavey came in after me and reported that the baby had stopped crying. They were probably feeding her. But Isha wasn't in the mood to be comforted. 'Or they've killed her,' she said bleakly.

'Why would they bother to fetch her just to kill her?' I asked. 'They could have just left her where she was.'

Did I talk about the possibility of a baby being killed? Those words seemed to come from another universe, a place I could barely imagine. I was aiming for consolation, but Isha didn't seem convinced and put her head in her hands. Her long, shiny, black hair, escaping the clips that held it back, fell over her shoulders and covered her face. Mary stretched an arm round the young mother and held her close, then looked at me and shook her head, in what I took to be disbelief at the events unfolding around us. Me too, I thought, me bloody too.

Gill joined us, offered comforting words to Isha, then beckoned me to an empty pair of seats. She spoke quietly but firmly.

'That's *enough*. You've captured all of them apart from whoever is in the driver's cab, and that can't be more than two as there's no room. Leave it to the police now.'

I thought about it for a moment. 'Gill, I'm truly grateful to you for saving my life. You're right, there can't be more than two in there. But what are the police going to do? Shoot them with snipers? At this speed? Blow up the front of the train? There's a baby in there, for god's sake. Either way, the drivers and the baby will probably be killed, and the train will crash and leave the rails.'

I didn't know what we could do, but waiting for the police didn't seem to me to be an option. Things would only get worse. We had to try something. Only I didn't know what. Gill sighed and passed me her phone. 'Talk to them.'

I nodded to Gill and took it. 'Claire Fitzroy here. I believe you've had regular sit reps, what are you proposing to do?'

After a slight pause, a woman's voice answered. 'ACC June Heatherington. Hello, Claire. If you can marshal passengers to the back carriages, Euston is being prepared for the train's arrival.'

'What does that mean?'

'I can't go into operational details on an insecure line, but saving lives is our priority and procedures are being put in place to ensure the best outcomes.'

Something didn't sound right in this management-speak. 'Best outcomes for who? The passengers, the drivers and the baby in the cab? Or the workers, residents and buildings in and around Euston?'

'We're concerned with everyone's safety, Claire.'

'Are you going to shunt us off onto another line? You can at least tell me that.'

'It would be hard to do that at the speed the train is travelling.'

'Tell me if I'm wrong, June, but I imagine the priority is to protect lives in the capital, and you've just got your fingers crossed that with all the passengers at the back, there won't be too many fatalities on the train. I expect some passengers are already texting their loved ones about the possibility that they may be considered collateral damage.'

I had no idea if anyone was suggesting we were going to be sacrificed, but it was worth a try, if only to make them think of the bad PR.

'Claire, we have the experts, and they are working out the best solution. Do not attempt to storm the cab. Secure the prisoners and prepare the passengers. You have achieved a great deal, now leave the rest to us.'

I was getting the message. They hadn't found any smart solution. 'Crossed fingers aren't enough.'

I handed the phone back to Gill, who shook her head, exasperated. 'Have you considered that they might give themselves up when they reach Euston and see the reception they are going to get? But if you go in now, it might pre-empt whatever gold command are planning?'

'There's no scenario where I see them surrendering. Nothing about our encounters have suggested that.'

But the truth was, what could we do, with the baby and the drivers in the cab?

> *[June Heatherington testified that she ordered you, in no uncertain terms, to go to the back of the train. She said that would have been police protocol in order to protect members of the public. She said you hung up. – Loretta]*

> *[I can't remember the conversation exactly. It was a long time ago. Recollections may differ. – Claire]*

India was in the seat behind, checking her gun. Tuesday morning, a young, smartly dressed woman on an intercity train in England, checking a gun in full sight. She looked proficient, even with the large plaster on her forehead.

'Are you OK?'

She nodded. 'Just a scratch.'

'Your shot was pretty accurate.'

'Not accurate enough, though.'

I hadn't realised she had meant to hit the hijacker. Stupid of me. We were all quiet for a moment, and I decided to check on the train manager.

One of the train door windows in the vestibule between carriage B and the cafe carriage had been shot out – the bullet must have ricocheted off the door frame – and the wind was whistling through. It felt good to feel cold fresh air and I took a deep breath. I realised just how bad the train smelled – stuffy and airless and something unpleasant beneath it. There was blood on the broken glass, I assumed where people had knocked more of the glass out for safety.

For a moment, it was just me, the speeding train and the buffeting wind. Then I heard it: the helicopter was back. I looked out the window as it flew past over the adjacent fields, then disappeared. But the noise of the engine and rotor blades was still loud, so it had to be close, and I wondered if it was at the front of the train. Just the sound of it made me feel better. But I thought of what I'd said to Gill. It was no use to us at all. There was no point trying to winch people off, it would be slow, dangerous and help very few passengers. I couldn't see them trying to shoot the hijackers in the cab – not when there was the driver, assistant driver and baby all in there. For now, it was just an eye in the sky.

I turned away from the thoughts of rescue and made my way into C, the smell of blood immediately hitting my nostrils.

Scarface lay on the floor, his eyes shut, with Geoff kneeling beside him, bandaging his bleeding wrist, and Deavey close by. Rita and Melanie sat together at a table, looking exhausted, Rita with one arm round Melanie, who was slumped down into the midwife's shoulder.

'Is he badly hurt?' I asked Geoff.

'Don't think so. He just passed out as they were taking him through.'

'How's Nik?' I asked, dreading the answer.

Geoff shook his head. I felt sick. The train jerked and suddenly the hijacker's right arm pulled Geoff to his chest, as if to embrace him.

'Come any closer and I'll fuckin' kill him, I've got a knife,' Scarface snarled, his arm firmly round Geoff's neck, who was struggling to get away. Hearing that, Geoff went still. I couldn't see a knife, but the hijacker's undamaged hand was behind him.

'All of yer – get back.' He began to crawl backwards in a semi-sitting position, pulling Geoff with him.

'It's all right, mate, just stay calm. I was only trying to help,' the paramedic said softly.

I still couldn't see a knife. I could see Deavey backing up against the train wall, but not really moving away.

Scarface continued to pull Geoff back, but I could see he was finding it difficult and was in pain. I wondered if he'd just stab him and then run to the cab while we helped Geoff. Just because we couldn't see a knife didn't mean there wasn't one. It was quiet, apart from the constant noise of the train. I couldn't see how this would end well.

All at once Melanie screamed, 'No!' Scarface jerked his head towards her, distracted, and Deavey leapt on the hijacker, knocking him out with his gun.

> hijackers on train we're fighting back. love you.

> crap joke.

> wish it was. will you marry me if?

> ru pissed?

> jesus, just seen news yes yes yes, come back safe. Love love you.xxxx

15

TINA

COACH C

12:57

> Claire, I'm so sorry please text me you're OK. I love you.

Geoff recovered quickly. 'Not the first time I've been grabbed. Like a Saturday night after the clubs shut. But I wasn't sure if the wanker had a knife. Great scream, Melanie.'

She seemed shocked. 'I didn't do it intentionally.'

'Did the trick, though,' replied Deavey, who was busy tying Scarface up. 'No knife, which is what I thought, Geoff, by the way. I couldn't see one.'

I looked at the unconscious man. And suddenly felt so weary. 'Why don't you all head back down the train?'

'I'm not leaving Nik,' said Melanie flatly. The poor young woman looked rung out.

'You did everything you could. Nik's at peace now.' How trite the words sounded to me, even as I spoke them.

Geoff replied, 'We couldn't save him, but we're not leaving him.'

'Not till it's over,' said Melanie.

'Dr Patel's back down the train dealing with the shot hijacker and someone having an asthma attack. He'll let us know if we're needed,' Rita added. 'Did someone say something about a baby?'

I nodded. 'They took a baby from her mum, Rita. We tried to get her back but couldn't. She's with them in the driver's cab.'

'Oh my god. How old?' asked Rita.

'Nine months.'

'Why on earth would they do that?' Geoff sounded incredulous.

'To stop people storming the cab? It's all madness. They left her alone in a carriage then sent a young driver to fetch her. I was surprised the train has two drivers, Melanie. Is that usual?' I was forcing myself to think, to speak.

Melanie answered calmly, almost mechanically. 'Sometimes. Nik said there was an extra in the cab today. We both know the driver Joe, but we hadn't met the assistant before. What was his name? Nik told me… It's Lee. Yeah. Lee something. They're trainee drivers really, more than assistants.'

She stopped and shook her head as if to clear it. Then added, 'Poor bloke. Not what he was expecting.'

'Not what any of us were expecting. Hopefully he can look after the baby. We think he might have fed her because she's not crying anymore.'

'The mother,' said Rita, 'should I go to her?'

'Someone's looking after her, Rita, thanks. We had to stop her trying to get to her daughter. She's staying put for now, but she won't move back here. If we can find a way to get the baby, we may need you then.'

I fought to remain focused and to push away the part of me that just wanted to sit down and stare out of the window. A thought struck. 'Melanie, do you have a pass key for all the doors on the train?'

She reached into her pocket and handed me a chunky piece of metal. 'Yes. This is… was… Nik's.'

'Will it open the driver's cab?'

'Yes. It has to, in case a driver becomes ill, or something.'

Or something just about covered it, I thought.

'Are you going to try and rescue the baby?' she asked.

'Only if we can figure out a way to keep her and the drivers safe.'

I realised I needed to move, I couldn't stay there. I stood up and walked to the door, leaving the three good people who had done everything in their power to keep the manager alive. I stopped, suddenly full of emotion.

'You made Nik's last minutes as comfortable as possible, and he was surrounded by kindness,' I said, my voice choked. 'I believe that matters. And it will matter to his family. Nik Bhatia couldn't be saved, but he was comforted and cared for by good people. That was his last experience of life, not the horror that came before.'

I don't know if it helped them to hear that. But I believe it must make a difference, to be surrounded by kindness as you leave your life. It was something my brother never had, dying alone, off-base, surrounded by hate from men he thought were allies.

Standing in the vestibule heading back into B, I pressed my face up against the cool unbroken window in the other external door. I tried to be analytical, detached. How many were in the cab? How could we rush them without them killing the baby, killing the driver, crashing the train, killing everybody, setting off the bombs? Would I see my wonderful children again, Jim, another sunrise? Would any of us?

I couldn't think what to do. I just wanted to be somewhere else.

A hand gripped my shoulder. It was Paul. He handed me a miniature brandy. 'Drink.'

I screwed the cap off and knocked it back, feeling the harshness of the alcohol in my sore throat.

He spoke gently, his hand still firm on my shoulder. 'We need to start a proper search up front. You know that old World War Two acronym, TINA?'

'There is no alternative,' I replied.

'That's how I feel about our situation. We have to do something to limit loss of life. The mouthy one, he's kept going on about IEDs on the train, taunting the people holding him about it. I had a chat with him just now.'

His calm voice, and the shot of brandy brought me back. 'And?'

'I don't think he's lying. I'm guessing any IED is going to be in the first carriage, we've checked everywhere else. And it makes sense. Close to the point of impact. I reckon it's in the storage area. Easy to leave without anyone noticing.'

'And not likely to be disturbed.'

'Exactly. We could be an armed missile heading straight for London at a hundred miles per hour.'

'The police are clearing the station,' I pointed out. 'That doesn't help us, but we still have some time to search the train.'

'Not if something makes it go off early.'

'But why would they do that? Surely it would cause maximum damage if the bomb went off at the same time as the train runs full speed into the buffers at the station.'

'Yes, but we're not talking about a trained and disciplined team. They get jittery when things don't go to plan, the mechanism could be unstable. It's not like they're built with quality control...'

I looked at him. 'If the terrorists up front know we've got their mates, it's up to them to finish it, and I imagine they're the worst nutcases...'

'And the IEDs are there or close by. That means the baby and the drivers will die too. And when the train buckles, or explodes, it's going to affect the rest of the train, with the very least, carriages leaving the tracks. I'm no engineer, but I don't think it will be contained all at the front. The carriages are all firmly linked together.'

I nodded.

'TINA,' I said. 'Let's go.'

16

The Search

COACH A

13:00

> whats up? txt me aokcab

> txt now aokcab

<u>**Extract from Cross-Examination of Deborah Atkinson
by Defence Barrister Eleanor Masters**</u>

DB. Miss Atkinson, you were in seat 24A in this carriage that I'm indicating on the plan of the train – coach G. Is that right?
DA. Correct.
DB. When did you become aware that something was amiss?
DA. About twenty minutes after the train left Manchester. I was doing the Telegraph crossword when there was some kind of hullabaloo from the carriage in front.
DB. Looking at the diagram on the screen, you were in carriage G – and you were seated looking forward towards carriage E, is that right?
DA. Correct. I like to see where I'm going, not where I've been.
DB. And what was the nature of the hullabaloo?
DA. A man came into our carriage with a large knife, shouting, telling us to put our phones in the aisle.
DB. Can you see that man in court?

DA. Yes. The one on the left in the dock with the blue shirt.

DB. You're absolutely sure?

DA. I wouldn't have said so otherwise. Adam Jefferson. He wasn't wearing a mask and he's unusually big with a rather distinctive face and extensive facial hair.

DB. Did everyone comply with his demand?

DA. I can't speak for everybody, but I did, and there were plenty of phones being put into the aisle.

DB. What was the mood in the carriage?

DA. Surprisingly calm. There were passengers with those things in their ears, including the young man beside me and I had to nudge him.

DB. What else do you remember?

DA. A girl made a bit of a fuss till someone told her to shut up. Generally, everyone was quiet.

DB. And how about the defendant? Did he seem to be in an excitable state? Aggressive even?

DA. To begin with. But when the phones started appearing in the aisle, and everyone was quiet, he seemed to calm down. Then he went through the automatic door behind me into the vestibule, I believe. I didn't look round, but someone whispered he'd gone out.

DB. That would be into the vestibule between coach G and coach H. Is that right?

DA. Correct.

DB. What happened next?

DA. There was more shouting. We were looking down the aisle or standing over the seats trying to work out what was going on. Someone said they were calling the police.

DB. So passengers were getting up – did any move into either of the next carriages?

DA. No, people were nervous, I suppose we all thought there must be others. Eventually Claire Fitzroy came in.

DB. From which direction?

DA. From the carriage behind us. That would be H.

DB. Had you seen her before?

DA. Waiting for the train, she got annoyed with my dog when he didn't get out of her way.

DB. *When you saw her coming in from Coach H, what was she doing?*
DA. *She was walking partly crouched as if she was making her way through a jungle in a war film. Shushing everyone. She had blood on her face, and on her shirt and there were a few people behind her.*
DB. *You were relieved to see her?*
DA. *Hardly. Blood on her clothes, knife in hand. Friend or foe, I don't think anyone was sure.*
DB. *She had a knife in her hand?*
DA. *Correct.*
DB. *Did she say anything?*
DA. *She told me to shut my dog up or take him back up the train. And then before Monty had a chance to calm down, that's what she did. Snatched my dog and handed him to some unknown female who hurried him away. It was horrible. It was no surprise that he ran away later.*
DB. *How would you describe your interaction?*
DA. *She was aggressive. He was only barking because he was upset. She looked absolutely terrifying, to be honest.*
PB. *Objection.*
Judge *Sustained.*

To: Claire Fitzroy
cc: Laurence Walker
From: Loretta De Silva
Subject: Miss Atkinson's testimony

Hi Claire,

Grace has told me that you're not happy with the inclusion of Miss Atkinson's testimony. I think you should reconsider. The questioning goes to the heart of what we talked about. If you had been a man who killed someone in self-defence, and then taken the lead in dealing with hijackers and saving lives, you would have been regarded as a saviour. (As many people do.) But the line of questioning by Ms Masters constantly pushed an unspoken agenda – that you were some kind of anomaly, that a woman shouldn't behave in that way. Surely that goes to the heart of why you felt you needed to tell this story? Please ring me, so we can talk about it.

Laurence says he still hasn't heard from you. Is everything all right? You know Ashgrove will do everything we can to push this book over the line. We believe you have an important story to tell and one that needs telling.

All the best,
Loretta

Loretta De Silva
Editorial Director, Ashgrove Publishing

The rest of the squad were in B, discussing the options and not coming up with many ideas. Paul came in behind me. We sat round two tables of four near the back of the carriage and talked quietly across the aisle. Everyone was subdued. Whatever successes we'd had were eclipsed by Nik's death – and the thought of baby Star in the cab. Deavey's hands were bleeding, and he was wiping them on a scarf. India handed him some plasters. Blood from the cut on her face was seeping out a little from the dressing, and I put another plaster over it. Kyo seemed oblivious to their bruises, and Alice to hers: she was studying a can of hairspray.

'Almost as good as pepper spray,' she said. 'Particularly if you can get it in their eyes.'

'You'd have to be up close,' replied Deavey.

'We will be,' said Alice.

Talking practicalities helped. Paul winced when he turned to look out up the aisle.

'You OK?' I asked.

'Fine. I'm not as young as I was. Arthritis. Hardly combat fit,' he replied ruefully.

'Apparently, yoga's the answer. And sudoku. I'm not convinced,' I said.

'Me neither. I'll be OK.' He looked at me with a reassuring smile.

We could still hear a helicopter but glancing out the window, couldn't see it. We'd been through Coventry I thought, and now were probably in Northamptonshire somewhere. Or Bedfordshire. Somewhere in a shire anyway. For a densely populated island, we do have miles and miles of similar-looking, flattish countryside dotted with a few houses, and nearly always a church spire somewhere in the picture. I caught sight of one now. Hundreds of years old and still standing.

A sudden flash of memory took me back to the church of my childhood: its musty, mysterious smell and a curiously welcome sense of enforced boredom. It was seductive.

I turned away from the window and gave full attention to what was going on.

Kyo described the layout of the front coach, A. About a dozen rows of seats, then an open door into a storage area much bigger than the luggage racks in the other carriages, used for bikes and bulky items. At the front was the door into the driver's cab, probably locked, but we had a key. Inside the cab, there was a baby, Lee the assistant driver, one or more hijackers and the driver, Joe Gupta.

Deavey had been on the phone to Gill, who told him there was still no sign of the walking corpse. I hoped he'd just been a passenger who had been knocked out, came to, and was now sitting comfortably at the back of the train. But hadn't mentioned it to anyone. If he was a hijacker and had been playing possum, he was staying quiet. For now.

Meanwhile, Gill had added that a few passengers had panicked about the out-of-order carriage K, anxious there might be explosives hidden there. So Anita had checked it out and said it was fine, there was no luggage and nowhere anyone could hide anything. There was no power, so no lights or heat. I wondered how she'd got in. It had been locked when I'd tried to hide in there, after seeing Patrick Harbour being murdered. Then remembered I had Nik Bhatia's key, so Melanie must have given hers to Anita.

I turned to Deavey. 'Paul says if you were putting IEDs in a train you were planning to crash, they'd be best at the front, as an added precaution in case the hijackers were caught and couldn't trigger them. Any impact would set them off.'

'Maybe. If they actually exist and they're not just lying. I'm not convinced.'

'We still need to check that storage area.'

'Are we storming the cab? What about Mr Sniper?' asked Kyo.

'Not with the baby there, and the two drivers. But, OK, let's do a discreet search in the storage area. And somebody needs to have a gun trained on that door in case hijackers come through,' replied Deavey.

'Just one hijacker, two max, given the space,' said Paul.

I thought for a moment. 'If we quietly check the storage area, keeping low, we might find somewhere to hide and stay close, particularly if there's a lot of stuff in there.'

'I saw a couple of bikes, plus boxes, cases, that kind of thing,' offered Kyo.

Deavey nodded. 'I'll cover with the gun.'

'I'll search,' said India.

'Count me in too,' added Kyo.

I looked at India. 'They seem to hate women. And you're tall. Easy target.'

'What about you?' asked India.

'I'm old and irrelevant. Kyo's small and good at tucking into small places. You can fire a gun, so we really need you ready to shoot, and further back, so you can see what's happening, and provide cover along with Deavey.'

She nodded slowly, as Josh joined us. He looked at India, concerned. 'Are you OK?'

'Fine. A scratch. Really nothing.'

He nodded, relieved. 'Everyone is close to the back now, apart from the volunteers for fighting. Gill's been busy moving them along.'

'How many volunteers?' I asked.

'We've got about fifteen people who want to help coming up to C. I'm calling them the reserves. When we go through to A they'll come up into B.' He paused. 'Alphabetti spaghetti. We don't want it to get so crowded that we can't move.'

Josh rolled his shoulders. 'The reserves are all up for it, armed with what they could find. And towards the back of the train, there are people at the doors, ready to defend their carriages. It's amazing. They've been passing on the news about the baby. It's made people angry. More united.'

'Good. Now we need to focus on the search.'

There were seven of us ready to head in and now a group of motivated people gathering in C, our backup team. Just Kyo and me to go in initially, with a second wave ready to follow. There wasn't much of a plan to be honest. I hoped that when we were in the storage area, something would come to mind. I had a few ideas but wanted to look at what was ahead of us.

Deavey suddenly looked at his phone, it was vibrating, and he answered it. 'Gill.'

He listened, then said, 'We'll wait,' and rang off. 'Hold on. Gill's got some information. She's on her way.'

Moments later she arrived in the vestibule between B and A, phone in hand, where we were clustered.

'The helicopter is using thermal imaging. There are three people in the cab.'

'Would it pick up a nine-month-old baby?' I asked.

She held the phone to her face. 'Yes, there's definitely a baby in there. Is that one of the three?' She listened for a moment, then turned to us. 'Perhaps. They couldn't get too low and close because of the risk of being shot at.'

'But if there's three including the baby – where's the hijacker?' asked Alice puzzled.

'They could have killed the driver,' I said. 'There's an assistant, remember?'

'The baby might not show up if it's being held and they still might have killed the driver. I think we should assume two,' said Deavey.

Gill took my arm. 'Listen, Claire. All of you. No one on the outside thinks you should try to break in. They'll probably kill the driver immediately. They are desperate, and you'd have to think the ringleader will be up front.'

'Are they known terrorists?'

'Not on any watchlists, at least the ones they've identified from the photos passengers have sent.'

'Whatever their motives, they're prepared to kill,' said Deavey, and the others nodded.

Gill spoke. 'They all have matching dumb phones, so there was planning behind all this.'

Dumb phones. 'Where are their phones?' An idea had suddenly struck me.

'Alex has a couple, and I've got one from the scarred-face man,' she said, and pulled it out of her pocket. 'They've had no luck working out the passcode.'

Four digits. The train. I tried 1012. And was in.

> HERO2: up and running
>
> BOND: stick to plan
>
> IRONMAN: check bro at back
>
> when we get off?
>
> is there real bomb
>
> BOND: no more chat unless

Gill and Deavey took a look.

'Bond,' said Deavey dismissively. 'Christ.'

Alice took the phone. '"Is there real bomb"? So does that mean it's all a bluff? They don't sound very organised.'

'There might be a bomb, or there might not be. Cell system terrorism at a micro level, not everyone knows everything – or just smoke and mirrors?' I said. Gill's sharp blue eyes assessed me for a moment, before she looked back at the screen and forwarded the texts.

'Whatever. Not much help after all, but gold command should know what they said and I'll ask what it is the hijackers want.'

I checked my watch and took a breath. 'OK. But the last text was sent fifteen minutes ago, so no current info and we have less than fifty minutes before we hit London. We still need to look to see if there really is a bomb on this train.'

I was walking towards the front coach, as the others were sorting out weapons, when Gill came up beside me. 'What?'

'Seriously, stop.'

'Not this again. No one has offered a happy ending when we reach Euston. So, no, can't stop, whatever the fuck gold command says.'

'You're well-meaning amateurs who could get themselves and others killed. More bodies. We've already got three – that we know of. Gold command has their mobile numbers now, they'll try to negotiate.' Her hand was on my sleeve.

There wasn't time for this. I stepped back from her.

'And probably won't have any success. They're not here, are they? They're not the ones likely to get blown up. And please take your hand off me.'

She dropped her hand and checked the phone, then sighed.

'Fine.' She looked at me. 'You've all done brilliantly.'

'That sounds patronising.'

'It's not. You have. Most of the train is in passengers' hands and you've captured armed hijackers. But enough. We need to get everyone to the back of the train.'

'What about the drivers? The baby? We can't go now. Not unless we get them out. And Isha won't leave her baby, so that's at least four more innocent lives. And they could blow up the train at any moment, as far as we know.'

'But it could all be a bluff.'

'Maybe, but it could be the ace up their sleeve.'

She shook her head. 'Come with me, just for a moment.' She walked up to the bags scattered by the door into the front carriage. I glanced at the team, but my curiosity got the better of me.

'They'll do what you say, and you could save their lives and the lives of most of the people on this train. You could also lead them to their deaths.'

'There isn't a leader. Nothing's going to stop Deavey, Alice or Paul.'

'I think you could. I've been watching you all, remember? And counterterrorism, they've been doing name checks, inevitably, including yours.'

I paused. 'That was a mistake. I regretted it.'

'Really?'

'You can check. Over before it started.'

I guessed she'd run out of arguments. I was wrong.

'Let me try and speak with them first, maybe they'll listen to a policewoman on the train, not a man in a helicopter. I've done some negotiation training. It's worth a try, but I need you to stay back. If you come barrelling through, we'll all be fucked. Give me five minutes.'

'If you tell them you're police, they might just try to kill you anyway.'

'The one, or ones up front might not be that killy. Might be feeling alone and prepared to negotiate as they've not heard from their pals.'

'Killy? Seriously, is that official police jargon?'

She chuckled. She had a deep throaty laugh and a smile that met her eyes. I found myself looking at her properly. I'd been doing what I hated people doing to me, making assumptions. Perhaps it was the blue hair. She looked back, an intelligent and slightly amused expression on her face, then sighed and pushed her blue fringe back with her hand. There was a tiny tattoo of a bee low on her neck, only partly concealed by the blue and pink striped scarf.

'No, it's a me thing, just popped out from nowhere.'

'OK. No barrelling, but I'll stay hidden and close, in case they decide to get killy.'

17
Gill

COACH A

13:10

> checkthis out try sell tv, sun mail. Passengers beat up hijacker! £££

Gill explained to the others, ignoring Deavey and Alice's doubtful expressions. 'I pull rank here. And this has been agreed by gold command. Just let me try, if they won't play, then, whatever… But they might just be looking for a way out. They might not want to die. If it's a no go, I'll come back and join you.'

Paul spoke. 'Done firearms training? You should take a gun.'

She looked at him, then nodded.

India handed hers over, and Gill took a quick, confident look. Before anyone could say anything else, she turned and walked carefully towards the front, her blue hair like a beacon, and I followed.

Deavey got into position flat on the floor in the vestibule, doors wedged open into the front carriage, his gun trained on the cab. We walked quickly past the rows of seats then I grabbed Gill by the sleeve and pulled her down into the partitioned area where some cases were stacked, giving us cover.

I whispered. 'Thank you again for saving my life. I hope I don't have to do the same for you, but I promise I'll do my best.

The door opens to the left, by the look of it. You should stay on the left too, so they can't see you. Maybe use that luggage by the door as protection?'

'No shit, Sherlock,' she whispered back, and winked. 'But I'll need to be close so that they'll hear me over the noise of the train.'

I noticed her fingers on the floor were tapping out a beat and remembered the headphones she'd been wearing on the concourse, a lifetime ago. Suddenly I didn't want her to go.

'What where you listening to, at the station?'

'All sorts. But the last track was "Rose Rouge". It's suddenly become my earworm.'

'St Germain.' I thought of the propulsive drumming. 'Perfect. Something about getting together?'

She nodded and smiled at me. 'Who'd have thunk it. Music mates. But for now, you stay here.'

I could hear the music in my head too, and suddenly had an image of one rare night, laughing and dancing to the track with my brother, and remembered that Jim had been there too, lit up by strobe lights in a gay club. Then Gill turned and started crawling to the door of the driver's cab.

Extract from Cross-Examination of Paul Horan by Defence Barrister Eleanor Masters

DB. *How long did you serve in the Territorial Army, Mr Horan?*
PH. *About thirteen years.*
DB. *You rose to the rank of major, is that correct?*
PH. *Yes.*
DB. *And when did you retire from the TA?*
PH. *Active service, about five years ago, but I remained on an advisory group until recently.*
DB. *Would it be fair to say you have a good understanding of command structure?*
PH. *Yes.*
DB. *Would you agree that as the liaison with gold command, Gill Kaplan outranked anyone else on the train, in terms of deciding on responses to what was going on?*

PH. Her input was certainly important.

DB. She was advising passengers not to confront the hijackers, wasn't she? For their own safety?

PH. As a former police officer her position was understandable, and she was being instructed by gold command who would not have been able to support civilians endangering themselves. That doesn't mean that what the passengers did was wrong. Caught in the action, you have to respond in the moment.

DB. Putting whether the responses were appropriate to one side for a moment, I wonder why you, as a former major, were not in charge?

PH. We didn't organise a command structure. Again, I think my input was helpful and, in the short time we had, response and action were more important than hierarchy. Gill Kaplan did ultimately pull rank, but I think that the passengers that heard her agreed with her position at that point, rather than just accepting whatever she said.

DB. But that happened with Ms Fitzroy's commands, didn't it? People did what they were told.

PH. In the moments we had to plan, ideas were raised and actions were agreed collectively. Claire, Ms Fitzroy, had good and fast intuitive responses and came up with proposals that we agreed on. Other people also made proposals that were agreed and acted upon.

DB. Consensus is usually time consuming. It sounds a bit chaotic.

PH. I think an armed hijack on a train is going to be chaotic. But the decision-making in response to that was in many ways surprisingly straightforward.

DB. But with your training and experience, didn't you think you should have taken charge, before Ms Kaplan got involved?

PH. It was working well as it was. I used my training and experience, as did other passengers who engaged. Everyone brought different things to the table. Most of all we had simple goals – try to stop those men killing or hurting anyone else. Simple goals make for straightforward responses. Modern successful armed forces allow for initiative in front line circumstances. Ultimately, if it works, it works.

DB. But it didn't work for everybody, did it?

PH. The actions that passengers took, in my opinion, mitigated against even worse outcomes for people both on and off that train.

Gill made her way to the left of the door into the cab and put her back against the wall. She looked decisive and confident as she started speaking loudly, her head close to the door hinges. 'Hello. My name's Gill. I've been asked to see if there's anything that can be done, any way that we can help you, to ensure that no one else, including yourselves, gets hurt. Can we talk?'

She leant back, away from the door as she finished speaking.

'Who the fuck are you, and who asked you to do anything?' The flat voice came from inside the cab.

I could see Gill take a breath, before she spoke. Her voice was warm, calm. 'Honestly, I'm here to help. To bring this to an end. If you tell me what you want, I can encourage the authorities to open negotiations. I'm sure you didn't mean it to go like this. In case you don't know, people have already died. But you haven't personally hurt anyone yet. That would really help you. You could give us the baby, that would be a start. And there could be a safe way out of this for you. I really want to help bring this to an end without the loss of any more lives.'

There was silence. Maybe she's getting through to them, I thought. She sounded so reasonable and reassuring. Gill spoke again. 'The baby would be a—'

She was interrupted by the screech of the train as the track seemed to slightly change direction. Thrown off balance I held on to a shelf and Gill stumbled away from the door, back into the left-hand corner against the dividing wall.

The shot was completely unexpected. It must also have been randomly directed, because I don't think the shooter could have guessed where Gill would be.

The flat voice came again from the cab. 'Keep the fuck away, Gill, or else the baby gets it.'

Gill slumped, looking at me, a growing dark stain appearing in the middle of the right-hand side of her pale blue denim jacket.

18
Thirty Minutes to Euston
COACHES B—A
13:20

> where are u get 2 cab now

> give up mate its over we got your pals

We got Gill into coach B and put her down in a wheelchair space. It was bad. Paul propped her up, supporting her, while Alice worked furiously to stop the bleeding with a sweatshirt. I crouched down beside her, taking her hand. Deavey took her mobile. Gill was pale, and there was blood all down her front, but Alice seemed to be having some success at stopping the flow.

I think I told her to hold on, Geoff would be with us soon. Deavey was telling the police that Gill had been shot. Someone gave me a bottle of water, and I held it to her lips for her to sip.

She took a few drops then pulled me closer. 'I have a wonderful daughter and grandson. And finally, a great bloke in my life.' She gasped for breath. 'I don't want to leave them yet.'

'You're not going to, Gill. Help's coming.'

She groaned in pain. 'Bit killy after all,' she muttered, then fainted.

Then Geoff and Rita were there, arms full of clothing and a couple of beach towels.

Someone going on a holiday, I thought. Alice, Deavey and I got out of the way. Paul moved to let Josh take over supporting Gill, and the four of us retreated to where India was still standing facing the front carriage, her eyes on the cab door, tears streaming down her face, and then I spotted Kyo – up at the front of coach A, lying flat and pushing a large metal case against the partition wall to the cab. I beckoned, and Kyo crawled along the ground to join us.

The train seemed to be going more slowly, or was that my imagination? We were moving inexorably to the capital. The clock was still ticking. We'd been through Milton Keynes – so the next station was Watford, about thirty minutes from Euston. I felt sick but had to believe that Gill would be OK. Kyo had picked up the gun which Gill dropped and handed it to Paul. We seemed to be talking like robots and avoiding each other's eyes, although I could see tears in Kyo's, and Paul's hand shook as he took the gun.

Deavey said quietly that the police hadn't made a decision about diverting us. There were technical issues, apparently. Josh joined us, and Deavey handed him Gill's phone. We still had to search for IEDs.

Suddenly there were shouts from carriage C. Paul and I rushed back in, passing the group with Gill. Near the back, a tall middle-aged woman in a red jacket stood yelling and struggling in the arms of a bearded man about the same age.

'We've got to get off this train,' she cried. 'We're all going to die. I don't want to die.'

I marched up to her and grabbed her arm. 'Shut up. That brave woman being treated up there has just been shot trying to save your sorry arse. Get to the back of the train and you'll be fine. Show some fucking backbone.'

The man looked appalled. 'My wife's sensitive.'

She was staring at me, her mouth open, her breath coming short and fast.

'So am I,' I hissed back. 'Pull yourself together. It's not all about you.'

I heard a cough, and turned to see the vicar with the woman in the embroidered coat. Expecting a sermon, I was surprised to hear him apologise.

'Sorry. She was upsetting people. We tried to isolate her, but she ran off. There are quite a few nervous people back there, and it's a bit squashed,' the vicar explained, breathlessly. Then turned to the woman. 'Come on, my dear. You're safer with us.'

He persuaded the couple to go with him and as they left, he turned. 'I'm so sorry about your friend.'

My friend? I thought of those few moments of conversation. I admired her, she was funny and brave. Yes, I'd be proud to have her as a friend. Not sure she'd feel the same way about me.

Alex arrived with Dr Patel behind him, looking flustered.

'We need your help,' I said.

'The shot hijacker, I wondered if we could move him somewhere more comfortable—' he started to say, until I interrupted.

'Forgive me if I don't give a shit. Gill, the policewoman, she's been shot.'

Deepak glanced over my shoulder and pushed past towards the little group at the front of the carriage. Alex and I followed, and when we saw Gill, I heard him sigh. Her eyes were open, and I was just thankful she was clearly alive.

I made myself focus. 'Alex, Anita has a pass key. Get her to open the end carriage, carriage K. Light and heat don't matter now. Move the passengers as far back as possible. Do what you want with the hijackers but make sure they're well tied up.'

'Is she going to be OK?' He looked at me.

'I hope so.' My voice broke. Focus. 'End carriage, Alex.' He nodded, touched my shoulder and quickly left.

They had moved Gill, who was now seated upright on a pair of seats, and I briefly joined them, remembering to hand over the vodka miniatures I'd taken earlier, in case they needed to clean the wound. I took her hand, which she squeezed, then headed to the front.

Silently, we took our places. We still had an IED to find. Or not.

Kyo and I crept back into coach A, climbing around Deavey, who, gun poised, was now at the front end of the vestibule. He was lying flat on his stomach, gun balanced on a hard case we were using to wedge the doors open, aimed up at the cab door. As soon as we were through, Deavey scooted out of the way, keeping his gun trained on the door. Remaining in the vestibule were Paul, armed with India's gun, to one side, and Alice, with a knife, on the other. India and Josh were behind in coach B, with the reserves.

The door to the driver's cab was firmly shut. I looked at the cab partition wall on the left where the bullet had come through and hit Gill. Her blue and pink scarf was caught about two-thirds down and from what I could see, appeared to cover any bullet hole. They wouldn't be able to see us. I silently thanked her.

Keeping low, avoiding stripes of blood on the floor, we entered the large storage area. Kyo and I each took a side. Mine included two mountain bikes. I checked, there didn't seem anything added to them which would turn them into IEDs. Besides the bikes, there was an assortment of bags, cardboard boxes and a large old case that was locked. Paul had earlier given us a quick rundown on what to do, and we had knives and knitting needles to use in the search. I carefully opened a box full of hairdryers and poked around gently. Was someone opening a salon? I took one back carefully to Paul in the vestibule, who looked it over and said it was fine, but decided he needed to be with us to look at the case. He had a screwdriver attachment on his penknife and began to undo the screws to the hasp.

Kyo picked up a golf bag, and, after Paul took a quick look, carefully wheeled it back to coach B.

We worked intently and quietly, occasionally the noise of a helicopter could be heard, and again, we heard a man's voice through a megaphone asking what they wanted. Kyo found two boxes of old books, which we checked, then quickly and quietly piled up against the partition wall as a weak form of protection.

Luggage was busted open. Clothes were scattered everywhere. Wrapped presents were unwrapped. Thankfully the noise of the train cloaked our activity. Then we noiselessly stacked as much of the unpacked luggage back into the storage area so that anyone opening the cab door wouldn't immediately see what we'd been doing.

It looked like the IED was a bluff. I shrugged at Kyo, who nodded, then pointed to a carton they'd just uncovered: a large box of Pampers. It was held together with strips of silver duct tape. I looked at it and wondered why you'd tape it. Perhaps it had been opened? But it looked new and full. It niggled. Kyo was just about to start on it with a knife when I shook my head and whispered to them to take it carefully to Paul, who had gone back into B. At the door, Deavey looked at the nappy box, then back at me, indicating that he might need to help, and they disappeared. I wedged myself partly under some shelves that we'd emptied, backing onto the driver's cab – across from where I'd advised Gill to stand. That comes back to haunt me most days. *No shit, Sherlock.*

With the luggage gone, I could wriggle into a small space where I was hopefully out of sight if anyone checked from the cab. Pressing my ear to the partition, I listened, hoping to hear something. Perhaps there was some murmuring, but I wasn't sure. India was probably keeping an eye on the door, but we'd discussed the possibility of a bullet hitting the wrong target. I didn't know what might happen if someone came out.

Suddenly, through the thin wall, I heard baby Star crying. The sound made my heart jump. I tried to block the picture in my mind of someone throwing her out of the window. Then the door slowly opened a few inches, the baby's crying growing louder. I gripped my knife and thanked something somewhere for the fact that Kyo, Paul and Deavey were out of sight.

'We know you're out there. Don't try anything or the baby gets it.' The message was chilling, and the flat male voice sounded almost mechanical. I held my breath. *We* know? How many of them were there? Was it a bluff? I had a feeling they didn't know they'd shot Gill.

'Fetch its mum. Knock when you get here. Just her and one of you. A woman. Unarmed. Or the baby gets it. And the driver.' It was as if he kept on thinking of new things to add. And repeating some old things. The door began to close then opened again. 'You got five minutes.'

Then it shut.

I heard my name being whispered and turned. Alice peeped over the barricade and beckoned me and I moved back to join her. 'How's Gill?'

'They've stopped the bleeding. So that's got to be good.'

Paul was investigating the Pampers box.

'They want the baby's mum. Given us five minutes,' I said.

Deavey nodded. 'You'll have to hold him off. Buy some time.'

'And then what? He says he'll kill the baby.'

Paul suddenly stepped back from the box. 'This has got to go now! While we're in countryside. Now!'

Everyone turned to him. He picked up a golf club and started smashing out the glass in the adjacent window. 'Tell the next carriage! Get down, get down!'

Alice and India ran past him. Outside I briefly registered rain-sodden fields, bare hedgerows. Normality. The damp clean air was whistling into the carriage. I expect we were all fighting a compulsion to run. But at the same time I couldn't move. I couldn't even think.

'Now, now, get back, get down, get back!' Paul fumbled with the box, grimacing in pain. Then Kyo and Deavey were beside him.

Crouching, I watched as they hefted the box and threw it through the window in one graceful movement. For a moment nothing changed. I was just wondering if Paul had been wrong, when a loud explosion came from behind us. The train seemed to jerk and wobble, then shifted on its axis and tilted, with a great metallic groan of pain. It felt like we had left the rails, were untethered to the earth. The lights flickered and went out, as the few people left in the carriage lost their balance and staggered across to the opposite side, clutching armrests or seat backs – anything to hold on to. We seemed suspended in space...

Then the carriage lurched back with a screech and bump. I pulled myself up and started running to coach C, everyone with me. Deavey caught me: 'Go back to the driver's cab and stall the fucker – we've got this.'

Still stunned by what had just happened, I walked up to the vestibule, trying to think what to say, when I heard shouting from the cab door.

'What the fuck was that? Are they trying to stop the train? Tell them…'

He seemed to run out of words.

'Your bomb went off. There are casualties.' I hoped there weren't. 'The mum's trying to get through. Please don't hurt anyone else. We're doing what you said. But it's chaos back here because of the bomb. Your bomb.'

The door was opened a couple more inches. 'Say that again.' The flat expressionless voice.

I repeated what I'd just said.

'Stop lying. There are no fucking bombs.' He didn't sound convinced. I lost it.

'The IED. In the Pampers box? It's gone off. Didn't you hear it? The police are hardly likely to bomb a carriage full of passengers.'

The door closed. At least there hadn't been another ultimatum. I turned back. And then I heard the screaming.

19

Shattered

COACH C

13:32

> sorry for all that went wrong Jools. all my love to the girls,

> take care of them and yourself. Deavey

> what you done now? don't let them down again.

> trying not to. hope to see them soon. love them 4ever.

I made my way back. B was empty and undamaged by the blast so I continued into C, dreading what I was going to find. The noise grew louder as I drew close. Not screaming exactly. I hear it now, when I wake in the early hours, jerking upright, heart pounding. A high-pitched moaning, groans, voices trying to reassure, the whistling wind.

On the side where the bomb had been thrown, several windows had blown in, spraying splinters of glass shrapnel into the carriage at high speed and into soft human flesh. I saw one man holding a bloodied shirt to the side of his face, with Isha holding his other hand and Alice with a towel helping someone sitting on the floor. I know now that it could have been a lot worse. Luckily there weren't many people in there. Even luckier, because it was still relatively cold, we were all wearing thicker clothing, which helped to protect people from the worst of the flying glass. Plus, most of them heard Paul's warning, and because they had ducked down, there were few facial injuries. But these were the brave souls who had come to help the fight.

I stood for a moment in the doorway taking it all in. There was no sign of Gill. I found out later that Melanie and Anita had already organised her removal into D. Paul was checking people and handing out bottles of water from the cafe. Out of six people with various injuries, only two looked serious. Geoff, Dr Patel and Rita, with a trickle of blood down one side of her face, were busy attending to them. At the end of the carriage, I caught sight of Anita, like me, taking in what was happening. Our eyes met, and she shook her head, then turned back into D.

I felt anger rising again and turned to see Deavey, who was putting a bandage on a young woman's hand, look up at me with a face that expressed what I was feeling. Was there another bomb in the cab? We would soon reach built-up areas on the outskirts of the capital, increasing the number of people at risk. The man or men in the cab showed no intention of slowing down. I was sure they planned to crash the train. We had to assume the worst – and try and do something about it, and fast. I thought about the impossibility of shooting our way into the cab without loss of life – and suddenly I had an idea.

20

The Cab

13:40

> OMG you weren't lying. praying for you will explain to lucy

There were enough unhurt passengers in carriage C to help the injured. The squad moved back into the vestibule between C and B, me grabbing my leather tote on the way. Paul's left hand was bleeding heavily through a makeshift bandage. He'd attempted to help a passenger and further hurt himself in the process. Someone had given him a wool scarf to wrap round as another layer, but the blood was already coming through the cloth.

I talked over the wind rattling the door and coming through the broken glass. 'You can't fight like that, Paul, it'll make it worse. Just stay back with the other gun.'

He shook his head. 'I can't fire the gun either. I'm left-handed. You should take it.'

He handed it to me, telling me what to do and I pocketed it in the leather jacket, while handing him the air pistol. 'Could work as a bluff?'

Once I'd explained the plan, everything happened quickly. The team gathered newspapers, and wrapping from the boxes we had unpacked, some flying about in the gusts of wind, and tore them into strips as we discussed our next move. Not perfect, but it might work. Someone found a plastic shopping bag, and we filled it with the scraps of paper. As soon as there was a decent sized bundle, Paul added bits of plastic wrapping, and I poured in the rest of the spirits miniatures I'd stashed away earlier. Kyo started shaking in the contents of a packet of Doritos.

Irritated, I said, 'It's not a bin.'

'They're highly flammable, I read it in an *Orphan X* book.'

I wasn't convinced but thought there was enough flammable material in the bag for a few crispy snacks not to matter. We moved it into the front coach.

I looked out of the window, to see where we were, and realised the others were too.

Paul spoke softly. 'Just north of Watford, then a lot of urban sprawl to Euston. It has to be now.'

Deavey handed me a lighter and I turned to Paul. 'Ready to call up the reserves?'

'On it. Good luck.'

Leaving the others, I carefully carried the shopping bag to the cab door, watching intently for any movement. The train seemed to be moving at full speed again. Deavey, Kyo and Alice positioned themselves further back in the storage area, armed respectively with a gun, a golf club and a knife, while behind them were half a dozen people carrying bottles, penknives and golf clubs ready for backup. Paul was at the back, ready to call up more reserves if needed. A few of us had scarves over the lower part of our faces. Together, we looked like a motley collection of pantomime bandits. Or were we just clowns?

All the time I was listening for any noise from the cab. The baby was quiet. Hopefully she was asleep, oblivious to everything around her, having sweet milky dreams. The alternative was too terrible to consider.

I scattered the sharp-smelling soggy mix against the cab door, opened my tote and took out the nail polish remover, unclipped the top and tipped the acetone over the pile, silently thanking the manicurist. Quickly, but nervously, I struck the lighter, one of those cheap plastic ones, trying to light a screw of paper. The lighter sparked but there was no flame. I bent down, tried again, holding the lighter closer to the dripping paper: again, just a spark. Only this time the high flammability of the acetone came into its own, catching me by surprise. There was a gentle swoosh and a bright flame fifty centimetres high appeared, catching the screw of paper in my left hand. It disappeared in the flame, burning my hand in the process. I stepped back from the door, heart thumping, trying to ignore the searing pain. Everything began to burn fiercely, and within moments a toxic black smoke was billowing.

I looked at Deavey, a cowboy, a triangle of scarf over the lower part of his face. We nodded.

I started yelling. 'Fire! The train's on fire! Stop the train! Another bomb. Stop the train. Get off!' Kyo added to the commotion at the top of their voice, and others joined in.

The smoke was increasing, choking, despite the small quantity of material on the floor. Alice threw me a newspaper, and instead of throwing it on the fire, I flapped it up and down to push the smoke into the cab. Deavey threw on some more empty plastic bottles. I thought of the baby's lungs and heard crying. She was alive, for now. Should I carry on doing this?

Suddenly, the train began to shudder, the baby's cries turned to a choking scream, there was shouting, loud coughing, then a screech of brakes. That was enough of a signal. Deavey and I exchanged a glance. I caught my breath, heart thumping, hoping I could keep my hand steady. My eyes were stinging, streaming, making it hard to keep them open. Deavey slid the key into the lock, turned it, opened the door. Struggling to see, I was aware of smoke and someone to one side, but with no time to think, I charged in, the gun in my good hand – and there was a loud bang as I was thrown back, and another bang, my hand jerking up as the force of the bullet that hit me threw me into the door frame and everything went black.

21

Off the Train

it's over! we're safe. home soon. love u

By the time the police came to question me early that evening in the hospital, they already knew a great deal about what had happened on the train.

Jim was with me. I'd come round from the anaesthetic to find him sitting whey-faced by my bed, lost in thought. I watched him unobserved for a moment. He was wearing a Paul Smith jacket I'd bought him, over a blue fine-knit jumper. His thick, grey-streaked black hair was unusually messy, and perhaps I saw tears on his handsome face. Funny how I can remember the clothes but am not sure about the tears. He didn't look like a man poised to leave me. He raised his head and caught my eye.

'Jesus, Claire.' He took my good hand gently in his.

I held tight. 'It's good to see you.' I meant it. For the time being. He leant over and kissed me, as a doctor and nurse arrived to tell me that my arm should be fine. The bullet had gone clean through, causing some muscle and ligament damage, but the surgery had been a success. I'd also had a blood transfusion as I'd lost a substantial amount. There was probable radial nerve damage, which might heal itself, but all in all it was great, apparently, that I could move my lower arm. There were questions

I desperately wanted to ask, but I wasn't sure if I could bear the answers, so asked about the burns damage to my hand instead.

'No deep tissue damage, no surgery required,' said the doctor, who looked about twenty-five and as if she hadn't slept for a few days. It suddenly dawned on me that I was in a private room, not a usual occurrence with the NHS. 'How come I'm on my own?'

'Police request,' replied the doctor. 'But I imagine you'd welcome the peace and quiet after what you've been through.'

What had happened after I'd blacked out?

While my brain was trying to piece things together, the nurse smoothed my bed. He spoke quietly. 'That's an amazing thing you've all done.'

The doctor shook her head. 'Let's not bother Claire with that at the moment.' Then she looked at me. 'Unfortunately, the police want a chat. Are you up to it? I'm happy to say no, but they're pretty anxious to get your version of what happened.'

My version? Were there other versions? My arm was beginning to throb. I started to cry, thinking of baby Star and the silence after the scream.

Jim sat up. 'My wife needs to rest.'

I couldn't feel joy in surviving. Instead, I felt fearful and distraught. As if I'd been shot and watched people dying. Oh yeah. I remembered that. But I had to pull myself together.

'I need to know what happened, but I think the painkillers are wearing off…'

The nurse bustled around a machine beside the bed. 'You've got a pump. Sorry, Claire, someone should have explained.' He showed me how to press the button, which I hadn't noticed, nor had I registered the line going into me. The relief was almost immediate. I came to love that button over the next few days.

'Are you sure you want to speak to them?' asked Jim.

The doctor looked at me. 'I'll tell them they can see you for ten minutes, and do a full interview tomorrow, how about that?'

I nodded.

I don't know if it was the top-up I'd just given myself of grade A drugs, but I can't remember everything that was said. Jim stayed with me and told me later that he wondered if I was hallucinating as what I described seemed so unbelievable. There were four of them, I initially assumed all police. One was DS Steve Chambers, who I'd talked to on Gill's phone. He noted my description of events calmly, as if he was already familiar with the bare bones. Steve turned out to be in his late thirties, studious looking, with floppy dark hair and wire-framed glasses. A uniformed constable, a young woman, took notes, and another man, Black, big and bulky in jeans, accompanied by a woman in a dark suit, came in and stood against the wall. 'Security,' he said to Jim, after being asked, as if they worked at the hospital. Later we realised they were from a different kind of security organisation; MI5 or Counterterrorism.

Steve and the woman in the suit did the talking. I answered a few of their questions, initially too frightened to ask my own. But as they realised what I didn't know, Steve filled me in on a few details.

When I'd entered the cab, I was shot in the left arm. The arm with the burnt hand. Then, as I fell back, I'd banged my head on the door frame.

The bullet went through my arm, fortunately missing the people behind. Driver Joe Gupta was sprawled across the controls with baby Star wedged in beside him. Lee Ellwood, the assistant driver, was dead.

'Oh my god, is the baby…?'

Steve replied quickly. 'The baby's going to be fine. Her mum's with her. Some smoke inhalation issues, but all should be good. There was no IED in there, by the way. And the driver, he's in ICU, and doing well. He had a heart attack.'

'But the assistant driver's dead…' I started to cry.

'Yes,' the woman in the suit replied. 'Bullet through the heart.'

'And what about the hijacker who shot us? Where's he?'

The policeman replied before the woman could speak. 'We are waiting on ballistics, but from what we can gather, it looks like the trainee driver shot you.'

'Did he miss – no – why did he have a gun? And who killed him?'

I hoped it wasn't one of the squad. In the confusion, I supposed it might be possible.

'Looks like you did, Ms Fitzroy,' said the woman.

22

Processing

Another death. Nothing made any sense. How could I have killed the poor man? I coughed and could still taste the acrid smoke. I felt sick and was breathing fast. Jim passed me a glass of tepid water.

'From what witnesses have said, you were shot and as you fell back your gun went off,' said Steve gently.

'So it was an accident,' said Jim firmly.

'As I said, we're checking everything. Can you remember, did you know it was loaded and had you taken the safety off?'

'Do we need to get a solicitor?' asked Jim furiously. 'My wife's been shot and beaten by these arseholes and you're asking if the safety was off?'

'We are just sorting out the timeline of the events,' said Steve, mildly. 'I'm sorry, we know Claire needs to rest. But people have died and we need to know how.'

I found my voice and spoke softly. 'But *who* shot me? Who else was in the cab?'

Or had it been one of the squad. Another accident.

'No one else,' answered Steve. 'The driver, the baby and the assistant driver.'

'So the assistant driver who died was helping the hijackers. Or was a hijacker?' asked Jim.

'We are looking into that. When the driver is well enough to help, I expect we will get our answers,' said Steve gently.

Before I could process all this, the woman spoke.

'Let me get this straight, Claire. It looks like you killed two men, a mixture of self-defence and accident.'

Jim looked at me, his mouth open.

I think I gabbled, 'I didn't mean to kill anybody. I didn't want anyone to die. The man with the gun in the toilet fell onto my knife when he was coming at me.'

The woman listened with a blank expression.

'But I don't understand about the assistant driver – how he was a hijacker. Was he in disguise?'

'No. He was the assistant driver,' said Steve. 'We're looking into him.'

'Right, that's enough,' said Jim.

Touching his arm, I shook my head. 'No, I need to know about Gill. How's she doing? Geoff stopped the bleeding.'

Steve Chambers replied. 'She's being looked after.'

I started to tell them how amazing she was. It seemed important to voice what I now felt about someone I had spent too long arguing with. But the woman in the suit intervened. 'Right now, Claire, we urgently need to know about the hijackers. I'm sure Gill's a hero, but we need you to focus on these men so we can be sure we've got the right guys for the right reasons.' She glanced at Steve. 'We are fairly sure that Ellwood, the assistant driver, was one of the hijackers.'

Now it made sense. I hoped he was. I took another drink of water and tried to focus. They wanted to know who I thought was the ringleader. I said I wasn't sure. The trainee driver, maybe, but I'd only seen him fetch Star. Scarface was dangerous enough but didn't quite seem the leader type. Definitely not the Nerd, or Black Jacket. I've no idea if they knew who or what I was talking about.

They asked if I'd heard any of them taking orders over the phone, and I shook my head. Then they wanted to know who had helped me, so I gave them as many names as I could remember. By this time, I was seriously flagging, and I could feel myself drifting away.

'What about their motive?' Did I ask that, or did they? I mentioned anti-Chinese opinions, incel attitudes, anti-vaxxers, religion maybe – it seemed such a pick and mix. I don't remember them leaving.

Jim stayed all night in a chair beside me. As usual in a hospital, I was woken early by a nurse and, with Jim's help, made it to the bathroom, trailing tubes and a contraption on wheels. I ached all over. But it felt good to brush my teeth and wash my face. What wasn't good was the face looking back at me from the mirror. Pale and drawn, I appeared to have aged a decade since I got on the train. Was that really only yesterday?

23
Details Emerge

The train finally stopped just north of Watford. It was as the smoke came into the cab that driver Joe Gupta had a heart attack and lost consciousness. When that happened, his foot eased off the 'dead man's pedal', the safety device fitted to most trains for just such an eventuality: more typically a health crisis, than a hijack. Pressure must be maintained on it at all times, or the train comes to a stop. Lee Ellwood, the trainee driver, had known about the pedal of course, and by threats to the passengers, and later to baby Star, made sure that Joe didn't release it earlier. That was what the jolt right at the beginning of the hijack had been: Joe's attempt to stop the train. Not leaves on the line, then.

I heard these details later and saw some of the news footage. The 10:12's final stop wasn't at a station, but a mile or so off from Watford and still about twenty miles from central London. The railway line at this point backs onto the gardens of rows of post-war housing and small industrial sites.

One police helicopter landed on the tracks, another stayed in the air. There was a news helicopter circling, and a medical chopper which landed in a car park adjacent to the tracks. Geoff the paramedic had reached the cab quickly, leaving Dr Patel with Gill, and did sterling work on the driver, Joe, while Rita and Deavey dealt with my arm, using a jumper as a tourniquet. Star was swiftly reunited with her mum, who had rushed to the cab, and Joe Gupta was quickly airlifted to hospital. Moving the bodies was handled with discretion. Meanwhile, Paul and a few others tried to keep people on the train, but for most passengers, understandably, that was now the last place they wanted to be. The squad all stayed on the train.

About twenty armed police arrived quickly. Initially passengers were in shock, standing on the side of the line, concerned about getting electrocuted until the police assured them the power had been cut. Somehow, through various access gates, ambulances and more police arrived. The hijack was big news. Some passengers on the train had been watching reports online, which must have been an odd experience. But that's our world. Many had phoned family and friends to tell them they loved them, and now were breaking the good news. Footage from the helicopter was dramatic, particularly the signs passengers had put up in the windows.

Community-minded residents plus the usual rubberneckers and nosy parkers living along the line came down through their gardens and, over hedges and fences, offered water or hot drinks – or just took pictures on their phones. Shiny thermal silver blankets appeared from ambulances. The police tried corralling people to process who was who, but they couldn't get enough officers on site quickly enough – gold command had sent people to a proposed rerouting of the train near Euston into sidings in a less built-up area. Apparently, a small army of police, fire service personnel and medics had been assembled. Whether or not that would have worked, nobody seemed sure, as the train would still have run into buffers at high speed, not a great choice for passengers – although the location would have limited any potential bomb damage in the central London area, which had been the aim of the plan.

Meanwhile, on the tracks beside the 10:12, an improbably social atmosphere developed. There was laughter as well as tears. Alice was handed a large glass of whisky from one old gent through a gap in his privet hedge. When the police emerged with the captured hijackers – followed by Alex and the team who had kept them secure – there were whoops and clapping.

I remember bits and pieces of this as I was fading in and out of consciousness. I'd lost quite a bit of blood, despite Deavey and Rita's best efforts, and the pain in my arm and hand was intermittently overwhelming. Relief was administered quickly after I was lifted off the train, some kind of morphine injection. I remember realising I was sitting at the back of an ambulance with a friendly paramedic who asked me to wiggle my fingers and raise my lower arm, as if this was the kind of thing that happened every day. I complied, and he said that was good news. I didn't tell him that my arm didn't even feel like it was attached to me. I did give him my phone and asked him to text Jim and say I was OK.

I remember people walking by wrapped in silver blankets and thinking they looked like giant turkeys ready to go in the oven. Then there was what seemed like a quiet moment. The morphine was comforting, and I drifted a little, thinking about Charlie, what he would have said to me now. My sweet twin. I must have seemed upset, because the paramedic reassured me that I was safe. I nodded and smiled, too weak to explain about my murdered brother.

That's when I saw Anita. Hood up, she was helping an injured man in a black coat with a bloodied scarf tied round his face, one of the unfortunate passengers hit by broken glass after the explosion, I assumed. I only spotted her because she turned to the ambulance and our eyes met. She was a few metres away. I called her name. She paused, then raised her hand in valediction and walked on. I thought she might have stopped for a chat. But it was just another small item to add to the 'nothing was normal' list.

24

Hospital

Gill was dead. Jim told me after my second night in the hospital. I sobbed inconsolably. I barely knew Gill – but somehow, I felt I did. I thought of our conversation about a French house dance track, and her bright blue eyes, full of life, and what she'd said to me after she'd been shot. I remembered how I'd disagreed with her professional advice, too often, I now thought. And hoped she'd understood it wasn't personal. I remembered her bravery and humour, and my suggestion about where she should stand by the cab door and wept some more.

When I think about how I was later described in the media, written by people who have never met me: 'steely', 'cool', 'emotionless', come to mind. They don't fit with the woman sobbing her heart out in a hospital bed mourning the loss of someone she'd known for less than an hour. Later I would hear that a man who'd been hurt by a piece of flying glass had died of his injuries (his family prefer that his name is not mentioned). Six unnecessary deaths, two of them hijackers. And at least two more passengers with life-altering injuries. It was overwhelming.

Jim didn't know what to do. He tried to talk to me, to hold me, but none of it helped. The nice nurse arrived, followed by a doctor, and then I was asleep again. When I woke in the late afternoon, woozy and upset, Jim was still there, and so was my daughter, who had flown in that morning. The previous day I had spoken briefly to both my children, hoping to reassure them. Now I could see I was frightening her so pulled myself together as much as possible. It would be no use to anyone if I was all over the place. I expect the drugs helped too.

In the end I was in hospital just under a week. It kept me away from some of the madness of the media and online dissection of events on the 10:12. Jim was there every day, and my daughter visited several times until I was able to reassure her that I was OK, and she could return to university. Both Jim and I wanted her safely away from the risk of any potential media intrusion. My son rang most days when his hospital shift ended. There was a 12-hour time difference so it became my morning call and we'd discuss injuries and recovery. He restrained himself to just one comment about the sanity of my behaviour on the train.

A few days after I'd been admitted, I woke from a nap to find Em and Derek sitting either side of my bed. I started telling them about Gill. I must have sounded upset because Em took my good hand, and spoke softly, echoing the words I had said to her what seemed like a lifetime ago.

'You know it's not your fault, right? You didn't ask for this, remember?'

They stayed for a while, and I was grateful they'd come all the way to see me. Derek was unusually quiet. As they were leaving, I noticed Em glance at him. 'It was Derek's knife, wasn't it?'

I nodded.

'Just as well you had it.' She looked at me intently, and I knew the answer I had to give for Derek's sake, and perhaps my own.

'Yes, it was. Without it, I'm not sure I'd be here.'

He let out a long breath. 'OK.' There was relief in his voice. I knew he'd felt bad about giving it to me, as it had let the cat out of the bag regarding Jim planning to leave. Now I wondered if he'd thought I'd been threatened because of the knife. I couldn't face going into the details – Jim could fill him in.

'So. Thanks.'

I tried to sound chirpy, and it seemed to work as Derek let out a bark of laughter, and I could hear Em chuckle, and even Jim smiled, the insanity of stress, death, serious illness and family ties flowering into that surreal moment.

Some old friends visited, and Deavey, Paul and Alice came by to swap war stories and update me on the investigations – what little they knew. Paul's hand was stitched and healing, as was his shoulder. Kyo sent their love. Alice, now sporting an impressive black eye, yellowing nicely, said that she'd heard interesting things had been found on the hijackers' social media, but wasn't sure what. No one had heard from Anita.

I had many cards from friends, passengers and members of the public. I couldn't cope with reading them all, and asked Jim to filter them and take them home. There was one physical death threat, printed out in Comic Sans: DIE OLD BITCH, and placed inside a condolences card with a swan on it. I felt it was more an instruction than a threat and appreciated the brevity. Jim said he didn't appreciate my levity and handed it to a police officer who said they'd investigate and advised me not to go on social media. I stayed offline.

Apparently, there was an outpouring of support, but a trickle of the usual misogynistic hate, some more disgusting and disturbing than others, as well as mad theories, all revealing the dark underbelly of the social media universe.

The train driver, Joe Gupta, came out of intensive care after a couple of days. He was in the same hospital as me, and we exchanged get-well cards. The police dropped by on several occasions to ask me more questions and to avoid answering any. I agreed to a limit on visiting time for anyone other than family, and was able to have time to rest, sleep, do some physio and think. At one point Jim said that he loved me and we'd sort things out when I'd recovered. I agreed, but I knew I wasn't the same woman who had got on the 10:12.

When I wasn't running through what had happened on the train, I'd found my mind wandering back to my twin.

You never forget those phone calls. It was Jim who called me at work. I was sitting with a student who was struggling with her dissertation. I could tell from his voice something was wrong, and quickly wound up the meeting. I remember it with such clarity. Sunny outside, breezy with scudding clouds. The open-plan office had floor-to-ceiling glass on one side, with views across parkland. I watched two gulls circling on thermals as we talked. It took me a while to take in that Charlie was dead, shot close to his barracks in Helmand, Afghanistan, by supposed allies, some of the Afghani soldiers he had been training.

Losing my twin left me untethered and full of regrets. I tried focusing on my family, my career, but just felt like I was going through the motions. Life went on, we managed. Somehow, the grief becomes part of you and one day you find yourself laughing with your kids, and you're not pretending.

In a strange way, it helped me get through the breast cancer that emerged a couple of years later. There were times early on when I couldn't be sure if I was going to have to confront my own death sooner than imagined. Cold fear would grip, my heart would thump heavily, and I'd feel breathless, broken, useless. But I quickly learned: if I couldn't rule my body, I would rule my fear. Why allow desperation when you don't know the outcome? And after surgery and treatment the prognosis was good. The fear would have been a waste of time.

I realised that on the train I had used the same technique. If I couldn't control the hijackers, I could control the fear. And then we ended up controlling the hijackers too.

Jim had been by my side, when my family died, when I was ill, always reliable, always there, to cook, comfort, listen and amuse. My anger at his leaving me was because he was such a huge loss. Derek had assumed Jim had told me our marriage was over. I knew things weren't right between us but had been deliberately avoiding having that conversation. On the train, I realised, I'd worked that anger to push me on, just as I'd worked to control my fear.

25

Who Was Who

The police discovered the names of all the hijackers while I was recovering in hospital. Some had already been identified while we were on the train, linking criminal records to the photos passengers sent them. Steve had promised to come and see me before their names were formally announced, and I was hoping I could persuade him to share what they knew about the hijackers. I needed to put names to those men.

Paul had just left. He'd dropped by and made us laugh at his initial disbelief that such a thing as a hand clinic existed, which he'd been attending downstairs in the same hospital. There was a tap at the door and Steve appeared followed by a woman of about forty, in a tailored navy jacket and trousers, and a white shirt with a slim gold chain around her neck. She had short dark hair, swept down to one side, minimal make-up and a formidable manner. I'll call her Nancy. She was from the security services, I was told, and I realised she was the woman who had first questioned me. Nancy agreed to my request to let Jim stay. That told me she outranked Steve.

It had been five days. My strength was returning, although unless I pressed the magic button the pain in my arm and hand kept me awake at night.

Steve pulled out an iPad from his bag and found what he wanted. Nancy was watching me, a smile that didn't quite reach her eyes had appeared and quickly disappeared. Now I just registered impatience. But, I thought, she must have a lot on her plate. It's not every day a train is hijacked. And I knew there was criticism in the media of the security services alleged ignorance of any of the hijackers. So I understood why her right black leather boot tapped minutely on the floor.

'The man who died in the toilet was Jay Afiri, twenty-seven years old, from Liverpool. We have plenty of witnesses who saw him murder Patrick Harbour, the Scottish man in the seat beside you,' Steve said. 'Afiri had a drug problem and was recently released from prison. It's not clear where he got the CZ gun he was carrying.'

His age hit me like a ton of bricks. Not that far off my own son.

'His poor parents. He didn't look that young.' I could barely get the words out.

'Afiri was brought up in care, later in and out of prison,' said Steve.

Suddenly I thought of Afiri reaching over me, the smell of his clean shirt. Now I thought of him choosing it, carefully ironing it, on the day he was going to die. I was overcome with a sense of remorse, the terrible waste of a young man's life, and Jim, alarmed, put his arm round me.

'You don't have to do this now.'

'Sorry. It's OK. I just wish he hadn't died. He was so young.' I couldn't say any more.

'Patrick Harbour's sons wish Mr Afiri hadn't killed their father, a completely innocent man,' said Nancy. 'Did he say anything to you about his motivation for the hijack?'

'No,' I spoke more firmly. Sod her irritation. 'I've thought about it. He seemed to dislike women, or maybe it was just me. He was panicky and on edge. I assumed it was drugs because, as I told you in my statement, it looked like he had taken cocaine, or whatever people take nowadays. Monkey dust? What was he in prison for?'

'Various things, over the last few years,' she replied. 'The police have been looking for him with a warrant regarding a case of rape and violent assault. Not a nice man. I wouldn't waste any tears.'

My tears are my own to waste, I thought. If you work in prisons, you meet people who never had much of a chance to make something of their lives. But rape – it's funny how one word can change your attitude completely. Guilt had been getting in the way of clarity. I remembered what I'd seen Afiri do to Patrick Harbour, and there'd been no sign of remorse. I said nothing, but my tears dried up. I wanted to know about these men, needed to understand why they had done what they'd done and ended up changing – and ruining – so many people's lives. But understanding doesn't always lead to forgiveness.

Next, Steve showed me a picture on the iPad of a man still bristling with aggression at the police station.

'Black Jacket,' I said.

'Adam Jefferson, thirty-six years old, from Stockport. History of violence as a gang enforcer.'

'He came to the toilet door with Anita as a hostage.'

'What did he say?' asked Nancy.

'He was mouthy. We didn't know what was coming, we were already beaten, that kind of bollocks. Cocky, even after he was tied up. He said chaos was being unleashed – which didn't sound like something he would normally say, more like something he'd heard, or been told. He also hinted at IEDs. He probably spoke more to Alex and the others holding him.'

'Nothing clearer about motive?' asked Nancy.

'Not with any of them really. Some racist anti-Chinese stuff, incel crap, misogyny, Deep State nonsense, little bits of that kind of thing. I did ask what they wanted, but never got an answer.'

Steve showed me another picture. It was Big Guy.

'He had a horrible machete. I assume it was him who murdered Nik. We took him down in, I think, coach J. I never heard him say anything, but he was playing up to the passengers filming him, making it look like he was being hurt by the people who were actually trying to stop him killing anyone.' I shook my head, remembering. 'I'm guessing some of the footage makes it seem like they were treating him roughly. They weren't. Just trying to contain him. Who is he?'

'Mo Abadi, thirty-seven years old, from Birmingham. Big Mo is his street name. Dealer, enforcer, and latterly, apparently, a religious convert,' said Nancy.

'Was he a person of interest to you already?'

Nancy looked at me sharply. No fake smile now. 'No. No alarm bells. And you are right about the footage, but the general reaction is overwhelmingly supportive of the passengers.'

Next up was the young one, still looking nervous behind his glasses.

'The Nerd. Looks like a sixth-former. He was controlling coach E by claiming his phone could set off an IED. Honestly, he looked like he didn't really want to be there. He was out of his depth.'

'Shane Rees, he's twenty-two, a chemistry student,' said Steve.

'He said something about Deep State, and claimed the phones were being blocked. Were they?' I asked Nancy.

She shrugged. 'Don't think so.' Not exactly a no then, but I wasn't sure if it was even possible.

'He also picked on a Chinese-looking boy in a racist kind of way. But that was all I heard that might have anything to do with motive. He was frightened, though. Armed with a knife, and very on edge. But as far as I know, he didn't hurt anyone. It was just threats.'

Then it was Scarface's turn. His hatred seemed to surge off the screen.

'He was frightening. Properly scary.' Just seeing his picture made me recoil. 'I got the impression he'd be happy to kill anyone. He came into coach E. We had a bit of a tussle.'

I looked at his angry face, and a shiver ran through me. 'Amazing that boy Ty managed to get him down with my water bottle. But he got away from us, somehow. Deavey and Kyo got him again later. But he still managed to attack Geoff, even when he was wounded. Who is he?'

Steve answered. 'Sim Targut, twenty-eight years old. People trafficker, enforcer. Probably done more evil things than we'll ever find out. Any indication of motive from him?'

I shook my head. 'I hope he's in agony.'

'He's recovering from a fractured skull among other injuries,' said Steve.

'No doubt sustained when he tried to escape,' added Nancy.

'He was going to kill me. Gill saved me. I couldn't care less if he was hurt.'

I remembered the moment and shut my eyes.

'None of them mentioned their aims or reasons?' asked Steve gently.

I shook my head and thought for a moment. 'The thing is, we couldn't negotiate. They weren't interested when anyone tried. And people did ask what they wanted. Gill tried with the trainee driver, but didn't get an answer. Maybe he spoke to Joe Gupta? Ellwood threatened the baby when we didn't know it was him doing the talking. He said he'd kill her. I don't know...' I trailed off. Would he really have done that? Had he been that monstrous?

'What do you know about him?'

Nancy checked her iPad.

'Lee Ellwood. Twenty-nine, failed his psychological fitness exam for his TDL – train driver's licence – the first time and had just resat. You can only take the exams twice. He seemed convinced that he'd already failed. He blamed the rail company and specifically the new MD, May Leung, for the fact that he wouldn't be given another chance, although it is standard procedure across all railway companies. He took it very personally, apparently.'

'To go from that to hijacking a train, kidnapping a baby, shooting people – that's a stretch.'

'Yes,' agreed Steve. 'But there's also conspiracy stuff. Shared online activity. Have you heard of NoSinoChan? An anti-Chinese site. There are others. They wind each other up. All these guys spent a lot of time online. They really didn't seem to have lives.'

Nancy looked as if he shouldn't have spoken, but I found it interesting.

'No wonder he failed the psych test,' I said.

Nancy nodded. 'That's the world of conspiracy theorists – it makes strange alliances. I expect when we've finished with his computer we'll find out that Ellwood was going down all sorts of alternative-truth routes.'

'We thought Ellwood was a victim.'

I remembered he took the baby's bag. 'Perhaps he wouldn't have hurt the baby, though. An empty threat.'

Nancy was dismissive. 'One, he shot Gill Kaplan and could easily have killed you. Two, when you watched him pick up the baby and the bag, he was in character, remember? The assistant under threat from the non-existent hijacker in the driver's cab. He picked up the bag to shore up the idea that he was a good guy, a victim.'

'Yes. Of course. It's so chilling he would do that. Particularly with the baby.'

But it made sense. 'The driver's told us he had to persuade Ellwood to take over the driving and let him feed her, after he threatened to throw her out the window because her crying was annoying,' Steve added. 'The driver believed he was quite capable of doing that. He couldn't be more grateful, by the way.'

Again, how quickly guilt can disappear. Ellwood didn't deserve it.

Nancy spoke. 'There is a clear anti-Chinese element in Ellwood's posts, but his focus, unlike the others, is linked to the new MD of the rail company, May Leung. Her parents are from Hong Kong, but she was brought up in Liverpool, with the accent to prove it.'

'She sent you silk flowers,' said Jim, 'and a nice handwritten card.'

I'd forgotten that. They'd arrived the day after, when I was still in a daze.

Steve leant forward with another picture on his iPad.

'He was the one Deavey shot. I saw him first when he came in holding Isha. Beardy the 'roid man. All muscly at the top and skinny chicken legs. He's the one who referred to women as femoids. The tin can lad managed to hit him until he let her go. He deserves something, that lad.'

'Beardy's name is Joe Rodrigues,' said Steve.

I thought about the young mother separated from her baby. 'How is Isha? Can you give her a message from me? Jim, could you get me a card, and perhaps, Steve, you could give it to her. She had a horrible experience. Her baby…'

'She's doing OK, Claire,' said Steve. 'The baby's fine and Mum's very grateful to you too, like her dad.'

'Did you know?' asked Nancy.

'What?'

Steve answered. 'The driver, Joe Gupta, is Isha's father.'

I took this in. 'Then Star is his granddaughter?'

Steve nodded.

The penny dropped. 'The trainee driver, he'd know who she was. Her dad might have said his daughter and Star were on the train.'

'Joe says he didn't, but he's still an ill man, and probably doesn't remember.'

'I wonder why she didn't tell us that it was her dad who was driving the train?'

'Perhaps she felt she couldn't trust anyone. She couldn't be sure if there were more of them, hiding among the passengers,' Jim suggested.

Steve looked at his iPad. 'Joe Rodrigues, Beardy, is twenty-nine, from Kent. He does a bit of labouring, bit of drug dealing, posts a lot of online abuse and threats to, well, all kinds of people, LGBTQ+, vaccinators, women, all sorts. For which he was already being investigated. He also featured on the same website as Ellwood.'

I leant across to pick up my laptop from the table beside the bed. 'I must check out that website, group, or whatever it is. They sound charming. NoSinoChan?'

Steve shook his head. 'You won't find it. Disappeared. We've seen little bits due to reposts, but it's been taken down and tracking back hasn't revealed much. Whoever's behind it knows what they're doing and probably doesn't want to be linked with the hijackers.'

'It might just be coincidence anyway. They all used lots of the same sites,' said Nancy.

'Is the train company owned by a Chinese company or the Chinese government?'

'No, a British and European consortium,' answered Nancy.

'So why pick on them?'

'The fact it's not owned by a Chinese organisation doesn't stop the conspiracy theorists saying it is, and using Leung as proof. Although her family left Hong Kong before it reverted to Chinese rule.'

Jim sighed. 'These people never let facts get in their way.' His phone vibrated and he checked it, then angled it to me so I could see who was calling.

'Sorry, love. It's Adi from work, I have to take it.'

'No problem. I've got the security services looking after me. And have a break, go for a walk. You could do with it.'

'Are you sure? Anything I can bring you back?'

'A proper coffee. But no rush.' I smiled and he left the room. He'd shown me the screen because he wanted me to know who it wasn't. Was that thoughtful or annoying? I couldn't decide. But I bet eagle-eyed Nancy had noted it.

I was feeling tired, and my arm was hurting, but I had another question. 'Have you found Anita, has she come forward?'

'No,' replied Steve. 'As access was difficult for the emergency services, a significant number of passengers just walked along the tracks to Watford station and disappeared. You saw her going past in that direction, didn't you?'

'With the injured man.'

'We checked that as well. People with flying glass injuries were treated, but none that matched his description. It may have just been a scratch, and the bloke went home. Some people don't want to be involved, Claire. They're frightened, or they're illegals, or they were supposed to be somewhere else. Lots of reasons.'

'Anita was so calm, even when Black Jacket, Jefferson, had her by the throat. What about CCTV footage from Watford station, is she on that? Surely she'd make a good witness?'

'There are plenty of witnesses. If she wants to be in touch, fine, but if not, there's not much we can do. Looking for her is a waste of resources,' said Nancy.

I thought about her wave to me. It did somehow look final. Nancy was fiddling with her phone, her voice dismissive.

'Then there's the mystery of the man who wasn't dead. She thought he was.'

'Easy mistake to make if you're in a hurry, and someone's unconscious,' said Nancy, not looking up.

'He did look... the way he was slumped across the table. I mean, I suppose we were told he was, and didn't have the time to investigate.'

Nancy shrugged, as if to say *duh*.

'You didn't check his pulse?' asked Steve.

'No, because I thought Anita had.'

'You weren't the only people fighting back. The man might have been injured in a fight with a hijacker, came to and gone back down the train,' said Nancy, finally looking up. 'Or played dead because he didn't know who you were.'

It was odd. But the whole journey had been odd. Not just odd. Terrible.

'Anyway, he wasn't a hijacker. So, again, not a line of enquiry that's worth pursuing.' She started checking her phone again, as if bored, and then frowned. 'OK, I've got to pop out to deal with something. Sorry. I expect Steve can help if you have any other questions. But I suggest you rest as much as possible.' She smiled. It looked like she was out of practice. And then she was gone.

'Busy woman,' I said.

Steve smiled; his was real. 'She's right about you getting some rest.'

It was unsatisfying. It felt like I was being told to calm down and forget about an astonishing and dreadful ordeal. How does anyone do that? I knew I wasn't being entirely fair, and perhaps what I was experiencing was part of the natural comedown you might expect after the adrenaline-fuelled journey on the 10:12. But it felt like I was being told I was no longer part of the story.

His phone pinged, and he checked it. 'Ah. Unless you want to have a look at the Watford station CCTV, in case you see your missing man? I've just been sent it.'

Back in the game.

'Yes. I'd like to see if I can spot him.'

Opening his tablet, he scrolled through some pictures, before handing it to me. On the screen were grainy images, clips of footage. I flicked through, and then stopped.

'I think that's Anita.' The clip was of a woman, hood up on her sweatshirt, and carrying a backpack. She walked past the camera, head down. 'Her hood was up when she waved to me. I remember that.'

He took a look. 'A lot of people in hoodies with backpacks. Scroll on. See if there's anything else that catches your eye.'

I recognised a couple of passengers, not by name, and then I saw the mac. I went back and looked at it again. The man had short dark hair, quite tall, and a black or dark mac. He was looking down. I showed the screen to Steve. 'The man who wasn't dead, we covered him with a similar mac, maybe it was his. It was Burberry, or a fake, I saw the lining.'

'Didn't he have a hat on?'

'Yes, a beanie, rust coloured. But he might have taken it off.'

I felt like he was indulging me. And looking at the images I could see how it would look to anyone else. You couldn't see either of their faces. In fact most people were walking with their heads down, either on their phones or probably thinking of what had just happened. I wasn't confident about the identifications. Steve must have noticed my expression.

'Maybe it was him. But he's not a person of interest, as Nancy said.'

I hadn't noticed Nancy slip back into the room. 'What are you looking at?'

'The footage came through to me from Watford. Just thought Claire might like to check.'

'And I thought we were going to let the poor woman rest.' Was there a touch of irritation?

'I think the man in the mac was there, maybe, and Anita. Possibly,' I told her.

'He wasn't a hijacker, he doesn't seem to have done anything apart from fall deeply asleep. None of the hijackers have mentioned a missing person. As for Anita, if it is her, she looks fine. Maybe she'll get in touch at some point in the future. There are more important things to worry about, Claire. When you're feeling better, we may need to go over the timings again, and what Gill told you to do. Steve, we need to go.' The mention of Gill was a good way to shut me up and a reminder that I hadn't done as I'd been told. Again I thought perhaps she was just exhausted – I imagined how the security services must have been working without a break since the first calls came in.

Steve was putting his tablet in his backpack and Nancy was looking at me, perhaps wondering why I'd finally gone quiet, when there was a soft knock and Jim came in.

'We're just going to give you and your wife some peace,' said Nancy, ready to go.

Jim glanced at me. He seemed to have something on his mind. Then put his hand on Steve's shoulder. 'I've been thinking, is Claire, or are any of the other passengers who grappled with those monsters, in any danger from the hijackers' supporters? I've found it hard to get a straightforward answer about that from anyone.'

'We don't think they necessarily have any supporters, Jim, but we are keeping a careful eye on things and will let you know if there are any suspicions. We've got someone here at the hospital too,' replied Steve. I could see he was taking the question seriously.

'It hasn't helped that they've picked on Claire for most of the media coverage,' Jim added, and I suddenly realised how rattled he was.

'Yeah, that's unfortunate. That's not us, by the way, it's other passengers. And, mainly, it's because everyone just thinks she's a heroine.' Steve smiled at me. 'And no one's named your children, as you requested.'

Jim had told me there were reporters outside the hospital and that his phone hadn't stopped ringing. I'd left mine turned off and had only switched it on a couple of times to pick up messages from the kids, or the squad.

'It'll die down,' said Steve, 'become yesterday's news. Until the court case, anyway.'

It suddenly seemed overwhelming. Nancy had been lingering by the door looking impatient, but now she suddenly appeared to remember she was dealing with someone who had been shot and was potentially traumatised.

'Are you feeling well enough to go home?'

'Almost. Looking forward to it,' I replied.

She put a card down with a number handwritten on it. 'Ring me if you remember anything else, won't you?'

I nodded. She paused at the door. 'You did a great job, now let the professionals get on with it.'

'What do you mean?'

'Obviously you're curious and have lots of questions, and I know it might be frustrating, but I think when we reach the trial, you'll get your answers, Claire.'

She was wrong about that.

Steve followed Nancy, looking slightly irritated by her, and Jim fussed, making sure I had everything I needed. I could tell he wanted to say something, but I wasn't going to help him out. When I was settled in bed, he sat down beside me.

'I'm so very sorry, Claire, that you had to hear that from Derek.'

I looked at him. He didn't want to talk about it, and neither did I. But we did. What we said is between just us two, but when he left I think we understood each other better than we had in years, and we held each other close for a few minutes. After he'd gone, I closed my eyes. Everything was going round and round in my brain with a thumping headache as accompaniment. I wanted to go back to where I was before I went to Manchester. I wanted to be sitting in the shade on a small sunny island listening to the waves. I wanted it all to disappear.

I pressed the magic button and floated away.

[Claire, I understand your wish for privacy but given that you had that devastating news just before you got on the train, it must have influenced how you were feeling, and how you reacted. I presume you talked about that with Jim. An explanation of your motives in fighting back could really be helpful, don't you think? – Loretta]

[Loretta, I didn't defend myself and other passengers because I'd heard my husband was leaving me. I was upset, angry, hurt – all those things. But I believe I would have acted as I did either way. Perhaps my jangled nerves made me more attentive to what was going on, and more prepared to react in a decisive manner. But what we said is between us. I won't include anything more, but I wanted to make it clear – to the readers and my children – that I harbour no resentment towards him, despite what he did. – Claire]

Extract from Cross-Examination of Stuart Deaver by Defence Barrister Eleanor Masters

DB. Mr Deaver, were you previously in the military?
SD. Yes.
DB. And did you see active service?
SD. Yes. With the Fusiliers.
DB. During your service did you ever fire a gun at the enemy?
SD. I did.
DB. You won marksman competitions while in the army and have exceptional shooting skills, is that correct?
SD. I'd describe them as good, not exceptional. And it was quite a few years ago. I don't use or own a gun now. I'd be nowhere near as good as I was.
DB. But you still managed to shoot Joe Rodrigues while he was behind Isha Gupta and at the far end of the coach to you.
SD. I winged him. He wasn't just standing behind her, he was threatening her with a knife. I didn't think I had a choice.
DB. If we could get back to the beginning. You described earlier how you first came across Ms Fitzroy, in the toilet of the second to last carriage, J, as indicated here on the screen. What prompted you to go there, apart from the obvious of course?
[Laughter in court.]
DB. Where were you seated, to start off with?
SD. I was sitting near the front of the carriage.
DB. You had a first-class ticket.
SD. No.
DB. Why were you in that seat, then?

SD. I'd almost missed the train and ran on to the first carriage I came to. Which happened to be first class.
DB. You could have moved through the train to the second-class section. Or were you intending to purchase an upgrade?
SD. Does it matter? I was taking a breather, and fully expected to move at some point to my reserved seat in coach D.
DB. Just clarifying for the court, Mr Deaver. Were you aware of a disagreement between Ms Fitzroy and the passenger sitting next to her?
SD. No.
DB. You didn't hear any argument at all?
SD. I was reading messages on my phone, not worrying about what was going on at the back of the carriage.
DB. So what eventually drew you away from your phone?
SD. When Afiri stood up and started shouting, telling everyone to throw their phones in the aisle. I looked up and saw him waving a gun about.
DB. Had you noticed him before?
SD. Maybe vaguely registered him, he looked like a druggie to me, but I wasn't really interested. His business.
DB. After he shouted, what happened?
SD. People started doing as he said. They were scared.
DB. What happened next?
SD. I couldn't see that clearly from where I was sitting, but it looked like the passenger I know now to be Patrick Harbour stood up to Afiri after he threatened the pastor lady.
DB. So, he attacked Afiri?
SD. I didn't say that. I think he remonstrated with him. He was concerned about the lady and having someone wave a gun in your face and tell you what to do is pretty provocative.
DB. Could you see a gun in Mr Harbour's face?
SD. It looked like it was being pointed at him. It was obvious that everyone in the carriage was at risk.
DB. That was your estimate of the situation. Others saw it differently.
SD. There was a clearly unstable man shouting and waving a gun. I think most people would agree that's a pretty strong definition of a risky situation.

DB. *That's presuming the gun was loaded and that the man holding would fire it, wouldn't you say?*

SD. *Humans have to make presumptions. If a caveman saw a lion coming towards him roaring, he'd presume the lion was going to attack. Afiri gave every impression of possessing the ability to act violently, and he was armed. If someone's carrying a gun you have to assume they will use it. Mr Harbour was a brave man who acted to save lives.*

DB. *Wouldn't you say Mr Afiri was defending himself, when he shot Mr Harbour?*

SD. *No. Mr Harbour stood up, unarmed, remonstrating with him and Afiri shot Mr Harbour with a gun that was already in his hand. It was a one-sided contest.*

Judge. *Move on, Ms Masters. These facts have been well-established and there should be consideration for Mr Harbour's family having to hear the details again.*

DB. *What did Mr Afiri do next?*

SD. *Passengers were upset about Mr Harbour and Afiri was rattled. I was relieved to see him disappear into the vestibule.*

DB. *This would be between coach J and K?*

SD. *Yes. He shouted for us to stay seated. I think he said if anyone moved, he'd shoot. Then he wedged some bags to keep the door open and smashed the lock on the toilet door.*

DB. *Could you see him do that from your seat?*

SD. *I heard someone saying he's smashing it.*

DB. *You didn't see him do it with your own eyes.*

SD. *No. But I saw what he'd done to the door with my own eyes when I got there.*

DB. *And how did that happen?*

SD. *Another hijacker turned up. Jefferson arrived in the carriage from coach H and grabbed Anita. He had a knife. He was more together, less edgy than Afiri. Told us all to shut up and stay calm, or the woman would get it, and pulled her down the aisle, calling for Afiri. His brother, he called him. Then they went into the vestibule. I took the opportunity to crawl along the aisle as quickly as I could. I grabbed a bottle from a table on the way down, not that* it would have been of much use, but it felt good to have something in my hand.

DB. And you took this action because?

SD. Because my training kicked in. Twelve years in the army and I'd just seen an innocent man murdered. I didn't want to have to see anyone else get hurt and there was a chance I might be able to help stop that happening. Otherwise I don't know if I could live with myself. That good enough for you?

DB. It's to clarify for the court, Mr Deaver, not for me personally. What did you see when you arrived at the toilet door?

SD. I'd edged up to the automatic door which Afiri had wedged open. I could see Jefferson holding Anita at the toilet door. His back was to me and someone inside was talking, then something happened, Jefferson's body stiffened, and I moved in.

DB. What did you plan to do?

SD. Probably hit him over the head with the bottle? I hadn't really thought it through.

DB. What did you find?

SD. When I got to the toilet door, I could just see past Jefferson, and saw that Claire was pointing a gun at him. I dropped the bottle, grabbed his arm to free Anita, and it was all over pretty quickly.

DB. What could you see inside the toilet?

SD. Not much to begin with. But eventually, I saw Afiri on the floor, bleeding.

DB. Did you see a knife and a gun?

SD. She had the gun in her hand. I didn't see a knife at first.

DB. Were you surprised by what you found?

SD. I think relief was my main emotion. But there wasn't much time to think.

DB. Did you take the gun off her and point it at Jefferson?

SD. She gave me the gun. I think she said she'd only ever fired a water pistol.

[Laughter in court.]

DB. Ms Fitzroy was making a joke as a man lay dying?

SD. He was already dead. And it was more a statement of fact than a joke.

DB. *Did you recognise the gun?*

SD. *If you mean the make, then yes, it was an old Czech handgun. An antique, really. They're not used in the British Army, but I'd heard about them. They've been knocking about Europe since the whole Balkan business.*

DB. *When Ms Fitzroy handed over the gun with her statement of fact, what else did you notice? There was a lot of Mr Afiri's blood we've been told on the floor and on her clothes, did you see that?*

SD. *There was a lot of blood on the floor and there was some on her clothes. I thought at first she'd been wounded.*

DB. *Did you help her before helping Mr Afiri?*

SD. *Mr Afiri was already dead.*

DB. *But did you check?*

SD. *It was obvious. I've seen dead bodies before. But yeah, I did check for a pulse.*

DB. *Was this after you'd helped Ms Fitzroy?*

SD. *She didn't need help. She was fine.*

DB. *Fine? She'd just slashed a man's throat who had bled all over her and she was 'fine'? Didn't you think that was odd behaviour for a middle-aged woman?*

SD. *By fine, I mean she was calm. I'm sure she wasn't fine in the sense that everything was OK. Because it wasn't.*

DB. *So Ms Fitzroy was remarkably calm having just killed a man.*

SD. *I didn't say remarkably. She had that calm I've seen in soldiers who've been under attack and come through. Sort of exhausted and relieved at the same time.*

DB. *And at what point did you see her knife?*

SD. *I can't remember. It was later.*

DB. *And what did you think about Ms Fitzroy having a knife like that on her?*

SD. *Given the circumstances, I suppose I thought it was a pity it wasn't another gun.*

[Laughter in court.]

Judge. *My learned friend, perhaps focus on the train of events?*

[Some laughter in court.]

DB. *Yes, Your Honour.*

DAILY MAIL

HIJACK HEROINE IS MARTIAL ARTS EXPERT

by Sam Dean

Manchester train heroine Claire Fitzroy expert in Krav Maga – deadly martial art used by the Israeli Forces.

Speaking exclusively to the Daily Mail, *ad exec Dominic Bell, 32, reveals he met Claire in a Krav Maga class in trendy Hoxton, East London in 2019.*

'Claire was so good it was scary. She was the oldest but I'm not sure any of us could have taken her down.'

Krav Maga, which means 'contact combat' in Hebrew, is a defence system which uses techniques from boxing, martial arts and street fighting. Its purpose is to finish a fight quickly and aggressively. Attacks are aimed at the most vulnerable parts of the body, and the techniques used can permanently injure or cause death.

Black belt trainer Jack Kahn, 43, who runs the classes said women often took classes to feel safe on the streets.

'We have three grades: practitioner, graduate and expert. Claire was a graduate. She took classes seriously but wasn't obsessed. I'm sure the training kicked in when she found herself in such a dangerous situation.'

Claire Fitzroy was one of the passengers who bravely tackled hijackers on the infamous 10:12 from Manchester. Fitzroy's actions resulted in the death of at least one of the suspected hijackers. There has been considerable interest in a woman of her age being able to overcome much younger male assailants.

Mr Bell said, 'I'm sure it evened up the odds. No one would have been expecting her to know how to fight.'

The trial starts next week at the Old Bailey.

26

Before the Trial

Those strange, half-muttered conversations on the train with people who stepped up to help come back to me now. They seemed to think they needed to prove they were up to it, to justify their decision to volunteer. But what was demonstrated was that people aren't defined by their jobs, their body type or how old they are. By itself, digital marketing might not seem relevant to a life-threatening situation, but if that job needs quick, flexible thinking, then yes, good skills to have when facing danger. And passengers who were involved in sport demonstrated fitness, commitment, the ability to take a bit of punishment maybe, and push on. But someone could also be rubbish at sport, and a sandwich short of a picnic, and still make a difference, by their bravery or kindness.

Perhaps we were all trying to find something within ourselves to make us feel less helpless when confronted by cold-hearted murderers. It wasn't just about persuading others, but about persuading ourselves. Either way, I'm grateful that there were passengers of all ages, genders, classes and ethnicities on the 10:12 that day with the courage to step forward and risk their lives for the sake of others. When I think about those brave people it challenges my usual pessimism about humankind.

In the long months running up to the trial, a number of 10:12 passengers circulated snippets of information, or offered support to the 'squad'. There was even a WhatsApp group – but then we were officially told not to talk to each other, and the group was shut down in case we jeopardised the case. I hadn't engaged anyway. Too many people, too much digital noise.

Deavey, myself, Alice, Paul and a few others kept in touch, sharing any information that the police gave us, which was next to nothing anyway. A group of people had gone through a traumatic experience together. It was only natural that we might want to communicate with others who understood what we had been through, and I said as much to the police when they expressed their concern about anything that might invalidate the prosecution. Our contact was largely along the lines of *How are you doing?* and *Have you heard about the trial date?* If the prosecution had read any communications between us, I don't believe they would have found cause for complaint.

Haunted by the memory of her crying baby, I fretted about Isha. But a few weeks after leaving hospital, DS Steve Chambers turned up with a thank-you card from her, saying she and Star were fine, and her dad was improving. That helped, and I worked hard at the physio exercises, determined to regain full strength and mobility in my arm and hand, and tried to focus on small pleasures, like listening to music, gardening and sketching. Enjoying books or films was more difficult as it was hard to maintain focus: my mind would wander, and I'd lose my place in a story or miss a whole section of a film plot.

I couldn't forget about the 10:12, although I tried. It took a while to recover physically, and Jim and I needed time alone and with the family. For obvious reasons I won't write much about our children; they deserve and need their anonymity. But they were loving and concerned, all you could hope your children would be in the circumstances.

Jim told me that Monty had been reunited with his owner and I was pleased for her. He'd run off when the train stopped, and there were lurid stories on social media about his fate. He was found a few days later. So, that's one happy ending. Jim was bemused, he said people seemed more interested in the dog than the victims. One theory was that I'd silenced the dog. A canine killer. Threats were made online, people claiming to be supporters of hijackers. Or dog lovers. I didn't look.

A bunch of dead flowers were found at the hospital addressed to me with '*4 youre grave*' written on the card. The CCTV wasn't enlightening. I suspect they were stolen from a grave because who keeps a bunch of flowers around until they die. It showed a bit of effort anyway.

Compared to what politicians or celebrities put up with, the threats were minimal. But perhaps because of the strangeness of the ill-assorted hijackers, I felt unsure exactly what team they were playing for, and therefore who any enemy might be.

They didn't seem religious. Anti-Chinese – but not all of them. Anti-women, mostly? Anti-vaccine, maybe some, anti-Deep State, whatever that was, some secret organisation that was secretly taking over the world? So anti… things. But not all anti the same thing. Just united by being anti something. I turned this over. We are all anti something, I imagine.

Me: people talking on speakerphone on public transport, queue jumpers, the term 'influencers', oh, and political liars. People who rip off the vulnerable. Lack of kindness. Unnecessarily large cars. I kept turning what I knew over in my mind, going down the same culs-de-sac and getting nowhere. Sleep was difficult anyway, haunted by nightmares. It was an unsettling couple of months. Watching spring turn to summer, I had a sense not of completion, but of waiting, for what I didn't know.

Then a few months after the hijacking, the security services suddenly decided we had to move, for my safety, and we were placed in a nondescript flat in a nondescript area outside London. However much we pressed, they were vague about what had prompted the decision. It was 'precautionary' they said, and I shouldn't worry – we'd been moved to a 'safe' house. I wondered how that was supposed to work. There was some respite. I was given permission to visit our son, who lives on another continent – our daughter had come home a few times – and then Jim and I took a break in Scotland. Every time I asked if there had been specific serious threats against me, I was told there had been 'murmurings', whatever that was supposed to mean, but nothing too worrying. In which case, I said, I wanted to return to my own home, but it was decided that our address was easily discoverable and we should err on the safe side.

The situation was designed to create paranoia. Occasionally, walking alone, I wondered if someone was following or watching me. I changed my appearance, just a little, and sometimes just a little is all it takes to make you unrecognisable to people who don't know you personally. Trying out different looks could be fun, and Jim and I treated it a bit like a game. We tried to keep his name out of things – it helped that we have different surnames – and he continued working. There are always new developments that need planning advisors to steer them through to construction. Mainly, he worked from home. After the initial upset, I was more concerned for him than for myself, and on the days he went to the office, I insisted that he took different routes and travelled at different times. The police said his risk was minor, but I was worried about his proximity to me and eventually moved up to Scotland on my own.

I had no job and was done with academia. It was certainly done with me.

[Do you want to mention that you left after a disagreement, where your objections to a complaint were not upheld, as I understand. Or were you fired? – Loretta]

[No. And no. I disagreed with them passing a student who they had initially agreed I was right to fail. It was symptomatic of the problems in Higher Education. – Claire]

My intention before the hijack had been to apply for community arts jobs, if there were any around, or return to prison teaching. Now, it wasn't only my notoriety which stopped me – it would be impossible to pass a DBS check. I might not have a criminal record, but it was uncontested that I'd killed. The police said to wait till the trial was over. But I needed something to do and was used to earning an income.

The place in Scotland belonged to a friend of a friend who only asked for energy bills to be covered. On my own and with no distractions I started to paint again, and for the first time in years really enjoyed it. As for solitude, we had all become used to Zoom meetings and lack of physical contact during the pandemic, and it didn't seem so different. I kept in touch with friends and family and, unrecognised, could shop or visit galleries. Thanks to contactless payments, no one checks a name on a debit card anymore. There were a few meetings in London with security services and lawyers, but again, much of that could be done online. Jim and I would meet for a weekend somewhere, every now again, and that felt romantic, with the promise of a fresh start.

To: Claire Fitzroy
cc: Laurence Walker
From: Loretta De Silva
Subject: Family matters

Hi Claire,

I know you weren't keen to involve your family, but as the 'kiss and tell' was widely reported, we do think you should address the subject – not least to indicate the pressure you were under pretrial. I believe from speaking to Laurence that Jim did have some kind of a fling, if not the love affair that was suggested. If that's not the case, then perhaps we get rid of the article and have a sentence from you about the lies in the media?

Speaking of family, I know you have included something about Jim being supportive to you during the court case, but there's almost no information about your family life. I understand the security concerns, but surely it's possible to say something without putting them at risk? I know I've said this before, but given the aggressive image of you that's been portrayed in some media, it would be a good way to humanise your reputation if you could include more family information.

Do keep in touch, we've been having a few problems getting hold of you.

Happy to meet if you want to chat!
Best,
Loretta

Loretta De Silva
Editorial Director, Ashgrove Publishing

Occasionally there would be another 10:12 story in the media and I might get a mention, but usually the facts were wrong. Sometimes they were amusing; sometimes, I admit, they made me feel good. The interview with Carla Johns, seeking her five minutes of fame in the tabloids, however, hit me hard. Jim rang to warn me the night before it appeared, after the paper had contacted him for a comment. We had a difficult conversation. The warning didn't stop me feeling humiliated and alone, despite Jim saying it was well and truly over, as he'd promised.

DAILY MAIL

HIJACK HEROINE

HUBBY'S LOVER

Petite blonde, Carla Johns, 39, (pictured) bravely speaks up about her secret relationship with husband of train hijack 'heroine', Claire Fitzroy.

Carla met Jim Laine, 55, at the Argyle Partnership, one of the top planning consultancies in London. Laine is a senior planning consultant and Johns was his assistant.

'Jim's quiet, a bit of a silver fox, but a gentleman, and we hit it off immediately. I knew he was married, so I didn't want to take it any further. But she seemed to be away a lot and never took his name, so I wasn't that surprised when he said the marriage had broken down and he was leaving Claire. That's when our affair started.

'Some weeks later, Jim said his wife had found out about us and he was moving out as soon as he could. I think he was scared of her. He said she had a terrible temper.'

The relationship continued until the hijack, when Laine broke it off, claiming his wife needed him.

'It's horrible what happened on the train, and I feel for all those affected: the train manager's family, the policewoman and that poor lady whose dog they killed. What kind of monster does that? Claire seems to have the right mentality to deal with that sort of thing. I was heartbroken that Jim gave in and ended it with me. But you wouldn't want her as an enemy, would you?'

Carla is moving to Spain to work as a holiday rep. 'I'm looking forward to a fresh start with sun, sea and sangria!' she said.

The hijackers' trial is due to start next month at the Old Bailey.

Then a letter was passed on to me which put my problems into perspective.

Dear Claire,

I'm sorry it's taken me so long to reply. I tried loads of times, but just ended up with a few words, and a lot of tears. I didn't want to use email, it seems impersonal, and you never know who might end up reading them.

People have been kind. Geoff and Rita have really helped, talking me through Nik's last minutes, and although the whole thing is just terrible, at least I know he died with kindness around him, and that he wasn't scared or in pain. It helps a bit with the nightmares and sleeplessness. (Who wants to sleep when you only have nightmares.) Mel, who worked with him, and who I know tried hard to help keep him alive as well, sent me a letter.

She's obviously devastated having experienced the whole nightmare and because she'd worked with Nik for a couple of years. Lots of thoughtful messages. May Leung and NorthRail have been good too.

So, you want to know about Nik and why he was on the 10:12. The second bit is the easiest. The 10:12 was a common run for him, and he could get home in reasonable time to where we live in Hulme. He'd had a couple of days off with a bad cold. He didn't have to go back, I'd asked him not to, but he liked his job and they were short-staffed. My sister says I can't beat myself up over it, but I'll regret letting him walk out our door that day as long as I live. I just gave him a quick kiss and said 'You love your Pendolinos more than you love your wife', or something equally stupid. I was rushing too, in a hurry to get to my job. I work in HR for a bank. They've been very good.

All the things I wish I'd said. How much I love him. How much the girls love him. Everyone loved Nik really. He was one of the good guys. We went to school together and started going out when we were fifteen and have been together ever since. We were married at twenty-three – I'm six months older – he always used to call me his cradle snatcher. The reasons I started going out with him at fifteen pretty much continued to be the reasons we stayed together. Nik was kind, funny, clever, handsome and sexy at fifteen, and was still all those things at forty. Plus, by then he was also a brilliant husband and dad to our three daughters, Anji (14), Arya (11) and Ruby (6). The girls were everything to him, and then next came cricket. And me, of course.

He loved cricket, watching it, playing it – his team did a guard of honour at the funeral. He was a good batsman. Cricket isn't very family-friendly, taking up all of Sundays, but his Irish mum, Kath, used to come with us to watch, and somehow, we made it work – plus, working shifts for the railway meant he could be around at other times. He was a cricket coach for the junior league and passed his love of the game to our Arya, who plays for the local club.

Nik was fun to be around and had lots of friends, of Indian heritage and white – actually all sorts. Pakistanis, West Indians, all the cricket nations, he used to say. He wasn't religious, although his dad was Hindu and his mum used to be Catholic. Nik always said cricket was his religion. He was a fan of Oasis, not Blur, and liked Drake and Ed Sheeran, old Tamla and some Indian classical music. He liked cooking, trying out new things, and nearly always managed to burn a pan. He'd have the occasional beer or glass of wine but was never much of a drinker and he loved our family beach holidays in Spain and Turkey. He stayed fit, running all year round, and doing nets in the winter. He liked watching crime dramas on TV and took the mickey out of his 'girls' for watching Bake Off – but somehow always ended up staying in the room.

Nik started as an apprentice with the railway when he was eighteen. Twice, it was suggested he move to a management desk job, and I think he planned to do it next year. His reluctance was because he liked people, dealing with them face to face. NorthRail valued Nik and used him to help train new apprentices to deal with customers. Or as he always preferred to call them, passengers. His mum and the girls came with me to the British Hero Awards ceremony where he, Joe Gupta and Melanie were given medals – he would have been so proud of Anji accepting it on his behalf. And if it only had been different circumstances, we would have all loved having tea with Prince William and Kate, who were very friendly. I know the girls will never forget it. Nik would have probably asked what all the fuss was about.

Most of all, Nik was kind. He looked after his mum, who moved near us when his dad died, and through his railway job trained as a listener for people who felt suicidal and then went on to become a Samaritan, doing several shifts a month. But he never made a big thing out of it, and most people didn't know he did it. I had a lovely letter from them.

So there's this massive Nik-shaped hole in our lives. The girls and me, and Kath, his mum, we've just got to try and get through it. My mum and dad are doing what they can, and we're all getting bereavement and trauma counselling. But that's about us, not Nik. I still wake up some mornings, and before I'm fully with it, I think he's in bed beside me. It crushes me when I remember. I want to turn over and never get out of that bed again. If it wasn't for the girls, I don't know what I might do.

I sometimes imagine how it would have turned out if I'd been there, if I'd tried to stop him annoying those scum so that they killed him. Or if someone else had stopped him. You said in your letter, and lots of people said at the trial, that he was a hero. It's difficult, isn't it? If he'd put his family first, he might have lived. Or he might have died anyway along with a lot more passengers, as the police said to me. He did save lives, I'm sure. He was brave. But a bit of me wishes he'd been a coward.

I attended the trial for a day but found it too much. I hope they all rot behind bars and die miserably with no one caring about them. They must be such sorry excuses for human beings to do what they did. I won't even say their names. I'm glad you shot the traitor in the cab. How could he do that to the people he worked with? And taking the baby – what a monster that man was. It's still hard talking to the girls about it. But they are very proud of their dad and both their schools have been amazing.

Nobody has ever had a bad word to say about Nik. And all I can really tell you is that he was the best man I've ever known, and I loved him to bits and my heart is broken.

Thank you for your letter and condolences. We're planning a memorial next year, a celebration of Nik's life, *and hopefully I'll be more with it by then and really hope we can have a talk.*

*Best regards,
Sian Bhatia*

To: Clementine John
From: Claire Fitzroy
Subject: Sian's letter

Hi Clemmie,

Sian's letter came late but I'd already taken out the bit about Mel. Sian sounds like a lovely woman. It was Geoff who told me Melanie was in love with Nik and they were having an affair, so it was difficult for her when Nik only wanted to talk about his kids and wife as he was dying. Apparently, she was in a bad way at the funeral, seeing his wife and kids only made it worse. But whatever his marital problems, Nik Bhatia was a much-loved brave man whose actions saved lives. And that's what the world needs to know, I'm sure you'd agree.

Claire

27
Old Bailey

The Crown Prosecution Service website
'Terrorism'
The Terrorism Act 2000 defines terrorism, both in and outside of the UK, as the use or threat of one or more of the actions listed below, where they are designed to influence the government or an international governmental organisation, or to intimidate the public. The use or threat must also be for the purpose of advancing a political, religious, racial or ideological cause.

The specific actions included are:

- Serious violence against a person;
- serious damage to property;
- endangering a person's life (other than that of the person committing the action);
- creating a serious risk to the health or safety of the public or a section of the public; and
- action designed to seriously interfere with or seriously disrupt an electronic system.

The use or threat of action, as set out above, involving the use of firearms or explosives, is terrorism regardless of whether or not the action is designed to influence the government or an international governmental organisation or to intimidate the public or a section of the public.

Action includes action outside the United Kingdom.

It is important to note that in order to be convicted of a terrorism offence a person doesn't actually have to commit what could be considered a terrorist attack. Planning, assisting and even collecting information on how to commit terrorist acts are all crimes under British terrorism legislation.

What you quickly realise when you get caught up in a criminal trial is that you are told next to nothing. Things change without warning. You find yourself in a world you assumed you would understand, but then discover it operates by its own arcane rules that are rarely explained by those in the know. When they do attempt to clarify things, it's usually in the way that people who are immersed in their own world try to explain something – incomprehensible to anyone on the outside.

Initially, it was indicated that the trial would be at the court located next to Belmarsh prison, in South East London, where many terrorists are held, and where legal professionals apparently bemoan the lack of wine bars and high-end eateries. Although I enjoyed teaching at the prison, I didn't have many happy memories of it and imagined a concrete-walled room with no windows. But then it was moved to the Central Criminal Court. Relief. You've likely seen it and think you know what it's like inside. Scores of film and TV dramas have represented court cases at what is better known as the Old Bailey, the most famous criminal court in Britain. You imagine yourself in that wood-panelled room with bewigged legal representatives. I remember thinking at least it will be familiar, a help when you're battling with nerves.

The trial date changed several times. I'd ring the police and be reminded how lucky I was that the case had been given special priority, as some criminal prosecutions were taking four years to come to court. I didn't bother explaining that I don't think it's lucky to find yourself on a train that's been hijacked by armed killers, and waiting for a trial is its own kind of torture. You can never put it out of your mind.

Eventually the day came. We arrived early. I wanted to walk around, get my bearings, try to calm my nerves. Normally for a journey to the city from our then home, the suburban train route would have been the best option, but Jim decided I could do without another train on my mind and booked a cab. I was glad not to have to worry about it. I had been on suburban trains since the 10:12, but it was never easy, and if carriages were crowded, I'd let the train pass. No intercity. Planes were also difficult. I was always looking over my shoulder, checking other passengers.

Our conversation was sporadic. We ran through what we'd been told about the legal process, and the charges and sentences the hijackers were facing, until I ran out of any inclination to say much at all. While I had been trying not to think about it, thankfully Jim had researched everything – he said he didn't want there to be any surprises. He held my hand, and I was grateful for our easy silence, his support and the simple fact of his presence. These were things I had always loved about him.

He took us straight to a local convenience store nearby where someone had the financial foresight to set up a service looking after the phones of people attending court. You can't take a phone in with you. The shop owner's low-tech system involves a sticker with your name on the back of your phone, a locked cupboard and the electronic handover of a couple of quid. The man behind the counter didn't look at me and I wondered at all the other witnesses from other, possibly life-changing, trials who must have handed their phones over to him to be placed in the scruffy MDF cupboard sealed with a small cheap padlock next to the cigarettes and spirits.

It was a warm sunny day and people were on the streets, moving with purpose. With time to spare, we headed to the front of the court for a proper look at the building. St Paul's Cathedral is nearby, and the pavements were busy with tourists mingling with office workers. It appeared so normal – people were chatting and smiling, delivery drivers were pulling up and dispatching their parcels. But it felt unreal, like the set of a film.

Too bright, too normal, compared to what I was going to have to relive in the next hours.

I was worried there might be a horde of reporters and photographers outside, and there were perhaps a dozen, evident by large cameras, chatting to each other, who initially took no notice of the middle-aged couple having a look at a famous landmark from across the road. An Italian female journalist was doing a piece to camera. A hedge conveniently planted at the edge of the pavement provided some cover, and we stood behind it studying the main entrance. It's the kind of historic building you pass all the time if you live and work in London; you register its presence and its purpose and don't think any more about it. This time I took a proper look.

There was the famous golden statue of Lady Justice, sword in one hand, scales in the other, gleaming in the sunshine and poised dramatically on top of the roof sending out her message of impartial justice. I wondered if someone regularly climbed up there to give her a polish and keep Justice shining. Directly to the front of the building, another statue caught my eye, less famous, but as it turned out, more relevant. Over the main entrance are stone carvings of three women, a central hooded figure with two others, one on either side. Of course Jim had done his research and told me they were the Recording Angel flanked by Fortitude and Truth. As the days went by, I thought a great deal about those last two and how much of one I was going to need, in order to discover the other.

We were turning away, when there was a shout: 'Hey, Claire!'

I glanced at the gaggle of reporters as Jim grabbed my hand. They were looking over at us, lifting cameras, moving to the edge of the pavement. Unexpectedly I'd been recognised, despite wearing a bucket hat and dark glasses, hoping to blend in with the tourists. Jim muttered that we should walk away slowly as if the shout hadn't been directed at me. Fortunately, the lights changed, and traffic flowed, preventing the reporters from crossing the street for a few moments. A pub stood behind us, but it was shut, so we walked slowly up a side street then quickly dodged around another corner. Jim knew the area, having worked on a development project there some years before, and he took us through a small alleyway which most people would have just walked past. A little out of breath, we eventually ended up on the street where we needed to be, and Jim left me in a doorway while he checked ahead and came back with the all-clear.

There was no grand entrance for us, thank goodness. We had been told to come in via a side door, where we went through airport levels of security and Jim was directed to the public gallery. The trial was in Court No. 1 apparently one of the largest rooms. Climbing up to the third floor where the court is situated (lifts were available only for those with disabilities), I was struck by how dark the stairwell was, with old-school tiling on the wall, cracked and gloomy, and paint peeling off the woodwork. It felt like a physical representation of the state of our criminal justice system. My stomach was churning, as I thought how it wouldn't only be the hijackers who were going to be judged. I'd been told the cross-examination might be uncomfortable – why, I'd asked, I didn't hijack a bloody train. The police officer replied that as the barrister would be representing the men whose behaviour I would be describing, he or she might pick at my statements to paint their clients in a better light. I wasn't sure how you could portray armed hijackers who had murdered innocent people in a good light. The officer said it was a question of degree and, appearing rather embarrassed, pointed out that as a result of my actions there had been deaths, however justified. It was all about proportionate use of reasonable force, and in the second instance there were plenty of witnesses to it being an accident. But that wouldn't stop the defence giving me a tough time. We left it at that.

I was led to a functional waiting room where several people were already seated, one of whom I recognised as Miss Atkinson, the dog's owner. She gave me a dismissive nod, then returned to her crossword. There were two other women and an older man in a smart navy suit, and he looked up and nodded. Perhaps that was witness room protocol. I nodded back. Another woman in her thirties stared at me briefly then pointedly turned away. I found out later it was Gill's daughter Abigail, who was due to be called because of a phone message her mother had left her. The hard stare shook me. Steve Chambers had advised me not to contact her, after I received no reply to my condolences and explanation of what had happened.

'She needs time to process it all, I think,' he said, which I suspected was a polite way of saying she blames you for her mother's death.

The others in the room were probably support staff. The blue-suited man gave me an encouraging smile, and a thumbs up when he was called first, which made me feel a bit better. I found out later from Jim that he had been one of the passengers who had helped subdue Mo Abadi and, in his testimony, gave a spirited defence of the actions of the passengers and praised the squad. Thank you, Mr Blue Suit. Betsy, a thoughtful witness support volunteer, now sat by me. She said she hoped I wouldn't be kept longer than two hours before being called to the witness stand. But her expression suggested any hope may be in vain.

Betsy complimented my outfit. I'd pondered hard over what to wear and settled for a tailored linen-mix midi dress in teal with three-quarter-length sleeves. It was warm and sunny, so I didn't need a jacket and my legs were bare and ended in low-heeled black sandals. I'd added a silver pendant round my neck that the kids had bought me, and a pair of pretty silver drop earrings Jim had given me years ago. I was aiming for neat and minimal, feminine and practical, not threatening in any way. With that in mind, I had swept my hair back into a tidy French pleat and applied a subtle lipstick and some mascara – not that anyone would notice the eye make-up behind my large, grey glasses. Clothes and make-up can be armour for women, and it certainly made me feel better that I was comfortably but smartly dressed.

The plan was to join Jim in the public gallery after I'd given testimony, depending on how I felt. As a witness you're not allowed to watch the trial until you've done your bit. Having gone through the security arch to get in, it was clear that I couldn't have smuggled a phone in, even if I'd wanted to. But it meant

I couldn't chat with friends, and I assumed witnesses weren't supposed to talk to each other, so there were few distractions as Betsy had other clients and was coming and going from the room. I skimmed a paper I'd picked up, but Betsy had suggested I didn't read about the trial, and I couldn't relax enough to do a crossword or a sudoku. Instead, I went over the reminders I'd jotted down in a notebook, trying to keep the timeline and the people involved clear in my mind. And when the words started swimming in front of my eyes I tried sketching the Recording Angel and her mates from memory. Fortitude turned out to be particularly tricky. Betsy bought me water and offered biscuits – but I felt sick. The thought of talking in detail about what had happened that day was giving me waves of nausea and I knew I had to get a grip on myself and my intermittently thumping heart if I was going to give clear and accurate testimony. It was a hard wait. Possibly harder than waiting on the ward before being wheeled down to have cancer surgery. At least then I'd had some drugs to enjoy.

Just over two hours after I'd arrived, I was called. Betsy was there to wish me luck and then an usher took me in. As I was led to the witness box, people were moving around, whispering to each other. I glanced up to the public gallery: the first surprise was its size – it was so small. The front row was taped off, a security precaution applied in some courts, I found out later, perhaps to stop visitors from dropping things onto people's heads. It was scruffy, like a crime scene. There were two rows of seats, perhaps thirty people in all. I was relieved to see Jim in the second row. He discreetly raised a hand, and I nodded.

The room, as expected, featured large amounts of oak panelling, and where the panelling ended, green painted walls. The jury was on one side. I didn't want to stare, but a quick glance seemed to indicate the usual London mixed bunch – a range of ages and ethnicities and a mixture of men and women. The judge, a thin middle-aged white man with wire-rimmed glasses low on his nose, looked like he was born to wear the grey wig. His seat was higher than the rest of the court, facing the room, in an oversized green leather chair – rather throne-like – with similar chairs, empty, on either side of him, as if he was waiting for late dinner guests. He was busy looking at his computer, it seemed, and then at notes in front of him. There was a pile of legal tomes stacked to one side and a KeepCup, from which he occasionally sipped.

At the next level down, and directly in front of the judge, was the court clerk, a middle-aged Black woman, who also seemed busy on her computer. There were about ten people in black gowns and wigs, scattered round the side facing the jury. I couldn't tell who was who, apart from Hugh Delaney, the prosecuting barrister and his assistant, Cyril Adewale, who I'd met very briefly to go through my testimony. Cyril flashed me a friendly smile. There was a low hum of hushed chatter and people and passing things to each other or going in and out of the courtroom.

I worked out who I thought must be the defence team, led by Eleanor Masters. She was of average height, in her forties, blonde hair escaping from the wig. She had a habit of using a pair of glasses in her hand as a prop, I noticed, as she talked with a young man beside her. She glanced my way. I didn't respond.

I avoided looking at the dock. It didn't matter that I despised them. It's hard to be rational about someone whose monstrous presence haunts your dreams, and leaves you gasping for breath and clutching at your throat when you wake. That was what Scarface, Targut, meant to me. But I had a strategy and focused on breathing steadily, then made myself turn to face the dock.

It turned out to be a spacious raised area, surrounded by what I assume are toughened glass panels. I looked at the men who were sitting in a row at the front, various papers in front of them. They were dressed in shirts, but no ties – as if the dress code on the invite was smart casual. Like me, they were doing their best to look unthreatening. They seemed smaller. Almost insignificant. If I could have forgotten what they'd done.

Shane Rees caught my eye and looked away. He looked even more like a child. Rodrigues was fidgeting, cracking his knuckles. Mo Abadi appeared to want to look as if he was asleep. But Targut stared at me for a moment, a sneer on his face, then picked up a sheet of paper and began studying it. The look caught me off guard. Anger, hate, aggression... or was I reading too much into an expression. Their security team, whatever they're called, were two young women and two men, seated to one side of the accused and behind them. One of the young women looked like she was reading a magazine – the hijackers seemed not to be regarded as a threat, but there were murderers among them. They looked like bored patients in a waiting room on a hot day, with ingrown toenails or prostate problems, which made the appalling seem pedestrian.

Standing in the witness box, I felt uncomfortably on show. The clerk asked if I wanted to 'swear or affirm' and I affirmed I would tell the truth. A lawyer had said to me that even though I'm an atheist, it's better to swear on the Bible or Koran, as research indicated that people didn't trust the word of those that affirmed. But I couldn't possibly start my testimony with a lie, however bad it made me look. As it was, there didn't seem to be much of a fuss about it. I wondered what the men in the dock had said, and glanced their way, but then decided I would try and avoid looking at them, as the witness support officer had suggested, although somehow, my eyes kept swivelling back to that glass box while I waited for the questioning to begin.

I could see Delaney going through papers as if he'd just seen them for the first time. It gave me a moment to look round the courtroom again. No, it was not like the versions I'd seen on TV. Wood panelling, tick; coat of arms, tick; wigs and gowns, tick. But what surprised me was the mess.

The room was not designed for modern media. There were electrical leads trailing everywhere: up to screens that faced the jury, or across the court so that the public gallery could see what was being shown on them. No health and safety gone mad in the Old Bailey. Extension leads were strewn on the floor crossing pathways between seats – a clear trip hazard. And despite the screens and laptops in front of just about everyone, this was no paperless procedure. Mountains of files and sheets of paper were scattered across tabletops, along with empty and part-filled plastic bottles of water. Delaney appeared to have made a den out of what seemed like clipboards, sheets of paper and law books to prevent prying eyes looking at his laptop, or perhaps it was just to beat light reflection.

The room was messy, even chaotic. But the atmosphere wasn't. I became aware that all eyes were focused on me. I could feel my heart thumping again. I looked across to the judge, who appeared to give a slight nod of recognition. Hugh Delaney coughed. 'Ms Fitzroy, if we could take you back to the day in question…'

Extract from Examination of Shane Rees by Defence Barrister Eleanor Masters

DB. *Was the intention of your group that day to cause disruption to the rail service?*
SR. [unintelligible]
Judge. *Speak up please, Mr Rees.*
SR. *Yes.*
DB. *Was it also the intention of the group to kill and harm passengers?*
SR. *No. Just threats.*
DB. *How do you explain the IED then?*
SR. *I don't know who put it there. Or if it was there.*
DB. *So what was the aim of hijacking the 10:12?*
SR. *Like you said, disruption. Making a point about who was taking over our country. And…* [unintelligible]
DB. *And money, did you say? Ransom money?*
[silence]
Judge. *Mr Rees. Please answer the question.*
SR. *I don't know about that. I wasn't in charge.*
DB. *Did you personally hurt anyone physically?*
SR. *No.*
DB. *Did you know if violence was planned?*
SR. *No, I'm sorry people were hurt. I'm sorry.*

28

After the Trial

After giving evidence, I opted to stay in court. Jim was there, and I knew he'd report back, but I was so shocked by Eleanor Masters' questioning that I suppose I wanted to hear someone stick up for me, and for all the others who put their lives at risk to save passengers and crew. I couldn't believe what Masters was doing. I still wonder how she sleeps at night. I know they have to defend their clients, but it felt personal, nasty. A distortion of the events on that day.

The way she implied what happened to Gill was somehow my fault, chilled me to the core. Then hearing that Melissa Ngozi and Deborah Atkinson had portrayed me as some kind of Rambo-crazed monster just made the whole thing seem surreal. As I stepped down from the box, I was shaking. But I noticed Deavey and Alice at the back of the gallery; they must have come in while I was being questioned. He looked at me and shook his head, and Alice gave a friendly smile and a subtle hand gesture towards the defence which almost made me laugh out loud. I read their statements later. They were concise, measured and fair, explaining how Gill liaised with gold command but also helped us. Deavey took full responsibility for how Jefferson had been treated. We needed to contain him, he told the court, not just because Jefferson was aggressively trying to escape but also because Jefferson revealed there were other armed hijackers, and implied there were explosive devices on the train. And it was containment, not unwarranted force, as the defence barrister seemed to suggest. I am grateful that they had my back. The explosives expert stated that the IED was timed to go off at Euston and would have done so in the event of a crash, which made Paul feel more comfortable about the decision to throw it off the train.

To: Claire Fitzroy
From: Clementine John
Subject: Ngozi's testimony

Claire, I tracked down the transcript of Ngozi's testimony. She seems fairly restrained? Please find attached.

Clemmie.

Extract from Cross-Examination of Melissa Ngozi by Defence Barrister Eleanor Masters

DB. *You had several confrontations with Ms Fitzroy, we've heard. When she killed Mr Afiri, later when she told you to stop filming on your phone, and when she tried to stop you and the other passengers who wanted to negotiate from going forward on the train to try and talk to the hijackers. How would you describe her manner and attitude?*
MN. *Forthright. Assertive. Confident.*
DB. *Aggressive?*
PB. *Objection.*
Judge. *My learned friend, leading questions again?*
DB. *Apologies, Your Honour. Ms Ngozi, did you agree with Ms Fitzroy's actions?*
MN. *I thought there was value in attempting negotiations to avoid further bloodshed. Ms Fitzroy was on another path, one of confrontation.*
DB. *Was she the leader?*
MN. *It looked like it.*
DB. *Is it fair to say you thought that approach would mean more violence with inevitable consequences?*

MN. Obviously, I couldn't know for sure. But it seemed highly likely. Meeting violence with violence doesn't tend to de-escalate a problem, it has the opposite effect.
DB. What made you think the group led by Ms Fitzroy had violence, not peaceful negotiations in mind?
MN. They were armed. Guns, for goodness' sake, and all sorts. And we can see where that led. They weren't just for show, were they? People who carry guns tend to end up using them. Claire Fitzroy shot a man dead.
PB. Objection!

To: Clementine John
From: Claire Fitzroy
Subject: Ngozi's testimony

Clemmie, She stated that I was taking a violent approach whereas she was all peace and understanding. The gun went off when I was shot. It was not intentional. The takeaway is that I was the aggressor. And nothing about the risks of her filming! Still not happy about the inclusion. Similarly to Masters' examination of me – it's what she implies. Which is why I don't want them included.

Claire

The guilty verdicts, which should have been cause for triumph, afforded little consolation for me. It was trumpeted as a big success in the media and a tribute to Gill, Nik and the bravery of the 'squad' and Joe Gupta. Paul, Deavey and Gill, as ex-service and police, Geoff and Rita, as NHS staff, as well as the younger members of the team ('not all Gen Z are snowflakes… gives us hope for the future' *Telegraph*) were rightly praised for their actions. I was occasionally the 'hijack heroine', but my involvement in the death of two men and the descriptions of me in court led to an ambivalence about my behaviour. As Deavey said, it was OK for an ex-soldier to shoot someone, but not a female art lecturer.

THE TIMES

SCENES OF CHAOS ON BOARD THE 10:12

Gasps could be heard from the Old Bailey public gallery yesterday during the trial of the 10:12 hijackers. The defence team showed a compilation of films made by passengers on their phones which portrayed chaos as several of the passengers known as the 'squad' attempted to stop others from filming.

Claire Fitzroy, 58, one of those credited with overcoming the hijackers, could be seen wrestling a phone from another woman and shouting in an intimidating manner. Stuart Deaver, 37, a former army corporal appeared in several clips waving a gun and swearing, while some passengers were arguing, and captured hijacker Mohammed Abadi was apparently being manhandled by others.

The woman involved in the altercation with Fitzroy, Melissa Ngozi, 48, a Christian pastor, stated in the witness box that she had been intimidated by Fitzroy and that she had completely rejected any suggestion of negotiating with the hijackers. But Paul Brady, a former major in the Territorial Army, and one of those who retaliated, said the reason for the fray was that there had been a real concern that footage would be uploaded on social media and seen by the terrorists, thereby revealing that passengers were fighting back and had captured hijackers. He said that one of the accused, Adam Jefferson, 36, had told them there were explosives on the train.

'It was constantly on our minds that an IED could be set off and we didn't want hijackers further up the train feeling threatened enough to do that. Passengers filming what was going on potentially put us all at risk.'

The trial continues today.

In the weeks after the case, when the media fuss began to die down, there was no resolution for me. The judge had made a point of commenting on the bravery of the team of passengers who had outwitted the hijackers. But the undercurrent, a murmuring, about my behaviour, continued. There were memes, which I didn't find funny, of Ninja Gran. The *Daily Mail* ran an article – by a female journalist – that, while purporting to support my actions, also described it as menopause rage and said she'd often felt the same way. The same way as what? Defending herself against murderers? But she wouldn't have gone 'as far' and managed to suggest that there was something strange in a woman doing what I'd done. So apparently people died because I had falling oestrogen levels. I was post-menopausal, but why let facts get in the way.

This was followed by another glut of memes about menopause rage with my image superimposed. 'My hormones called, they wanted to arrange an appointment to shoot you,' was typical. There were even murmurings again that I'd killed the bloody dog – who as far as I knew was living happily with its owner.

You're not supposed to look at these things. But, I discovered, you just can't help yourself.

A few op eds popped up in the more serious papers about underestimating women of a certain age, usually written by women of a certain age. More troubling were suggestions in the 'out there' social media that I was an undercover agent.

Steve Chambers warned this might encourage retaliatory action from any pick-and-mix messed-up person. He suggested a holiday.

I'm not sure you can take a holiday if you don't have a job, but Jim took time off work and back we went to Scotland, this time to a remote cottage on one of the Shetland Islands, somewhere we loved. But we hit bad weather, biblical rain and wind, and I spent far too much time staring out of the window wondering why those men had come together to hijack the train. The conclusion people seemed to draw from the trial was that they were a group of inadequate psychopaths seduced by conspiracy theories. But was that the whole story? To me, their actions on the 10:12 appeared too directionless, too chaotic.

Deavey suggested I let it go, get some talking therapy. It had helped him, he said, with his PTSD and he'd had a few sessions since the hijack. Alice said they were a bunch of confused, if dangerous, halfwits, no wonder it was a mess, and suggested the core team got together for a boozy night out. I thanked them, but I wasn't ready for either a piss-up or a psych over. Instead, I put on wellies and walked out into the rain, or when it was too wet even for that, made notes and lists, interspersed with sketches of the hijackers and some of the passengers.

Initially people assumed the hijackers were 'regular' terrorists. Because who else would do something like that? It was no *Taking of Pelham 123* – there wasn't a bank vault under the tracks between Manchester and London. No gold bullion on board, or army payroll (Westerns galore). And no political demands. Did these hijackers imagine death and glory, or had they believed there was an escape plan? Were they violent misanthropic psychopaths? Perhaps that was true of Targut. Or lonely and dysfunctional men who had been duped? Young Rees, maybe? There had been nods to conspiracy theories; the aggressive anti-vaxx badge, incel misogyny, use of the term 'Deep State', the assertion of a Chinese plot. Adam Jefferson had been a muddle of all of that. I knew conspiracy theories created unlikely alliances, interconnected largely online, ranging from crusties with dogs on strings to neo-Nazis. During the pandemic, I had come across a demonstration gathering in Trafalgar Square, and couldn't think what had brought all these disparate groups together – coked-up white supremacist EDL types, dreadlocked hippies in a miasma of cannabis, normal-looking people with strange placards about paedophilia – until I heard a conventional-looking woman speaking from the platform, aggressively threatening doctors and nurses for the heinous crime of administering the Covid jab.

The men weren't hijacking a train to stop vaccinations, but they weren't saying much apart from anger against a perceived Chinese plot. When asked – and various passengers did – the answer seemed to be a variation of 'you'll find out'. But we hadn't. They'd revealed little from the dock. The media described them as anti-Chinese conspiracy theorists, but their motivations seemed more muddled than even that broad term implied.

This was no lone wolf action, these men were doing it together. They had discussed it, planned it. These plans appeared to include the potential death of scores of innocent people, and possibly their own. How much hatred would that take? In court, Rees said there had been no intention to kill anyone. The threats were to keep people in line, to keep them safe. He cried. It was an action designed to create chaos for people to notice that the Chinese were taking over the world, Abadi said, throwing in Deep State, the *Matrix*, the illuminati, and confusing anyone listening. He also said the man I'd killed in the toilet hadn't really been one of them, then clammed up. What did that mean? There seemed to be genuine confusion about why they were doing what they were doing and what they expected to get out of it, which reflected their own varied chaotic motivations. Was it just for people 'to take notice'? That's clearly a motivation for a lot of people – but in such an extreme way and at such a high cost? None of them appeared to know Afiri personally, but according to the police had met online. Prison appeared to be a link, but not all of them had been inside at the same time. Nothing about them suggested they were friends or even liked each other. But somehow, they had been brought together in this bloody enterprise.

'Do your own research', the mantra of conspiracy theorists (which in reality seems to mean not trusting traditional and tested sources but going down digital rabbit holes where your paranoias are not just welcome, but enhanced and linked to others), seemed to fit what these men had been doing, finding each other in the process. But killing people is still a big step from theorising alone.

I often thought about Nancy's advice, her assumption that I wouldn't let things go and wouldn't be able to leave things up to the professionals. She was wrong. Between coming out of hospital and going to the trial, I did just that. But now it was different.

The Scottish rain offered up no solutions, although the windswept waters of the Atlantic and the North Sea helped me find some clarity. The all-clear came from the security services – the

10:12 was yesterday's news: life moves on in our media-heavy world. There was always a war, global catastrophe or celebrity scandal somewhere to fill the insatiable demand for content. I returned home after a month with no answers. I had been responsible for the death of two men and deep down was haunted by the prospect that I had been partly responsible for what happened to Gill. There had to be a reason for the hijack and the needless deaths. And a way for me to come to terms with the horror.

29
Art Therapy

I finally took Deavey's advice. Several counselling sessions gave me a few tools to deal with the processing of that day, memories of which were occasionally overwhelming. Along with seeing old friends and family, and checking in with the squad occasionally, going back to making art was the best thing I did. When I painted, it calmed the need to find answers. There was no dithering about the subjects; landscapes, it seemed, were what I wanted to paint – framed by a window, which might have been a train window. As I applied paint to canvas, I needed the shape of that frame. Some have figures in the landscapes: a farmer looking up from a tractor, people watching from a block of flats; sometimes a woman with a baby or a man wearing a black mac. A few canvasses include reflections in the window: a blind partly down, a suggestion of a crowded carriage, a person looking out. I was doing the kind of art I'd sometimes encouraged my students to do at the prison, expressing what was haunting me.

I completed a dozen paintings in all. They were done as a personal project, not for anyone else. Then an old art school friend visited and took photos of them, and the next thing I knew I had an offer for a short exhibition at a new small East London gallery building a good reputation. I dithered, then phoned Steve and told him about it and he came to see the collection with someone from the CPS. They thought there was nothing that would upset any legal process. Nancy also came, this time in a grey pinstripe trouser suit and pink shirt. She said very little but used her phone to photograph all the paintings. She did say something about me being a professional and that she'd hoped it had been cathartic and helped to put the whole business to rest. I didn't know what to say to that, so merely nodded.

The paintings wouldn't say the 10:12 or even 'train' to anyone, and I added some landscapes I'd done in the Shetlands and used my married name, with initials. It felt like one of the few positives in my life at that time, with an empty nest and no employment. Jim was doing his best to keep my spirits up and stop me worrying about money, but it wasn't just that: painting gave me some hope for the future, when no one would employ me.

The gallery staff hung everything beautifully. I'd used acrylics, and the paintings were a similar size – a little smaller than a train window. The gallery wanted to use my dubious fame for publicity, but I said no. I invited some of the crew to the private viewing and was pleased when Deavey, Alice, Paul, Alex, Mary, Kyo, Rita and Ty all showed up. They had a particular response to the paintings, and I guess in my naivety I hadn't really thought how other visitors would pick up on that. Rita hugged me for a long time, someone else cried, and Ty just stood with a shaking head in front of the one with the woman and baby. I guess someone noticed the unusual reactions and did some digging. Within days there was a small item in the *Telegraph*, then the *Mail*. I even got a half-decent review in the *Guardian*. And the publicity did help sales. There were three I was keeping, but the rest sold for the best prices I've ever made for my work, one anonymous buyer paying double the price listed for a train window view.

Dear Claire Fitzroy,

I have sent this to the address your letter came from. You wanted to know why I was on the train. I was going to visit my girlfriend Shelley who lives in London. Once a month she comes to Manchester, and once a month I go to London. My father told me it was wrong to hit women and girls and he was right. He also told me I had a good arm on me which means that I am good at throwing. The nice lady Isha came to see me with Star when I visited Shelley again and we went to the park. I'm glad I threw the cans although I didn't get them back and they were for dinner that I was going to cook Shelley so we had pie and chips instead.

I'm glad you didn't kill the dog. I don't mind you calling me the Tin Can Man. Shelley says it's funny, like a superhero.

I cannot come to see your paintings as they are there on days that I am not in London. I hope you are all better now.

Tony Rossi

As agreed, the exhibition closed after three weeks, and I went to the gallery to collect the pictures I was keeping. The owner was happy. The exhibition had really put them on the map and he showed me the visitors' book, packed with comments. I sat down with a cup of tea and started to read what people had taken the time to write: mostly thoughtful and with insight, some kind, some inane, a few critical of the art, mostly very positive. Including one that read: *Congratulations. It brought it all back. Hope you have recovered. Anita xx*

30

Isha's Story

Anita was another missing piece of the jigsaw. With the exhibition out of the way, the questions came flooding back. I didn't want to go back to counselling, I wanted answers. I needed to talk to other people on the train that day – perhaps they'd have pieces of information which could help form a complete picture. Why the 10:12? There were fewer carriages than normal, so it was easier to manage, but did they know that in advance? Who had shut the last carriage – was that connected? At the trial it emerged that fewer carriages than normal appeared on the booking system for the 10:12, which went unnoticed, and unexplained, accepted as a glitch. The electrical problem turned out not to exist – a fault in the system, apparently. Was this a coincidence?

I wanted to speak to passengers before hijackers – if I could even speak with them – and first on the list was Isha to see if she could tell me more. There was something that didn't sit straight. I wondered if Ellwood had found out from Joe Gupta that his daughter and granddaughter were on the train and deliberately used them to make Gupta compliant.

Isha sent me a message via the police, saying she hadn't been able to face being in court. She had given video evidence with her face concealed. I decided to get in touch with Steve again. He's a decent bloke and I thought although it was possibly outside his remit, he would help. I emailed asking him to let

Isha know I'd like to talk, attaching a letter to her, and eventually there was a reply.

Hi Claire,

The nice policeman passed on your letter. Yes, happy to meet up sometime. I couldn't face the trial and I need to protect my privacy. I'll explain, but first I want to say thank you again. By the time you came in the carriage I was sure we were going to die, but instead you and the others saved our lives. I honestly believe that. And it's given me a chance to start a new life with Star. Dad's moving down too, after his medical retirement goes through, so a fresh start for all of us.

Why was I on that particular train, the 10:12? First off, it was an important day for me as I had managed to get away from a violent partner and was planning to start a new life down south. He went to prison for what he did to me, but he's got these friends outside, and the Oldham refuge where I stayed received threats. I didn't want to stay at Dad's because he didn't need more trouble in his life.

I know what Zain's like. He'll never stop.

Dad arranged for me to stay with a relative in London, and I was on the 10:12 because Dad was the driver, and he wanted me safe and close. He didn't tell people, because he was worried about anyone knowing anything about me, in case of Zain. And he'd told me not to say anything either, and I'm sorry I didn't tell you earlier, but I don't think it would have made much difference.

I've wondered a lot about why that hijacker picked on me. Dad says he never mentioned me to that excuse for a human Ellwood. It was Jefferson who grabbed me first of all. He told Rodrigues to watch me. I thought maybe it was because a mum and baby look vulnerable and if you can hurt them, you can hurt anyone, which makes the hijackers look even more scary. Does that make sense? I guess it was just a coincidence. I'll never know as he wouldn't talk in court, would he. I read about it and Dad told me he wouldn't answer questions and was really arrogant.

You'll probably think I'm mad, but I still can't help wondering if Zain had something to do with it. I even thought I saw him on the train. He always could mess with my head. He was a conspiracy theorist too, but then so are a lot of people.

I did tell the police about him, but Zain was in prison when it happened, so he definitely wasn't on the train. His full name is Zain Rhind. I hope you never come across him. He is Star's biological father, but if I have my way, he'll never have anything to do with her.

By the way, some passengers tried to help before you arrived, until they saw Rodrigues's knife. I begged him to not hurt the baby, and I don't think he would have. But who knows?

I'm in East London – ring and I'll give you the address. Let me know when would suit you. Best if you come to me, and best in the morning as we'll get more peace and quiet. Star has a right pair of lungs on her. I'm just so grateful she's too tiny to know what was going on. Sometimes when I get down about what happened – and what might have happened – I look at my baby. Do you know what, she's nearly always smiling! Better than any pills.

Love Isha

I loved hearing about the therapeutic effects of baby Star's smile on her mum. It did me good too.

This, however, was the first time I'd heard the name Zain Rhind. No one else had mentioned him. It was probably nothing, but I checked with Steve Chambers, who told me they had looked into Rhind, but that he was locked up in Belmarsh at the time – coincidentally the same prison where I had once taught, and where I still knew people.

Isha was living in a flat on the thirteenth floor of an unexceptional, tatty, concrete twenty-storey tower in East London, probably built in the 1980s. For admission, there was a locked external gate and call system to be negotiated, then a walk through a sparse garden to the block reception, another buzzer system and a concierge, and then a lift. This wasn't maximum security, just standard for so many developments in London. The block itself was probably ex-council and now full of young people and migrant families – a mix of owner-occupiers and renters, judging by the lively posters on the walls of the shuddering lift. Isha had a spyhole, and after I'd rung the bell, she opened the door on a chain.

'Claire?'

'Yes, it's me. I know, my hair's different.'

She unfastened the chain and let me in. 'Looks nice,' she smiled.

Inside, there was a buggy in the small lobby and slipping past it she took me into the living room. She agreed to let me use my phone to record our conversation.

The walls were painted white, and it was simply furnished IKEA style, with a sofa, armchair, TV, table, highchair, grey carpeting and a couple of boxes of kids' toys. There were bright cushions and Isha clearly liked houseplants, a selection of which draped down from shelves. But what took my breath away was the view. The living room had a large window at one end leading onto a balcony with views across the city. Isha noticed where I was looking. 'Amazing, isn't it? And me with a fear of heights.'

'How's that working out?'

'I try and avoid going out there, but I've had to chase off the pigeons a couple of times. I just don't look down.'

'Definitely the best tactic.'

'Being scared of heights seems stupid when I think about what happened.' She shook her head.

I barely recognised her from the desperately unhappy woman on the train. Isha is pretty. She'd put on a bit of weight, which suited her, and her black hair was glossy, nails painted bright colours, but the biggest difference was the frequent smile on her lips. She offered me coffee or tea and I settled for a glass of water before sitting down at the table. Star, now a toddler, was having a nap.

'This is temporary. A charity got me the place, and I was sharing with another young mum, but she's moved on. When Dad moves down, we're going to get a place together. But in some ways, I'd like to stay here. What's been great about it is how safe I feel. My own fairy tale tower. The police even arranged for extra locks on the door.'

'Have you been threatened by supporters of the hijackers? Or is it your ex, Zain, you're still frightened of? Isn't he in Belmarsh?' I asked.

Isha sighed. 'He scares the living daylights out of me, but he's going to be locked up for a while yet. It's his mates I'm worried about. And maybe some mates of the hijackers? Or maybe they're the same people.'

I was surprised. 'Seriously? You think Zain knows the hijackers?'

Isha shrugged. 'I asked that nice policeman, Steve Chambers. People move around a lot in prisons. Some of those men were in the same prison as him at the same time. They might have known each other. And apparently, he's all committed Muslim now – hard to believe, given his drinking, gambling and the rest when he lived with me.'

'What was the rest?'

'Making money illegally. Online, identity fraud maybe, but it wasn't like I could ask.'

So Zain Rhind clearly knew his way round a computer.

'Excuse me for asking, but are you Muslim?'

'I'm not much of anything – culturally Hindu, I suppose.'

I wondered about what she'd said. 'That's a weird coincidence, him knowing some of the hijackers – with you being on the train. You said in your letter you thought you saw him too.'

Isha nodded. 'Yeah. I told the police. Getting off, I caught a glance of the back of a man, something about him... But they looked into it and Zain was definitely locked up when the hijack happened.'

Another mysterious man possibly sighted on the train. But apparently definitely not on it.

'But how would he have known you'd be on that train?' I asked.

'He could've known Dad was going to be driving the train. Easy.'

That seemed weird. Did this guy have superpowers? 'How?'

'Zain used to work on the railways, digital systems. Maybe he accessed the train shift schedules. But I can't prove anything and he always makes me paranoid, so I'm trying not to overthink it, you know?'

Had her fear manifested her abuser, I wondered. I'm sure it could happen. On the other hand... 'What does he look like? I went right through the train.'

Isha shook her head. 'I've got rid of his pictures. Creeped me out. Average height, shaved black hair, olive skin, average build. Doesn't help much does it.'

She paused for a moment. 'He's super smart about all tech stuff. Obsessed. Like he had all these screens and computers at home. I wasn't allowed anywhere near.' She shivered. 'I really don't want to talk about him. It kind of gives him power. Anyway. He was in prison.'

Why did another man who wasn't there seem so suspicious? One could be an accident – but two? It felt like too much of a coincidence. There were explanations. But it niggled.

She paused. 'How are you doing? Are you all recovered? Dad sends his best, he was pleased you were coming to see me.'

I shrugged. 'I'm fine. Bit sick of the online comments.'

'Yeah, I can see it's not great, but there are nice things, that you're tough and stuff like that.'

'I'm not sure it's that nice.' I thought of the dead flowers, and the occasional anonymous threats and challenges to fight 'real' men with the implication that they would hurt me and I'd be put 'back in my box', as one had said.

'But the people who count, they know what you did,' she said. 'Like that soldier Deavey, and Alice and the other ones who helped. You know, Mary's been to visit a few times, the nice woman who stayed with me. She bought some lovely things for Star. And Rita rings to see how I'm going on. That's helped me. I know I'm lucky, that me, Star and Dad are all alive.'

She sighed and looked down.

'How are you and Star?'

Isha immediately seemed more cheerful. 'She's walking now. Getting up to all sorts of mischief. I take her to a nursery three days a week and I'm working a few shifts at the local hospital as a play therapist on the paediatric ward, which I'm loving. I feel like my life is finally starting again. I know he'll be out in a couple of years. But I might try and emigrate to Australia or something. Get away from the monster. Or get a gun. I bet that's what you'd do.'

She half laughed. But I was thinking about connections between Zain and the hijackers. I had to ask. 'Do you really think that the hijackers might have known who you were and that's why they targeted you?'

'When I heard some of them had been in the same prison, he might've known what they were planning and could've helped them with the train stuff. That would have made him feel important. He was sacked by the rail company, and had a massive grudge against them, because of that. And against my dad.'

'Why your dad?'

'When Zain broke my jaw, a few weeks before Star was born, Dad was furious. He went round and smacked him one. It was lucky it happened in the street, cos I think Zain would've killed him, but some passers-by stopped him. Dad's almost sixty. And with his weak heart. It wouldn't have ended well. But Zain will hate Dad for humiliating him.'

I was astounded. No one had said anything to me about Rhind's connections to the 10:12.

'The police know all this? That he's a tech expert with a massive grudge against NorthRail, as well as being pissed off with the driver? That's two big red flags.'

She nodded. 'But they can find nothing to link him to doing anything or helping anyone. And he was in prison.' She paused. 'There I am, talking about the bastard again.'

It was one thing to have a vendetta against your ex – but that doesn't usually end up with organising a train hijack, a bomb and murdered passengers. However, a violent ex, particularly one with tech skills was not to be ignored. I'd had a friend whose ex always seemed to know where she was. He worked in IT. She eventually worked it out.

'I'm sorry. But did they check your phone and computer?' I asked.

'What for?'

'Spyware.'

She looked surprised. 'But that's like in films, isn't it? Spies and stuff.'

'Does Zain play computer games?'

'All the time when he wasn't gambling or doing all the other shit he got up to.'

'I think you need to get the police to check your phone and computer.'

'You think he might know I'm here? But he's in prison, how could he do that?' She looked horrified. The relaxed happy young woman had disappeared. Because of me.

'I don't know. I hope not. Why don't I ring DS Chambers now? And you get your phone and laptop.'

'My laptop got broke when they grabbed my bag from me and threw it down. I haven't replaced it yet. It's in the cupboard in case they need to transfer stuff? And my phone screen got smashed, and because it was an old phone, Dad bought me a new one. That's what he said anyway. Or…' She thought for a moment. 'Do you think Dad might have thought Zain was tracking me?'

Dear Ms Fitzroy,

I trust you have recovered from your injuries. I know you wanted to meet, but I'm not a social body at the best of times. However, I feel I have perhaps misjudged you. Although I don't think there's anything in particular that I can help you with, I did think it was interesting that you talked in your note about everyone having different reasons for being on the train and behaving the way they did. So I will tell you a little about me, not least because I suspect you think I am a certain sort of person, and I don't think I am the person you think I am. Mainly, I am a woman who dearly loves her dog.

Before I caught that dreadful train, I hadn't been on one since my Harry died. Perhaps once or twice a year, we would take a day trip to London to see a matinee or an exhibition. It would be a long day, but we preferred it to staying over and had a lot of fun planning what we would see, where we would eat and so on. We packed a whole holiday into one day. When I lost Harry suddenly in 2018, our small world became my even smaller world. Harry was the talkative, social one. I'm more of a homebody. Harry worked as a bookkeeper at a local engineering firm and I was a computer programmer with the local council. We retired at the same time.

When she died, and as the shock subsided, I became aware of the silence. The loneliness, I suppose. The pandemic saved me, as through complicated circumstances I ended up with Monty.

Apart from my years with Harry, having Monty was the happiest time of my life. Walks in the park resulted in meeting other dog owners, and there'd be doggy-related chit-chat that could carry one happily through the day. In the evenings, Monty and I watched TV together, him across my lap.

I was on the 10:12 that day as it was the anniversary of the first London trip Harry and I made together many years ago. I hadn't been able to manage it before. I'd decided to visit St James's Park and have lunch there, walk through Westminster and down through Whitehall then along the river to Tower Bridge, before getting the bus back to Euston. I could enjoy happy memories of our London trips with Monty for company.

Perhaps my little existence seems pitiful to you. You're one of the modern women, nothing you can't do. If you were a lesbian, I'm sure you'd have a rainbow flag flying from your house, and perhaps you despise Harry and me for our timidity in these changed times. But Harry used to say – what we are is Debs and Harry, who love each other. We don't need labels.

When you snatched Monty, I was upset and still think it was unnecessary. He would have calmed down. However, there were killers on board and I suppose you didn't have time for niceties.

This is a nation of dog lovers, I've come to realise. Monty died of old age just before the trial and I had many kind messages. Now I volunteer at the local dog charity, WOOF, cleaning kennels and playing with the dogs, which has helped. As several people have said, dogs are more deserving of our compassion as they are not killers, unless humans have made them so.

If you put any of this in your book, which I doubt, then I want the text to be agreed with me first. I've taken advice from a fellow volunteer at WOOF, who works at a solicitors, and this is a legal instruction.

Apart from that, I'm sorry you were injured, and I wish you well. I do think you were brave.

Yours faithfully,
Deborah Atkinson

[Clemmie, Don't mind this being included. As for dogs not being killers, foxes and rabbits and even some humans may beg to differ. – Claire]

31
Scotland Yard

Several days later I had an appointment with Steve at Scotland Yard. I'd rung him and asked to talk about Isha's revelations about Zain and we had the usual to and fro about that not being my business, nor his role, even when I pointed out that she emailed him giving her permission. It was a polite no. So I was surprised a day later when a text popped up saying he'd meet me.

I knew he liked me; we had somehow hit it off; perhaps the contact we'd maintained while I was on the train meant we shared something. I don't know. Sometimes you meet people in life and just click. It wasn't romantic. I'm no femme fatale and he's not a hard-drinking detective. Or perhaps I've got it all wrong and Steve had been told to find out what I was up to and why.

Steve's a tall, angular man. With his floppy dark hair, large tortoiseshell glasses, striped shirt and dark trousers, he looks more like an academic than a police officer. I hadn't been surprised to learn he'd come in on the graduate scheme. He seemed tense as he joined me in the small anonymous room where I'd been taken, and I told him so.

'You make me tense, Claire,' he answered with a smile. 'I've got ten minutes for you to ask me your annoying questions and see if I can give you any answers.'

'Isha told me you found spyware on her laptop and that you think her old phone would have been compromised too.'

'If Zain Rhind put spyware on her laptop, he could easily have put it in her mobile. She said he'd often take her phone and computer away from her as punishment.'

'So he could have known she was on the 10:12 by reading her texts to her dad and aunt?'

Steve shrugged. 'Rhind was in prison.'

'I know that doesn't mean he's as cut off as we'd like to imagine. Remember I worked in one. Maybe he tells his mates who are planning a hijack to choose that train and deal with his ex and her dad at the same time?'

'Wow, Claire. An entirely parallel narrative – where did I come across one of those recently. Ah yes, the deluded hijackers.' He shook his head. 'No evidence of that. None of them said anything about Rhind. We did ask. If anything, they were puzzled. Abadi said picking Isha was random, she had a baby. More terrifying.'

'And you believed them.' I couldn't keep the irritation out of my voice.

'It's not a question of belief. It's a question of evidence. Five people who don't deny they hijacked a train, in a plot against Deep State, the Chinese takeover of the world, etc.'

'The hijack would be rather hard to deny.'

'Exactly. And that means they haven't got much reason to lie. They were ready for their "martyrdom" – but none of them mentioned Zain Rhind. If we found evidence, we'd be all over it. But we looked. And looked again.'

'He was tracking Isha. She was on the train.' Steve was generally calm, but I could sense my persistence was testing his patience.

'Yeah. That's straightforward.'

'From prison.'

Steve leant back in his chair and sighed, then spoke. 'There's a half-brother called Addi, who's younger, intellectually challenged and in thrall to his big brother. He's coughed to it. Says he was helping Zain because it was wrong for him to lose his daughter. Zain told him how to access the tracker. Says he was keeping an eye on Isha so they'd know where the baby went, his niece.'

That did make sense.

'Why was Zain in Belmarsh? Cat A. Isn't that unusual for his assault sentence?'

Steve shrugged. 'It's wherever they've got a bed, nowadays. He's somewhere else now. Claire, don't waste your time running after red herrings, causing chaos. The hijackers were found guilty and sent down for a long time. CPS have grins on their faces – and that's a rare sight. Justice was served. Zain Rhind is still in prison for what he's done, and we are talking to Isha about the possibility of additional charges, evidence based, over the tracking software. We don't see Zain as the big brains, or any kind of brains involved with the hijack. Did he know about it? Possibly. Did he give them information about trains? Possibly. Was he the mastermind? No. I think a group of sad losers found each other online, talked each other into more and more crazy theories and ended up on that train, probably pushed along by Targut and Abadi, along with Ellwood's revenge fantasies, and encouraged by the nonsense websites online – all the incel, xenophobic, Deep State, red pill *Matrix* stuff. They are just the kind of men to be sucked in.'

He was right. That's the great thing about conspiracy theories, everyone's welcome. Access from all areas into these unreal worlds.

Steve looked at me. 'You do not want to be responsible for undermining a completed and successful case by walking over everything with your size sixes.'

'Six and a half. I'm not investigating, Steve, I just…'

'What?'

'It doesn't feel right. Jay Afiri, Ellwood, Shane Rees – they're not much more than kids. Boys being told what to do.'

'Exactly. By various someones, or AI, writing shit on a computer in a dark basement any place round the world.'

'And Rhind was definitely locked up on the day in question?'

Steve sighed again. 'Please, Claire. Let it go. He was under observation all that day.'

With vague reassurances that I'd mind my own business and keep in touch, I got up to leave and Steve accompanied me through the police HQ to the door. The offices were largely open plan. Was it my imagination, or did I see people eyeing me discreetly as I walked out? Did they know who I was? Or was it paranoia? Walking down another pale green corridor, a forty-something woman in a smart black uniform with silver buttons glittering paused in a conversation she was having with a younger man, gave me a brief nod and muttered: 'There should be a George Cross with your name on it.'

Steve raised his eyebrows as she walked away. 'Wow. ACC and a fangirl.' I looked again, it was June Heatherington. And I assumed she'd hate me.

It was only when I was home with a cup of tea that I thought about the odd way Steve had referred to Rhind's imprisonment – under observation all day. Why not just say locked up?

32

Belmarsh

If Jim had been around, he would have tried to stop me obsessing. But he was away visiting our son. I had been supposed to join him, despite our now semi-separated status, but decided there was too much unfinished business for me to feel comfortable about leaving the UK. Perhaps he left because my obsessing was driving him a little mad and he needed a break from the whole hijack thing. I didn't blame him: I'd have loved to take a break from the 10:12, but try as I might, couldn't let it alone. One train ride changed my life and had, additionally, left me with the kind of notoriety which made ordinary life difficult. No one in their right mind would employ me. I had killed people. I found myself waking in the early hours and going out for a walk or run as it became light and the streets were largely empty. I tried to make yoga a habit, and failed; podcasts, TV, films, none could keep my attention. My mind kept returning to the men who had risked everything to hijack the 10:12.

Twenty-seven-year-old Jay Afiri, in care, then prison, on the run, now dead. Why hadn't he been enjoying his freedom, or concentrating on keeping it, instead of getting involved in something that would almost inevitably end badly for him, let alone everyone else? Although I doubt he ever imagined it would lead to his death.

Adam Jefferson and Mo Abadi were more understandable perhaps? Both in their mid-thirties and not long out of prison, each had a history of violence – but again, what had led them to decide it was a good idea to become involved in what could have ended in mass murder? Were they psychopaths, religious fanatics, conspiracy theorists or a mixture of all three?

Shane Rees, at twenty-two, was the baby of the lot. He had been a chemistry student when he was convicted for working in an illegal drug lab, a hard leap from university to prison. And then surely an even harder leap to hijacker. I recalled his expression when we came face to face, how he looked like he couldn't believe what was happening, his eyes blinking behind his glasses as if he'd just realised he'd got on the wrong train. The boy who had helped Isha on the station concourse. How did he fit in?

Sim Targut, 28, people trafficker, drug dealer and gang enforcer who looked and acted like he didn't care who he killed. Probably a psychopath. Probably enjoyed it.

Joe Rodrigues, 29. Convicted drug dealer. History of online abuse of women, no history of physical violence and had initially engaged with the court. Nasty misogynist. Probably weak and insecure. Steroid addictions. He seemed to not quite believe what had happened. Until he suddenly shut up.

Lee Ellwood, 29. Full of bitterness, anger and self-aggrandising vengeance – but to take rejection that badly was surely a stretch. There was what he said in his so-called manifesto, shown in court, about not all of the men having the same values. But then none of them seemed to trust each other. And in the end, no one did betray them. Or did they? Were they expecting help?

Ellwood had started well at NorthRail, but after a year or so things began to go downhill. He found getting up in time for shifts difficult. The police uncovered a strong weed habit, which he'd more or less been able to fit around times in the cab in case of blood or urine tests, carried out occasionally by NorthRail. But the weed hadn't helped him retain the information from his training. He was also in debt due to a late-night online gambling habit, and his psych tests indicated poor attention and lack of judgement in stressful situations. Other secrets emerged at the trial. There was the NoSinoChan connection – he had regularly visited the site to vent his frustrations against NorthRail, and its CEO in particular. The gun had been his father's, a former serviceman who had brought it back as a 'souvenir' after serving in Kosovo and later left his wife and young son, along with the firearm, when he emigrated to New Zealand. Ellwood boasted about it, in dark little online corridors. There had also been links to IED-making instructions on the NoSinoChan site, apparently.

A mixed bag: Jefferson and Abadi had expressed some religious sentiments, but with backgrounds that didn't suggest any deep convictions. As for the others, there were shared attributes: violence and criminal activity, misogyny, and most commonly, shared prison time.

I'd known prisoners serving long sentences for violent crime when I was teaching in Belmarsh. A percentage of those men would be released and commit acts of violence within months, sometimes days, and be back inside before their porridge was cold. But others I'd never see again, particularly if they found the right support.

Targut and Rodrigues I would put in the first group. Possibly Jefferson and Abadi. Men marked as dangerous who seemed unable or uninterested in finding other ways to live and who would probably end up dying in prison or on the street. Afiri struck me as a weak but dangerous man, a woman hater and probable rapist; a drug-addled screw-up with a short fuse and anger issues. Perhaps he shot Patrick Harbour in order to prove himself to the group. But we would never know for sure. Ellwood might have been late to the party, but he was generally regarded as the ringleader, perhaps it had all been his idea – but we couldn't ask him either.

Now, after the trial, several of the culprits were in Belmarsh, the very same high security prison where I had worked, and which was the Ministry of Justice's popular choice for the incarceration of terrorists. They had largely stonewalled in court – but might they open up to me? Extremely unlikely. But while there was the slightest chance of a 'maybe', I would do what I could to try and talk with them.

I applied for visiting orders. With the trial over, now locked up and having to come to terms with their long sentences and new lives, perhaps they'd be more talkative. What did they have to lose? Maybe status. All prisons have hierarchies, and in some it's the gangs and others the militant Islamists at the top of the tree, a position once held by the IRA and before that, a long way back, by bank robbers. Perhaps they had kudos from some sections for the supposed motives for their crime, and that could carry a lot of weight, and more particularly protection, in a prison. Which after all is what hierarchy is all about – protection and power.

I left it a few weeks, but there were no responses to my requests. Either there was nothing in it for them, or they weren't talking on principle, or it was fear of losing their status. But I had another card up my sleeve. Although it had been years since I worked there, I still had contacts, some of whom had been in touch to wish me well when the 10:12 was all over the news. It wasn't hard to get a message through, asking for their help. I explained that I just wanted to talk about that day and wasn't trying to cause anyone any trouble. Not all my contacts were in the 'going home at night' category. A few were banged up and could vouch for me. I had remained friendly with two prisoners in particular, I'll call them Tom and Jerry; intelligent, thoughtful men, who had taken a wrong road early in life and ended up in prison with hefty and justifiable sentences. Neither of them now thought they had been incorrectly sentenced. Both were rather capable artists, in different ways, and had used their time to grab whatever education they could. These prisoners were trusted by the staff, but more pertinently they were trusted by most of the other inmates. I hadn't been great at visiting, but we had exchanged letters, and over the years I'd sent in various books and magazines that I'd thought might be of use or interest to them and helped arrange for their work to be exhibited and sold on the outside. Not that they'd see the money, it had gone to a charity, but it established their reputation, which should help when they finally got out.

When I contacted Tom and explained my situation, how I couldn't really understand what had happened and it was driving me nuts, he replied saying he'd listen out for anything about them, and perhaps talk to them if he thought there was a chance they might be persuaded to see me. He'd enrol Jerry too, he said. He welcomed having a bit of a mission, something to relieve the monotony, but told me not to hope too much. This is what our exchange meant, but it wasn't committed to paper (or spoken of on the phone) in such direct terms, or the prison authorities would have probably stopped us communicating. It was versed somewhat differently, in a way that hid the real meaning unless you knew how to read it. I also used my married name – which Tom and Jerry knew, as that was the name I had taught under.

A few weeks later a message got through. Targut, Abadi and Jefferson walked tall, but to try a request again with Rodrigues and Rees who were in a different wing – and eventually I received replies. The visit was on.

Belmarsh is close to the Thames, surrounded by industrial estates, marshes and the large 1960s housing development Thamesmead, which was used as the location for the controversial, dystopian film *The Clockwork Orange* in the 1970s. Despite the thousands of additional new homes that have been built along the river corridor since I'd worked there, the area still maintains a certain wildness: windswept, open skied with patches of remaining marshland among the building sites. It wasn't hard to imagine the prison hulks, overcrowded decrepit ships brought into use due to overflowing gaols, that had been moored close by on the river in the nineteenth century. But all that disappears when you go inside. Outside is irrelevant because you can't see it; apart from snatches of the sky when you're taking limited exercise in the yard, or, if you're lucky, very occasionally from a window. What you see are walls, corridors, doors and bars. But none you can order a drink from.

Memories came flooding back when I stepped through the gate into that sealed-off world. I remembered the times when the authorities declared a lockdown after keys had gone missing. No one was allowed to leave; not guards, teachers, even the governor, until everything had been checked, which could take hours. I'd have to call Jim from the prison landline if the kids needed picking up. I registered the distinctive odour of a prison, which to me was the smell of hopelessness, but was probably caused by a lack of fresh air and lots of bodies. When I'd first started working inside, I developed migraines, and almost gave up in the first month. The bleakness was palpable. But as I came to know my students and discovered unexpected talent and curiosity among them, I began to accept the surroundings like an old lag. Until the day came when I realised that I needed to escape. But that's another story.

Permission to visit Rees arrived and I booked a date. My first impression was that the prison was much the same, but bigger, and I could see more tech in the shape of screens, keypads and cameras. Whether they would allow me in had caused anxiety, but the staff dealing with visitors had been privatised and none of them were from my time. I'd also changed my appearance again, just a little, since the court case and no one seemed to notice me. I knew the procedures, so was prepared for the search, the handing over of the phone, the photographs and biometrics, the queues and the waiting. Visits were limited to one hour. With over 900 prisoners incarcerated on the site, it was busy.

The walls were painted a pale pink with some interesting prison art but mainly landscapes and pictures of flowers. To me, that would be a painful reminder of the loss of the real thing. Guards were dotted around the perimeter and were watchful but not overly intrusive. The tables were perhaps a metre away from each other so it was possible to overhear what was going on beside you.

With his black hair cut tight to his skull, Rees looked even more like a sixth-former, a boy who had seen very little daylight in the last year or two. We faced each other across a battered laminate table. I'd bought him a coke and a chocolate bar, and a cup of tea for me. His glasses were broken, taped with a sticking plaster, and behind them his brown eyes moved around, seldom resting in one place for any time and only glancing at me occasionally.

'What do you want?' he asked quietly, unwrapping the chocolate bar.

'If you send me your prescription, I'll get a new pair of glasses sent in.'

He looked at me. This young man with a twenty-three-year sentence, about the same length as his life outside. He'd not injured anyone, not physically anyway, but he'd been part of the conspiracy.

'What do you want?' he repeated.

'I suppose I want to know why you didn't tell the whole story in court. What you did say didn't make sense. Even you didn't look convinced.'

He shrugged and said nothing.

'You agreed to my visit.'

He shrugged again, his hand twitching. 'I'm only seeing you because someone suggested it would be a good idea. Prison's boring, when it's not horrible, and I get a coke.'

He drank from the paper cup.

'And you don't get many visitors.'

He looked away, checking the room, who was in there. 'You used to work here.'

I nodded. 'Art teacher. You doing any ed classes?'

'Not yet. I will when I can. Maybe.' He sounded detached.

'You might be able to finish your degree online.'

'Yeah?' There was a tiny bit of interest.

'It's possible. I might be able to help.'

'It was chemistry. They'd say I'm planning to make bombs.'

'Was that why you chose it?'

'No.'

'If they are worried about that, I expect there'd be some linked science degree they'd allow you to do, and maybe you'd get merits for what you'd already done. In some ways it's easier now, post-pandemic. So much is done online. So why chemistry?'

'There are always jobs for chemists. I was quite good at it at school. And my mum wanted me to get a profession.'

'You missed a lot of classes, according to the media.'

'I don't have rich parents to support me. I was working shifts in restaurants, warehouses, whatever I could get. Some students never have to work, they have an easy life.'

'Then you found a more lucrative income stream that utilised your knowledge of chemistry making illegal drugs that ended up with you going to prison.'

He stared at me. 'What do you want? To rub my nose in it? Remind me how shit my life is? I don't need reminders.'

That was true. I paused for a moment. 'Speaking of money, I've put twenty quid in your account. Should buy you a few canteen treats. What I want is your help. To find out what really happened that day and why.'

'You were there too. And at the trial.'

'I was watching you, in the witness box, your eyes kept on flicking to the gallery. Was someone there, making sure you didn't say the wrong thing?'

He sat back and looked down. 'I was looking to see if my mum was there.'

'Was she?'

'No. Don't want nothing to do with me. She wrote, says I'm no longer her son.'

'Things change, over time.'

'You don't know my mum. Great believer is my mum. God's told her to abandon me, she said. But she'll "pray for my damned soul".'

He said this in a Jamaican accent, and I remembered his family was from the West Indies.

'Christian?'

'Evangelical. At church most of Sunday. Big collection of hats.'

'I expect you've caused her a lot of embarrassment.'

Rees snorted. 'Forget embarrassment: shame. I've brought shame and misery upon the family.'

There was pain in his voice as well as anger. I let that sit for a moment. 'I suppose you have, Mr Rees. You've got other family apart from your mum, haven't you?'

'Sister and brother, no dad around, certainly not one that would want to own it now.'

His eyes continued to scan the busy visiting area and suddenly he became more agitated. 'What's this about? I don't want to talk about my family with you.'

'I'm trying to understand why you got involved with the hijack. You just don't seem the type.'

He shrugged. 'Your problem.'

'No. You're the one in here until you are a middle-aged man. If you survive that long.'

He looked over his shoulder, an almost involuntary twitch, then muttered, 'Your visit ain't gonna make me survive any better.'

I looked down and fiddled with my hair, twisting my head, so that my hand was partly blocking the view of my face as I spoke quietly. 'When we finish up, you should stand and tell me to fuck off. If they ask, say I'm writing a book about the hijack and you thought you'd try to find out what I was going to say. If they ask why you agreed, say your lawyer told you to, and your mum. She does, by the way. She thought it might be helpful for you to talk to me. I met her last week.'

That really got his attention. 'How is she?'

I sat back. 'Sad. Missing you. They don't understand either. Your sister Chanelle is doing OK. Working in a nursery where they don't know about her link to you. She told me to tell you she still loves you.'

'I don't want them to see me here.'

I didn't tell him his mum's sadness was still tempered with anger at what he had done. 'I think you'll get a letter soon.'

'What about my brother?'

'Not so good. He got some shit at school, so he's moved and gone to college, where they don't know he's your brother. Your mum thinks he'll drop out. He's not been the same, since it happened. The police questioned him a lot. She's worried about him.'

He frowned and rubbed his face, he seemed overwhelmed by the consequences of his actions. He'd had enough. 'Why are you visiting my family? You've no right...'

But he tailed off half-heartedly, then stood up. 'Fuck off!' he shouted and kicked his chair.

As he was told to quiet down by the guard, he looked at his shoes and muttered, 'I don't want them hurt. Leave them alone.'

The newspapers had found where the hijackers were from almost immediately. Shane's family had lived in their council house for years, and were on the electoral register.

They'd agreed to meet me. I think his mum was still trying to find answers. She couldn't believe that her quiet studious son had ended up where he was. His first sentence had been the result of him being persuaded to use his chemistry skills in an illegal drugs lab – someone's scuzzy kitchen – to pay off debts, largely incurred through gambling. It wasn't a long sentence, but prison can be a dangerous place for a vulnerable young man, and I imagine he'd gone under the wing of someone who had pushed him to fly in a direction from which it was hard to turn back, or just introduced a lonely and scared boy to the world of conspiracy theories. Now perhaps he could be kept in line with threats to his family, but threats from whom? Perhaps just the whole prison omertà thing. I still couldn't work out what Shane thought he was doing on that train and why.

But Rodrigues didn't seem vulnerable in that way. My prison friends must have continued their efforts because before long I received a message that Rodrigues would see me, but not in the public visiting hall. I pulled in some favours and some days later found myself in a small dingy room in a different part of the prison. Rodrigues was waiting for me, with a guard at the door.

33
Rodrigues

He was sitting at a table facing me as I walked in. The window was opaque glass – light but no view, walls pale blue and unadorned. Inset into one wall, a sheet of dark glass reflected the room. I had been advised we would be watched, but not recorded, as a security measure in case of any violence. This was highly unlikely, given that Rodrigues was cuffed to the table, clearly regarded as more of a risk to me than Rees. An opinion I shared.

I could see he'd been hitting the gym or exercising hard in his cell. He'd put on weight since the hijack, and it wasn't fat. Stretching, he did some shoulder rolls to emphasise his physical strength, in case I had any doubt, so something of a peacock, then. There were intricate tattoos visible on his arms and neck, bulging out of a blue Adidas T-shirt. He must have been behaving; you don't get to wear your own clothes in prison unless you follow the rules. He was still wearing the grey prison-issue jogging bottoms, maybe he kept his own trousers for best. He looked at me disdainfully from under hooded eyes.

'Like the hair,' he said. 'Knocks years off. You could be seventy.'

'Thanks,' I smiled. 'You're looking dandy yourself. Prison must suit you. Just as well, I suppose.'

He gave me a hard look. That didn't work either.

'What you got for me?'

'I've put twenty in your account. Buy you a few canteen treats.'

He snorted. 'That's it, is it? Biscuits and bodywash. Great.'

'Were you stitched up?'

That got his attention.

'What do you mean?'

'Simple really, were you expecting the 10:12 to go down the way it did, and if you weren't, what were you expecting? What had you been told?'

'It went the way it went.'

'It is what it is. What will be will be. *Que sera sera.*'

'What? You got the dementia or somethin'?' There was the wrinkle of a frown, and he glanced at the one-way window.

I sighed. 'Why bother stating the obvious? Of course it is what it is, and it went the way it went. That's how history works. But *why* is what's important, isn't it? For you too, I'd have thought. You've got a hell of a long time to mull it over. Twenty-three years, isn't it? You'll be well in your fifties by then.'

'Time off for good behaviour. I could be in my forties. That's like ancient history to you.'

He was working hard to keep a wall up. But he had agreed to see me. Then again, perhaps a visit from me was marginally better than looking at his cell wall.

'Why the tedious snark, Mr Rodrigues? I came here to find answers that might also help you.'

'How's that gonna work exactly? Like, how's helping you, even sayin' I could, going to help me, apart from providing a few chocolate bars and some better shampoo?'

'There are always deals to be done.'

'What, you'd throw in the conditioner?'

'Sentences can be looked at again,' I said, wondering if that was true.

'Yeah. But anyone looking again is still going to be looking at a gun.'

'Who gave you the gun, by the way?'

'Just appeared in my hand.'

'Was it Zain Rhind?' It came from nowhere. I suppose I just wanted to see his reaction to the name. I find it hard to let things go. I suppose I should speak to a therapist.

He paused. 'Who's that then?'

'I thought you might tell me.'

'I'm supposed to know him?'

'You were in prison together. Forest Dean for a bit.'

'You meet all sorts in prison. They come, they go. I don't usually bother with names.'

'Not even the men you share a cell with?'

'Shared a lot of cells. Can't tell my cellies apart. See, they all wank, fart and moan too much. That's cellies for ya.'

Another brick wall.

'So why were you on the 10:12? And why did you attempt to hijack the train?'

'Like I said at the trial. You heard.'

'But you started to say something about it not being what you'd signed up for?'

'Well, life's full of surprises isn't it. Nobody expected Ninja Gran.'

'I'm not a gran, or even a ninja for that matter, but never mind. If you hadn't met resistance, what did you expect was going to happen?'

'What do you think?'

'I've no idea. Seems mad to me. That's why I'm asking. Did you want to kill everyone on the train?'

He looked away. 'No.'

'Who did you want to kill?'

'If people had done what they were told, people like you, no one would have been hurt.'

'But you planned for the train to crash. And the IED.'

'Who said it would crash? And there was no fucking IED.'

'Of course there was. There was an explosion, remember.' None of the hijackers had seen the damage it had caused, perhaps only seeing was believing.

'Planted. Fake news. You know that and you're lying, or you're stupid.'

'Were you told it was a bluff?'

'S'obvious.'

'You're wrong, there was a bomb and I have no reason to lie to you about it. In a box of nappies in the baggage space behind the driver's cab. I saw it. You were at the trial. You saw the photos of the damage it did to the carriage and the railway bank—'

He interrupted. 'Yeah. So easy to fake. Like, the train exploded, didn't it? Oh no, it didn't, it didn't stop. Funny that. Believe everything you're told, and you think you're so fucking smart. Women believe any shit.'

'I saw what it did. The smashed glass hurt a lot of people. Killed someone, remember? And I was there when they threw it out the window. I heard it go off.'

'Course you did.'

I gave up. 'What was the plan, if it didn't involve IEDs?'

He shrugged then spoke softly. 'Said all there is to say about that, innit.'

I waited a moment, and then began to put my jacket on. The muddle on the train, the mixed motives – what had they been thinking?

'You agreed to see me, in more secure conditions than the visiting hall. I'm wondering why. And you haven't mentioned religion since I've been in here, although you did on the train.'

'My religion, my business.'

I tried again, anything to get him to open up. 'So you're happy here, are you? Happy the way things turned out?'

He looked at me belligerently. He wasn't going to tell me anything. I stood up.

I couldn't resist. 'Beautiful outside today, by the way. Sunny and warm. Perfect for a barbecue.'

Finishing buttoning my jacket, I glanced at him again. He was staring at the table. He looked lost. His eyes met mine and he glanced across to the one-way screen. Then back to me again.

'I'd stand if I could.' Some of his bravado was back. 'Always taught to be polite to old ladies.'

He swivelled his eyes to the screen and back.

'So why did you hijack the train, Mr Rodrigues?'

'God told me to.'

'You got a phone call, an email, or was it a personal visit?'

'Don't mock my religion, old lady.' This was said half-heartedly.

'Sorry if I offended you.'

I walked to the door, knocked once and it was swiftly opened.

Looking over my shoulder, I said: 'Enjoy your chocolate.'

His face, turned away from the screen, was desolate. Suddenly he stood up and began shouting.

'I'm not a fucking slave, get these fucking chains off me!'

He was pulling his arm, attached to the ring and yelling at the top of his voice as I was quickly hustled out of the room.

To: Claire Fitzroy
From: Loretta De Silva
Subject: Anonymous letter

Hi Claire,

Attached is a copy of the letter I left the messages about. Please let me know what you want to do about it. Were you really trained by MI5?! I'm assuming they're a tinfoil hat wearer! (Certainly not keen on accuracy when it comes to names.)

Clemmie and I have tried to get hold of you on the phone without success. Apologies if you didn't want us talking to Jim, but we were concerned about your well-being. He told us that you sometimes go 'off-grid' and not to worry. We didn't say why we needed to speak with you. However, we would be grateful for a quick response on this.

Best,
Loretta

Loretta De Silva
Editorial Director, Ashgrove Publishing

FAO: Loretta de Silver
Ashgrove Publishing

Dear Ms de Silver,

You may wish to know that your newly signed author Claire Fitzroy is not what she seems. I met her on an MI5 course some years ago where we were being trained in surveillance. I came to my senses and left. She was a detached woman, lacking humour or sociability, and probably did well. I was surprised, and then not surprised, that it didn't come up at the trial. Take from that what you will.

For obvious reasons,
Anonymous

34

Warning

I left the prison after the usual formalities and was crossing the car park to my unfashionable old Prius that never seemed to go wrong so gave me no excuses to upgrade, when I spotted Nancy, leaning on the bonnet, looking at her phone, wearing a dark mac, grey trousers and black loafers. No bag apparent, so I guessed she had a car nearby.

'You Ubering now?' she said by way of a greeting, nodding at my car and putting her phone in her mac pocket.

'Hello. What do you want?'

'I want you to stop. Stop digging around. You could be putting people's lives in danger, do you realise that?'

'Whose?'

'You've got two or three degrees, haven't you? Use your brain. Don't you think we're already pursuing leads regarding NoSinoChan? You could really mess that up with your meddling.'

'How?'

'There are nut jobs on social media who'd happily get rid of people they thought were traitors or the enemy. Baby Rees and Mr Rodrigues in there, for example, could end up, well, ended.'

Rodrigues I didn't much care about. Rees was different.

'Plenty of loonies in prisons happy to do the job. Anyway, there are also the nutters who aren't in prison. Your friends, family? You're happy to put them at risk?'

I caught her arm. 'Have you heard of any threats to my family?'

She shook me off. 'Unfortunately, we don't hear everything.' And walked away.

[Claire, Was 'Nancy' threatening or warning you? Sounds scary! Had she followed you? We may have to clear this, though? Also, I was talking with Loretta, and we were wondering if you shouldn't explain a bit more about getting a private room, to speak with Rodrigues? How did you manage that? It seems to indicate that you have connections high up at the prison – more than a former teacher would, surely? Amazing though! Also, Loretta's hoping for a reply to a letter she sent you? Said to tell you it was urgent. – Clemmie x]

[Nancy was warning me off. Don't know if she was following me, she may have had business there. She was annoyed I might mess up their investigations. Also, prison authorities are super conscious about who can be leant on and terrorised by other inmates, if you are thought to be 'talking'. No one loves a snitch and horrible things happen. I said I was writing a book, so they'd have thought of me a bit like a journalist. They were probably protecting Rodrigues. Either that, or someone on the other side of that screen was tasked with finding out what he was saying to me, perhaps Nancy herself. Much easier than trying to listen in the visitor's hall. Maybe both things.
Reply to Loretta in hand. – Claire]

The interviews were frustrating but revealing. I didn't think either man spoke freely. And the name Zain Rhind seemed to get a reaction. My prison friends told me that Rhind had been moved back again, was well behaved and keeping himself to himself. This was unusual, but he was coming up for parole in the next year which explained why he was attempting to keep his nose clean. I hadn't realised his parole hearing was due so soon and wasn't sure if Isha knew. For her sake, I hoped new spyware charges would keep him locked up.

For various reasons, I was no longer in the family home, although Jim and I were still friendly. I'd moved around for security reasons before the trial and was pleased to find a small flat where I could settle for a while. There was a cheap conservatory at the back with a ribbed clear plastic roof and ill-fitting framed uPVC windows: boiling in the summer and freezing in the winter. However, in spring, with a plug-in heater for cold days, it worked well as a studio and the high-fenced overgrown garden at the back, full of buddleia and ivy, made it feel safe. The birds agreed. On warm days I'd leave the door open and hear blackbirds, robins, a wren, and bought a bird feeder to hang from a misshapen lilac which attracted blue tits and goldfinches. It had brought me some peace, but now I kept on thinking of a man who broke his pregnant girlfriend's jaw.

I called Isha, to see if she knew Rhind was coming up for parole, but the line was dead. Worried, I immediately phoned Steve, left a message and fretted till he rang back. When I asked if Isha had been told that Rhind might be getting out soon, all he'd say was that the police were aware and were taking precautions. I told him I hadn't been able to get hold of her. He said Isha was safe and that was all he could tell me. I pushed about her father, and he said he'd check.

'You know Rhind has a big grudge against him as well, don't you?'

'Claire, it's a domestic violence case. The local police are dealing with it.'

'I'm a concerned friend. There could soon be a violent man on the loose who is out to get her.'

'If he's freed, it won't be for a while, and I'm sure precautions are being taken to keep them safe.'

'Please just make sure they are, Steve.'

I could tell he was irritated, aware I sounded bossy, and couldn't blame him for his reaction. But the next day Isha rang. She sounded rattled. She knew about Rhind but said she still felt reasonably safe in the flat. The police had added extra protection to the door and CCTV. She'd changed her phone and number. I asked her to tell me more about Rhind, and she explained that she had actually been introduced to him by her father.

'Dad still feels guilty about that. But Zain can turn it on. He can seem like a lovely bloke. He fooled me and my dad, and probably a lot of other people as well. They met at the local railway workers cricket club. Dad loves cricket and Zain used to play. Dad always used to say you could trust a cricketer.'

'I know you don't like talking about him, but he seems a mystery and I'd really like to know more about him. It might help us figure out if he's still a threat. You said he might have been involved in identity theft.'

She sighed. 'I know he earned extra money doing jobs on the side for people.'

Could some radical terrorist group have been a client? Had the police missed the connection?

'Like what? What sort of people?'

'He wouldn't tell me.'

Another dead end. Isha thought for a moment.

'I think he believes he's been, I don't know, short-changed, cos he didn't go to uni and people didn't see what a genius he is. He could have gone to a university, he's got A levels, but ordinary unis weren't good enough. He told me he applied to Stanford, Harvard, Oxford, places like that. I don't know if he did or not. Zain's world gets confusing. I'm not sure he always knows what's true and what's not. He always thinks he's the cleverest person around. And he kind of is in some ways. But then there's all the conspiracy nonsense. The world run by… cob something.'

'Cabals?'

'He got worse during the pandemic, it was a government conspiracy, or a Chinese conspiracy. He said the Chinese were taking over the world, that the virus had been engineered and released by them. Vaccines were part of the plot. When the new head of the rail company turned out to be Chinese, he went full on. I don't think he said anything publicly at work, but he was smoking a lot of weed, missing days, working from home, but not really working. Telling his colleagues they were idiots. Then he was sacked. And who else was there to take it out on in lockdown? I stopped disagreeing by then and nodded along like an idiot. Not that that stopped him.'

She went quiet.

'Are you OK?'

'Yeah. Bad memories. Some of that conspiracy stuff seems to make sense, until you take a step back and really think about it. Also, I worked with kids with disabilities, kids that get sick a lot, and parents who have a lot of real problems. It put things into perspective. Zain has no perspective. He can justify anything.'

'Anything?'

'He was making money through illegal online stuff, so it wasn't a big leap for him to believe the law couldn't touch him.'

'You thought it was identity fraud?'

'Yeah, but maybe scams too, hacking? It's not like he told me. Sometimes he'd get really psyched up, you know? Liked to boast. He'd put one over on somebody, or an organisation. He loves that.'

'What about family?'

'His younger brother, Addi. He's no mastermind. Zain used to use him like a servant. Addi's on remand and was inside when the hijack happened. Liverpool, I think. Some robbery gone wrong, threatened someone with a knife. Turned out the victim was not only a kickboxer, but an off-duty policeman too. Typical Addi. But he'd do anything for his brother. Their mum died young, and I don't know what happened to the dad. I think another family, or something. Zain mentioned a half-sister. He never liked talking about his dad and would get angry if I asked. Mad, isn't it. Why didn't I see what he was?'

'Don't blame yourself, Isha. People like that climb into your life and wrap themselves round you before the poison shows.'

'I s'pose. But he was such a bad choice.'

'And you got away. Where do you think he'll go when he gets out?'

'No idea. I just hope it's nowhere near me and Star.' Over the phone I heard her catch her breath. 'I was just getting my life sorted, and now I'm back to being scared again.'

That optimism and humour she'd shown when I'd last met her had evaporated. She sounded defeated. 'I'm so sorry, Isha. If you ever want me to come and stay for a few days, I'll sleep on your sofa, whatever. If it makes you feel safer. Anytime. Or come and stay with me. Just ring.'

'Thanks, that's really nice of you. I've tried to avoid getting my friends involved, because then they become his targets too.'

'Seriously, I think I can handle that. If you need me, just ring, OK? Would your dad talk to me about Zain? Could I ring him?'

'He'll talk to you but not on the phone. He's become paranoid because of Zain.'

She told me her father was staying with his sister somewhere on the outskirts of London. 'He's gone completely old school – anxious about Zain's ability to access anything online. I'll give you their address. He'd prefer a letter. I'm sure he'll say yes. But, Claire, don't tell him I'm scared. I don't want him to worry any more than he already does.'

To: Loretta De Silva
From: Claire Fitzroy
Subject: Anonymous letter

Hi Loretta,

As I said on the phone, I had to check something before I spoke to you about that toxic little note from Anon. To clarify, after my twin was murdered, I felt I had to do something but had no idea what. MI5 had advertised for middle-aged women to be trained in surveillance, on the grounds that they were already unnoticeable. Amazing but true.

I signed up, thinking I could – I don't know – help find potential murderers? I was lost in grief, to be honest, and, long story short, I left pretty quickly. It was a weird time. I've a pretty good idea who wrote that note. She got kicked off the course right at the start for boasting about it in a pub when she was pissed. An off-duty cop quite rightly ratted on her. She wanted my support, and got a firm no.

The security services take a dim view of former employees blabbing about other employees, some of whom might be working undercover in dangerous circumstances. Not me, obviously, but who knows what else she might say? Like me, she signed the Official Secrets Act. I understand she will be reminded of that and will cause no further trouble. Not in a scary way. Just a phone call.

It was a few weeks of my life, which went by in a blur. Afterwards I had grief counselling. I hope that puts your mind at rest – I wasn't an undercover agent. If I had been, perhaps things would have gone a lot better on the 10:12.

Regards,
Claire

35
Joe

Joe Gupta, Isha's dad, was in his fifties and had been a train driver for almost thirty years. His sister's house turned out to be a comfortable 1930s semi in a quiet road, near a busy underground station. His reply to my request had been warm and friendly and I was looking forward to meeting him.

The house was small and well-kept, with a tiny front garden lush with greenery, and wheelie bins kept tidied away to one side. A short crazy-paved path led to the front door which Joe opened quickly after I'd rung the bell – I suspect he'd been watching out of the net-curtained window. The sister had made herself scarce, and Joe and I settled in the comfortable front room with a pot of tea and a variety of Indian sweets and snacks. I'd not been in court for his testimony and it was good to see Joe now, smartly dressed in a striped dark brown shirt with a plain brown tie, and brown leather slippers. His thick dark hair was greying at the temples, there were reading glasses on a chain round his neck and overall he looked fit, if tired.

Pale striped wallpaper backgrounded many framed family photos. We sat on a leather three-piece, me on the sofa and Joe in an armchair with a footrest. A large TV, an ornately carved dark wood coffee table and a few shelves with ornaments including a statue of Ganesh, plus a row of books, completed the room. Joe was concerned about my health, and I briefly reassured him that I was fully recovered. He wasn't forthcoming about his own health, only saying he was fine, but that some ongoing heart problems ('nothing serious') meant he wouldn't be able to drive trains anymore. He was sad about that, he said, in some ways. But he'd had a good run. And he was possibly going to be doing a bit of training for the rail company at some time, and meanwhile he was looking forward to spending more time with Isha and Star.

I explained that I wanted to clarify a few things that had me puzzled. 'I remember the train lurched, seemed to almost stop and then started up again. Was that when Ellwood revealed what he was up to?'

Joe thought for a moment. 'He pulled the gun pretty quickly – remember the announcement?' He shook his head. 'I was trying to think of something, anything I could do. But I didn't want to rush it, and he knew his way round the controls. First thing he'd done was switch off the radio.'

'And the dead man's pedal?'

'Of course, he knew about that. But I eased off it, quickly, hoping it would make him stagger and I'd get the gun. He did – but he shouted that he knew Isha and Star were on the train, and had someone with them ready to…'

He sighed, and I nodded. 'But when you had a heart attack it was too late for threats. He must have been trying to get to the pedal.'

'When you came through the door. The police worked out the timeline. I just remember the pain, and thinking I'd failed my family.'

He looked stricken. I felt dreadful that I'd taken him back to a dark place and took his hand. 'But you hadn't, Joe. You saved so many lives by keeping calm and driving the train safely under unimaginable stress. And, actually,' I added, 'your heart attack meant the train stopped before the station. And if the bomb had still been on the train and we'd crashed into the buffers… Mad, isn't it?'

He brightened up and our conversation moved away from the 10:12. I agreed that his granddaughter was beautiful and clever, and told him about my children. He talked about the death of his wife from Covid. Isha was his only child and his wife had died in the early days of the pandemic. She'd been a care worker, he told me. He seemed to be avoiding the 10:12, or perhaps he just needed to talk about his family.

'Tell me about Zain Rhind,' I said.

'I don't even like hearing that man's name.' He put down his cup of tea, rattling the saucer.

'I understand, but his name keeps coming up, Joe. You know he knew some of the hijackers from prison? I need to know more about him. How did you come to meet him?'

'It were all my fault she got involved with the bastard. The train company has a cricket club. I'm a keen member, although my playing days are over. Rhind was a decent spin bowler. Aye, all spin. That's him. He presents well. But you never know what he's really up to till it's too late.'

'Did you know him at work?'

'Yes. Believe it or not, I admired him. Working-class lad, immigrant parents, worked his way up in digital systems without ever going to uni. A decently paid job. People who worked with him said he were a genius. That he'd go far. But that were never enough for him. Butter wouldn't melt with me, but he kept on having rows with his bosses, and then in lockdown, working from home, he often wasn't.'

'Isha met him at the cricket club?'

'Isha was sad, missing her mum, and I thought he seemed like a good lad – so I introduced them at a cricket club social. Worst decision of my life. Before long, she's living with him, which I didn't approve of, but initially she seemed so happy. I should've done something. But I was still grieving for her mum. Isha had a good job with the disabled kiddies, he had his career, they seemed nicely set up. Little did I know what was really going on behind closed doors. The devil.'

He looked down at his hands and shook his head.

'He went to prison for it, and Isha escaped, all with your help,' I pointed out.

'But if she'd never met him…'

'Then you wouldn't have Star.'

He sighed. 'I hope she inherits his brains, but not his personality.'

'Don't know about his brains. Isha says he's a conspiracy nut.'

'Aye. There's that as well. You're right. Star doesn't need anything from him.' Joe spoke more firmly.

'Do you know anything about his family? Where he grew up?'

'Bury, maybe? I met his younger brother, not much up top, worshipped Zain, and he mentioned a sister, or half-sister, somewhere abroad, like Dubai or something. They were orphans he said. His dad was Scottish, and his mum Pakistani and they'd died in a plane crash when he and his brother were little. Didn't make sense really. I wasn't sure where the sister came in. He made it sound mysterious, but I just thought, little kids come up with all sorts if they don't remember their mum and dad.'

Joe told me he and Isha had sent formal letters to the police and parole board, arguing against early release. He asked how I thought Isha was doing and I told him she'd spoken positively about herself, her job and Star. Joe was starting to look tired and I didn't want to overstay my visit. I suddenly remembered something.

'Joe, who shut the end coach, K?'

'Ellwood, or Nik, I think. It was on the manifest, because of electrical problems. Nothing showed up on the controls, though, but obviously you don't take chances.'

'But it was official.'

'Yes. It happens from time to time. You can't unlink the carriages, so it's easier to run it closed and hope you can squeeze the passengers in. Or they get a refund.'

I nodded. Joe was looking weary; it was time to wrap up. After I was cajoled into eating a few more impossibly sweet but delicious treats, I stood up and wandered over to the shelves.

'Ganesh, isn't it?' I said, pointing to the elephant-headed statue. 'Doesn't he bring good luck?'

'Amongst his many attributes. Intellect, wisdom, also new beginnings. And he's...' Joe thought for a moment, 'a remover of obstacles, you might say.'

'Sounds like a useful god.'

He nodded. 'There's certainly one obstacle I'd like removed. When he does get out, I'll be ready.'

He looked out of the net-curtained windows, his hands clenched. There were pots on the windowsill, a couple of orchids and some busy lizzies. I wondered fleetingly if he shared Isha's love of indoor plants or whether that was the sister. I didn't know what to say to calm his anger. I thought of the dark ripples that spread from an act of violence. They had pulsed through me too. 'Don't let him get to you—'

He clearly didn't want to discuss it and interrupted. 'Here's me going on, how about you? Are you just being brave, or has everything really healed up all right?'

Physically, yes. I stuck with that. I patted Ganesh's head. Like a dark cloud on a windy day, the anger passed, and I left shortly after, not wanting to overstay my welcome.

To: Claire Fitzroy
From: Alice Hartley
Subject: How I ended up on the 10:12

Hi Claire,

You couldn't really make it up, but I was on my way to an accountancy seminar. I can see the yawns now. I was running a session on factoring, but I won't bore you with that. So, yes, I'm a trained accountant with PwC, and I've been at their Manchester office for some years. I had intended to run through my presentation on the train and was nervous as there were a few high-powered people attending, who wouldn't necessarily agree with me.

(I ran the session a couple of months after The Train – and I couldn't have been less bothered at the thought of any disagreement. Silver lining, I suppose. In the event no one challenged me – perhaps they were scared!)

You also said you wanted to know what led me to step forward, as you put it. As well as being an accountant I'm also a rugby player, which means being up for running towards trouble. I'm not the best, but when I was younger, I was county level and I play at a good club now. As a team player, you need to be strategic, thinking about what others are doing and not just the opposition. I love rugby in a way I don't love accountancy, although I know it's a necessary service. But in both areas I enjoy being a team player.

This is sounding like a bloody job application. That might be all I should say, but there is something else. I'll ring and talk to you, before I decide whether I want it in. Or whether you do! So here goes.

It took The Train to make me realise how angry I've been. I'm mentioning this because of how the defence went after you, suggesting you were furious with your husband and that's why you acted the way you did. You didn't seem that angry to me. More focused, if anything. Apparently, it couldn't be just because you wanted to save lives. If you'd been a bloke, of course, it would have been different. Believe me, I've heard all the shit imaginable about being a woman who plays rugby. Obviously, that means I'm a lesbian (I mean, some are, my best friends, etc. – not that it matters) and not a 'proper' woman.

I lived for six years with a man I'll call Jon, because that's the prick's name. We bought a house together in Altrincham and had a cat, Mr T. Jon made it clear he never wanted children, and with mixed feelings I went along with it, because I loved him. Then he dropped the bombshell, he'd fallen in love with someone else. Five months after he left me, Jon and his new girlfriend, eight years younger than me, became parents to a baby girl. He kept the cat too.

My initial pain and shock gradually turned to anger, and I think it had been simmering away until we took action on the 10:12. When an option in life is taken away from you, perhaps you think about it more, and I was surprised to find myself deeply hurt to be denied the possibility of becoming a mother, given what fertility rates are like when you're nudging forty.

I don't want to use the word catharsis for the horrible things that happened that day, but at least I was able to use the anger for a good purpose, instead of letting it rot inside me. My best friend Lal told me I was failing at dating because any man who spent time with me could sense I was ready to explode. I was pissed off with her at the time, but she was right. And I'm not like that anymore, which is good in every way, apart perhaps from my approach to rugby, but then I'm qualifying as a ref and will stop playing soon anyway.

Like you, I think of the people on the train most days. They were so brave. The best people. I hope you can face coming to Nik's memorial, it will be good to see you.

Finally, I know you thought I was an arse for going off-piste, and I was, as it put us both at greater risk. But being a team player, I just couldn't let you go into that carriage alone. Sorry! You were right, it made Targut notice us and caused more problems. I won't forget him threatening to kill me unless you did what he wanted. And I couldn't shut up because I was so nervous! Mind you, least said about your Scottish accent. Seriously, we did what we could. When I saw you right at the beginning, after Afiri had been killed, I could see a woman with purpose and determination and I'm so glad you were on the 10:12 – although I'm sure you're not.

Let's talk on the phone about the personal stuff. In some ways I'd like people to know what a shit Jon was. He'd been seeing her for over a year before he told me. But I'm over it. They're getting married, so he's her problem now. And you know what they say about marrying a mistress and creating a vacancy. And then there's Deavey. Bit of a surprise that, chalk and cheese – I mean, he's actually a United fan while I'm City all the way through. That surprised him, given the rugby. But, weirdly, so far, so good. Really good tbh. Who knows?

Talk soon, and good luck with the book.

Your annoying friend for life,
Alice

36
Digging

The text came through just after one in the morning. But I didn't read it until I was sitting with my morning coffee, watching blue tits on the feeder and decided to check my phone.

> stop or you'll be sorry NSC

I dropped the phone on the table as if the threat could leak out and infect me. It took me a moment to work out NSC – NoSinoChan – then a few more to email Steve Chambers from my laptop. How did they get my number? Admittedly I'd never changed it as the police had recommended, because no one unknown had tried to contact me on it. Which was stupid of me. Joe Gupta had the right idea.

Funny how in a matter of moments a haven suddenly doesn't feel that way anymore. I checked the front door and the back garden and thought of Isha's flat, secure from any break-ins. I took the SIM card out of the phone and switched if off. It felt tainted.

Steve replied quickly and before long I was in his office again, handing over my phone. On the way, I'd dropped my laptop off at a little one-man computer repairs place I'd used before, tucked away in a small unit on an industrial estate. I asked the heavily bearded middle-aged man who ran it to check for spyware, or anything odd at all, and he gave me a price and told me it would be ready the next day, as if my request was the most usual thing in the world. He had an array of cheap second-hand phones for sale, and I bought one, and a SIM card, explaining that someone had got hold of my number who shouldn't have, and he explained how to access my phone book. He was kind and the visit made me feel a bit better.

Steve told me he'd get my phone checked out, but not to get my hopes up as they'd probably used a burner. He'd been in touch with the security services and their combined assessment indicated risk was low, but as the place was temporary anyway, it might be best to move. I'd miss the blue tits, but as luck would have it, a friend of mine with a secure riverside flat in East London on the eighth floor was going to Spain for a few months and was happy to let me stay. I didn't know the area well but thought it would be fine. Jim would have had me back at our old home, but I didn't think that was a good idea. I'd found that I needed time and space alone and wouldn't be great company anyway.

The computer guy was as good as his word and gave my laptop the all-clear the following day, by which time I had already moved into my friend's spare room. I had a new phone number and a new email address. I was good to go and wasn't going to let 'NSC' get to me – probably some inadequate living with his mum who had followed the court case and spent too much of his life online. I'd probably overreacted.

I met Steve in a cafe near his office a couple of days later. In person felt safer than digital.

'Nothing of use from the phone, I'm afraid,' he said over a double espresso and pain au chocolat.

I shrugged, told him I wasn't too worried, and gave him my new address. We agreed it was handy to have mates with second homes.

'The spooks want to know if you're still digging. I said you'd been concerned about Isha, and that was it. Is that true?'

'I'm talking to people from the train – but that's not digging, just pulling together different experiences. It might be a book, if anyone's interested. Why Nik Bhatia was on that particular train, Geoff the paramedic's experiences, that kind of thing.'

'And the hijackers?'

'I feel a bit sorry for Shane Rees, and think he was caught up in something he didn't understand. I told you I saw him helping Isha on the concourse with her luggage before the train set off. I'm worried he'll be picked on in prison. He's just a kid, really.'

'It's too late for Rees, he made all the bad decisions himself.'

'He still deserves to be safe. He didn't hurt anyone.' I paused. 'Could it have been Rhind who sent me the message?'

Steve sighed. 'How would he have got your number?'

'He's a tech wizard.'

'Who is currently not allowed any digital access because of the discovery of spyware on Isha's phone, and only supervised phone calls. I don't think even Gandalf could get round that.'

We parted with him telling me to be careful and keep in touch, but his relaxed attitude made me feel better. A nutter had got my phone number. Happens all the time. Doesn't it?

I had been economical with the truth. For one thing, I had the feeling I was being followed. I tried to dismiss it while wondering why I saw the same people on the Tube at different times. But were they the same? One day at the supermarket, I was convinced that a hard-looking man in his thirties was trailing me – he had next to nothing in his basket. I moved swiftly, shaking him off. Then saw him at the checkout, with a woman and child, laughing as he put the few things from his basket into the overflowing trolley being propelled by the girl. After that, I tried to stop my imagination working overtime. I didn't like to think I was becoming paranoid. Or scared. It didn't fit with the image I like to have of myself. But that policy has its own risks. Just because you're trying not to be paranoid, doesn't mean they're not trying to hurt you, as someone didn't quite say. In my case, it was more a concern that if I let myself be overcome by fear about my own and my family's safety, it might mean I missed the bigger picture. But did a bigger picture even exist?

To stop going round in circles, I had to focus on what I did know. Once I was settled in my friend's flat with its views across the river and the city beyond, I opened my sketch pad and listed the hijackers, filling in what little more I'd learnt from various sources, starting with Jay Afiri. A social worker who'd occasionally been in touch with him after he left care described how during lockdown he had become increasingly angry, believing the world was unfair, that women, Jews and the Deep State were largely responsible for everything he didn't like.

May Leung's appointment just happened to coincide with Ellwood's decline due to his drug and gambling habits, and he decided it was her fault that he would lose his job for imposing unfair conditions on him. That the rules were universally applied, and that there's general acceptance of the 'two chances to pass' rule for the train drivers' exam was irrelevant. He didn't mix with his colleagues and was convinced he was picked on.

Ellwood fitted the lone wolf terrorist model: an isolated, disturbed and bitter man. But then he'd become the leader of a gang?

The general agreement that a bunch of loners, who were troubled and violent men, had been caught up in conspiracy theories and that this had prompted their mad actions did make sense, but Rhind's connection to NorthRail still bugged me. I knew he couldn't have been on the train as he'd been in prison, but maybe he had told them about the trains, or somehow orchestrated it? I emailed May Leung about the end carriage being locked. She came back with the information that its closure had been officially scheduled the day before, and seats reallocated. It had come up on the manifest. But her staff couldn't find any reasons for it be locked, it was just a glitch. Nothing wrong with the electrics. But I remembered Anita saying the lights and heating weren't working. But then, perhaps, they hadn't been switched on. Because the end carriage hadn't played any significant part in the hijack, the police had never investigated.

I couldn't see Rees as a hardened, violent criminal. Steve felt Shane was another young man already trapped in a spiral of drugs and prison before the hijack. To me, he seemed more like a lost boy. When I contacted Belmarsh for another visiting order, I was to discover that he had been moved to a prison in

Cambridgeshire which not only had a bad reputation as a hotbed of Islamic radicalism but housed a special unit for highly dangerous inmates. Several guards and medical staff had been injured in a particularly nasty attack a few years back. I wondered how the boy would cope. In his position, if you don't accept an offer of protection from a powerful group – protection which always comes at a price – you can be used, bullied, hurt or worse, by anyone who decides they want to. As for why he had been moved, I knew these things were part of a complex juggling act in an overcrowded system that meant prisoners could end up somewhere they really should not be.

I emailed a request, suggesting a video call visit if he preferred. But prisoners are only allowed one of those a month and they last just thirty minutes, so I was pleased when I was offered an in-person meeting. All this took a few weeks to organise and, in the meantime, I had some science books sent to him and transferred £20 to his canteen fund.

On the day, I set off early. Cambridgeshire is only an hour or two's drive from where I was then living in London and I arrived to find the prison was on the edge of a pretty, ancient market town with gracious old buildings and a lively river flowing under an old bridge. After lunch in a friendly, peaceful cafe, that without the vegan specials and complicated coffee menu could have come from an earlier era, I drove to the outskirts of the town and a different world. Surrounded by small, tatty industrial parks stood the prison, its harsh, concrete, windowless exterior enough to make any new inmate abandon hope.

The visiting hall was smaller, scruffier and more depressing than the one at Belmarsh. There were no pictures on the walls, only posters with instructions: 'No Touching' was a popular one. There were perhaps twenty tables, and most were taken, with a prisoner on one side, mainly in grey sweats, facing one or two visitors. Rees was alone in a corner, the table next to him empty. If I thought he'd looked scared before, the young man I faced across the table seemed like a ghost of himself. His glasses were still fixed by tape, only now they were also smudged and dirty, and I had to stop myself grabbing them off his nose to give them a wipe. Any chippiness was gone, he was almost friendly, and I realised he probably had few, if any, visitors. He sounded drugged, speaking more slowly than when we last met. He seemed truly a lost boy.

'Have they put you on some medication, Shane?'

'Yeah. Anxiety attacks.' His voice was a whisper.

'Does it help?'

He shrugged and looked round. 'The reasons I'm anxious are still here. I shouldn't be in this place. Make them send me somewhere else. Please.'

His head shifted from side to side, like a deer sensing a hunter.

'I wish I could. Have your family been to see you?'

'Don't want them to. It would freak them out. My mum's written, though. And Chanelle. Thanks. Mum said it did her good to meet you.'

'Did you get the money and books?'

'Yeah. Thanks.'

The polite hijacker. It was hard to reconcile this nervous lad with the shouting man on the train.

'Have you signed up for ed classes?'

'No. Don't wanna be here that long. It must be a mistake. Why have I been moved here? They won't tell me. I shouldn't be here.'

He shook his head vehemently, muttered something, then seemed to catch himself.

'Belmarsh was bad, but this place…'

He was twitchy, not paying attention.

'Shane, do you have your glasses prescription?'

He shook his head.

'Request an optician visit. It's your right. Email or write to me if it doesn't happen and I'll see what I can do.'

He looked at me. 'Why are you trying to help me?'

'Because I'm an idiot? An idiot who wants to know what was really going on. An idiot who thinks that perhaps you had no idea what you were letting yourself in for.'

'Which makes me the idiot.'

He looked at his hands, then whispered. 'This place is a nightmare. There are people here, they want me to join them. They think I'm one of them. They pretend to be your friend, but,' he looked around, 'but they're fucking monsters.'

'You are a convicted terrorist.'

He blinked. 'It wasn't supposed to be like that. It was gonna be exciting, showing people what's really going on.'

'What is really going on?'

He looked at me. Then at his hands, rubbing them together. Then it all came out in a spate of words bursting from his lips as if he'd been holding it in, going over and over it all, waiting for the moment he could tell the world the truth. Only it was said in a quiet monotone, without conviction, like an answer learnt by rote.

'The Chinese government secret takeover, deliberately releasing Covid all over the world and buying up our country. The Deep State plots against us, trying to control our brains through the vaccinations.' He paused, as if remembering. 'The Jews controlling all our money. Women, taking over. Men not being allowed to be men.'

'That's the lot, is it?'

He shrugged.

I leant forward. 'Interesting. Can we break that down a bit? The Chinese government and Jewish people are in this together, are they? And what are we doing, women that is, that stop you being men?'

'Jobs and that. Not you older ones so much.'

Thanks. 'It's not about sex, then. Incels.'

He looked away, embarrassed. Another grievance on his crowded agenda.

'What job do you want, that a woman stops you getting? There are many more male scientists than women, aren't there. And you understand how vaccinations work, don't you?'

He didn't answer. He checked out the room again. This wasn't helping.

'Anyway, that's what you believe. Help me try and understand. Why was threatening to kill hundreds of innocent non-Deep State passengers, with no members of the Chinese government apparent, but possibly some Jews, and obviously a lot of women – a good plan? What was that going to achieve?'

He paused. 'That we couldn't be pushed around. That we would stand up for our rights.'

'But you were being pushed around, weren't you? Someone was doing the pushing, pushing you towards the 10:12.'

He blinked several times and studied his hands. I leant closer and he looked up.

'Shane, seriously, do you really believe all that stuff? Or even if you did then, do you now?'

He picked at his fingers. I noticed blood round his nails, which were bitten ragged. I wanted to grab his hands and hold them still.

'I dunno. Not all of it. It wasn't supposed to be like it ended up.'

He began rocking in his chair and I saw a guard notice, then look at me. I wondered if Shane was neurodivergent in some way. He was certainly distressed.

'Shane, it's OK. I'll stop. Here.' I pushed over some chocolate bars and a coke that I'd bought at the refreshments counter. He stopped rocking, unwrapped a Snickers bar and ate it.

'I suppose,' I said gently, 'I just wondered about the moment when you all decided to physically do something, as opposed to talking online.'

The chocolate seemed to perk him up, or perhaps it was talking about something specific. 'At the meeting. It was in this like sports club, in a field. Cheshire. I went up just to meet the others. We got the message and then were sent the code to get there.'

'The postcode?'

'No, what3words. More accurate.'

I knew about the location code that relates to a map of the world where you can find any place using the right three words on their app. An ordinary postal address might have been just as good. Just less mysterious. I wondered how they had all kept quiet about this at the trial. But then none of them were keen to volunteer information. And 'met online' seemed to cover what was needed for the conviction.

'I don't have a car. Can't drive anyway. So I went by coach, train's too expensive, get to the place near Stockport. I think it's shut up, empty. But we were told another code to get in, you know, one of those security locks. Some of the other guys are there already. First time we met. It was weird. But inside, there's a laptop computer, just a crappy old Acer on a table, and we switch it on at 14:15, like he told us, and he starts talking to us from it. Telling us how it'll work out, and then saying where we can find a gun.'

'Who's telling you?'

He opened the can of coke and took a swig.

'Not even fucking cold. Sorry.'

I realised he was apologising for swearing.

'Did you know the guy?'

'It was Bond.'

He saw my face and smiled for the first time. Now he really looked like a kid.

'That's his handle, it's a joke. From NSC, NoSinoChan. He's, like, the guy who... saw our potential.'

'Who is he? Did you ever meet him in person?'

He smiled again. 'Nah. He's too clever for that. He called himself Bond, but not James. Really clever dude. Like, a brain-iac. So, as he tells us the plan, it's like fucking *Mission Impossible*. Targut argues, wants to know how much money, but Bond says he'll do the negotiations while we're on the train. We're not to say why, cos the Chinese won't want a big fuck-up on their line, so they'll cough. Sorry.'

'Why did you all trust him with the negotiations?'

'Cos it was obvious he was well smart.' He seemed surprised I'd even asked. 'He knew all about cyber blackmail. All the code, the tech things. Stuff no one else could do. And he'd already put money in our pockets.'

'How? Was it a lot?'

'Not talking about that.'

He looked around. I suppose he was worried about being done for something else. And that someone might be watching him. I had to get him back on track. 'OK. I won't ask. I'll stick to the 10:12.'

He nodded slowly.

'So let me get this straight. The Chinese government was going to give you money? Why?'

It was as if I'd opened the floodgates. This boy needed to talk. Perhaps to make sense of it, but he became excited too, featuring in his own adventure story.

'Probably the train company too, maybe. And our government. Bond had it all worked out he said. Hacked into their systems. Showed us some stuff to prove it, like the train company server. He accessed confidential stuff, about their security. He said he could really mess them up.'

'So it was all about money? Blackmail? Money they'd pay for you not to do – what?'

'Not to mess up their computer systems, not to reveal what they were really up to.'

'And not blow up the train with innocent people on board.'

'No. That was just a threat to make them listen. But mainly about, you know, the rest of it. Tell the world we're being taken over. But also the money.'

'How much money?'

'Bond said millions. Because it would fuck them up so badly it would cost them billions. Like their share prices and stuff. The cost of repairs and stuff. Like their reputation...'

He seemed excited, and then frowned, as if it didn't make sense to him. I could almost see an internal battle playing out in his features.

'Why did you all plead guilty, if you'd been fooled?'

'Looks weak otherwise. We did it. Own it. That's what... Gotta own it, take pride. And there are the other brothers working towards the same stuff. Protect them.'

He sat up straight for a moment.

'There were more of you?'

'Doing all the deals.'

The deals that never existed. 'And you never met Bond?'

'Nah. That's not the way these things work. We only revealed our identities at the meeting because we knew we were working together. Some of us used fake names. Mine was Dmitri.'

I thought about his chemistry studies. 'From Dmitri Mendeleev? The Russian who came up with the periodic table.'

'Yeah.' He looked surprised that I would know him.

'Nice touch.' It sounded like a secret club organised by pre-teens.

'How did Bond communicate with you?'

'He had this cool avatar. And he'd made his voice come out like Daniel Craig.'

He opened the Twix and took a big bite. It looked like he hadn't eaten in weeks.

'It wasn't Daniel Craig, though,' he added.

'No. I don't suppose it was,' I said, trying to remove any hint of sarcasm in my voice.

'He told us to open a drawer in this, like, kitchen bit. And there was the gun, and a load of green phones. I picked up a phone and said if you shouted that you could set off a bomb with it, people would do as you say. I'd seen it in a film.' The boy smiled for a moment. 'He said that was a sick way to take control.'

He had another bite of the chocolate bar.

'Targut says what if we make some real bombs. And Bond just says, why waste time doing that when the threat's enough.'

'And everyone agreed, including Ellwood?'

'Targut was grumpy, but didn't say no. Ellwood wasn't there.'

That was interesting, already with his own agenda maybe. Or he *was* Bond.

'So, no explosives.'

'No need. That was the great thing. It was all supposed to be a threat – but no one gets hurt.' That fleeting smile again. He looked about twelve.

Enough of the fairy story. 'But there *was* an IED. People were hurt. Someone died. If passengers hadn't thrown it off the train, more people would have been killed. Remember? At the trial?'

He looked down and started rocking again. I wanted him to know the cost of his actions but needed to know why they'd done it.

'And how were you supposed to escape?'

He seemed glad to have another question, to distract him from the victims.

'Bond said there'd be another brother with access to the cab who knew all about trains and had a fail-safe system to make it stop, that the driver couldn't do nothing about it. Dead man's handle, or something. This other brother was gonna get in the cab and pull the driver off the pedal. Bond said he had chosen the perfect place, where we could get off the train, and there'd be a van waiting. Another team was doing all the bank transfer stuff, then we'd all rendezvous and celebrate. He called us the Brotherhood.'

'Bond' could be talking about himself, Ellwood, I thought. Maybe it did fit. He didn't want the train to stop, though, and there wasn't a van waiting. Otherwise he could easily have made Joe release the pedal by threatening Star. Ellwood must have been on a suicide mission.

'Only that doesn't seem to have happened,' I pointed out.

'Abadi said they didn't get Bond or the other guys. The money's waiting for us, he reckons. So we need to…'

He stopped. He was falling off the raft floating on fantasy river. He muttered more in hope than certainty. 'Bond will sort it…'

He paused, remembering. Then spoke slowly and quietly. 'It went all kinds of wrong. No one should've got hurt. When we were planning, it felt great. At the trial, one of the guys said Bond probably got the money and we'd get our share after we get out. Have you heard anything like that? That the train people paid up?'

I shook my head. How stoned had they all been to believe this crap? 'No one got any money. Who told you that?'

'Can't remember. NorthRail would keep quiet about it anyway. Bond told us companies always do when they pay ransoms. Looks bad for them, if they admit they've paid out.'

I knew that could be true. But not this time. I wondered again about this strange group of men. 'Were you all a happy team, at this meeting you had in Cheshire?'

'No. Targut was whining, he said they'd track us down. And Bond said, not in Panama they won't. Palm trees, beaches, new faces and IDs if you want them.'

'Where do you think he is now?'

'Best guess, a great beach somewhere. But I don't know.'

Perhaps he thought if he said it out loud it might be true.

'You don't think Bond was the assistant driver Ellwood, who got shot?'

He looked at me then. His eyes focused suddenly, as if he was just remembering who I was.

'That you shot.'

I nodded. 'By accident, when he shot me.'

'Accident-prone, aren't you.' He leant forward. 'Bond wasn't on the train. He wouldn't be that stupid.'

A prisoner, a big guy wearing grey sweats and a white kufi cap sat down at the table adjacent to us, and was joined by a visitor, a younger serious-looking Black man. The big man looked over at us. I saw Shane flinch.

I muttered, 'I'm your old social worker, OK,' to Rees. He took a moment, then nodded. We talked about his family for a while, and I made comments that I hoped made me sound like a social worker. Shane played his part, until his anxiety about the man across from us was too strong for the medication he was on, and he started rocking again. Then the other men seemed to become engrossed in their own muttered chat, and Rees looked at me, his eyes full of tears and whispered, 'It's all crazy, isn't it? It doesn't make sense. I'm really sorry about everything, sorry to everyone. Tell them I'm sorry. Can you get me moved? Please?'

I drove home feeling mixed emotions. Most of all, I felt strongly that he shouldn't be where he was. He deserved a prison sentence, not a death sentence. But those thoughts were put aside when I arrived home and found a letter, forwarded from the publishers. A printed address label, care of, a plain standard white envelope. Inside was a postcard with STOP written in large letters on the back. On the front was a picture of Amsterdam, where my daughter was studying.

37
Coincidences

Steve looked at the envelope. He was wearing blue nitrile gloves. He had decided to visit me for a change.

'There was a bit of publicity about me signing with Ashgrove after the London Book Fair. You wouldn't think these people read *Publishers Weekly*,' I said, trying to sound amused.

He looked again at the postcard. 'To be honest, I doubt we'll get anything. The postmark's E3, so London, Bow or Mile End, high-density living areas. Have you told your daughter? We'll contact the Dutch police.'

'She's not there. She's at a university in the States for a semester and won't be back in Amsterdam for months.'

He looked up at me, his eyes twinkling through his tortoiseshell specs. 'That must be a relief for you.'

'It is, not just because she's not there, but also because they obviously don't know that. Which means they don't know everything. But that must mean you think it's serious?'

'Probably not. Your daughter was in Amsterdam before the hijack, you know young people and social media. She would have been easy enough to track down. But obviously we need to investigate and take precautions.'

I thought about that for a moment. Steve said: 'Everything else all right?'

I shrugged. 'I've been getting a bit paranoid, feeling like I was being followed.'

'Driving or walking?'

'When you're paranoid, it's both. I use public transport or walk mostly in London, and after the NSC text, I thought I spotted the same people popping up. But why wouldn't they? Inevitably, the same people use the Tube and the buses on the same routes as me. But paranoia makes it look sinister.'

'What about driving?'

'There's a van, a white Ford, parked up outside where I'm staying. I'll show you, if you like. There's often a bloke sitting in it. I know, there are hundreds of blokes in white Ford vans, and I'll inevitably catch one in my mirror when I'm driving, and I can't say it's always him with any certainty. But when he's parked up, he seems to just sit there, late at night too. I've got the number plate.'

I told him, he checked his computer and nodded. 'Yeah, Mark Layton. His wife kicked him out for getting too friendly with her sister. He's living in the van.'

I was taken aback. 'That's scarily police state.'

'I wish. He was checked out a while ago.'

'Why didn't you tell me?'

'I said we'd keep an eye out, an extra patrol or two.'

'I thought you were just saying it to make me feel better.' Steve did tend to make me feel better. Perhaps it was because he always stayed calm, and his sarcasm was gentle, even when I must have been annoying him.

'So cynical. Anyway, I'll let Nancy and the spooks know about the card.'

'Great. She'll just give me more shit. Look what I'm stirring up. Keep my nose out.'

'She's got a point. They may have missed that your daughter's away, but…'

'Who are "they"?'

'NoSinoChan followers maybe?'

I sighed. 'Could you tell the Dutch police anyway, in case they hear of anything. I'd feel better. Also, please tell Nancy I'm not trying to Miss Marple it. She might believe you. And I want to see if she can help get Shane Rees moved. It's not about investigating the hijack; he knows bugger all. Some fantasy about them all ending up rich with money from the Chinese government, on a beach in Panama, having shown everyone how the world's being taken over. A NoSinoChan fantasy, with some avatar telling them what to do. But, Steve, he is seriously at risk and shouldn't be where he is.'

I was worried about the boy, and felt I had to try to get Nancy to help – she seemed to be the only one who might be able to. I wondered how many NoSinoChan supporters there were in the prison – perhaps my visit had alarmed them and resulted in the card. Maybe it would help her to know that. I'd left her a couple of messages after my visit. Now she could ring, and probably crow a little.

Steve stayed for a coffee and to admire my view of the Thames, and we watched planes landing and taking off at City Airport, while the cormorants perched on an old jetty aired their wing feathers and kept an eye on the incoming tide. I felt better, knowing the police were keeping an eye on my home. As soon as Shane was moved, I'd leave the 10:12 alone. Apart from the book.

Nancy returned the call twenty-four hours later. There were no niceties. 'You didn't take my advice, then.'

'My visit to Shane Rees might have been misconstrued. It was about his welfare. Maybe you need to check out his fellow prisoners.'

'Oh, why didn't we think of that?'

I ignored her sarcasm.

'Shane is every kind of vulnerable, he shouldn't be in that dangerous prison, Nancy. He's a low risk to society.'

'Other passengers on the 10:12 might disagree, given, you know, that he was willingly involved in a violent hijacking. Your limited prison experience is informing this quest for mercy, I suppose. Weren't you an art teacher?'

I could hear the omitted 'just', as if she'd said it. Sarcastic *and* patronising. 'Yes, and my students talked about their lives inside, while they were creating art. Plus, this was maximum security, the sharp end of the justice system, and I'm not blind. But seriously, where he is now, it's even worse. He shouldn't be in there. Come on, even on the prison scale, you know it's a truly scary shithole. Why's he there? If he gets hurt, I'll have to say something.'

'For his own safety, as I understand. The other hijackers. And really, don't make threats, Claire. You're making them to the wrong person.'

She was right. 'What did he do to upset the others?'

'Talk to you? They probably decided he was a weak link. And they were right, weren't they?'

I didn't want to think about that. That I'd put him at risk. I hadn't cared much given what he'd done. Until I met him.

'He's sorry. He's trying to help in his muddled way. There are other options.'

'I don't think he'd thank us for putting him in with the nonces.'

The woman was exasperating.

'That's not the only option, and you know it.'

'So, what has he said?'

I told her all Shane had revealed, and she listened without interrupting.

'I thought you said you weren't digging.'

'He just came out with it. We'd been talking about him getting back into education. And the trial was about justice, not about finding out what actually happened. I've had emails and letters from passengers explaining how they came to be on the train, for example. I'm just trying to find the fuller picture.'

'Claire Fitzroy, truth seeker. Isn't that what the conspiracy nuts call themselves too? Nothing to do with your Zain Rhind obsession?'

'I know he was locked up, but there are coincidences.'

'There often are. That's life. When I was backpacking after uni, I found myself sharing a room on a remote cattle station in Western Australia with a girl I'd never met, who turned out to be the daughter of my mother's hairdresser back home in Wigan. And a few weeks into that god-awful job in that god-awful place, I was bored out of my mind looking at her photos, when I recognised a handsome boy she'd shagged in Thailand a couple of months previously – he was the bestie of my former university boyfriend.'

It was a long speech, but she sounded bored. I said nothing. She spoke again, the boredom dissipating. 'Frankly, it's irritating that you don't think we checked, because of course we did. Mr Rhind was in prison, and although he might have been able to get the odd message in or out, there's no way he could have gone full on digital Fat Controller. Some other dick may have done that on NoSinoChan, or it might be a figment of your poor boy's imagination. We do check this stuff, Claire, very, very thoroughly. And we have way better methods than those available to a rather obsessive, possibly traumatised, art lecturer. Or should I say successful artist. Why don't you stick to what you're good at, and we'll stick to what we know best? I promise to only pick up a paintbrush to decorate my tired-looking kitchen, and you leave the snooping and sleuthing to us. And there'd be an added bonus – no one would be making threats against your family. You could stop putting them at risk. There's a bit of NoSinoChan stuff in Australia too, how long before some Aussie fruitcake connects you to a young English doctor?'

Taken aback by her vehemence and mention of my son, I made conciliatory noises, and we ended the call. Was I putting my family at risk? But I didn't believe everything the spy said. She had a point about Rhind, but no way was Nancy's accent from Wigan.

I didn't try to contact Rhind, as I didn't want to put myself or my family in his toxic, digitally knowledgeable sights. Shane and I kept in touch with a few short letters. Jim didn't understand why, but Deavey and Paul did. They both understood that a vulnerable young person can be swept up into something they only later realise has been a terrible choice. Then the prison ed department told me he'd been moved to another Cat A prison elsewhere in England. I did some checking and was relieved to find that his new home sounded safer than the previous one. A few weeks after that, we had a video call. He looked better, seemed calmer, and told me he'd had constructive discussions with the education department about completing his degree and they'd said it might be possible if he maintained good behaviour.

In the meantime, he'd started some remedial courses. And he had a new pair of glasses.

'Thanks for helping me get out of hell. I mean, it's no hotel here, but it's better. My cellie, he's an old guy, and he's OK. Showing me the ropes, he says.'

'I don't know if what I did helped. The prison service is a mystery. But you got new glasses too.'

He nodded, and was quiet for a moment, looking into his lap. 'I've been thinking about everything. Like, I was just a stupid kid with debts when I first got into trouble and got sent down.'

'From trying to pay the uni fees?'

'No. Online gambling. Thought I was so clever. But that seems like another life. I'd never do that now. I was just a kid with not enough money who believed in the fantasy and got sucked into even more debt. And then – and then it all went to shit…' He trailed off.

'At least you can't gamble where you are.'

He looked up and into the screen. 'There's always gambling. But I don't do it. I wish…'

I waited. He took his glasses off and pulled up his white T-shirt to wipe them. There was the child again, but there was none of the rocking to and fro. He was in control of himself.

'Like, I can say sorry to you. I mean, I am, really sorry. And, see, I wish I could say sorry to everyone, not that it would make it better, I know, but I think I need to stay quiet for now. I mean, I don't know how I ended up here. It's… like… mad, my life. Hundred per cent. But sometimes I think I'll wake up and… Maybe it's a parallel universe and somewhere else there's a Shane Rees with a degree in chemistry working for a pharma company on a new anti-cancer drug, with a nice girlfriend and a flat and all that. My mum proud of me.'

He paused, then gave a sad laugh. 'I hope he's appreciating what he's got.'

He trailed off again. I was sure he wasn't lying. But he had threatened people's lives, and here I was feeling sorry for him.

'My family's been to see me. Chanelle brought Mum. She cried a lot but said God had answered her prayers. I'm a sinner returned to the fold. I'm going to church here to keep her happy, but it's kind of helpful too, with the anxiety and stuff. Chaplain's good to talk to. I've just got to take it a day at a time.'

He paused. 'When I think how long I'm going to be banged up, I want to give up. But my cellie says I can't do that. Day at a time. I can't hurt Mum again.'

To try and cheer him up, I told him I'd put another £20 in his canteen fund, and he thanked me politely. I could see his parallel universe too, how it would run alongside his real life, where he would be locked up for many years to come. I asked if he was going to the gym, and he said no, it didn't feel safe. But he'd heard there might be football happening sometime soon. He hoped so.

Something suddenly nagged at the back of my mind. 'That sports club where you had the meeting, what sort of sport did they play there?'

'Cricket. And what was clever, it was the NorthRail cricket club.'

38

Memorial

Memorial services are usually held some time after a person's death, the idea being that the bereaved will have processed the initial shock and grief and are now ready to celebrate the life of the deceased, not mourn the loss. I'm not sure it always works that way; but perhaps the bereaved still adrift in mourning are comforted by the presence of people around them who also knew and cared about the person they loved and lost.

Nik's memorial was two years on. I'd been dreading it. I've never been that great at socialising in large groups at the best of times, and since the 10:12 I was even worse at coping with a crowd. I hadn't been well enough to go to his funeral and had skipped the formal anniversary event held in Manchester. A few of the squad went. Paul told me he felt he had to be there for those who'd died, and I think the others felt the same. I just couldn't. But I knew I had to go to Nik Bhatia's memorial: for his widow's sake and because Gill's daughter was going to be there.

As it was, I almost turned back. I'd driven up, alternating between listening to a podcast debunking conspiracy theories, 6 Music, and Glenn Gould playing the Goldberg Variations. I flipped restlessly between all three for the first two hours of the drive before opting for silence. I stopped at a services to use the loos. It was busy with people queuing for the expensive coffees and artery-hardening pastries. At the side of the grimy, panelled building there was a patch of worn grass with benches, much of it being used, unappealingly, as a doggy toilet stop. But there was an empty picnic bench, so I sat down, pulling my wool coat around me against the chill of a rather lovely, sunny autumn day.

Sian Bhatia had requested everyone wore colourful clothes, she didn't want her girls to be surrounded by black suits. I've always found the idea of colourful clothes at funerals an understandable request, but hard to pull off. Black keeps things simple. In the event, I wore navy wool wide-leg trousers with a matching jacket, over a floral shirt covered in dusty pink roses, against a blue background, which I hoped was enough to mitigate the dark suit, and I'd thrown my camel wool coat in the car in case it was chilly.

Sitting there in the sunshine, I didn't want to carry on driving north. Gill's daughter Abi hated me, I was sure. I remembered her look in court, and dreaded having the conversation about her mother, who regularly appeared in my nightmares. And if that wasn't bad enough, I'd be walking into a room full of people who knew me as a killer. This fact tends to put me apart from regular people. Some of my ex-services friends talk of it as duty performed – but I wasn't wearing a uniform.

I sat for half an hour watching an assortment of dogs defecating and their owners wrapping the deposits in plastic bags, then stood up. I'd stop at the memorial for half an hour, talk to Sian and her girls, keep close to the squad – then leave. I picked up another coffee and hit the road.

May Leung ensured that NorthRail footed the bill for the whole event. The venue turned out to be a rather grand traditional hotel on the outskirts of Manchester, off the road and tucked away, while the gathering itself was in a charmless but functional nineties-built annexe surrounded by mature trees in the grounds, hidden from prying eyes behind the main hotel. There was tight security, people with lanyards and black clothes who checked names and IDs. Several police officers were on duty as well, plus those who had been invited, including Steve Chambers, so it felt relatively safe.

Luckily, the first people I saw were Deavey and Alice, outside with Ty, who was smoking. Deavey wore a brown sports jacket with a bottle green shirt, and Alice was in a green trouser suit.

Ty looked uncomfortable in a pale pink shirt and navy trousers. Scrubbed up well, I said to him, and received an embarrassed shrug. The squad feels like family to me now. Not instead of my own family but added to it. They are easy to be with. We all know and accept each other's foibles, understanding that our shared experiences sometimes make normal life feel remote. It's not like we talk about that kind of stuff much. It's there – but left unsaid.

We spoke briefly, but I needed to pay my respects to Sian and her family so made my way in. I don't think it was my imagination, but people seemed to part as I approached – with a smile or nod, it must be said. Clearly people hadn't forgotten what I looked like. I wanted to walk back out, and had paused, wondering what to do, when I felt a hand on my arm. It was Paul. He'd got the same dress memo and was wearing a navy suit and light blue shirt, with his concession to colour being a rather beautiful floral silk tie. We exchanged greetings and I explained I needed to talk to Nik's wife. I'm sure he could see I was nervous, and it helped to have him close as we made our way to Sian and her girls.

Pictures of Nik were scattered throughout the room on tables and on the walls: playing cricket, on the beach with his girls, in his NorthRail uniform. I passed Geoff, Dr Patel, Kyo and Jason who were deep in conversation – Jason looking up, giving me a smile – and then I reached Nik's widow.

We spoke for a while, other people evaporating around us. Sian, in a cream and green maxi dress, was calm, and glad to see so many people, she said. Grief was still etched round her eyes, but she spoke with warmth and kindness. Melanie had been unable to come, as her grandmother was ill, but they'd exchanged emails. Sian introduced me to her girls, who were pretty and smart in pink dresses, and attentive to their mum. Then she introduced me to other relatives, and to Nik's cricket friends, and I shook many hands and had to listen to too many people telling me how brave I'd been. To which the only reply was no, Nik had been the truly brave one. There were at least two hundred people there, including May Leung, who came over and joined our conversation. She seemed shy but spoke well and told us that NorthRail along with the other major rail companies were setting up a special award in Nik's honour for acts of bravery and kindness by railway staff. Geoff appeared, then Rita, and I left Sian in their capable hands and moved on, promising to keep in touch.

Joe and Isha were with Star, who was being made a fuss of by people I assumed were NorthRail staff. I spotted Mary, sharing a huge hug with father and daughter. Isha caught my eye and waved. Paul pointed out Miss Atkinson, standing with Tony Rossi, the Tin Can Man, still in a hi-vis jacket. We walked across, and as we got closer, I realised she was holding a puppy in her arms, and Tony was happily stroking the dog. We exchanged a few words, and I patted the pup. It was important to me to know that they were both OK, but Miss Atkinson appeared more concerned about my welfare, which seemed odd, until I noticed my hands were shaking.

I made my excuses and began walking away. Paul tapped me on the shoulder.

'There's Abi, Gill's daughter, over there in the blue dress,' he said softly.

I looked across at the young blonde woman who had blanked me at the Old Bailey. I could see the likeness to her mother. Her eyes met mine, and as I started to move towards her, she nodded, then turned her back on me. It hurt, but I didn't blame her.

The event was taking on an unreal, dream-like quality. There were arrangements of brightly coloured dahlias and chrysanthemums in vases around the room. The soft music was eclectic: sometimes Indian ragas, interspersed with Coldplay, Taylor Swift, and Tamla and soul classics. I reminded myself to breathe slowly. I was here for Nik, Patrick Harbour, the man killed as a result of the IED, and Gill.

There were many conversations: a blur of faces, Paul usually by my side and filling in the spaces when I ran out of things to say. Eventually, needing a break, I went off to the ladies. While I was washing my hands, May Leung walked in. She looked around, as if to check we were on our own.

'How are you now, Claire?' she said softly, in her Scouse accent.

'Not bad, thanks. How about you? Has the trolling eased up at all?'

She shrugged. 'It's died down. They've found someone else to hate, I expect. I did get a lot of positive messages too, which helped. How about you?'

'Don't know. I've closed all my social media. Not something a rail company can do.'

'No.' She paused. 'How are you managing?'

'I've gone back to painting. Which you know, because you bought one anonymously. 'Other Line', wasn't it? With the tractor? And you paid more than the price listed. I asked the receptionist at the gallery to describe the buyer who had made her bosses so happy.'

She smiled. 'I didn't buy it just to help you out, by the way. It's worth it, really good.'

I thanked her and finished drying my hands.

She checked her watch. 'It's good you've gone back to what you love. I've got to make a speech. I still don't find it easy. But this wouldn't be the place to show cowardice, would it? See you, Claire. Good luck.'

I drifted back into the hall, keeping near the door. At one point, Deavey came over and whispered, 'Claire, you should speak to Pat Harbour's sons. They've been trying to catch your eye, and they've come a long way.'

Deavey walked us over to two dark-haired men in their twenties, both in dark suits and black ties, glass of wine in hand. One introduced himself as Douglas, the son who had written and then introduced his brother Rory. We talked for a while, and they clearly wanted to go over what had happened. Somewhat reluctantly, I started to tell them about their dad getting up to help Melissa Ngozi, and suddenly felt sick.

'I'm sorry. I just can't at the moment. Your father was a brave man.'

I had to get away; Deavey could see it and grabbed my elbow, steering me towards the door while making our excuses. I heard one of the brothers say: 'I thought she'd be tougher than that.'

Out of the corner of my eye, I saw Abi watching. She had been standing near the brothers and I hadn't noticed.

When we got outside, Deavey took me round a corner to a low wall and we sat down. In front of us was a thick copse of mature trees, mainly beech and oak, already turning autumnal russet and gold. I no longer felt sick, the overheard comment had seen off my nausea. To Deavey's surprise, I laughed.

'What?'

'I thought I'd be tougher than that too.'

He laughed as well. 'You don't want to be any tougher, it's not good for the soul.'

We sat for a few minutes in easy silence.

'Gill's daughter can't even look at me.'

He shrugged, not sure what to say. 'How's Jim?'

'OK. We see a lot of each other and speak most days. It's all very friendly.'

'Do you think you might…?'

'No idea,' I said. 'We're both deliberately not deciding anything.'

'Yeah, probably best not to rush to any decision.'

'Like you and Alice you mean? How's the flatshare going?'

A wry smile appeared. 'She told you, did she?' He paused. 'I can't believe my luck. And my kids love her too.' He checked his watch. 'She'll be wondering where I've gone, I better go and find her. Will you be OK?'

'Yeah. I'll just enjoy the sunshine for a bit longer.'

He left me on the wall, and I closed my eyes. The weak sun felt good on my face, but I was tired, and worried about driving back. Another fifteen minutes and I'd leave. I felt a tap on my shoulder. It was Abi. She handed me an envelope.

'Abi. I'm so sorry—'

She interrupted, but gently. 'I wasn't sure whether to give this to you. Read it when you have a moment.' She had her mother's eyes. Before I could say anything, she'd gone.

The envelope was simply addressed to Claire Fitzroy.

I opened it.

39

An Old Friend

Claire,

I'm not sure if you'll be there today, and I don't want to talk about this with people around, so thought I'd try writing instead. It's difficult. I did feel that you had some responsibility for what happened to Mum. If you'd just done as she told you, then perhaps I wouldn't be writing this. But Geoff told me what Mum said, and although I didn't take it in properly at first, Mike, my husband, said I should believe what she said: that it was the right thing to do, no one forced her. It's time for me to accept that. Mike says think about who the real bad guys are, and I know he's right.

I know Mum's been recognised as a heroine, but all the papers just described her as an ex-police officer, single mum and grandma. She was so much more than that. I would like you to include something about her in your book. If I can explain a few things, then maybe you and me could have a chat sometime about what to put in?

Mum was a widow. Dad, who was also a cop, died suddenly when I was nine after a heart attack. Mum told me later she almost left the force, the hours are useless for a single parent, but Nan and Grandad lived in the next street to us, so I spent a lot of time with them. I resented her job, to be honest. It was only later I realised two things. One, that I was lucky to spend time with grandparents who loved me and taught me useful things. Thanks to them I make a good Victoria sponge, know how to grow runner beans and have been known to win the odd game of poker. Two, Mum enjoyed being a police officer, but it came at a price. When I was kid, she always went to work with a scraped-back ponytail, and no make-up. Years later, she told me that female officers often tried to look unattractive to avoid harassment from the male cops.

Mum didn't have much time for herself. When I went to uni, she should have been able to pick up a social life, but by then Grandad had dementia and Nan wasn't well either, so she ended up becoming a carer for them. Not that she ever complained about it. She'd batch cook meals when she got home from work and fill their freezer, take them to hospital appointments, and work weekends to make up the time.

You said to me in your letter that my mum was brave, smart and kind. All true. The thing about Mum, though, that no one mentions is that she was fun. She'd do the housework dancing around the room to Meat Loaf (never ABBA) and later house music at full volume, often joining in and singing at the top of her voice. Loved it when I was a kid, totally embarrassed by it when I became a teenager. After she'd reduced her hours, she started electric guitar lessons. And then came the band, which she loved. Called the RPs (Real Police – three of them were retired coppers), Mum was a vocalist and guitarist. Keith, the drummer, was at the trial. He and Mum had been living together for a few months when she was murdered. They were very happy.

She was on the 10:12 because she'd been in Cheshire with Keith for his daughter's 30th. Keith stayed on but Mum wanted to get back as she collected my son from school a couple of days a week. I wish I'd just said to her we'd manage, and then she could have stayed on and come back with Keith. He's still destroyed by the fact that he wasn't with her and couldn't protect her. It breaks my heart too.

Mum had just started living for herself and having the loving relationship she so richly deserved. All taken from her, by that murderer. She was so much more valuable to the world than any of those scum.

I try to focus on all the good times we had, what a great mum, daughter and grandmother she was, and a pretty good rock guitarist and singer too. I'm glad she had some time with Keith but hate the fact that all their plans, a round-the-world trip, more gigs with the band, will never happen. I miss her every day, as does her grandson, who adored her. He's only seven. Perhaps the medal will help, at least he'll know she was a hero. I hope you'll be at the ceremony, perhaps then we'll be able to talk. You're getting one too, aren't you?

Thanks for telling me what happened, how she saved your life and how you admired her. I think I understand now why you did what you did, but I wish the pair of you had never got on that train, or at least stayed at the far end away from the driver's cab.

Best wishes,
Abi

I held the letter gently in my hands. They were no longer trembling. I sent a silent undeliverable message to Gill, then looked up.

'Anita!'

I stood and hugged her – not my style, but rocketing emotions and the occasion seemed to call for it. She smiled. She looked different. Her hair was short, and a pair of large, black-framed dark glasses was on her nose, which had lost the piercing. She was wearing an unfastened beige coat over a dark pink jumper and black trousers.

'How are you?' I asked.

'Fine. Sorry I didn't stop the last time we saw each other. You must have thought it was odd.'

'In terms of that day, probably one of the least odd things that happened,' I replied. But I was waiting for an explanation. 'You came to the exhibition.'

'Yes, the paintings were amazing.'

'You signed the book. You wanted me to know you'd been.'

She shrugged. 'Just in case you were worried. To let you know I was OK. I didn't have your number or anything, and I don't do social media.'

'Have you spoken to Deavey, any of the others? I know they'd like to see you.'

She shook her head. 'No. It was you I came to see. To explain.'

'OK.'

'I'm not legally in the country.'

'I'd never have guessed. Your accent's completely southern counties. Where are you from, then?'

'I went to boarding school in Kent. And university. But my right to remain ran out a long time ago. I just wanted to explain.'

She still hadn't said where she was from.

'The police said it might be something like that. You weren't the only one who didn't come forward. Who was the injured man I saw you with?'

'Him – oh, just a guy I was helping. He'd been cut by the glass and was a bit shaky.'

'Was he the man who wasn't dead?'

'What?'

'In coach D, next to the cafe. You found him.'

'He wasn't dead?'

'No. He disappeared.'

'Wow. He looked very dead to me. No, not the same guy.'

It sounded flippant and I was struck by her apparent lack of knowledge about who died on the 10:12. 'Do you know someone called Zain Rhind?'

She shook her head, with a frown. 'No. Was he a passenger?'

'I don't think so. I mean, no he couldn't have been.'

She seemed puzzled. 'So why are you asking?'

I didn't know what to say. 'No reason, really, just… loose ends.'

There were suddenly voices behind us. She looked over my shoulder, and I instinctively turned. There were two men coming round the corner, deep in conversation, one was Steve. She spoke quickly.

'I've got to go. I hope you're better. I'm trying to find a way to stay legally, and when I do, I'll get in touch. Please don't tell anyone you've seen me.'

She started to move away.

'Where are you from?'

She looked over her shoulder.

'Egypt and Lebanon mostly. And Kent, of course. Good luck, Claire.'

She walked away into the trees. What on earth had that been about?

Steve had stopped and was listening to the other man, some head honcho at NorthRail who dealt with security. I looked back at the copse of trees, their autumn leaves russet and gold. Then walked quickly towards them, following Anita's path.

The patch of mature woodland turned out to be a strip only about ten metres in depth. As it thinned out, I could see an access road, and Anita getting into a parked car, a silver Golf. The engine started and the car moved away, and I tried to memorise the number plate. Anita had climbed into the passenger seat. So not on her own.

By the time I'd got back to the wall, picked up my bag and rooted round for my phone to make a note, I could only remember the first couple of letters. I suddenly thought about what I was doing. Someone had given her a lift. So what? I sat down on the wall, annoyed with myself. Then a distraction came in the shape of Steve, now on his own.

'You OK?'

I nodded. 'Just needed a moment.'

'Who was the woman you were talking to, was she on the train?'

I nodded again. 'I don't remember her, though. Bit embarrassing.'

I'm not sure why I lied, but I suppose it was because Anita had asked me not to tell anyone she'd been there, and I assumed she ran the risk of being kicked out of the country, which didn't seem fair given the circumstances. Sorry, Steve.

'Can we have a quick chat?'

I nodded and he sat down beside me. He was holding a glass of wine, and although he wasn't drunk, I had the feeling it wasn't his first.

'Claire, I've been thinking about your situation, your need to know everything. I do understand that. Really, I do. But one of the things I've learnt as a police officer, is that in complex cases you often don't discover everything. In fact, the criminals involved often don't know everything themselves. I think you should decide that we know enough, and that you and your team did a good thing and saved lives. A far, far better outcome than might have been expected. We probably know as much about what led to that day as we ever will. And please try and accept that. For your own mental health, apart from anything else.'

I hadn't expected that from Steve and thought about what he said before I replied. His version was better than Nancy's and expressed genuine concern. But. 'It's not Agent Nancy who's put you up to this is it?'

He shook his head. 'You see, there you go, looking for conspiracies. No, Claire, I'm a big boy and came up with that all on my own.'

I could see he was telling the truth and smiled. 'Sorry. I know there's sense in what you've said. I'll take it on board.'

After a quick goodbye to Deavey, Alice and Paul, I left. Traffic was heavy and I felt weary and unsettled. Paul had wanted to come with me on the return journey, but I'd said no, now I wasn't sure why. Despite the kindness and warmth of the event, and Abi's letter, the afternoon had been upsetting. Seeing all the people from the train had brought vivid and unwanted memories to the surface. When I noticed the car was edging over 90 mph, I realised I wasn't fit to drive. Near Knutsford there was a Travelodge at a services, and I pulled off the motorway, became confused by the layout, and eventually took a wrong turn into the services car park, where I stopped, to take a moment to calm down. And there was a silver Golf, a couple of parking lanes in front of me, the number plate starting with GL. The only letters I remembered from the car Anita had climbed into.

There are probably hundreds of silver Golfs with a number plate starting GL. But I couldn't help myself. I really wanted to know who was driving. Might it be the man in the black mac? And if it wasn't, maybe I could forget all about him. Fortunately, the car park wasn't full – but wasn't empty either. I moved into a space closer to the Golf, making sure I wasn't conspicuous. The car was empty, but moments later, a woman came out of the services and got into it. Even spies have to pee. It was Nancy. Pure coincidence, no doubt, that the silver Golf she was driving had the same first two letters on its numberplate as the car that Anita had stepped into. Pure coincidence that she was only twenty miles or so from the memorial. Anita seemed to have disappeared. She had form there. The Golf drove off and I felt a slight moment of triumph: I'd outspied a spy.

40

End of the Line

I checked into the Travelodge, took off my suit, fell into bed and was asleep almost immediately. Sometimes anonymous places can be easier to sleep in than your own bed. But I woke suddenly, thinking about Anita, the man who wasn't dead, and Nancy. Staying at a twenty-four-hour services has its advantages. At two in the morning, having pulled on trousers and a coat, I wandered over and bought a chicken burger. I didn't notice whether it was busy or what the weather was like. Deep in thought, with three people revolving round my head, I walked back and ate the fast food with a cup of instant coffee.

No one, apart from Isha, Joe and me, seemed concerned about Zain Rhind. And I was the odd one out. The other two knew him. Why was I so obsessed? The train company link was there. But there was the incontrovertible fact: he was locked up, inside. And I'd had that from the police, as well as Nancy. For everyone in the squad, for Jim, and even Joe and Isha, that meant he was not on the train. I had even briefly wondered if Anita was the half-sister that Joe had mentioned. If she wasn't helping us but hindering. Then I only had to think about her actions on the train – she did help. I was beginning to think I was going mad – but why did Nancy drive Anita to the memorial? The woman she'd told me couldn't be found?

I didn't trust Nancy. I suppose it was the job. The secrecy, the historic cover-ups. I trusted Steve Chambers, though, despite stories about cops gone bad. But a lack of honesty seemed part of the spy's job description, whereas liar cops seemed to be more individually motivated or part of a corrupt group. Or maybe it was just Nancy's manner that put my back up. I decided not to confront her for the time being and think it over.

Was Anita undercover on the train? Was she an agent? I couldn't see it. If she was there in a professional capacity because of the hijack plot, she wouldn't have been there on her own. It occurred to me that she might have offered information about the hijackers, in return for right to stay, hence the secrecy. But what could she have known that we didn't?

I was home before ten. Jim and Paul rang, but I didn't mention Anita or Nancy. Perhaps everyone thought I'd gone a bit mad too and this would only confirm their suspicions, even though I could say Steve Chambers had also seen her. Then I remembered I'd told him I had no recollection of the woman. I tried to get on with my painting; it was a study of the statues of Truth and Fortitude over the Old Bailey door. Only Truth seemed to be developing Anita's face, and Fortitude began to look a little like Nancy.

What was I left with? Much was made by the prosecution of the websites the men had been using. Even more was made of them by the defence, who asserted that they had been groomed into their decision to hijack the 10:12 by some unspecified mischief makers, whether foreign state actors, or cult cranks.

Did that mean they had no responsibility for their actions? I don't think so. But I do think they were adults who were easy to manipulate. Angry, lonely, detached and needing a 'tribe'. NoSinoChan gave them that. A group of criminal misfits tricked into causing misery and mayhem on a train, by someone, possibly Rhind from inside prison, or by one of the hijackers pretending to be one of the duped, although he was in fact the duper. Ellwood? He hadn't been at the Cheshire meeting so he could have been Bond. But when he had spoken to me on the train he had seemed genuinely surprised, in fact disbelieving, about the presence of an IED. Was that an act? The police thought it was probably Targut who had brought it on board. They don't require any special skills to make, apparently. You don't need to be Bond to do it. Either way, the hijackers schemed to do something that, whatever they claimed, would almost certainly cause unnecessary deaths. Six people had ended up dead, two by my actions. But many lives had been saved. Maybe that was all I'd ever know. And as Steve said, it would have to be enough.

But was it? Perhaps one last throw of the dice. I rang Nancy, and twenty minutes later she rang me back. I went straight to it. 'Why did you drive Anita to the memorial yesterday?'

There was a brief silence then she said briskly that she would meet me by the bandstand in a park a mile from where I was staying, in an hour. When I agreed, she hung up.

It was raining. I put on a waterproof jacket and picked up an umbrella. I decided to walk, to give me time to think about what I wanted to say, but I still hadn't worked it out when I reached the park.

The rusty wrought-iron gates opened into a scruffy open space, with mature trees, bushes, lawn and a pond – none looking their best at this time of the year and in this weather. Water was dripping from the trees, there was the strong musky smell of fox and there'd been a party at one of the battered iron benches, judging by the crushed cans and an empty bottle of cheap vodka scattered on the ground – beside an empty bin. There were few other signs of life on the way to the Victorian bandstand, apart from dog walkers and a couple of runners.

Nancy was already there when I arrived, wearing a brown coat, knee boots and a scowl. She put her hand out. 'Your phone.'

I frowned.

'You'll get it back.' She was brusque. I handed it over and she looked at the old model for a second, scoffed, and gave it back to me. 'What makes you think I was with Anita?'

'I followed her. Nice Golf, by the way.'

She started walking along a path edged by tired-out flowerbeds. I opened the umbrella, but didn't offer to share. Nancy spoke and, as usual, sounded irritated. 'I tracked Anita down. What she said to you is true. She's illegal. I asked her to speak to you, to put your mind at rest about the man you saw her with and thought was Zain Rhind. You know, the Zain Rhind that was actually locked up in prison. I'm worried about your obsession, Claire. I thought speaking to Anita might help.'

Somehow, I didn't see Nancy motivated by a wish to help me. 'Why the secrecy about your involvement?'

A young man with a jaunty felt hat walked past with three small dogs on leads. One snapped at Nancy, who grimaced in annoyance, and the man looked at her and smiled. 'She's a cheeky girl, thinks she's a Rottweiler.'

Nancy waited till he was out of earshot.

'You wouldn't believe me, and so needed to hear it from her. But also, because she's not legally here and technically I should hand her over to immigration.'

'Perhaps you offered to help her stay if she said what you wanted her to say.'

She laughed. 'Give it a rest. You are seriously at risk of joining the other bunnies down the rabbit hole. She'll probably get residency; she has a good case. But I won't be helping.'

I wondered if Nancy was the cheeky girl or Rottweiler. There was no contest. We continued walking, and the drizzle continued drizzling. I could see doggy man ahead, pausing to talk to another dog owner, a middle-aged woman with an overweight staffie mocked by a pink kerchief round its neck. Did MI5 employ dogs as accessories? Were there secret kennels somewhere with doggy Martinis? Lack of sleep was leading me in strange directions. A wind suddenly picked up, blowing a flurry of leaves and, catching my umbrella, lifted it out of my hand and into the lower branches of an old horse chestnut tree, laden with green spiky cases bursting with shiny conkers. As I tried to reach it, I caught a tight smile on Nancy's face and realised that under the thin veneer of make-up she looked exhausted.

She checked her watch ostentatiously and started walking again. I abandoned the umbrella, pulled my hood up and joined her. 'The NorthRail cricket club, just another coincidence?'

'No. We assume Lee Ellwood set it all up. He didn't play cricket, but he attended at least one match there. You seem to forget that he wasn't at the meeting. Not in person anyway. Didn't that give you a big fucking clue? Ellwood was your Bond, your mastermind, but he wasn't very good at it.' She kept her gaze firmly ahead, and didn't turn to me.

'I'm sure he didn't know about the IED.'

'One or more of the other hijackers planted the IED. You know we found "How to make an IED for idiots" sites on Abadi and Targut's computers – my money's on Targut. And he didn't tell Ellwood. His reasons were different to theirs. Ellwood was a computer nerd, and pretty technical, so it was quite within his capabilities to make one, but as you said, he didn't seem to know about it. His plan was simply to crash the train.'

She stopped suddenly and turned to face me. There was definitely something quite intimidating about her. She spoke softly, but clearly.

'Ellwood was bitter and deranged. But Targut's a psychopath. There are other indicators I can't go into, but it's our belief that Targut placed the IED, probably with Jefferson's help. Maybe Abadi knew, possibly Rodrigues. Not your little boy Rees, I'll give you that. Targut thought they'd be off the train before it exploded.'

I thought over what she was saying. It made sense. But she took my silence for obduracy. She sighed.

'I've got more important things to do than worry about an obsessive woman who won't accept the truth, who is fixated on an obsession which could have consequences for her and her family. You carry on digging into crazy world, the crazies start coming for you. You know there must be people around fixating on you already – you're quite the challenge for a certain type of man. Then there are the political-stroke-religious ones who seek vengeance for their comrades, and might consider your family legitimate targets, as well as some of your squad pals. Who don't appear to share your concerns about a prisoner locked up in Belmarsh, by the way.' She paused, staring hard at me.

'I'm only—'

She interrupted. 'You've already had threats. And your daughter might not be in Amsterdam now, but she's going back there, isn't she? I'd have thought you'd see the benefit of a quiet life, if not for yourself, then perhaps for the people you care about. But it appears not. Are you missing the spotlight?'

'Fuck off.'

She suddenly came up close and, looking me in the eye, muttered, 'This is my world, Claire. You think you know about it, but you don't. Your digging is risky for anyone close to you. You're becoming batshit crazy, seeing conspiracies everywhere. You are a hapless idiot messing with things you don't understand. You need to go back to counselling. And get the fuck out of my world.'

She strode off, leaving me reeling from the verbal onslaught. I walked around the pond to calm down, then paused, looking at the algae-covered water, at the few stately ducks cutting a trail through the green. A flock of pigeons landed, cooing around me, hoping I'd ignore the signs about not feeding the wildlife. Perhaps Nancy was right. What I'd suggested would mean conspiracy at a high level. And for what?

Something startled the pigeons, and they flew off, up into the trees. Was Nancy threatening me? I thought about her angry words. Then suddenly I could hear Charlie. *You're doing it again. She warns you about the risk, and you decide she is the risk. She gives you the facts. You decide she's wrong. Calm down, take a breath, get over yourself. Focus on making the most of your life, the future.* The future you were denied, Charlie, I thought, wiping moisture from my face, rain or tears, then made my way back to the old horse chestnut to collect my umbrella.

The conker tree had a wide girth, hundreds of years old, with a battle-scarred, gnarly trunk. The leaves were largely yellowy brown, and many had fallen, the conkers not quite ready to follow. I stood underneath for a moment, looking up into the branches, then stretched to see if I could reach the lowest one. Scrambling, feet on trunk, I pulled myself up and onto it. I managed to snaffle the brolly and fold it down, balancing on the slippery branch, happy I hadn't lost my old tree-climbing skills.

There had been an ancient apple tree in our garden, tall for a fruit tree. Although the apples were wormy and sour, the blossom was pretty, and it added character to an otherwise bland garden. My parents talked of chopping it down every year, but never did. Perhaps they knew Charlie and I used to hide there and indulged us, for once. They probably didn't know about the cigarettes.

    The drizzle was easing up, and weak sunshine leaked through the clouds. Nancy's attitude was provoking. But did I really want to spend precious time digging into these men's miserable lives to try and make sense of something nonsensical? I caught a whiff of cigarette smoke, a more uncommon smell in London nowadays than cannabis, and started down the tree. I slipped and slid inelegantly onto the ground – so much for my climbing skills – and found myself sitting in wet leaves and, my nose quickly told me, Monty's revenge. Fortunately, Nancy wasn't there to enjoy my hubris. I couldn't see anyone, but I had a sense of Charlie leaning back against the trunk and smiling.

Dear Claire,

I am writing to inform you that Ashgrove was the subject of a recent brief cyberattack. On behalf of the company I would like to reassure you, as we are reassuring all our authors, that we have taken all relevant steps to ensure the security of any personal details, as well as all manuscripts. There is no evidence of any data breach, and our systems have been judged as adequately robust. However, extra levels of security have also been added, and we will maintain a continuing cyber security protocol.

    Please contact John Simons, our head of security, on ext. 2035 if you have any further questions. At the moment, it appears to be a phishing expedition for data that failed, and was possibly a mistake in the first place.

    Your sincerely,
    Loretta De Silva
    Editorial Director, Ashgrove Publishing

To: Claire Fitzroy
cc: Laurence Walker
From: Loretta De Silva
Subject: Re: Family matters

Hi Claire,

This is how the MS is looking now. Let me know if you're happy to press go. Great to hear you've been in touch with Laurence and given the OK re the serialisation. You'll have had my letter about the possible cyberattack by now, sorry it delayed my getting the MS to you. It's sorted with no apparent consequences, although the source remains a mystery. Maybe we should put you on to it!

    All the best,
    Loretta

    Loretta De Silva
    Editorial Director, Ashgrove Publishing

SECURITY LEVEL PLATINUM
[Official Secret Cat A]
...encryption 8...

Attn: Senior HHSSO (ops)
RE: FITZROY REPORT (2)
Attached is the Fitzroy train hijack book MS (not yet signed off, redactions to come) and correspondence envelope sourced from publisher's server, etc. *[No traceability]*

Overall assessment.
1. Team view is relaxed. Concerns about Fitzroy's investigation into Rhind have been allayed. She identified him as the possible source of hijack, linked the personal angle, and made the assumption that he was behind the NoSinoChan seduction site for conspiracy theorists (now maintained under different handle, etc.). However, she has not uncovered his links to us, and her investigations haven't prompted the plods to further investigate. They've had their day in court and are now on to more pressing business. Ellwood, the dead trainee driver, has proved a useful scapegoat. Rhind will keep his mouth shut.
2. The handler responsible for Rhind's freedom to commit his jolly has been vigorously debriefed and dismissed, and systems put in place to ensure strong oversight into any future off-book prison-based informant day releases.

    The handler was blackmailed by Rhind, who discovered nasties on the handler's computer. The handler believed Rhind was going to meet his girlfriend for sex, and, as he had supervised Rhind's visit to a sex worker before, thought there would be no problem. The handler now works for a low-level security company. We helped him get the position and he believes we have eyes on him. That, plus his abject humiliation and fear of arrest over said porn, should ensure no further complications. As far as the prison, MoJ and the police are concerned, Rhind was undergoing terrorist-related interrogation with MI5 on that day and was secure in a murky basement somewhere. That intel has a support line, and team is confident it will stay tight.

3. The handler's supervisor, 'Nancy', has appeared before the disciplinary committee and her frontline career is effectively over. Her lack of oversight of the situation was, she claimed, due to an unreasonably heavy caseload. But as she did not pass that concern upstairs, this was not accepted to the degree she had hoped for. She has now been relocated to the backroom. 'Nancy' did a reasonable job clearing up the mess re Fitzroy and Rhind, although reading Fitzroy's account, her heavy-handed tactics with text and postcard may have served to increase Fitzroy's curiosity. The unauthorised use of undercover agent J (see more below) at the train manager's memorial, intended to allay Fitzroy's fears, seems also to have backfired, although it's accepted it was an attempt to protect the service from further investigations.

4. Re events on the 10:12, Agent J from Manchester office, known to Fitzroy as 'Anita', became aware of a possible planned minor incident on the train via investigation of chatter on NoSinoChan. This was assumed to be along the lines of a fake bomb warning, orchestrated by Rhind. She discussed this with her team leader 'Nancy' in London, but as Rhind was developing a habit of myth-creating, it was not given priority. J took it upon herself to travel on the train. During the hijacking, she discovered Rhind in an empty carriage. A disagreement ended with her knocking him out to prevent his discovery, as he appeared unstable and talkative. (Fitzroy's 'not dead' man.)

Later, using threats and flattery, she was able to persuade him to hide in the closed end carriage to which she had obtained a master key, and contacted 'Nancy', who instructed her to remove him from the train, with the object of avoiding any involvement in the police investigation. J was successful in this. According to her report, Rhind was delusional and desperate to see how his 'masterpiece' played out. He planned to watch the CCTV feeds from the train manager's office, or take refuge in the end carriage, the closure of which he had organised in order to have somewhere to hide. He was vague about how he would have dealt with the manager and showed no remorse about the man's death, despite knowing him from a work sports club.

He denies he chose the 10:12 train because his ex and their infant daughter, and his ex's father would be onboard. But spyware found on the ex's phone, as well as unauthorised access discovered on NorthRail's staff allocation site, prove otherwise. What he ultimately planned to do is unclear. But as 'Bond', he instructed the hijackers to grab his ex and daughter and take them to the front, the most dangerous part of the train. By withdrawing Rhind from play, J's actions saved the service a great deal of grief. She has been commended and a promotion is in the pipeline.

5. The failure to gain any accurate foreknowledge of Rhind's actions is of considerable concern and will be the subject of a forthcoming report from Group C. For what it's worth, I think Rhind initially made a reasonably effective informant. Assessment of intel he provided does indicate some usefulness in terms of names, locations and motivations of certain dangerous actors in the CT area, and to a lesser extent, religious extremism. His claim to have set the hijack up to deliver us the 'brothers' appears on one level to be true. He certainly did not attempt any negotiations, there were no backup plans for the hijackers and he kept his identity from them on the train. Ellwood closed the end carriage when he joined the train before departure, a closure Rhind 'authorised' by accessing the rail company's server. He had his own pass key. There was one IED near the front. Rhind claims no knowledge of this, which is probably true. CCTV indicates it was planted by Targut. Fitzroy is convinced Ellwood was also surprised by the explosion. The IED

was standard basic build; 'how-to' details easily found on the dark web. Interrogation of surviving hijackers suggests that Jefferson knew. The others were told that threats of IEDs would be enough to frighten passengers into obedience. The hijackers all have slightly differing opinions as to the reasons for the hijack, which fits with Rhind's assertion that he 'gamed' them. This also fits the conspiracy theory world: nothing is as it seems, don't believe the official narrative and, most of all, everything is connected.

6. A number of matters pertaining to Rhind have emerged since the events on the 10:12, and our analysis and actions are outlined below.
    - Rhind's claim not to have informed us about the train because he wanted to pull off the 'undercover coup of the century and present it to us on a plate' may be true but would never have worked. He has become detached from reality (see attached psych assessment).
    - The threat he poses means he will have no access to any digital tech while serving the remainder of his sentence. Parole will not be granted. The psych assessment reveals a strong narcissistic personality disorder linked to increasing delusions, more extreme than when he was first recruited. He may also be suffering from double-agent syndrome, identifying with the causes he was supposed to be undermining. The security assessment is one of potential threat in various areas on his release.
    - Rhind was behind the deaths of four citizens, promoted and fostered hate crimes, as well as being a violent abuser of his former partner. He is a continuing threat to her and her father, according to the assessment. Team proposes discrete termination shortly after release.
7. The anonymous letter writer and former dept trainee, correctly identified by Fitzroy, has been dealt with. A clear explanation of the consequences of breaking OSA with

assurances that we would pursue to the max and that she would end up in prison, plus a small ex-gratia payment for her 'trauma', encouraged her to sign a new agreement in addition to OSA and deliver an abject apology.

8 We recently had a meeting with Fitzroy. Our offer to keep a watch on socials, etc., in case of any serious threats against her, her family or her 'squad' on the train, was well received. In return, she agreed to modify or take out certain elements in the book as you see it now, namely the discovery of 'Anita' with 'Nancy', and their subsequent meeting, although not her view of agent 'Nancy' (which you may find amusing). She also requested protection for Rhind's ex-partner and her family on Rhind's release, which we turned down (agreement might have raised Fitzroy's suspicions), while suggesting the police were better for that role. It will be a short one.

9 Finally, we have accepted assurances from Fitzroy that mention of her limited freelance surveillance work for us during her time teaching at Belmarsh will not appear in any form. She has more to lose. We've told her she can go ahead with the book – her publishers and agent were becoming frustrated by her refusal to sign off, and as some of her history with us is now known by them, we don't wish to create a situation where they may suspect further involvement because of the delay.

By the way, I recommend the book. She was probably a loss to the service.

Errol

Acknowledgements

One thing leads to another.

Without the Crime Writers' Association, this book would probably not exist. Their annual Debut Dagger Award (now Emerging Author) offers the wonderful opportunity for would-be crime or thriller novelists to enter with a synopsis and extract from a novel. Winning it – and what a shock that was – with *The 10:12* led me to my agent, Stephanie Glencross at David Higham Associates, whose wise words and encouragement helped improve the book in so many ways. Stephanie then led to Therese Keating, my editor at Raven, a happy collaboration, with Therese's questions and suggestions helping to clarify what I was trying to achieve.

So big thanks to the CWA, and all the people at DHA and Raven/Bloomsbury who have helped in the birth of *The 10:12*.

Professor Colin Divall, the railways expert, kindly helped me understand elements of contemporary train function. *The 10:12* is loosely based on a Pendolino, but is a train of the imagination. Any train inconsistencies are mine, not Colin's.

Thanks to friends and wider family for their encouragement, my sons for their enthusiasm – and Stephen for the kitchen knife. Brian Hill, my first reader, despite taking issue with my placement of commas, has been a continuing support. My thanks for that, and so much more. Long may it last.

And finally, if you've made it this far, thank you reader for choosing this book. I hope you enjoyed it and that we will have more adventures together.

A Note on the Author

Anna Maloney has written for TV (one BAFTA win), film and radio and taught screenwriting. Previously, she worked in factual TV, journalism and PR as well as being a qualified playleader and sometime usherette. Anna lives in south-east London.